BY LONNIE BUSCH

Without a Face
Assimilation
The Anything Room
Cargo Hold 4
All Hope of Becoming Human
The Baldwin Hotel
The Cabin on Souder Hill
Push Me:Feisty Stories of Love & Loss
Turnback Creek; a Novella & Six Stories

(More about Busch's books at end of Project Übermensch)

PROJECT ÜBERMENSCH

LONNIE BUSCH

UBiQ PRESS

No AI was used for any part of this book

PROJECT ÜBERMENSCH

A UBiQ PRESS BOOK

North Carolina, USA

https://lonniebusch.com/

Cover Art by Lonnie Busch

ISBN: 978-1-964024-04-2 (hardcover)

ISBN: 978-1-964024-03-5 (paperback)

Library of Congress Control Number: 2024905700

First Paperback/Hardcover Editions, April 2024

Human Authored Reg #: 3864951, https://authorsguild.org/human

CONTENTS

1. 1943, US NAVY YARD IN PHILADELPHIA   1
2. 2024, KLEARY CREEK, NC   3
3. TWO BEAUTIFUL ROSES   9
4. DARK DESIRE   15
5. GOODBYE VERONICA   19
6. MEETING COLETTE   23
7. THE LODGE   27
8. A UNIVERSE THAT THRIVES ON BALANCE   33
9. IMPERMANENCE   37
10. DEAD JOGGER   43
11. FRAUDULENT PROFITEER   45
12. A DARK MEMORY   49
13. CARNIVAL CHARLATAN   53
14. COMFORT OF STRANGERS   63
15. OUT OF YOUR MIND   67
16. SOMETHING HUGE IN THE POPLARS   73
17. ANOTHER BODY   79
18. THE BEAST   83
19. ON YELLOW MOUNTAIN   89
20. CARLY AND MELISSA   97
21. IN THE SILENT WOODS   101
22. DEEPEST FEARS   105
23. NEWTON'S THIRD LAW   107
24. EXTRA EYES   113
25. STRIEBER MOUNTAIN ROAD   121
26. BAD NEWS IN BRISTOL   127
27. RUBBERNECKS   137
28. BRISTOL: MORNING OF THE SEMINAR   141
29. ELIZABETH ZAHN   145
30. THE PLEDGE   149
31. THE DEFECTIVE ALGORITHM   155
32. CONCRETE EVIDENCE   159
33. FEEDING THE BEAST   165
34. UNEVEN FURY   171
35. NIGREDO, TENEBROSITAS   177
36. A GREAT STORM   179
37. BARBARIC HUNGER   187

38. A NECESSARY LIE   193
39. SOMETHING IN THE ROAD   197
40. FULL MEASURE OF THE DAMAGE   201
41. NOT LIES, EXACTLY   207
42. A TIMELY ACCOUNT   211
43. A POWERFUL THOUGHT   221
44. A PACT WITH SATAN   225
45. THE MANTRA   229
46. NO LONGER ABSTRACT   235
47. A LIFELESS HUSK   241
48. MIRACLES   245
49. DEAREST FRIENDS   255
50. TWO HUNDRED AND FORTY MINUTES   261
51. IN LEAGUE WITH DARK FORCES   265
52. THE AGRICULTURAL ADJUSTMENT ACT   271
53. NEVER UNDERESTIMATE FEAR   281
54. ONE LAST THING   289
55. THE ESCAPE   293
56. THE LONG DRIVE   297
57. FIFTY MILES FROM BOZEMAN   305
58. THE VEIL OF ILLUSION   313
59. A LIFE OF NORMALCY   321

About the Author   329

PROJECT ÜBERMENSCH

1

1943, US NAVY YARD IN PHILADELPHIA

THE WORLD WAS AT WAR. Operation Watchtower was drawing to an end as American forces took Guadalcanal after several months of savage fighting on land, sea and air, effectively ending Japanese expansion plans, and perhaps marking the turning point in the Pacific campaign. Rome, Italy was decimated under its first significant bombing raid, and a week later, Mussolini was arrested, and Italy appeared ready for a peace settlement with the Allies. North of Norway, the pride of the German Fleet, *Scharnhorst*, a German battleship, was sunk through a clever tactical maneuver by the HMS Duke of York and its escorts.

That same year, seeking advantage in the war, the US Navy conducted test trials with an unconventional electromagnetic force-field technology which bore aspects of Einstein's Unified Field Theory. The technology, if worked as purported, would *cloak* U.S. war ships, rendering them invisible to enemy radar. However, the experiment went nightmarishly awry, inadvertently tearing a rift in the space-time continuum. The laws of nature were violated with near apocalyptic results— time bent toward the future, then buckled back, looping in on itself. The *USS Eldridge* vanished from the Philadelphia Navy Yard, then rematerialized just a few moments later with horrific consequences; crew members helplessly and hopelessly embedded in the decks of the ship. Bodies and limbs gruesomely merged with solid steel. Some encased to their necks, others with only their arms and part of their torso exposed, many with half their bodies dissecting metal bulkheads. Numerous among the crew dead. Third mate Peter "Smitty" Smithwick, whose legs were planted to the knees in the steel deck near the hedgehog mortar weapon, was unconscious, but still had a pulse, his feet and calves now part of the ship.

Amidst the eerily green ion-charged mist floating over the ship, and the chaos that ensued after the incident, a small group of "men" were rumored to have convened on the deck of the *Eldridge*. No one recognized them, their faces hidden beneath hoods as they searched the carnage for survivors. The group was believed to have been involved in the experiment, maybe even the arbiters of the technology responsible for the disaster. The mysterious individuals managed to excise third mate Peter Smithwick from the steel decking by amputating his legs just below the knees, then hauled him away to an undisclosed location. One account claimed that a pair of the hooded individuals returned minutes later to remove healthy legs from one of the embedded dead sailors, then placed them in a large case and carried it off the ship.

The catastrophe at the Philadelphia Navy Yard would live on in a fog of mythologized infamy, known only as *The Philadelphia Experiment*. None of the hooded individuals that boarded the doomed *Eldridge* that day were ever seen again. The technology the Navy had experimented with was ostensibly the groundwork for stealth capabilities of fighter jets decades later. Crewmen who had lived through the invisibility experiment, ones not merged into the bulkheads, either died or were eventually discharged from service as mentally unfit. The Navy denied anything of the sort ever happened.

Third mate Peter "Smitty" Smithwick, after much rehabilitation and advanced forms of surgery unfamiliar to medical science at that time, would have to learn to live with new found capabilities, one which was the gift—or the curse—of delayed aging. It would take years for "Smitty" to discover this, and not until Amanda, his eventual wife, would be the one to point it out. Due to this anomalous malediction over aging, and his eventual divorce from Amanda, Peter Smithwick found it necessary to change his name and go into hiding. In order to destroy all ties to his past, he assigned himself a new moniker, Geoffrey Cannon.

2024, KLEARY CREEK, NC

ALMOST A QUARTER-CENTURY into the new millennium and not much had changed. Not really, not for Orvin and his wife Colette. Phone apps existed for practically everything now, but after forty years of marriage, Colette still wrote out her grocery list on a scrap of paper, then handed it to Orvin so he could pick up groceries on his way home if he wasn't too beat from painting houses and climbing ladders all day. Orvin knew where the list was, in his shirt pocket, but this morning, he couldn't find the photo of his five-year-old granddaughter. He always kept the picture on the dashboard, just to the left of the speedometer. Did it blow out when he stopped at McDonald's earlier that morning? Swerving his pickup onto the gravel shoulder, he came to a skidding stop in front of a long row of mailboxes and inspected the clear plastic panel that covered his gauges to see if the picture had slid down inside the dash. It never had before. He checked the passenger-side floor, reaching his hand around the paint cans and shop towels. He raised both knees up alongside the steering wheel, giving the area below his work boots a visual check before rooting under the rubber mats and the brake pedal. He pushed the seat forward and rummaged through the tangle of dried and broken paint rollers. Why was he saving those?

Then he remembered. He slid his fingers down inside the breast pocket of his shirt and there it was, with the folded grocery list. He pulled the photo out, giving it a gentle kiss before securing it back on the dash, recalling he'd carried it into McDonald's to show Del, the contractor who was building the new strip mall on Main. Pushing the brake in, Orvin put the pickup in gear, then reached up and lightly held the silver cross hanging from his rear-view mirror.

He pulled his vehicle onto the highway and within just a few miles was making the left turn onto Strieber Mountain Road. Even though he hadn't painted homes up here in years, he still had a couple of friends, mostly previous customers that hadn't moved away yet. Today he was going to quote a potential house painting project near the top of the mountain. Surely it would be a large house, a substantial job that may require additional help. At Orvin's age, he wasn't sure how large a task he wanted to undertake anymore, but of course, he and his wife could always use the money.

The road was steep, twisty and narrow, like most of the mountain roads in this area. With barely enough room to creep past one another without trading car paint or losing a side mirror, Orvin kept his eyes and ears open for approaching vehicles. He had gone about a mile up the road when he noticed a home that had sat vacant for almost three years, but now had a vehicle in the driveway, an older model Land Rover. Seeing that the house could use a coat of paint, and wasn't very large, he decided to pop in and introduce himself, maybe leave a card and tell the new occupants about their church, *The First Pentecostal of Kleary Creek*.

Orvin steered his truck into the gravel driveway and put it in park. He grabbed a business card and a brochure for the church, then got out, straightened his trousers, tucked in his shirt and went up the wooden steps leading to the front of the house. What an amazing view the property had of the surrounding mountains. It appeared that the entire front of the house was glass, or more exactly, three twelve-foot-wide sliding glass doors opening onto a massive deck.

Walking up to the first set of glass doors, Orvin was about to knock when he saw movement inside, first a woman, then another, and as his eyes adjusted to the darkened interior, he saw they were both naked and he quickly looked away. His heart was jittery and he felt his skin flush, turning to go back down to his truck. Just as he spun away, a voice rang out.

"Hey there," a man said.

Orvin turned to see a tall, well-built trim young man—uncombed black hair, thirtyish, his chin blackened with stubble—lashing the belt of his robe. "I'm Geoffrey Cannon," the man said, briskly jutting out his palm. "And you are…?"

4

"Orvin," he answered sheepishly, shaking the man's hand. "Orvin Littney."

They stared at each other a few moments before Orvin blurted out, "Have you found Jesus?"

Geoffrey's eyes flew open, his mouth spread to a surprised grin. "I can only imagine some of the answers you get to that question," Geoffrey said.

Orvin hurriedly shoved the church brochure into the man's hands, hoping the naked women wouldn't be joining them on the deck.

"Thank you," Geoffrey said, eyeing the brochure, then glancing past Orvin to see his truck. "Ah, a painter. My place could use a fresh coat."

"How long have you lived here?" Orvin asked.

"Actually, I just closed on this place about a month ago. I love this area, all the mountains and waterfalls... And it's close to Asheville, and Knoxville and some other places I am just familiarizing myself with. Like Blowing Rock, Boone, and Charlotte. Absolutely beautiful."

"You know your deck could be saved with a little work," Orvin interjected, still uncomfortable with his decision to stop. Why did this man have two young women parading around in their birthday suits? And were there more than two? Was Geoffrey Cannon a human trafficker, or maybe the head of a prostitution ring? Or a pimp? Orvin was very uneasy.

"So, what would you suggest?" Geoffrey said.

"I wouldn't suggest anything," Orvin said. "I'll just be on my way..."

"Wait, wait... what about my deck? I thought I'd have to replace it, but you said I could save it. What do I have to do?"

"Power wash first, then a few coats of stain. May need some sanding before the stain but wouldn't know until we got the algae and gunk cleaned off... Those walnuts trees are causing all those black stains..."

"Is that something you do, power washing and staining?"

"Yeah, here's my card."

Geoffrey took it, looked at it just a moment, then shoved it down in his pocket. "Say, do you have a minute or two?"

"No, I really have to go. I have an appointment up the mountain."

"Well, I was just wondering if you could tell me more about your church, here," he said. "I was just going for a short walk, and being new around here, I really don't know anyone. Your church might be the perfect place to meet some new people."

Orvin relaxed at this comment; maybe Mr. Cannon wasn't some criminal eluding the law, hiding out in the mountains of North Carolina. He seemed like a nice enough fellow, but Orvin was still vexed by the naked women.

"I guess I could walk a little," Orvin said, glancing at his watch, even though he had not given his prospective clients an exact time he'd arrive.

"Great! I'm just going to throw on some shorts and a T-shirt," he said, glancing down at his bare feet, "and some sneakers."

"Okay. I'll just wait down by my truck," Orvin said, anxious to get away from those huge glass doors. Just as he was turning away, one of the naked women came through the living room hooking her bra behind her back. She was still without under pants. Orvin hurried down the steps.

Geoffrey appeared on the front deck wearing shorts and a faded black T-shirt, shifting his head side to side, as if looking for something. Orvin jumped from his truck. "Down here...."

Geoffrey bounded down the steps, taking some two at a time. "A magnificent day, Orvin!" Geoffrey said, coming up near Orvin's truck. Orvin could only nod, unable to meet this young man's exuberance head on. It was hard not to notice the huge scars beneath the young man's knees, some kind of major surgery, Orvin suspected. The man was athletic looking, so maybe old football injuries, or maybe a car accident, Orvin imagining firemen cutting the young man from a mangled automobile using the jaws of life. Geoffrey smiled at him and walked down the driveway past Orvin's truck and stepped onto the macadam, walking right up the middle of the country road. Orvin looked both ways, even though he knew it was not a high-use thoroughfare; it basically dead-ended at the top of the mountain.

"So, let me tell you about our church," Orvin said, a bit out of breath, finally falling in stride with Geoffrey.

Orvin explained about the intimate size of the congregation, how most folks knew each other, and the choir, which Orvin was especially proud of, and their drives to raise money for the school, bake sales and carnivals and whatnot. "We have a carnival coming up in—" Orvin started to say, but stopped, suddenly short of breath. Geoffrey stopped and padded back a few steps to stand next to Orvin. Orvin bent over and placed his palms on his knees, trying to take deep breaths, the pain in his chest growing. He tried to swallow and his mouth felt like tissue.

"Are you okay?" Geoffrey said.

When the feeling passed, Orvin straightened and looked around, focusing his eyes on the valley below, the sawmill so small it looked like a train board building. After taking another deep breath, he let it out slowly, then smiled. "As I was saying, we have a carnival coming up in a couple of weeks," he said, resuming the trek up the steep mountain road. "Lots of rides for the children and teenagers and—" This time the pain struck like an ax. Orvin's palm went to his chest, as if to squeeze out the piercing discomfort, but the thundering pang shot through his entire body, causing him to pass out. For a split second Orvin felt himself falling, everything going black, then nothing, no sense of the hard pavement beneath his body, no awareness of the scrapes on his knee where he'd cut himself on the loose gravel. Then bright light. Bright blinding light. It took a few moments for Orvin's eyes to adjust, a peace and calm pouring through him like warm milk. Orvin felt himself floating, seeing himself ten feet below, his lifeless body lying in the road, his veiny, right hand resting at his side, no longer clutching his chest, his eyes closed, lifeless. The vision of himself didn't frighten him, as if his entire being was now wrapped in tranquility. Then he noticed Geoffrey leaning over his body, the young man's hand under the back of Orvin's head, as if to protect it from the hard surface of the road. Orvin felt himself smiling, a wonderful mixture of joy and serenity pervading his senses. Just then, Geoffrey turned his head upward, his eyes friendly, aiming his smile directly at Orvin's disembodied consciousness. *You're going to be all right*, Geoffrey said. Orvin couldn't hear him exactly, not with his ears, but the words were clear and lucid. *I've called an ambulance. By the time you come back it should be here*, Geoffrey added. *But isn't it glorious?* It was glorious, Orvin thought, this new domain he found himself in, but couldn't understand how Geoffrey could see him, or communicate, or... but then, Geoffrey and the macadam road began to shrink from view as if Orvin was swiftly rising away from them. He could still make out Geoffrey kneeling next to his own lifeless body, then oddly, Geoffrey smiled up at him as he placed his palm gently on Orvin's unbeating chest. Suddenly, Orvin found himself in freefall, a dizzying descent culminating in blaring sirens and strobing red lights, the clatter of metal wheels on pavement, the rush of voices, of urgency, the hurried footsteps of emergency medical technicians, the smell of exhaust, aftershave and perfume, the hissing drone of oxygen, the pinch of syringe needles, the restrictive weight of security straps adding gravity, machines beeping and buzzing, the searing pain resurfacing in Orvin's ribcage and the metallic doors slamming with a numbing, soundless finality, and even though Orvin could feel every turn and twist in the road winding down the mountain, he rested the last of his waning awareness on the white metal ceiling, the tiny heads of rivets, lending them his attention as he fell slowly away.

3

TWO BEAUTIFUL ROSES

LILLIAN, seated across from Geoffrey Cannon in the front of his Land Rover, talked about her job which she hated, her ex-boyfriend whom she hoped would stop texting her, then about growing up in boring Iowa, and her dream of moving to New Zealand at some point in her life. "But not until I've shopped every store in Europe, and visited every museum," Lillian said.

Geoffrey smiled.

Veronica sat as quiet as a turnip in the backseat of the Land Rover, with her body pulled to the driver's side, directly behind Geoffrey. She listened impatiently to her narcissistic best friend drone on about her life. She loved Lillian, and hated her in equal measure. And the previous night, the two of them making love to the same man at the same time, well... Mr. Cannon hadn't been the first. There had been numerous liaisons since college. But Geoffrey Cannon was Lillian's latest conquest.

The previous afternoon, at the seminar in Asheville, Geoffrey had chosen them from the audience to come up on stage and help him with his talk, which would require them to sit in front of an audience of nearly five hundred people in a Marriott banquet room, on display like prize livestock. Mortified by the prospect, Veronica wanted no part of it, but Lillian insisted, saying it would be fun. So they went up, people applauding their courage, or maybe their stupidity, Veronica never able to quell the quaking inside. Lillian sucked up all the attention, her ego expanding like a supernova every time the crowd cheered or laughed, growing exponentially friskier, and bolder. When Mr. Cannon asked her what she wanted most in life, Lillian talked about her stupid red Ferrari dream and everyone went looney for it, even Cannon.

After Cannon had finished with them, he magically produced two live flowers from behind his back, handing each of them a perfect red rose. It was impressive, Veronica had to admit. And he was charming, but she couldn't wait to get off the stage.

When the seminar ended, it was Lillian who hatched the plan to wait for Geoffrey in the Marriott parking lot. Already she had put herself on a first name basis with this enigmatic man who had penned several books, and piloted metaphysical healing seminars all over the country.

"Let's ambush Mr. Cannon, see if we can get a meal out of him…" Lillian's eyes were hungry for more than dinner; she had lusty cravings, and loved the pursuit, the danger and machinations of maneuvering unsuspecting strangers into threesomes. Men and women, didn't matter.

Veronica wilted, intrigued by the idea, but weary of the subterfuge. "Come on, Lil," Veronica had said. "Let's just go grab something to eat, get a couple of drinks. I'm beat." Veronica learned early on what her role in this friendship would be—white-knuckling it in coach, while Lillian performed wing rolls and stomach-dropping loop-de-loops from the cockpit. Lillian got her way, as she always did, and the two women waited near the Marriott entrance, walking up to him as he exited the hotel, flashing their winning smiles, holding up the beautiful roses he'd given them and thanking him. How could anyone resist?

"How about you, Veronica? What are your ambitions?" Geoffrey asked, jolting Veronica from her reverie in the back seat of his Rover. She could see his face framed in the rearview mirror.

"Paying off my school loans," Veronica said, miffed about the past twenty-four hours. During the seminar, she had explained that she was a registered nurse, and that she was a little angry that she had to limp by on her salary, just to pay rent and buy groceries and make her car payments. She'd spent all that money on her nursing degree, only to have to shell out wads of cash every month to pay back the loan."

"I'm not complaining, but you finish school and get your dream job only to have to scrimp to get by again, like you're still in college…" Veronica said.

Lillian rolled her eyes, mouthing the words, *Oh, brother*, but it obviously wasn't lost on Geoffrey. He glanced over at her, then fixed his attention back on the road, the radio playing low, forecasting the weather, the thrum of the highway a constant undertone.

"Sorry," Veronica finally said. "Didn't mean to rant and spoil the afterglow." At times she couldn't stem the sarcasm, rerunning a tape in her head from the previous night's sex, how uncomfortable she'd been, needing to be by herself for a time. Now she bristled with embarrassment over her money-problem disclosure; it demonstrated a certain uncoolness that Veronica seemed to exude with greater regularity around Lillian.

"Nothing to be sorry for," Geoffrey said, finding her eyes in the rearview mirror.

If only that were true, Veronica thought, knowing full-well her appetite for self-abasement, often comparing herself in unflattering ways to Lillian, who would quickly rush to rescue Veronica's sagging self-image, propping her up with flattery and praise. It seemed to be the hallmark of their relationship.

Presently, Veronica wished Geoffrey would have offered something more pithy and profound than, "Nothing to be sorry for," but what good would it do anyway? At the seminar she had been transported, feeling more buoyant, the group dynamic lifting her, the shared experience of hundreds of people in some kind of mass hypnotic spell. But now, after the crummy night she'd spent trying to keep up with Lillian's gymnastic physicality and lust, the helium was gone.

Veronica was quiet, as if searching the landscape speeding past her window, knowing that once she spiraled down into this dark cave, there was no way out. She couldn't start making jokes, laugh it all off; these troubling emotions were like spikes in her gut, the bleeding wouldn't stop.

When they approached the city limits of Asheville, Geoffrey asked if the girls were hungry. Lillian said she had to get home, that she had a date that night with someone she'd met online. Veronica looked in the mirror to find Geoffrey's eyes, then shrugged and said she was fine.

"Just drop us at the Marriott," Lillian said. "I can take Veronica home before my date."

Geoffrey turned the Rover into the parking lot of the big hotel. Lillian, leaning forward in the seat, directed Geoffrey to the location of her car. "I think it's this row," Lillian said. "Is this right, Veronica?" Veronica said nothing. "Oh, oh! There it is, Geoff! The blue Mazda!" She smiled over at Geoffrey. "Not a cherry red Ferrari yet!"

Geoffrey chuckled, stopping near the trunk of her car. Lillian popped the passenger side door open and grabbed her purse, her eyes snagging

Geoffrey's attention. "Well, Mr. Cannon, that was a delightful evening," Lillian said, leaning into the car, her hand resting on the seat. "We should do that again real soon."

Geoffrey reached over and placed his hand on top of hers. "Truly remarkable," he said, his eyes glinting with soft light. Veronica pushed the back door open and got out, closing it behind her, walking slowly around to the passenger side of Geoffrey's Rover.

"You ready to go, Ronnie?" Lillian said.

Veronica blenched, cutting her a hard look. "You know I hate when you call me that..."

Lillian flushed with embarrassment. "Sorry... sweetie. You ready to hit the road?"

Veronica shifted her attention to Geoffrey. "Is that invite for dinner still on the table, no pun intended?"

"Of course," Geoffrey said. Veronica climbed in the front seat next to Geoffrey and shut the door, then busied herself with the seatbelt. Lillian leaned in through the open window and kissed Veronica on the cheek. "Have fun," she said. "And call me later. I'll probably need a good confessor after this date tonight..." Lillian smiled at Veronica. Veronica returned a pleasant, but somewhat difficult smile. When Lillian took her eyes past Veronica, she placed her fingers to her lips and swept an airy kiss toward Geoffrey.

Geoffrey turned to Veronica and asked what sounded good for dinner. "Mexican? Italian? Sushi?"

Veronica looked over at Geoffrey with tears in her eyes. "I know it's a long drive, but can we just go back to your place?"

Geoffrey nodded, and said nothing. She was glad he didn't pry and ask questions, because she had no answers. For a while she drifted in and out of the present moment, feeling the breeze through her opened window. *This is the most important moment of your life.* Geoffrey Cannon's words had drifted over the crowd at the Marriott like the hush of a slow-moving wave. Veronica could still see him standing there on the event room stage, his lavalier mic clipped to his yellow Izod polo shirt, baggy army-green cargo shorts and worn sneakers with no socks. The stubble of beard along his jaw betrayed his boyish flop of dark hair and slender figure. The crowd of almost five hundred people sat rapt on metal folding chairs, without a sound, not a squeak or creak from one of the metal rivets. Their minds were open and receptive, almost like a trance, a voluntary assemblage of energy.

"Are you on vacation?" Geoffrey asked.

"No, shift work right now. Four on, four off. Long days."

She glanced over at him before taking her attention back to the highway. After a moment, she asked him if he believed what he'd said in the talk he gave the day before. Geoffrey asked what she was referring to.

"You know, the part about *this being the most important moment of your life*. Do you believe that, that the present moment is the most important moment?"

"No," Geoffrey answered. "I know it."

"But... the past and future are pretty important too."

"Maybe so, but they don't exist."

Veronica felt a little slippage. They existed for her... and for everyone else she knew. How could he claim they didn't? Geoffrey regarded her a moment. "I see your confusion. What University did you attend?"

She told him, glad he was changing the subject.

"When did you get your diploma?" he asked.

"I don't know. Four years ago, I guess." She knew absolutely when she'd graduated, but what did it matter?

"Where were you when they handed you the paper?"

A troubling heat crawled through her chest. Was this some kind of tricky metaphysical doublespeak? "I was at Duke," she said. "Brooks Field in Wallace Wade Stadium."

He shot a quick look her way, then said, "Back then, when they handed you your diploma, and you took it in your hands and looked at it, feeling very proud of your accomplishment, did you say to yourself, 'Wow, this feels like four years ago?'"

Veronica wasn't sure she understood. "You mean that day? Of course not."

"Right, because in that moment, when you accepted your diploma, it was that day. The present moment..."

Veronica scoffed, shaking her head. "Well, yeah, but that doesn't—"

"Name one time, any time in your life, that you did something, one thing, that wasn't in the present moment."

Veronica started to say something, then felt stumped. "Well, I did a lot of things in my past, so—"

"But you didn't do them in the *past*... you were in the present moment when you did them. You couldn't have done them at any other time, because there is no other time. Only the present moment..."

Veronica was getting a headache, feeling caught in a game of verbal

Sudoku. She understood his point, but it didn't negate the existence of her past and future. "Okay, if I concede, can we move on?"

Geoffrey laughed, nodding his head. "Let's grab a pizza on the way to the house."

"Sure," she said, smiling. Maybe some time in the future this would all make more sense, but in the moment, in this present moment, which seemed to be an inescapable moment if Geoffrey Cannon were to be believed, she wasn't able to board his philosophical train. Then she wondered about some future moment when it all clicked, and realized, that when that moment came, that moment would be the present moment. It had to be. She was about to concede his point... that everything actually did happen in the present moment, and yet, the notion still pricked her brain like a bramble.

4

DARK DESIRE

VERONICA strode naked from the bathroom, stepping barefoot, up on her tiptoes, over to her side of Geoffrey's bed and slid beneath the covers, pressing her body against his. Veronica had hardly said two words on the forty-five-minute drive back to Geoffrey's mountain home. Geoffrey hadn't minded, giving him time to practice what he preached; focusing on the highway, the thrum of the tires on the imperfect surface, emptying his mind of all deadening thoughts. Now, in this moment of solitude, he let his being fill with the warm sensation of Veronica's flesh pressed to his, the smell of her hair. It would have been easy to rewind the past thirty minutes of lovemaking, but instead, chose to fix himself in the present moment, the little sounds she was making, the slight adjustments she performed to fit her body to his, her fingernails sliding hypnotically along his stomach, just barely grazing his skin. When he felt his mind begin to drift, he opened his eyes, finding the most mundane objects in the room, then tilted his face toward Veronica's hair, her scent pushing into his senses, filling his head. A moment later, Veronica's breathing turned to a rhythmic soft purr, unhurried and peaceful.

Just as Geoffrey's thoughts turned to food, trying to picture what was in the refrigerator, another impulse broke in on his otherwise well-behaved thoughts; he suddenly wanted to stretch his fingers around Veronica's slender neck and squeeze the very life from her, watch the last breath leave her throat, witness her ethereal body floating above his depraved eyes, his hands still clamped to her throat...

Geoffrey shuddered, shooting upright in bed, disturbing the blankets.

Veronica stirred, regarding him with shock. "Everything okay?" she said, pulling the sheet up to cover herself, as if suddenly self-conscious over her nakedness.

Geoffrey had experienced this dark desire occasionally with other women, but that was a long time ago; although of late it had become more frequent, more pronounced. He focused his attention on the ceiling fan above the bed, on the thin chain that hung down from the motor, the individual links that reminded him of the drain stoppers found in bathtubs and sinks from an age long ago.

"I bet you're hungry," he said, jumping up from the bed, his gaze settling just a moment on her graceful, fragile neck.

"Let me help," she said, getting up to join him.

They rummaged the kitchen and finally found enough food to create a hodge-podge meal of instant rice, scrambled eggs and store-bought chocolate chip cookies.

"What happened with that ambulance this morning, before we drove back to Asheville?" Veronica asked, biting into a cookie. "Was that old man okay?"

"He had a heart attack. He'll be fine."

"How do you know?"

"That he had a heart attack, or that he'll be fine?"

"That he'll be fine."

"I don't know…I just do…"

That evening they watched a movie on Geoffrey's streaming service, then decided on a midnight stroll up the mountain. Geoffrey found some jogging shorts that fit Veronica, a sweatshirt and some flip flops.

"You're so lucky to live in such a beautiful place," Veronica said, as they headed up the dark asphalt road. "It's so peaceful."

Geoffrey smiled. She was right of course, it was a charming, secluded area and he was grateful to ET for finding it. "This will be a good home base," ET had told him. "Central to all the cities we want to engage with, but with the seclusion you'll need to recharge." Geoffrey didn't want to ponder too long on the notion of *recharging*; he never felt in need of replenishing his resources.

He and Veronica walked another half-mile, coming to a dirt side-road overgrown from lack of use, when Veronica turned to him, kissing him with a passion that caught him off guard.

"Make love to me," she whispered. She pulled the sweatshirt up over her head, dropping it to the ground. Geoffrey raised his palms to her breasts, then slid his hands up to her throat, wrapping his fingers around her tender neck. As if making an offering of herself, she let her head fall back gently as her eyes went shut. She moaned, pushing down the jogging shorts he'd loaned her, stepping free of them, then worked on the button of Geoffrey's cargo shorts, using her toes to drag them down to his ankles.

With his fingers cupped around her neck, he gently increased the pressure until she moaned louder, her breathing growing coarse and uneven. She reached her right hand down to manage him a moment, then worked him from his boxers. Hooking her right leg up around his hips, her left hand clasped over his shoulder for balance, she guided him inside her. Geoffrey's hands, directed by a force outside himself, tightened his grip as Veronica's moans turned to strained groans and muffled grunts, her hips writhing, her upraised leg clinging to him like a vine, holding him close. Now she was screaming, pushing into him until she started choking, fighting for breath, digging her fingernails into Geoffrey's hands, trying to peel his fingers from her throat. Just then, like a faulty clasp, his grip malfunctioned, releasing its hold, and Veronica moaned loudly, her breathing erratic, strained. Several moments later, maybe a minute or more, with the ebb and flow of their bodies winding down, she went limp in his arms, lowering her leg, placing her foot on the ground. She reached down to pull up her shorts, then went back for the sweatshirt, dragging it down over her head, tugging at the bottom to straighten it. Geoffrey pulled his shorts up.

"You okay," he said, ashamed by his behavior. This wasn't the conduct of a healer, of someone who had dedicated his life to helping the lost find their way, the unhappy to discover joy.

"That was... otherworldly..." Veronica said with a curious tone, leaning into kiss Geoffrey on the lips. She drew a deep breath, then let it out slowly. Even in the delicate light of the moon, Geoffrey could see the red marks he'd left on her neck. "I mean," she said, her lips wet, "I've never experienced anything like that before. I've heard about it, but never tried it..."

Veronica must have thought it was some kind of breath play, sexual asphyxiation, pleasure through hypoxia. But nothing could have been further from the truth; Geoffrey had no idea what it was, had no sense or control over what he was doing; it frightened him that it had gone as far as it did; he was only glad he hadn't killed her.

5

GOODBYE VERONICA

GEOFFREY WENT for a short run when he woke, leaving Veronica sound asleep in his bed. It was still early, the sun barely burning through the thick canopy of leaves and limbs. He stopped a moment to take a drink of water and catch his breath, then pulled his phone out and dialed his business manager, ET. Edward picked up on the third ring. "Geoffrey, how are you?"

"I'm good," Geoffrey said, knowing there was no reason to ask ET if he'd woke him up; ET needed little sleep. "Are you free later?"

There was a hesitation and Geoffrey wasn't sure ET had heard him. "ET?"

"I'm pretty tied up today. A little glitch with the Knoxville seminar needs ironing out. I have a few minutes now, though."

Geoffrey really preferred to meet in person, but that desire was trumped by his overwhelming need to talk. "It happened again, the thing I told you about," Geoffrey said, trying to be discreet even though there was no one around for miles. But he never really trusted cellphone technology.

Another quiet interlude from ET's end of the call. "Did anyone get hurt?" Edward finally said.

"No... not exactly." No one had. Nevertheless, Geoffrey was a bit embarrassed explaining to ET how far it had gone. In the past, it had been confined to a powerful desire, one which Geoffrey had always managed to suppress. This felt very different. "I had my hands around her throat..."

The silence that followed this time was unbearable. "ET... say something, I'm freaking out here..."

"Was this one of the women from the conference the other day?" Edward said.

"Veronica."

"Did you frighten her?"

"No, I don't think so. She thought it was some kind of sexual game. I think she actually enjoyed it..."

"Where is she now?"

"At the house."

"Where are you?"

"Jogging."

"As soon as you get back to the house, take her home. Does she live in Asheville?"

"Yes. Okay, I will. Should you and I talk later?"

"Stay by yourself tonight, Geoffrey. *Alone.* I'll call you later when I get free." Edward disconnected the call. Geoffrey slid the phone back into his pocket and cut his run short, deciding instead to head back to the house. By the time he reached the front deck, the sun was stretching long morning shadows across the badly weathered boards. He tried to see past the reflections in the glass sliding doors, hoping to catch Veronica dressed and ready to hit the highway. When he went in, she was still buried under the blankets, unmoving. Had she called in sick to work so she could spend another night with him, without her friend Lillian? Veronica, for all her beauty, talent and intelligence, appeared to be a very troubled young woman.

When he walked to the bedroom, he was surprised she hadn't stirred. "Veronica?" he whispered. Then said it again, a bit louder. "Veronica? You awake?"

Nothing. He stepped closer and touched her shoulder, then shook her gently. "Veronica?" Feeling a peculiar uneasiness, he carefully peeled back the blankets, then the sheet until he could see her face. "Veronica? Are you all right?"

Her eyelids fluttered, then opened, her eyes unseeing, as if still caught in some ambitious dream. A moment later, her consciousness seemed to break through.

"Good morning," she said softly. She pulled the sheet back, scooting over to welcome Geoffrey back to bed. He undressed and slid in next to her.

"I've been jogging," he said, touching his armpit, as explanation for any possible body odor.

"I don't care if you've been running a 10K marathon," she said, rolling him onto his back and straddling him. When they finished making love, Geoffrey was uncomfortable breaking the news.

"Veronica, I need to get going this morning," he said. "I hate to—"

"Hey, no worries," she said, pulling herself from the bed, heading for the shower. Geoffrey dressed and made a quick breakfast for them. On the highway, Veronica had little to say, content to stare out the window. Geoffrey was okay with the lack of conversation, but felt there was something on Veronica's mind, figuring she was uneasy sharing it.

"I couldn't help but notice your tears when we left the Marriott parking lot yesterday," he said. "Are you sad about something?"

She sniffled, then brought her eyes to his, her hair tossing luxuriantly under the draft from the open back windows. "Lillian," she said. "She's my best friend in the whole world... and I can't stand her. I hate her so much..."

Geoffrey kept his eyes on the highway, thinking how Veronica's declaration lacked the vitriol usually associated with such a keen emotion as *hate*. She glared over at Geoffrey, almost as if she were surprised he hadn't responded, then shifted her attention back out the window.

"Everything works out for her, her job, her finances, her dates... everything," Veronica said. "I don't know what she sees in me." She was quiet for several minutes before she said, "You must think I'm a shallow, jealous bitch..."

"You know I don't think anything like that," Geoffrey said, disliking the sentiment she had placed at his feet.

She sniffled and wiped her eye with one knuckle, keeping her face turned toward the window, sheltered from his view. "I don't know what's going on with me. I've been so miserable."

Geoffrey was approaching the first Asheville exit and wanted to ask where he should turn, at the same time not wanting to interrupt her internal inventory.

"Take the second exit," she said, filling her chest with a deep breath, releasing it slowly as if to organize her emotional landscape. At the top of the exit, Veronica instructed him to make a left turn. Less than a mile down the road, she told him to make another left and pull into the lot by the first apartment building. Geoffrey pulled into a parking spot, then turned off the engine.

"Want to come up?" she said, then grimaced. "Of course you don't... who would want to spend time with a nutcase like me..." She threw open the door, then gathered the few things she had from the front floor of the Rover, and stared hard at Geoffrey, her green eyes irradiated by a fresh well of tears. "Thank you for last evening," she said, holding the door open, peering across the seat at Geoffrey. "I'm really sorry."

"Please, Veronica," he said. "Get in and close the door."

For a long second she didn't move, didn't blink, just stared at him, a few errant tears sliding down her smooth cheeks. "I'm just going to go, okay? I'm fine, really."

"You sure?"

"Will you call me sometime? Oh, never mind," she quickly added. "Lillian tells me I'm too clingy! Isn't that a wonderful thing to tell your best friend!" Veronica toggled her head back and forth, as if rewinding her statement, flushing with embarrassment. She slammed the door and hurried toward the entrance of the three-story building. Geoffrey rolled his window down and called to her.

"I'd like to phone you sometime," he said.

Ostensibly, in response to his statement, as if directed from some deep and involuntary chamber of her heart, her lower lip puffed out and quivered, before she spun away and dashed through the glass doors.

6

MEETING COLETTE

THOUGHTS ABOUT VERONICA faded on the drive back, but the anguish she must have felt never left him. Before arriving home, he picked up groceries, filled his gas tank, and stopped for an ice cream cone, which he ate at the picnic table outside the little shop. He had decided on one last errand. Guiding his Rover into the hospital parking lot, he easily found a spot a short walk from the emergency entrance. The doors slid open and closed as Geoffrey walked to the reception desk.

"Can you tell me which room Orvin... Orvin Littney is in, please?"

The woman checked her monitor and told him Mr. Littney was on the fifth floor, room 512. Geoffrey smiled and went to the elevator. When he entered Orvin's room, he spied a woman sitting near the bed, holding Orvin's hand. Orvin, with eyes closed, appeared to be asleep. The woman twisted in her chair to face Geoffrey, appearing to experience a moment of shock, her eyes wide, hard, frozen like a corpse.

"Hi, I'm Geoffrey Cannon... I called the ambulance the day Orvin had his—"

"*Geoffrey Cannon!*" she said, life coming back to her body. "That's your name?" This she stated with a steely chill, her eyes fixed on Geoffrey in an unnatural way. She remained seated, her features dull and gray with age. Geoffrey assumed she was Orvin's wife, and had expected her to offer him the other chair, but she just glowered at him. "Why was he at your house?" she said.

Geoffrey tried to explain that Orvin had just stopped by to be neighborly, and that he, Geoffrey wanted to hear more about their church, since he was new to the community. Of course, Geoffrey was lying to Orvin's wife, unable to tell her the full truth. That day, as soon as Orvin had appeared on Geoffrey's front deck, even before Geoffrey had laid eyes on the elderly man, he had sensed something wrong, and when he looked into Orvin's eyes, he knew he had a heart problem, but more than that, Orvin was on the brink of a major heart attack. Geoffrey had invited him on the walk to speed the event, knowing that he could save the elderly man's life if they were together. He had sensed that if Orvin continued up the mountain that morning in his truck, he would have had the coronary behind the wheel, and would have run off the road and down the steep mountainside.

Orvin's wife listened with disinterest to Geoffrey's account of that morning, her scowl unfazed by the innocent sounding details. Geoffrey couldn't help but wonder what Orvin had told his wife about that morning, about him. The glacial hush in the room was palpable. Mrs. Littney had not bothered introducing herself, and didn't seem to appreciate Geoffrey's presence there.

"Well, I'm glad to see that Orvin is doing okay," he said, and turned to leave.

"Geoffrey?" Orvin called from his bed. "It's good to see you."

Geoffrey moved cautiously toward Orvin, smiling, aware of the sour look on Mrs. Littney's face.

"This is my wife, Colette," Orvin said, turning to look at her, grabbing the remote control to raise the bed. The motor hum filled the silence.

"That was some deal," Orvin said, a new glow to his craggy features. "My lucky day, Mr. Cannon, having you right there to phone the ambulance. I guess I'd be dead if not for you..."

"Well, maybe if you hadn't been walking up the mountain with me, you may not have had the attack at all..."

Orvin's face sagged with a look of shame over Geoffrey's suggestion. "Colette said the same thing, but... the truth is, we'll never know. And I'm damn glad you were there, Mr. Cannon..."

"Mind your language, Orvin," Colette said with a blistering gaze, her mouth a fixed gray line across her face.

Geoffrey allowed the tension in the room to dissipate before he said his goodbyes. "I'm glad to see you doing so well," Geoffrey said. "When you're feeling better, I'd like to get the name of someone who could fix my deck, do that power wash thing you told me about and all that..."

"Well, no need to, Mr. Cannon," Orvin said. "I'll be up and around in a few weeks and I'll come up there and do it!"

"No, Orvin, you won't," Colette said flatly, then turned her unblinking eyes toward Geoffrey. "It would probably be best if you left now, *Mr. Cannon*. Orvin needs to rest before they bring his supper." Orvin launched a protest but Colette killed it with a severe, unshakable glare.

"It was good seeing you, Orvin, and please, call me Geoffrey." Geoffrey turned to Mrs. Littney and smiled, but she never made eye contact, instead directing her attention to a pamphlet the minister had left earlier.

7
THE LODGE

LATER THAT EVENING, after Geoffrey had made himself dinner and performed his meditations, he was about to go for his nightly walk to cleanse the noise of the day, when ET phoned. Geoffrey was glad to get the call and quickly voiced his concern over his strangulation fantasies, and how they had crossed the line into reality with Veronica. ET listened, then asked him a few questions to tease out Geoffrey's state of mind. Reluctantly, knowing the lecture he would get from ET, Geoffrey explained how miserable Veronica had been earlier that afternoon, then described his own distress over his inability to console her, or relieve her discomfort. "I just sat there, observing this lovely woman who appeared as though her entire life was collapsing! I didn't know what to say... I was mortified."

Edward, as was his way, remained still, only silence coming from his end of the phone.

"Then, as if that weren't enough," Geoffrey said, not waiting any longer for ET to respond, "I visited Orvin in the hospital—"

"Why did you do that?" ET broke in.

Geoffrey stammered a moment, trying to corral his reasoning; he hadn't given it much thought. "I don't know... I wanted to make sure he was okay..."

"That's not the only reason," Edward said.

"I wanted to help him! Why is that so wrong?" Geoffrey could feel himself growing impatient with ET, with the whole arrangement. "Orvin is a very troubled man and I think I could really make a difference." As soon as Geoffrey spoke the words, the image of Orvin's wife, Colette, rose up behind his eyes like a wrathful curse; the frosty reception, the fixed creases of her face, the unsmiling, immutable line of her mouth. Her hatred for him had been palpable, deep-rooted and seemingly unwarranted.

"Meet me at *The Lodge* tonight," Edward said without emotion. "Eleven o'clock." ET waited a few seconds before disconnecting the call.

Geoffrey's insides frizzled with dread. He hated going there, and didn't care much for ET's *associates*. Geoffrey glanced at the clock and thought he'd better change into long pants and a warm jacket, and put on his hiking boots. The drive to Yellow Mountain would take at least thirty-five minutes, then another twenty or so to get up the deserted dirt road, followed by a twenty-five-minute hike through the woods.

After finding his headlamp, he walked out to the Land Rover and slid in behind the wheel. The glow from the moon, which earlier had played across his deck and yard, was now gone; a filmy line of clouds cordoning off the last of its light. Geoffrey loved driving through the mountains, especially at night. Very little traffic if any, and occasionally he'd spot an owl swooping down to snag a fleeing rodent crossing the highway, or maybe a deer bolting across the yellow lines, caught in the beam of his headlights, even a bear once. On this night it was extremely dark, the trees and sky melting together into a solid black wall on either side of the SUV. Geoffrey tried to let the thrum of the pavement focus his attention, but failing this, switched on the radio and surfed different stations, his mind recalling Veronica's troubled mental state. How could he not have managed even one word that might have brought her at least a modicum of relief? Was his empathy that feeble, and fickle, a sort of drive-by compassion?

He reached over and turned the radio off, deciding to practice, quite literally, what he preached, which was, to rein in one's thoughts and quiet the mind. It took several minutes of acknowledging the images in his head, then letting them drift away, refocusing his attention on the tension of the tendons in his fingers wrapping the steering wheel, or the gentle rocking of his ankle joint to operate the gas pedal, the trees outside the windshield rushing by. It wasn't long before he was present, the world inside his head finally spinning to a halt.

When the highway narrowed to a two-lane road, Geoffrey had to stay alert so he didn't miss the turnoff, an unnamed dirt road not marked by any signs. Slowing down, he switched on his high beams when he saw the junction approaching. After making the turn, he slowed the vehicle and put it into four-wheel drive. Even with the extra traction, it was still tough to navigate the worn muddy road riddled with ruts, huge rocks and washouts, a formidable obstacle course even for a tank. He eased along, the road climbing steadily toward the top of Yellow Mountain, a destination usually reached by a hiking trail. This unmarked road was used mostly by hunters, who would come up in heavy duty pickups to construct their makeshift camps as an outpost during hunting season, so they didn't have to lug their heavy gear up the treacherous six-mile trail from the highway parking area. But this time of year there were no hunters, so if Geoffrey came to a downed tree across the path, or some other unimaginable hazard, he'd be on his own.

It had taken almost fifteen minutes and he'd only traveled about two miles, according to his odometer. It wasn't quite as long as the hiking trail to get to the top by this route, but it was still about five miles and felt like fifty. He hated when he had to come to *The Lodge*, the dark woods closing in on both sides of the vehicle. The higher he climbed, the narrower the road became, until it seemed as if he was in danger of scraping the paint off his doors on beech and locust trees lining the edge, while rhododendron leaves and branches shuffled along the hood and up past the windshield like car wash brushes. The understory seemed even more impenetrable since the last time he'd been up here. On the right was a small clearing that he could swing the Rover around for the return trip down the mountain. It was tight but manageable and Geoffrey got the vehicle pointed in the right direction and switched off the lights. Blackness fell over everything, so complete it was impossible to see. He pulled his headlamp from his pocket and fixed the strap over his forehead. After popping the door open, he switched on the headlamp, the LED illuminating the trees closest to him, dying out no more than thirty feet or so into the woods. He remembered the trail being off to his left, but walking in that direction he could still see no sign of it. Just then he noticed some scuffed dirt partially hidden by overgrown weeds.

Glad he'd worn his boots and long pants, Geoffrey pushed through the growth, stepping over fallen limbs and kicking aside smaller branches that could tangle in his laces; it was obvious no one had been up here in quite some time. Without warning, a huge bird swept down from the trees fifteen feet in front of him, its shimmering brown, orange and yellow feathers catching fire in the beam of his light for the briefest moment before vanishing into the overgrown forest. Geoffrey waited a second for his breathing to settle, figuring the huge creature for an owl, maybe.

It took about thirty minutes to hike the distance from his Rover to the bald at the top of Yellow Mountain, which was mostly a large expanse of scattered vegetation with few trees, dominated by sedges, red fescue and timothy grass. A few scraggly green alders grew out near the edges, but were impossible to see on this moonless night. Geoffrey switched off his head lamp and took his eyes to the impossible number of stars above him, more like massive dazzling smudges of light, speckled with smatterings of flickering pinpricks. A moment later, a huge object cut a black hole in the star-studded sky, growing larger as it descended toward the bald. Just then the lights underneath the object switched on, a dizzying display of gleaming spots and flashes, a luminosity radiating out with an aura-like luster. A second later, a brilliant beam shot to the ground, burning the grass in a glassy, whitish-blue light. There was barely any sound, a dull hum originating more in Geoffrey's chest than his ears. Instinctively, Geoffrey stepped backward from the enormous craft even though he knew there was no danger. He had never gotten use to these grand entrances, his body seemingly afloat, his head drifting out of sync, under the spell of some peculiar vertigo that always accompanied these meetings. The feeling would pass once they'd landed, but he had never quite learned to cope.

The enormous saucer was sitting on the ground, most of the lights dimmed until they had an almost dream-like quality, as if the ship had no real substance, a translucent chimera, an optical illusion. Geoffrey was still in a trance when ET walked up beside him.

"Are you ready?" Edward said.

Geoffrey could only nod when ET handed him the blackened goggles. Without question, Geoffrey placed the vision blockers over his eyes and Edward led him toward the entrance to the ship. Geoffrey was still under the influence of some bizarre intoxication, stumbling a bit as Edward supported his arm. There was never much Geoffrey could recall about these visits, and was never sure why these beings didn't want him to see them. He'd questioned ET about it on several occasions, ET assuring him it was for his own good.

Once inside the craft, Edward released Geoffrey's arm, then whispered to Geoffrey that he'd see him shortly, and was gone. Geoffrey stood waiting as he always did, his body swaying under some curious current, a hollow magnetism, strange noises circling him, low beeps and whooshes, as if he were being scanned with sound. No light bled through the dark goggles so he could never tell whether lasers or some other luminous technology was involved. After several minutes, or maybe hours, Geoffrey could never be certain, the experience so disorienting, Edward gently took his arm, speaking softly.

"You okay?" he said, leading Geoffrey away. In a few minutes they were standing in the sedge grass again and Geoffrey removed the black goggles. Just then, the craft grew bright, glowing, rising quickly into the night sky, its lights switching off suddenly above them, the craft now just a black hole against myriad stars, shrinking fast, vanishing instantly.

8

A UNIVERSE THAT THRIVES ON BALANCE

ON THE DRIVE back from Yellow Mountain, Geoffrey pondered how unusual it was for Edward to ask for a ride back to town. Normally ET would hitch a lift from the *beings,* as Geoffrey called them, never completely comfortable calling them *aliens;* Geoffrey had never seen them, and for all he knew, they could be some deep cover top secret government agents, or some elite military faction in possession of technology so advanced it had to be concealed from the general public. It was difficult for Geoffrey to wrap his head around the idea of aliens, little green men with floppy antennae sticking from their heads. Nevertheless, these *beings,* whoever they were, were in possession of amazing skills and powers. There was no doubt in Geoffrey's mind about that, and it seemed better to comply with their wishes than question their methods and requests.

Edward had been talking to Geoffrey, trying to explain what was going on, but Geoffrey couldn't compile the information. Obviously, Edward had noticed and told Geoffrey to pull to the shoulder of the deserted highway. Geoffrey slowed the vehicle and guided it to a stop, then put the Rover in park, the engine still running.

"Geoffrey," Edward said. "Have you heard anything I've told you?"

Geoffrey swallowed and let his gaze float toward ET.

"You have abilities we're trying to help you control," Edward said. "But you must listen to what we tell you, or… things could go horribly wrong." Even in the dark, Edward hooked Geoffrey with a gaze so hard Geoffrey felt like he'd been punched. Geoffrey, though sitting perfectly still, was stumbling inside, his brain faltering, staggering like a drunk. Geoffrey's thoughts would not cooperate, tossing up scenarios and recollections from the past, especially the *U.S.S. Eldridge* experiment, how ET's associates had rescued him from a certain and horrible fate. He owed them a great debt of gratitude. And Geoffrey was aware of his own powers, not the least being a kind of gradually-diminishing immortality. Geoffrey was aging, to be sure, but at a rate so slow, maybe a twelfth as fast as normal, as to hardly be noticed; a month of his aging equated to approximately a year in anyone else's life.

"I'm still a bit foggy," Geoffrey said. "I'm sorry."

Edward shifted his attention out the front windshield. A second later blue flashing lights snapped on behind them, a police car coming to a stop behind Geoffrey's Land Rover. Geoffrey looked over at ET, who shook his head and said nothing. The officer knocked on the window and Geoffrey punched the button. With the window down, the officer tilted his flashlight to look at Geoffrey, then shifted the beam to Edward, illuminating ET's face with a ghastly glare.

"Everything okay, fellas?" the officer asked.

"Yes, just needed to talk a moment," Geoffrey said. "Didn't want to be distracted while driving."

The officer paused, studying them both again, especially ET. "While I appreciate your cautiousness, this is a terrible place for a pow wow. Drunk drivers. Very dangerous." The officer hesitated a moment, then said, "Have you been drinking?"

"Me?" Geoffrey said. "No sir. Not at all."

The officer scrunched down to make eye contact with ET, illuminating his face again. "How about you sir? Have you been drinking tonight?"

Geoffrey was about to protest the question; it didn't matter if ET was falling down drunk because he wasn't the one driving, but before he could lodge his objection, Edward shifted his head slightly toward the officer, his eyes fixed and glossy on the rather large man and said nothing. After a second or two of tense silence, the officer stood up, placing his palm on the window frame of the Rover.

"You be careful now," he told Geoffrey, never asking for his license or registration; not even what they were doing out there in the middle of nowhere at this hour. In seconds the police car vanished over the next hill. Geoffrey, with his foot on the brake, eased the shifter into drive.

"Not yet," ET said.

Geoffrey again shifted the SUV into park. "Shouldn't we get going before he comes back?"

"He won't be back... and this is more important." Edward sat a moment, facing straight ahead, looking absolutely sphinxlike. Geoffrey had always considered ET an enigma, but the smart-dressing-silver-haired-middle-aged man was growing ever more puzzling.

"You have powers you don't realize, Geoffrey, and you must treat everything with the utmost attention. Like this strangling fantasy; it is disturbing... and, *The Associates* believe it is growing out of your persistent need to help... that—"

"What! That makes no sense... why should I have this power to manifest things, or to see illnesses, and not use them for good?"

ET's eyes glowed maniacally in the dark space of the car when he aimed them at Geoffrey. "As I was saying, your need to help everyone may be creating an unconscious need for balance, that all of your so-called good acts will need to be offset by beastly ones..."

"But that makes no sense, ET! Why would virtuous acts need to be balanced by—"

"The universe thrives on balance," ET interrupted. "Even if you don't see it, balance is how the universe maintains harmony, no matter how chaotic things may appear. For the average human, those virtuous deeds may proceed without consequence, but not always. TV preachers often fall into the trap, while sermonizing on family values and morals, their personal lives sink into the abyss of sex scandals and aberrant behavior, their psyches unable to bear up against the cosmic equilibrium. It is not a force to be trifled with... and for you, with your powers, it won't be a mere sex scandal you subconsciously create..."

Geoffrey wasn't even sure how to process what ET was telling him. Gazing out at the dark highway, Geoffrey noticed the police car coming back down the mountain, sure he would hit his lights any moment. But he didn't, his car rushing past as if the Range Rover was invisible. Geoffrey glanced at ET, then slid the shifter into gear and pulled from the shoulder.

The remainder of the ride was marked by a keen and convoluted silence, as if everything that needed to be said had been, and there was no space in this new vacuum for mindless chatter. In a short while, Geoffrey pulled the Rover into the apartment complex parking lot. With his thoughts so occupied by the troubling evening, he couldn't even recall how he had driven to ET's residence, how he'd made the necessary turns, stopped at stop signs, heeded traffic lights. ET popped the door open, and in seconds was crossing the lot without as much as a *goodbye* or *we'll talk soon*. Geoffrey thought it odd that this cryptic man lived in a development that was home to young Starbucks baristas attending Community College, midwestern retirees who couldn't afford fancy RVs, single mothers working two jobs while trying to raise a kid, and dead-beat dads hiding from the courts. ET, having lived in Kleary Creek for years, said he liked the area, the slow-motion atmosphere, the quiet, leisurely rotation, and thought Geoffrey would appreciate it too.

After Geoffrey lost sight of ET in the maze of parked cars and vehicles, he pointed his Rover toward the highway, a fifteen-minute drive to his mountain home, and couldn't wait to be there.

9

IMPERMANENCE

1979. Peter Smithwick had been married almost thirty-three years to Amanda Frost, a Miss Pennsylvania Pageant second-runner-up and could never truly understand his good fortune. To him she was the sky, moon and stars. They met by chance at a diner the night after the pageant. He'd been working the counter when she came in with two friends and Peter recognized her from the televised spectacle the night before. The girls sat at the counter, unaware of Peter's presence, him in white shirt and trousers, his black bow tie, and soda jerk cap made of paper tilted just so on his head, like a Norman Rockwell painting.

"Ladies, whatever you want, it's on the house," Peter had said, wiping the counter down with a damp rag where Amanda was seated. "We have a bona fide shining star in the diner tonight!" Amanda didn't seem to get traction on Peter's comment straight away, but when the other girls started giggling, looking in Peter's direction, Amanda turned toward him with a sly, unruffled smile.

They were married three months later, but never had children. Eventually they quit having sex with the goal of making little ones; they just made love and were happy, just the two of them, not needing a brood to complete their lives. Peter was secretly relieved, not sure how the experiment at the Philadelphia Navy Yard may have affected him, and the subsequent interaction with *The Associates*. Many of the survivors among the crewman were ruined for life, unable to keep jobs, quietly going insane, or dying. The Navy discharged all of them eventually; unfit for duty. A cruel pronouncement, since none of the men knew the risk that day; they were just doing their job. But Peter always figured the Navy had made that move so that if any of the men ever told what happened, their stories would be discounted as crazy and unreliable. Then there was the press, the publicity, especially after the barroom brawl when a few of the affected sailors actually disappeared in front of waitresses. But that was easily dispelled as the ravings of drunk barmaids and patrons and by the time the police arrived there was no one left in the bar anyway. The incident was reported in a small local rag, the article having the quality of a nonsensical dream, its impact fading swiftly.

Peter wasted little time on the hoopla around the Naval yard experiment. Most of it was written off as intrigue generated by fringe conspiracy theory nut cases. Until now. Peter was at the library reading a new book that had just hit the shelves, this one delving deeply into the phenomenon in October of 1943. The authors had originally set out to disprove all the hype around this urban legend, but soon, through their own research and contacts, had found themselves tumbling down a deep and slippery rabbit hole of incongruities that seemed to favor the veracity of the claim. This book could rekindle more investigation, UFO and paranormal researchers latching on to this new evidence never reported before. Phones would ring. Doors would be knocked on, people contacted, one person to the next, a relentless search into military coverups and misdirection, as well as the sailors who'd been on the ship that day. Peter always reasoned that if the Navy could make a three-hundred-foot cannon class destroyer escort disappear, how hard could it be to play a little hide and seek with official records and ship manifests.

"What kind of experiment was it?" the young woman asked.

"What are you talking about?" Peter said, looking up from the book, his gyro tossed off kilter by the odd question.

"The book you're reading there," she said, pointing at it. "Is it any good?"

The young woman worked at the library, maybe eighteen or twenty years old, several months pregnant. Peter had seen her several times during his visits, which were frequent, usually four or five times a week, yet they'd never spoken.

"The book or the experiment?" Peter tried to disguise his concern with levity.

The woman smiled. "Are you a college student? Temple? Penn? I just ask, cause you're always in here studying."

"No, ma'am. Just like to read. Never went to college." Peter never finished high school, enlisting in the Navy before he finished his senior year. Sarah and Devlin had urged him to wait until he graduated. "The Navy's always going to be there, son," Devlin had told him. Peter shot back, "But the war won't, and folks need help right now."

"You probably know more than most of those college kids anyway," the young woman said, picking up books people had left on the tables, stacking them on her cart.

"When's your baby due?"

"Two more months, but I feel like I'm about to pop." The woman wore a sad smile, arranging the books on the wooden carrier.

"You and your husband must be very excited."

She smiled again, not making much effort to appear happy. "Well, I better leave you to your reading or you'll never know how it turns out." She grabbed the handle of the cart with both hands and pushed it toward the stacks.

Peter knew exactly how it turned out and was hurrying home, a bit anxious over this new book. His wife Amanda knew nothing of his past, other than his parents had been killed when he was almost eleven, that he was raised by Sarah and Devlin McCoy, that he joined the Navy as soon as he could. That seemed to satisfy Amanda's need for the normal spreadsheet of the past, providing an orderly and palatable backdrop for Peter's otherwise helter-skelter, untidy life.

When he came through the door, he had hoped to convince Amanda that a move to another state, or even a new country, could give their inanimate lifestyle a much-needed boost. They were happy, and they loved each other deeply, at least he thought so, but there was no denying the relationship had built up a bit of static electricity over the years, accounting for the occasional voltage surge between them.

Amanda was sitting on the sofa when he walked into the living room, her eyes unhinged, as if she were in a daze. In her right hand was her whalebone-handle mirror with intricate scrollwork of marine life, the one he'd bought her for their third anniversary. He knew it was the wrong material for three years of marriage, but couldn't think of anything in *leather* that was suitable. She loved and treasured that mirror, but now sat there in her bathrobe holding it like a dead rat.

"What's wrong, baby?" Peter said, coming over near her.

Her blood-red eyes shifted, trapping him in her gaze. "What's going on, Peter?"

A chill squeezed up his spine. She always called him *Smitty*, his Navy nickname, until there was trouble; then it was *Peter* who was left to iron things out. He didn't know what to say, what she could possibly be referring to. He shook his head. She patted the sofa cushion for him to come sit next to her. When he sat, she pulled him close until his cheek was against hers. She slowly lifted the mirror until both of their faces looked back from the silvery surface. The image in the little oval glass was shocking. Until that moment, he had never noticed how much younger he looked than Amanda. The lines in her once creamy, unblemished skin now had the look of a furrowed and rutted road. Gray flames had sprouted near the dark hair at her temples, reaching up to her forehead, sweeping back like vines tangled in her otherwise luscious hair. The skin of her neck hung like a windless flag below her chin. She set the mirror on the cushion and stood before him and opened her robe. Her skin had taken on a wrinkly texture, much like crepe paper streamers strung for birthday parties and celebrations.

"What's going on, Peter? Why do you look so young? You're fifty-five, two years older than me, but you look the same as the night I met you."

At times Amanda's face had looked haggard, but Peter always made adjustments to compensate for her appearance; work, stress, age. Now he knew it was an unconscious strategy of denial on his part, the byproduct of an unflagging optimism maybe, or a convenient blindness more suitable than truth. She wasn't vain, but still appreciated her youthful allure, *second-runner-up in the Miss Pennsylvania Pageant.* Even so, she had the grace to accept the natural entropy of her beauty if only Peter had not been there as a constant reminder that they were growing apart in the most bizarre way, his face a cruel reflection of her own deteriorating vitality.

They would try for a while to make things work, but to no avail; Amanda sinking ever deeper into a gloomy quicksand of self-loathing, harboring contempt for Peter and everything he stood for. One night, after fruitless weeks of trying to fix the crack in their marriage, Amanda brought up his best friend and confidant, questioning who he really was, and why he was in their lives.

"Benny Goodman," Amanda said flatly. "Who is he?"

Benny Goodman, the man Peter had a remarkably important connection to, was no relation to the famous King of Swing. Peter had tried to convince her Goodman was a crew mate from the Navy years. But the late-night rendezvous and secret meetings had raised more than a little suspicion. There was no way to explain to Amanda how Benny functioned like an indispensable cog in Peter's life. Benny was for all practical purposes, Peter's *handler*, a go-between, a confidante who set up meetings with *The Associates*, another secret Amanda could never learn about.

Peter realized the lies were stacked too high and the tower of deceit and duplicity was toppling over; no way for him to stop its devastating collapse. He and Amanda cried, and held each other under the crushing weight of irreconcilable secrets and problems. There was nothing to be done. They both knew that, which made the issue hopeless, and maybe a bit easier in the long run; if something is so broken it can't be fixed, you learn to live with the loss sooner.

A week or so later Peter was gone.

He thought of the young woman who worked at the library, her whole life starting, her new child, her family. There would be continuity in her life, a thread running through it, holding it all together. A string of beads. She and her husband would spend countless holidays together, pictures to remember each one by, photos tracking the natural course of growth and aging. A kind of pliable durability, constancy, permanence.

For Peter, there would be no permanence. No family, no children, no wife to grow old with. No pictures and memories, no aging to track. Peter moved around, avoiding others, practically living in libraries along the way. He studied Buddhism and bodhicitta, Taoism, Jung's collective unconscious, Theosophy and Transcendentalism, Calvinism and Creationism, religions and mythologies, psychology and parapsychology, European philosophy, Kierkegaard, Sartre, Kant, Nietzsche, Camus, science, astrology and physics, quantum theory and relativity. He read extensively about the mystics, Meister Eckhart, Padre Pio, Helena Blavatsky, Dōgen. And Sai Baba, with his power to materialize objects and holy ash out of thin air. He explored the stigmata phenomenon, Francis of Assisi, Rita of Cascia, Therese Neumann. Peter distilled everything down, took it as a whole, and realized that the world viewed from one angle was solid and constant and predictable, but when viewed from a totally different perspective, it abounded with trapdoors, mysterious portals, secret passages and curving mirrors. A shifting set of veils. A malleable illusion; and it was time for Peter "Smitty" Smithwick to make himself disappear. His life as he'd known it was over now. He had to be more careful, more frugal about relationships and friends and acquaintances; his history was both a luxury and a burden he could no longer indulge. Luckily it was tied to a man named Peter "Smitty" Smithwick; that man was about to be erased forever. Smitty adopted a new moniker he'd come across in a library novel, a fictional character he'd admired for his altruism and generosity: Geoffrey Cannon.

10

DEAD JOGGER

GEOFFREY WOKE TO A GORGEOUS MORNING; fairly common for this part of the country, but he never took it for granted. With the air cool, and the sun barely clipping the tops of the walnuts, oaks and poplars, Geoffrey opted for the front deck to do his yoga. Afterward, he went for a leisurely hike up the mountain, followed by a shower and a simple breakfast of oatmeal and fruit, able to almost completely eradicate the events of the previous evening on Yellow Mountain. He was planning his day when the ringtone of his cell went off. Getting up to answer it, he glanced at the clock on the microwave. A few minutes before ten.

"Hello," he said, feeling renewed.

"Mr. Cannon? Geoffrey Cannon?"

"Yes, who is this?"

"Asheville Sheriff's Office," the man said, his resonant voice serious. Geoffrey knew the police funding drives always enlisted the troopers with the gravest voices, and was prepared to make a donation, receive his little get-out-of-a-ticket sticker in the mail, to be placed on the driver's side rear window, easily visible for any approaching patrolman. But then he wondered if this was about last night, the cop who'd pulled up when he and ET had been talking.

"Mr. Cannon, do you know a woman by the name of Veronica Carlson?"

Geoffrey didn't recognize the last name, but how many women had the name Veronica anymore. "Yes, I know a Veronica, but am not familiar with her last name." Which sounded horrible if this officer knew they'd spent a few nights together.

"We got your name from her best friend, Lillian Dellucci."

"Yes, I know Lillian. And Veronica."

"When did you last see Ms. Carlson?"

"The night before last," he said. "Actually, yesterday, I guess. I drove her back to Asheville."

"Drove her back?"

"Yes, we... spent the night together, and I—"

"That's the last time you saw her?"

"Yes. Is something wrong?"

There was an extended pause on the other end of the line. "Ms. Carlson is dead. Her body was found early this morning by a jogger."

Geoffrey's head was spinning. It wasn't possible. He pictured a trail running through the wooded neighborhoods of Asheville, imagined her body lying there in the dirt, maybe partially off the trail, or down a ravine in her running shorts and sneakers, maybe with her earbuds, listening to music on her phone, a jogger happening upon the ghastly scene. How long had she been there? All night? Or was she killed early in the morning? Of course, she wasn't just *dead*, or the police wouldn't be investigating. She was *killed*; the notion so repugnant to Geoffrey, like a dagger twisting in his gut.

"Mr. Cannon, are you going to be in Asheville in the next day or so?"

"Um... next day or so? No, I wasn't planning on it..." he said, a vice in his chest tightening.

Silence expanded out to fill the room, Geoffrey caught in its soundless turbulence. Unable to bear it a second longer, Geoffrey said, "But I can... I can be in Asheville today... if you think it's necessary..."

"We just want to ask you a few questions, Mr. Cannon," the voice said, his manner unhurried, his tone without condemnation. The policeman gave Geoffrey directions to the Sheriff's office and hoped they could see him around one o'clock that afternoon, then thanked him and disconnected the call.

Geoffrey lowered his cell phone to the table, setting it down softly as if it were an explosive device, his attention lost somewhere in the infinite depth of the blue sky beyond his sliding glass doors.

11

FRAUDULENT PROFITEER

IT HAD BEEN three days since his trip to the Asheville Sheriff's office; Geoffrey in a daze since. The meeting went well at first, until the police explained that Ms. Carlson, Veronica, had been brutally strangled to death, her windpipe crushed, left for dead in the woods. The coroner believed she had been murdered early that morning, maybe an hour or so before her body was found. Lillian, her best friend, during a tearful testimony, told the police that Veronica jogged at six in the morning, leaving time for her to shower and dress and get to the hospital by eight. Geoffrey's attention lost all traction upon hearing that Veronica had been strangled. Numbly, he sat staring at the dingy gray wall of the policeman's office, the detective's questions an unintelligible murmur, as if she were speaking to him underwater. She had offered much detail about the case, telling Geoffrey that they had questioned the jogger several times, the one who'd found her body. "He's our strongest suspect right now," Officer Taylor had said.

That had felt odd to Geoffrey, for Officer Taylor to have offered that bit of information. Had she been trying to gauge Geoffrey's reaction, hoping to detect some micro-expression of relief?

Geoffrey had phoned ET several times over the past couple of days, leaving messages, hearing nothing in return. He was about to phone again when he heard a knock at the front sliding door. He got up, hoping ET had driven over, but that wouldn't be his style. At first, Geoffrey didn't recognize the face. He slid the big glass door open and was about to ask what the elderly man wanted, until it hit him. "Orvin, come in," Geoffrey said.

Orvin smiled without moving. "No, no, I can't stay," he said, chuckling a little as if he were nervous.

"Well, you look fantastic," Geoffrey said, glad for the visit and the diversion.

"Thanks, so, yeah, I'm feeling pretty chipper. I uh... well, I just wanted to thank you for all you done."

"I didn't do anything, Orvin. Just called an ambulance. Anyone would have done that."

Orvin's pleasant expression faded somewhat, taking his attention to his shoes. He looked up suddenly. "I'm sorry, I can't recall your last name..."

"Cannon. Geoffrey Cannon."

"I'm sorry, Mr. Cannon, old age, I guess. Hard to remember things these days, but..."

"Please, Orvin, call me Geoffrey... or Geoff, okay?"

Orvin pulled his lips back into an uncomfortable smile. "I just wondered if you could talk a minute..."

"Why don't you come in?"

"No... no, I don't... I just want to ask you a quick question... then I must be going." He glanced at his wristwatch. "I have a follow up appointment with my heart doctor..."

Geoffrey waited, unsure what Orvin was so uncomfortable about.

"It's about the morning of my heart attack, and, well... I don't quite know how to explain what I saw without sounding crazy..."

"Just say it, Orvin."

"Okay then, well, after the pain dropped me to the pavement, I wasn't sure I could stand much more, then all of a sudden, well... the pain stopped!" Orvin waited as if to let this part of his story sink in. "Then, and this is the strange part, I found myself floating above my own body..." Here Orvin stopped again, looking over at Geoffrey with panic in his eyes. It took a few long moments for Orvin to begin again. "I could see you, and my body, and the road, just as clear as day, but I was up above it somewhere, or something..."

Geoffrey waited, unsure where Orvin was going with the story. Or maybe the elderly man just wanted to weigh Geoffrey's reaction to the events, to see if he would laugh, or roll his eyes, or be shocked.

Orvin cleared his throat, then curled his lips back until they covered his teeth. "So... did you see me, you know, floating up there? Because I could have sworn you did, that you even said something, like, telling me I would be okay, that you called an ambulance..." A few heartbeats later the elderly man added: "Then you said, 'Isn't it glorious!'" Orvin seemed to be trembling, his features steeled against a possible onslaught of incredulity. Geoffrey wasn't sure what to say, ET suddenly in his head, warning Geoffrey about trying to help too much. But he couldn't lie to Orvin.

"Yes, I saw you... and yes, I spoke to you."

Orvin relaxed, as if some valve released all the bound-up energy inside his muscles. He smiled and nodded his head with enthusiasm, his cells feeding on some vibrant new current. "I told my wife that," he announced. "But she said I imagined the whole thing. That only Jesus could come to a person as such... and only if it was our time. She said clearly it wasn't my time..." Here Orvin paused, his features sagging under a new weight. "She said, to suggest anything like what I mentioned, well... she said it was blasphemous to pronounce such a thing..."

Geoffrey wasn't sure how to respond. "What do you think, Orvin? Does it feel irreverent to you, like some slander against God?"

Orvin seemed to be disassembling, exhaling loudly, wrestling with the implications of such an act. "I don't know," he said, wringing his large, weathered hands together, as if washing them in some invisible sink. He swallowed hard, his Adam's apple rising and falling like a gavel. "I better go," he finally said and turned to walk back down to his pickup sitting in the driveway.

"Orvin?"

Orvin turned only slightly and kept walking, as if to catch whatever Geoffrey was about to say without stopping.

"Orvin, I'd still like to talk to you about the deck."

When Orvin reached his truck, he popped open the door and stood next to it, looking over the hood at Geoffrey. "I'll be in touch, okay? I really have to go."

Geoffrey waited until Orvin backed from the driveway and sped down the mountain road before going back inside. As soon as he stepped into the empty house, the gravity of Veronica's death dragged him down. He exhaled, and thought about yoga, or meditating, but knew there was no way to focus his attention. This should be simple for him; this is what he taught and preached and... maybe it was all a lie, maybe he was nothing more than a false prophet, or worse, a fraudulent profiteer.

He closed his eyes and was filled with a menacing dread. He opened them quickly. Each time he shut them, Veronica's face was right there, in the dark, her mouth twisted in pain, her eyes pleading for air, the veins in her neck bulging like electrical cords just beneath her skin. He could almost feel her fingernails digging into his own wrists, trying to rip his hands free. A moment later he would release the grip, allowing her to fall backward slowly, lifeless, her legs folding, her body floating to the ground, landing in slow motion among the leaves, her limbs bouncing slightly under the impact, then becoming impossibly still. He could see her black T-shirt perfectly, the name Jamie Cullum against a writhing decorative path billowing forth and ending with a piano. *Catching Tales.* The tour date distressed and illegible under numerous washings. Geoffrey had no idea who Jamie Cullum was. Had never seen that shirt before. Veronica's bright red running shorts clashed with the more somber hues of the design. Maybe the shirt was faded, he thought. Yet the details were so clearly visible. One of her running shoes had come untied in the scuffle, the right one, and was hanging off her foot, her pink sock pulled down to her ankle.

Geoffrey shot up from the kitchen chair, his throat constricted, his breath trapped. He rushed outside to the deck railing, gulping air into his lungs, exchanging it quickly for a fresh batch, then another, until the normal cadence of his breathing returned. After a few minutes he calmed himself, wishing ET would call, afraid to go back in the house and lie down, even though he was bone-tired.

12

A DARK MEMORY

IT HAD BEEN a week since Orvin had seen the heart specialist, and the prognosis was positive, and with a little restraint the doctor felt Orvin could return to some low-stress house painting, small jobs that didn't require a ladder, but wanted him to wait another month or so. "Exercise is good for you," the specialist said. "Just don't overdo it."

Orvin had been relieved by the pronouncement, but Colette just grumbled and cut him a hard look when he'd told her what the doctor said. She wanted him to stay home and rest on the couch, watch television, and maybe piddle around in the garage cleaning up his tools and the workbench and whatnot.

"No more painting, Orvin," she said. "It's just too stressful. Think about someone besides yourself."

Orvin was hurt by her comment. He felt he had always considered her feelings when making decisions. He watched her jerk the sweeper back and forth along the carpet, as if trying to remove a stain that would never come out. In high school she had been a grade ahead of him, and had never noticed him at all. She was on the cheerleading squad, sang in the church choir. Colette was never a devout Christian back then, often drinking and partying and dancing until all hours, but had the voice of an angel. Sitting in church, Orvin would watch her mouth form to the shape of the notes, but the sound itself issued from someplace deep inside her, as if it majestically flowed from every pore of her body like a trillion little speakers, the resonance of her voice filling the smallish church with rarified air. But everything changed her junior year. The rumor spread like oil on water, how several key players from the offensive squad of the football team had taken turns having sex with her after winning a major playoff game. The story had it that Colette and two other cheerleaders had promised this carnal party as an incentive for them to win, and that she had enjoyed keeping her word that night at a local motel. It was an ugly rumor that seemed to have some roots in reality, but Orvin could never tease out fact from fiction. Nevertheless, he'd been broken-hearted at the news of this event, having had a crush on Colette since his freshman year; a more beautiful girl he'd never seen. After the football incident, Colette left school, supposedly to have an abortion, which Orvin knew was a lie; Colette would never have done such a thing.

But she never finished her senior year, never graduated high school or went to college. Back in Kleary Creek, she took a job at her daddy's used car lot, doing bookwork and getting titles notarized, and even occasionally, cleaning out the interiors of trade-ins to get them ship-shape and sale ready. When Orvin saved enough for his first car, he went to her daddy's lot, not knowing she worked there. They talked and she seemed surprised to find out that they had gone to the same high school, and that she didn't remember him. And he was glad about that; maybe she'd feel no embarrassment over the football incident, figuring Orvin had never heard about it. They dated for a while, but never had sex until after they married, and even then, she'd never let him see her naked. Often, she would just lower her pajama bottoms enough to pull one leg out, to allow him his pleasure, then put them back on and leave the bedroom. He'd try to go to sleep in the darkened room after she'd left, but the sound of her prayers bled through the thin walls of their tiny apartment. It seemed to Orvin, that for every minute of sex, she felt it necessary to devote no less than thirty minutes of prayer, asking for forgiveness, pleading for her soul. And as the years went on, her commitment to God and Jesus snuffed out what little intimacy they had left. Eventually they bought a house with two bedrooms, so they'd each have their own. And every night, Orvin fell asleep listening to the murmur of her devotion filter through the wall like a ghost.

The memory pressed on Orvin so hard, he had to leave the house, escaping out to the garage to check paint cans, see which ones were dried and no longer of any use. Mostly he liked opening them, smelling the fresh paint; the odor always gave him a sense of renewal, of hope. He noticed his power washer over in the corner, and thought about Geoffrey Cannon's worn and tattered deck boards, wondering if he could give them new life with a wash and sanding and a fresh coat of sealer. For whatever reason, he liked Mr. Cannon. Geoffrey. Geoff. Maybe it was the bond they'd shared from the day of the heart attack, one Orvin felt even if Mr. Cannon didn't, or maybe it was something more, a sense that Geoffrey possessed some special gift, the ability to see past the veil of life, to peer past the frailty of human existence to glimpse the very core of someone's being.

"Why aren't you dressed, Orvin?" Colette said, standing in the driveway with her purse strung over her arm, her blue dress hanging like a bell covering her figure. He looked over at her, surprised, unsure why she was all gussied up.

"Church, Orvin. Saturday night," she said. "Did you forget?"

He had. He checked his watch and strolled toward his pickup truck, pulling his keys out of his pocket.

"You can't go dressed like that," she said. He looked over at her, suddenly weary, a harsh gravity pulling down on his limbs.

"I'll drive you, Colette," he said.

She hadn't moved from her original position. "You're not going in?"

He cleared his throat, then rocked his head back and forth. He hadn't missed church in, well, never; Saturday night services for Colette and him had been as regular as breathing, and Sunday services, well, those were life itself. And he was fairly certain he wouldn't be attending those either. Jerking the door open, he slid in beneath the steering wheel, then started the engine, waiting for Colette to join him in the front seat. He rolled down the window and let the smell of the fresh mowed lawn wash over him; nearly as bewitching as fresh paint. A few minutes later he heard the passenger side door open, felt the truck dip ever so slightly under the weight of another person, followed by the slam of the door. He checked his mirror, then backed down the driveway into the street. Colette muttered something under her breath as Orvin spun the truck around, but he lacked the will to ask her to repeat it.

During the drive, Orvin was thankful for the silence, even though he knew it was because Colette was upset. Relating the story to her of the morning of his heart attack, he'd purposely left out the part where Mr. Cannon had gently laid his palm on Orvin's chest, essentially restarting

51

his heart, calling Orvin back from the other side. Colette would not have tolerated a moment of that testimony, and even Orvin himself had been reluctant to bring up that detail with Geoffrey several days ago, but he knew it was true, the way he knew something profound had happened to him that morning, in the only way you can truly know anything; he knew it in his heart.

13

CARNIVAL CHARLATAN

GEOFFREY WAS surprised it was already noon; the morning half of the seminar in Knoxville had passed so quickly. He spent most of the early session on gratitude, (not to God, which was a debatable concept for many) but as a general appreciation, recognizing all the gifts one enjoyed in their life, many which often went unnoticed. This talk, which he had given numerous times, stirred only a smattering of raised hands when he first asked the question, *Are you thankful for your life?* Many people had trouble finding a place of gratitude in their hearts, when their minds were ravaged by bills, anger, betrayal, illness, jealousy, fear and pain. It was understandable, but Geoffrey's mission was to help them view their situation through a new lens, a brighter vision requiring a retinal read-justment of sorts.

He would start with grievances, calling on random people in the audience to give a short review of what was holding them back from gratitude. He would listen, smile, then call upon someone else. All the injustices shared a common foe; anger, and all the anger ultimately had its roots in fear, usually the fear of losing something precious. This crowd was no different than any other, the same problems, the same worries, the same hurt and annoyances and outrage, and yes, fear. There might be something consoling in the shared problems and pain, but Geoffrey knew they hadn't come to only air their grievances; they wanted help. And Geoffrey would do his best, first by telling them that what he was about to share, couldn't come from his lips, that it had to come from their own inner understanding, and to keep that in mind. "You must hear this from your own voice, your own mastery." He would pause, letting their minds align until his words became theirs, then he would say, "It is difficult sometimes to connect with our gratitude, because we take so much for granted. For instance, the fact that you are here today is cause for thanks, the fact that you woke to spend another day on this beautiful planet. That you are alive..." He would try to remind everyone of all their gifts, that maybe they owned the vehicle they had driven to the seminar, or had a friend so dear as to drive them, that they had eaten breakfast that morning in their home or apartment, benefitted from a degree of health that allowed them to make the journey to the conference, their ability to listen, to see, to comprehend, to have walked in on their own two legs, or had possession of a wheel chair, the list going on and on, Geoffrey trying to refocus their attention on not what they lacked or desired or had lost or what may have even been stolen from them, but on all the gifts they were blessed with, the love they shared; even their bills were proof that someone, most likely a total stranger, trusted them enough to extend credit, to allow them to pay over time. "This is not to minimize the challenges you all face, but to remind you of all that is going so right in your lives. If you allow it, your mind, your ego, will suck up all the bandwidth in your heart, constantly convincing you that everything is wrong in your life. And when that's the case, it becomes harder for things to go right..."

Geoffrey had tried to make them see the things that he could see from the stage, all the obvious reasons everyone in the room had cause for celebration and appreciation. Simple things, indisputable things that were often forgotten, or overlooked. That everyone in the congregation was alive and breathing and seeing and hearing, was incontrovertible. He had let his eyes swim over these lovely, beautiful, magnificent faces, sending out love and reassurance, knowing that what he had just shared with them was one of the most difficult ideas to assimilate. There was not one person sitting in the audience who didn't feel entitled to their anger, their pain, their disgust and hatred, even as it served no positive purpose in their life; a seductive construct of the ego, of the mind, its only value to stoke the embers of strife, misery and discord.

Geoffrey had thanked them all, and told them to enjoy an amazing lunch and he'd see them at two o'clock. Some people rose in front of their chairs joining pockets of applause, others filed out, some checking their phones, or talking to their friends next to them, their eyes on the exits. Geoffrey moved from the stage and stood near ET, listening to the murmur of the crowd departing the huge hotel conference room. He never felt more alive than when he was speaking to a room of interested patrons of his message.

"Let's grab something to eat," Edward said to Geoffrey. Geoffrey shifted his attention toward the exits, searching for the person who sat by herself near the back, a stocky woman in her fifties, fit, her back straight, sturdy shoulders, with nearly institutional auburn hair. He knew her from somewhere.

"Geoffrey?"

"Yeah, sure. Lunch sounds good."

Over lunch Edward brought up Veronica, the police, asked how that interview had gone. Geoffrey said they asked where he'd been that morning, if anyone could verify that he'd been home sleeping, how well he'd known Ms. Carlson. The usual stuff. Nothing accusatory. Then it hit him. Detective Katherine Taylor. That's who the woman in the back of the room was.

"The detective from Asheville is here," Geoffrey said.

"You sure?" Edward said.

"Yeah, she was sitting alone. I knew I recognized her…" Geoffrey put his fork down and wiped his mouth with the napkin. A complicated foreboding crawled through his stomach. Why had she driven all the way to Tennessee from Asheville? How could they suspect him? And yet, he suspected himself. A curious guilt formed along the margins of his thoughts. He cleared his throat and shifted his eyes toward ET. A complex set of transactions flashed across Edward's eyes, so instantaneous Geoffrey had barely detected them. "What?" Geoffrey said, wondering what had rattled ET's mind.

Edward checked his watch. "We should probably head back over…"

"What was that look about?"

Edward picked up the bill and walked to the register to pay. Geoffrey glared at him, then got up and walked stiffly to the parking lot, upset with Edward's inscrutable manner. Standing by the door of his Rover, Geoffrey slowed his breathing, measuring the air with intent, recalling his talk from the morning, feeling his own entitlement to his frustration over ET. Before Edward reached the vehicle, Geoffrey had managed to distance himself from his own ego's desire for anger, for conflict.

People started shuffling back into the large hall fifteen minutes before two. Without windows or access to the day outside, the afternoon felt like it was already bending toward evening, Geoffrey feeling some weird slippage as he watched attendees shuffle to their seats. Maybe it was the conversation with ET at lunch, or more likely, having just seen Detective Taylor take her seat at the back of the room. Why was she here?

Geoffrey had to focus, call his mind back from the disquieting game of *Why?* and *What if?* He checked his phone. Three minutes until he walked out, smiling, energetic, proving to his most adoring acolytes that staying present and giving thanks was key to calming a raging mind and harried soul.

"Don't give a thought to Detective Taylor," Edward said, walking up behind Geoffrey. "There's nothing to worry about."

Geoffrey was just about to dispute ET's claim, when he remembered the night they'd met at *The Lodge,* the police officer who checked on them sitting by the side of the road in Geoffrey's Rover, how ET had dismissed him with a look. Maybe there wasn't anything to worry about.

"You're on," Edward said.

Geoffrey checked his lapel mic and trotted out, his face shiny with manufactured joy, to a welcoming round of applause. Without stopping, he covered the stage from one end to the other, meeting eyes and smiles, so many bright faces abounding with enthusiasm, anticipation, and hope. Waiting a moment to let the crowd settle, Geoffrey stepped back to center stage until the room was quiet.

"Who here today is out of their mind?" Geoffrey asked, but no hands went up. "No one? Not one of you is out of your mind?" Still no hands went up, a few titters and smiles and chortles. "Well, let's see what we can do about that. Hopefully, before any of you leave today, you'll all be out of your mind!"

People laughed and fidgeted, adjusting themselves in the cushioned conference chairs. Others sat stoically, or smiled, fiddling with their glasses, clearing their throats, most sets of eyes facing forward. A few men near the front of the large room shuffled their feet, as if trying to find the most comfortable position. Women wearing snug jeans, dresses and shorts crossed their legs, or folded their arms with a pleasant grin. A few folks had their phones out, checking texts or emails after lunch, maybe work related, or a spouse, or from someone special who couldn't attend today.

"But first, I need to know who had a hectic week?"

In the crowd of over seven hundred people, at least eighty percent of the hands shot straight up. Heads swiveled, checking on their neighbors to see who shared such a frenetic week, finding comfort in the common-ality of this natural disorder.

"Hmm," Geoffrey said. "Must have been a rough week? Maybe the planets are no longer circling in harmonious orbit. Let's see. So, I need a willing participant, with Teflon skin, someone impervious to ridicule and torment!"

Numerous hands went up and Geoffrey let his gaze slide among the volunteers, settling on an attractive woman a few rows back with a generous curtain of jet-black hair pouring out from beneath her white Stetson. She appeared to be in her late forties, maybe early fifties, with bewitching features and the steely eyes of a rodeo bull rider. When she walked to the stage, Geoffrey couldn't be sure she wasn't wearing spurs. He took her hand and asked her name.

"Tess. Tess Landry," she said, holding his hand, enchanting the audi-ence with her sparkling smile.

"Landry? Any relation to the famous Coach?" Geoffrey asked.

"No sir," she said, her eyes glittery under the bright lights. "No Cowboys for me. A Sooner fan born and raised!"

"All the way from Oklahoma…"

"Oklahoma!" she shouted, spinning toward the audience, performing a solo two-step. "The greatest state in the world!" In fancy cowboy boots and studded jeans, Tess was going to be a live wire.

"Well, Tess, I can't wait to hear about your hectic days," Geoffrey said, clapping his hands together. While the audience applauded, Edward brought out a chair and a hand-held mic for Ms. Landry. Another stagehand brought a chair for Geoffrey. When they were finally seated, Tess gave a look to the crowd, then to Geoffrey, her luxurious black eyelashes like star gates to an exotic planet.

"So, Tess, can you tell us about these frantic days of yours?"

Tess started by telling everyone that it was the day before, when she was trying to get ready to drive up for Geoffrey's seminar. "I've been wanting to come to one of your gigs for years, and hell, I gave up on you ever coming to Oklahoma."

Yeah, she was going to be a handful. Tess continued talking about her boss piling more policies on her desk, explaining that she worked at a small insurance agency in Oklahoma City. Then, as if the extra work delaying her departure wasn't enough, she finally got on the road only to have a flat tire. She'd had to wait for Triple-A to come fix it, because she wasn't about to touch all that grime and grease and "unscrew those big damn lug nuts," which brought some laughter, mostly due to Tess's accent, with its charming power to transform the mundane into the comical. But her trials didn't end with road service, arriving at the hotel in Knoxville two hours later than she'd anticipated, only to find out that they had given away her reservation by mistake.

"Of course, there were no dang rooms left at midnight!"

The hotel called around the area trying to find her a room, but to no avail. Everything was booked because of a rodeo and a national cheer-leading competition and other events she couldn't recall. So, she ended up sleeping in the hotel parking lot in the front seat of her GMC Sierra, then in the morning got one of the rooms from an early checkout, which the hotel had brought in special staff to clean and freshen so she'd have a place to shower and take a nap. Hotel management apologized for the inconvenience and told her that her stay would be free, as well a voucher for a complimentary night if she wanted to stay an extra day.

People laughed and applauded and Tess took it all in stride, her moist red lips pulled back to reveal a brilliant set of white smiling teeth. Geoffrey waited for the audience to fall quiet before he continued.

"It sounds pretty crazy," Geoffrey said.

"I'm laughing up here now, and it don't seem so bad, but last night I was fit to be hogtied."

"Well, I can imagine. So, Tess, I want to perform a little inventory so we can understand this better. Is that okay?"

"Well, certainly, doll. That's why I'm up here, right?" she said to the audience, bringing more laughter and some applause. A stagehand rolled a large chalkboard out next to Geoffrey's chair.

"Oh, dear Jesus, I hope you don't want me to spell anything," Tess said, mocking a worried look for the audience.

"Nothing like that," he said. When the room fell silent, he asked her first if she worked at a desk, and sat most of the time, which she answered yes. He wrote a numeral one, then wrote *Sitting* beside it. He jotted the numeral two under it, then wrote *Sitting* beside it. "I'm assuming you sat while driving up here," Geoffrey said.

"Well, of course, doll," she said.

"Did you stand outside your truck waiting for road service?"

She nodded, then shrugged toward the audience as if confused by where Geoffrey was headed. He put a numeral three on the board and scrawled the word *Standing* beside it.

When he finished the review, the list had numerous entries, the actions either sitting or standing, except for the one where she slept in the front seat of her vehicle, which read *Lying Down*.

Tess leaned in toward the chalkboard as if she needed to be closer to make sense of the words written there, then looked at the attendees and shrugged again.

"If we look at this list, it would appear, Tess," Geoffrey started to say, "that most of your frantic day was actually spent sitting, followed by standing, then of course, one entry where you're lying down."

Tess screwed her lips into a complicated angle and cleared her throat. "If we go by that list of yours, well, I had me a routine day, doing nothing but sitting around and standing like a post? But that inventory doesn't tell the whole story, sweetheart."

"What am I missing?" Geoffrey asked.

"Well, hell, baby doll, the whole damn kit and caboodle is all! I mean, the mental roller coaster, the worry and hurry, the frustration, the waiting, the tension, the psychological torment of everything going to hell in a handbag!"

Geoffrey smiled, waiting for the laughing, followed by applause, to subside.

"That's kind of the point, Tess," Geoffrey finally said. "Everything went to 'hell in a handbag' in your mind only. Your physical self was never subjected to anything more challenging than standing up. Let's look at this another way. You're here at the seminar, you didn't miss a minute, and for sure, sleeping in your truck probably wasn't any fun, but you had a nice shower this morning, and I'm guessing, a nice breakfast afterward. And tonight, if you're able to stay another day, you'll sleep in a beautiful room with a comp dinner. I will talk to management about that."

Tess rolled her big brown eyes and sighed. "Well, that tension I felt in my chest was pretty real yesterday."

He could tell she was upset, as if he had minimized her experience. "I think you've been a real sport, Tess. Let's give our lovely friend here a big round of applause."

Tess managed a big Sooner smile and kissed Geoffrey on the cheek, leaving a red smudge as she strolled along the edge of the stage, smiling and waving at the crowd as if she'd just been named Miss Oklahoma, 2024.

Geoffrey watched her to her seat, allowing time for emotions to settle down. "The point of this exercise was not to make light of Ms. Landry's experience, but to call attention to how our mind tries to imprison us with our own emotions, run roughshod over our wellbeing and harmony. Is it a herculean task to disconnect from the ramblings of our tormented minds in times of stress? Absolutely! But that is the mission, that is the challenge of staying in the moment, never succumbing to stress in the first place. If we can be conscious of what is actually happening in the moment, as we live it, and fight the mind's craving to whip our thoughts into a maelstrom of past and future, anger and frustration, disappointment and indignation, we might just find that things aren't nearly as bad as we *think* they are."

Members of the audience clapped, nodding their heads, while others seemed to stew with grim, doubtful expressions, chewing on this idea like a rubber hose, which was neither palatable nor nourishing. Was it too abstruse? The schism between mind and soul? Was it real, was it illusory? Geoffrey told himself that new concepts could be finicky. There was always *resistance;* the ego's most potent weapon. Geoffrey knew all of that. He saw himself as a presenter of ideas. A kind of cranial chiropractor. That was the most he could do. But if it made a difference in one life, well, wasn't that enough? At least that's what he told himself.

Geoffrey finished the afternoon taking questions. When the Q and A session ended, he thanked everyone for coming, then headed toward the lobby. As people swept from the exits, Geoffrey positioned himself near one of the main sets of double doors to shake a few hands, and really apply his gifts, manifesting money for those who had voiced financial issues earlier that morning; Geoffrey recalled each and every one. One of his gifts; he had phenomenal memory. And the new money would just show up in their wallets, or in their purses or handbags, a hundred or so, or maybe fifty to cover the cost of the seminar. What harm could it do? No one would be the wiser.

Several people had more serious issues. The woman who had injured her back and was unable to work and was having trouble caring for her kids. Geoffrey held her in a hug, placing both hands on her back, his forehead against hers. In silence, he held her that way until he could see in his mind her damaged disc sliding back into place. After a few days the swelling would go down and she'd feel renewed, her energy returning. No one was aware of what he was doing; most folks thinking he was praying for them, the religious ones joining him in quiet reverence, thanking Jesus under their breath. There were others; a sprained ankle that wouldn't heal, migraine headaches, an obstinate skin rash that was painful and persistent. Those ailments would all vanish in a few days, at most a week, the participants experiencing a vigorous gratitude for their miraculous healing.

Then there was the woman who had spoken up earlier about a doctor's appointment she had great anxiety over. Geoffrey spotted her approaching with the crowd. When she made it to the front of the line, she said, "Thank you so much, Mr. Cannon. You've really helped me get over my fear." Even though she had no idea yet, this woman was gravely ill and the tests she was submitting herself for would reveal her situation. Which wasn't good. Geoffrey had felt her sickness all the way from ten rows back. Standing there now, he smiled at her, and placed his hands on either side of her face, resting his forehead against hers, hoping ET didn't see what he was doing. He held her until he could feel every perverted cell in her body align with new vigor. With no idea what he'd done, she smiled and took a deep breath and squeezed his hand, then turned and shuffled into the lobby. Her tests would all come back negative. A clean bill of health. What harm could it do, helping people like this?

It was the woman in the wheelchair who was his greatest test. She was in her sixties, youthful in appearance and spirit, at one time a lovely dance instructor. She smiled at Geoffrey and took his hand. A car accident ten years earlier. Took her husband instantly. Geoffrey knew he could make her walk, could see every circuit in her spine, each intricate broken connection, every filament of nerve tissue, every ruptured disc clearly delineated with glowing exactitude, but it was more than seeing, he could feel what needed to be done, knew precisely what to manipulate from inside the mechanism of his own being, how to establish the linkage between his own physiology and hers and he could lay his hands upon her legs, his forehead to hers, and she would rise from the chair, her legs weak but healed, her body restored. He fought the urge, as he had on so many occasions. "Undue attention," ET had warned him. "Side show," or "Carnival Charlatan," or "Worse." What was the "Worse?" ET reminded Geoffrey about the folks waiting on the return of Jesus, how they really didn't expect Him to show, so if He did, well... *the work of the Devil!* Satan! Beelzebub! People believed and didn't believe. They wanted Jesus to return but not really. The concept of a Jesus was easy to wrap a mind around, but the reality of a flesh and blood Savior who could perform miracles? It could only mean a couple of things. None of them good. "You remember what they did to Jesus, right?" ET had said. "They'll do it every time." Then there were the other problems with such an exotic brand of publicity, people lining up to be healed, no longer interested in growing, or becoming conscious, their own journeys thwarted by Geoffrey's *good intentions*. After all, wasn't that how the road to hell was paved? Geoffrey could only hold the woman's hand, and watch as her friend wheeled her away toward the front entrance of the hotel, disappointed he'd done nothing for her.

After the crowd had thinned, Geoffrey was about to head back inside and gather his things when Tess Landry caught him near the rear of the conference room.

"That was some show, wasn't it?" she said, walking right up to Geoffrey, so close he could smell the jasmine and strawberry shampoo in her hair.

"I really appreciate your—"

"I made up all that hooey, Mr. Cannon," she said, cutting him off. "Now don't hate me, okay?" Her big lashes, which appeared completely natural, blinked once across her glittery brown eyes and she seemed genuinely apologetic.

"Well, thank you just the same." Geoffrey smiled. A new first, a fake story, but he wasn't going to hold grudges. She took his hand, pulling back those full red lips to reveal her perfect set of dazzling alabaster teeth, pressing something into his palm. A sizzle of electricity passed between them, a subtle, sensuous charge. A second later, Tess in her white Stetson and her shining black hair, shifted away from Geoffrey, a half-moon movement that seemed to put the large conference room on tilt. Then she was gone. Vanished, the paper she'd deposited in Geoffrey's palm with the weight of an element from the periodic table. He opened his fingers, unfurled the note. 702. Nothing more. A room number. Her room number. What could she possibly see in me? Geoffrey thought, continuing toward the front of the auditorium. Once backstage, he went to the controls area and grabbed his jacket and his small duffle and headed to the parking lot, relieved that ET was nowhere to be found. Edward certainly wouldn't have appreciated Geoffrey's altruism, especially the clandestine healings Geoffrey had felt empowered to perform. Geoffrey reasoned that since no one knew, what harm could come from it? He saw no downside to his actions, feeling satisfied with his decision. He tossed Tess Landry's room number in the trash can and chuckled to himself, and was almost to the lobby when a woman called his name.

"Mr. Cannon? Geoffrey Cannon?"

14

COMFORT OF STRANGERS

DETECTIVE TAYLOR APPROACHED and introduced herself. "Detective Katherine Taylor. From the Asheville Sheriff's Department," she said, shaking his hand. "Remember?"

He nodded, feeling something slip off center.

"Maybe there's somewhere we could talk in private," she added, pointing him toward a nucleus of four cushy, pastel-colored designer chairs arranged in a small cross, a table in the center, sequestered from the main lobby by a wall of large plants. No one else was sitting there, so they took two chairs across from each other. Detective Taylor set a vinyl pouch on the table between them.

"Sorry to waylay you like this," she said. "I know you must be exhausted after speaking all day."

Geoffrey set his duffle bag and jacket on one of the remaining chairs. "I noticed you earlier," he said. "When I realized who you were, I was surprised you'd driven all this way."

"It's not really that far." She seemed to study his face, as if it were a roadmap of guilt. The uneasy sensation he felt was probably fatigue, he figured. Perhaps worry. Regardless, he must have looked criminal as hell the way she was staring.

"I just wanted to ask you a few more questions, if that's okay. I won't keep you long."

Geoffrey sat back in the chair and crossed his legs, nonchalant, nothing to hide. "Sure. Of course." Was this woman versed in body language? What did crossing one's legs indicate? He uncrossed his legs and sat with his feet flat on the ground.

"The suspect we had, well, he had a solid alibi, and so, you're the only one left," she said. "Do you have anyone who can vouch for you that morning?"

Geoffrey felt like he couldn't even vouch for himself anymore. He was going to explain he'd been with ET, but he'd dropped him off at his apartment around three in the morning, and didn't really want to bring him into it. Too many questions. And he certainly didn't want to have to explain about *The Lodge*, because he couldn't. "I was home in bed. By myself." Geoffrey shrugged as if there was nothing more to say.

Taylor picked up the vinyl pouch and slid out some new photos of Veronica from the trail where she was murdered. She set them before Geoffrey. "The lab was able to pull fingerprints from Ms. Carlson's neck," Detective Taylor said. "It doesn't always work, but this time they were pretty clear."

"Will that help?"

"Not if they don't match anything in our data base."

Geoffrey sat uneasy, something folding in his gut. It felt like Taylor was trying to *Columbo* him, make him say something incriminating, trick him into revealing a little-known fact about the case. But he didn't have any information to reveal, incriminating or otherwise. The silence between them grew exponentially, making Geoffrey more uncomfortable than he already was.

"Would you submit to being fingerprinted?"

Well now it was out there, the true reason for her journey from Asheville. At first, he thought why not; he didn't have any kind of a police record, nothing to hide. Then he realized the Navy fingerprinted him. An unsteady current flowed along his skin. Would they run new prints against the data base, or just check them against the ones they pulled from Veronica? He didn't care if they knew he'd been in the Navy, it was the *when* that would be impossible to explain.

"You don't have to," Taylor added.

"No… no, I will," Geoffrey said, hoping ET would have some ideas about how to wriggle out of this. "Can I come to Asheville later this week, say—"

"That won't be necessary," Detective Taylor said, pulling a small device from her pocket. "I can do it right here. Just stick your hand out."

Geoffrey exhaled rather loudly and eased his hand forward.

"It doesn't hurt," she said.

Holding his hand firm, she pressed the screen of the device against each fingertip, then asked to do the other hand. After checking the results, she pressed a send button, then turned it off and stowed it in her pocket. "That's it."

Geoffrey stood, picking up his things. "Okay, well, that was…"

She wore a pained expression and asked if Geoffrey could sit a moment longer. "Would you mind giving me a DNA swab?" she said. "You're not under arrest or anything. It's strictly voluntary."

Geoffrey sat down, putting his things back on the chair. "Sure, if it will help…"

Detective Taylor pulled a clear plastic sack from her pocket with a swab inside. Wearing gloves, she carefully removed the swab and handed it to him, directing him to swirl it around between his lips and gums and back in his mouth. When he finished, she held out the plastic bag for him to drop it in, then ran her fingers along the seam to seal it. "Thank you so much," she said. "I'll be in touch." She slid the photos back into the vinyl pouch and stood up, extending her hand. Geoffrey shook it and smiled.

"I enjoyed your seminar," she said, then turned and walked toward the hotel lobby entrance.

All at once Geoffrey felt like a dope, that he should have had a lawyer present. He hadn't even thought about that earlier. He picked up his things planning to head out to his car, when he decided there was something else he needed more. He walked to the elevator. The doors opened and he stepped in, then pressed the button for the seventh floor. Comfort of strangers, he thought, his center of gravity still out of plumb.

15

OUT OF YOUR MIND

THE COUPLE of weeks since the Knoxville conference had largely come and gone without consequence. After spending a few nights with Tess Landry in the World's Fair Hotel, and touring the old fairgrounds, all the buildings Knoxville had built just for the occasion, he'd been happy to get back to his mountain home, especially after Tess had told him she was married. Maybe because she wore no ring, and moved with an autonomous, unhurried grace, Geoffrey had assumed she was single. "Bad kismet, I guess, working together under the same roof," she had said, sitting naked on the sheets, sipping bourbon from a bottle she brought from her truck. "That's not a good combo, work and play, not in a marriage." Geoffrey had offered to grab some ice down the hall and fix her a highball. She declined with a swish of her manicured fingers, nails as bright as LED lights. "Your husband owns the insurance agency?" Geoffrey had asked, accepting the bottle from her and taking a sip. She'd spun toward him, her eyes glistening like razors. "Who said anything about him owning the damn place, Geoff? I said we work together. If the truth be told, and I'm nothing if not truthful..." Her eyes were suddenly full of mischief, the tip of her tongue slipping between those amazing teeth. "I started the damn agency years ago, before I ever met that dead-beat." Geoffrey had apologized but Tess hadn't seemed to care about his disparaging assumption, more interested in exploring the outer bound-aries of Geoffrey's stamina in bed.

The memory still weighed on Geoffrey as he stood at the glass doors watching Orvin pressure wash the old deck boards, amazed by how the wood seemed to glow after the removal of years of algae growth, grime buildup and walnut stains. Orvin had explained that morning about all the elements capable of destroying the natural luster of wood. "Most decks here in the southeast are built from southern yellow pine," Orvin had stated proudly, as if he himself had been responsible for the hearty trees. "#2 Prime. This is tough, treated lumber… last a lifetime if we care for it!"

Orvin told him they'd have to let it dry a few days before he came back and sealed it. "A little light sanding and we'll be good to go."

Geoffrey knew nothing about wood and stains and sanding, and appreciated how Orvin referred to it as *their* project, sharing the responsibility for its upkeep and longevity. They talked over a couple of beers when Orvin finished, Geoffrey sharing his plans about a housewarming deck party in a week or two, depending on if the deck would be ready for that.

"Oh, yeah, no problem there. Nothing but good weather for the next week or so," Orvin assured him.

Geoffrey explained how he planned on inviting his neighbors from the mountain, folks he hadn't met yet. "Thought I'd put a flyer on the mail box bulletin board at the bottom of the hill."

"Great idea. Nice folks up here." Orvin tilted his bottle back and took a short swig.

"I'd like you to come. You and Colette," Geoffrey said.

Orvin's gaze quivered under the spell of some unfurling complexity. He scratched his forehead and finished the last of his beer.

"Did I say something wrong?" Geoffrey asked.

Orvin spun around, his eyes meeting Geoffrey's full on. "No. No, not at all," Orvin said, almost apologetically. "Nothing like that, it's just, you see, Colette doesn't go in much for parties and whatnot." Orvin glared off into that same difficult space again, as if there were things written there he was unable to share.

"*You'll* come, won't you?" Geoffrey said.

Orvin stood up and picked his cap off the floor where he'd left it. "Let's see, okay. I want to get that deck done first… then, we'll see…"

Geoffrey walked Orvin out to the truck and waved as the elderly man pulled from the driveway. He started back up the steps, admiring the bright wood slats of the deck, swirled with knots and nebulas grain, a thousand miniature universes Orvin uncovered using nothing but water and pressure. It was like magic. Intricate and marvelous. Renewed. Geoffrey was standing in awe when his phone chimed in his cargo shorts pocket. He didn't recognize the number, but slid his finger across the screen to answer.

"Hello?" Geoffrey said.

"Mr. Geoffrey Cannon?" the deep voice said.

"Yes, that's me."

"I'm Detective Massanburg, with the Oklahoma City Police Department. Do you know a Mrs. Esther Landry? She goes by the name, Tess."

Geoffrey felt something snap, his eyes caught in the whirling eddies of wood grain at his feet. Esther? He'd had no idea that was her name. They hadn't talked about such things, hadn't talked much at all.

"Sir?" the voice said.

"Yes, sorry. Yes, I met her in Knoxville, at a seminar. Is something wrong?"

"Mrs. Landry's body was found a few days ago outside Knoxville. At a rest stop off the highway. Her husband reported her missing a week ago when she didn't return from the seminar. He showed us the brochure for your conference and we thought you might be able to help us with our investigation."

"Yes, of course. Whatever I can do."

There was a moment of silence amidst paper shuffling.

"*Are You Out of Your Mind?* Was that the name of your seminar, Mr. Cannon?"

"Yes."

"Why that title?"

Geoffrey tried to explain in the simplest terms possible the gist of his workshops, about being present in your life, how the mind can rob you of so much precious time. "So, in this context, being *Out of Your Mind* is actually a positive thing."

Massanburg cleared his throat, a quiet, *ahem.* "You said you met her, Mrs. Landry. How many people attend your seminars?"

Geoffrey explained that they usually numbered in the hundreds, but that that one-day workshop had attracted over seven hundred people.

"That's a big crowd," Massanburg said. "You personally meet every attendee at an event that large?"

"No, of course not, but..." Geoffrey's lungs tightened. "I ask for volunteers from the audience to come on stage and help with certain concepts..."

Another silence. Geoffrey could hear his own heartbeat drumming in his ears. This can't be happening again.

"Mrs. Landry was one of your volunteers?"

"Yes," Geoffrey said, terrified of the question that was coming next. He couldn't lie, but telling the truth was going to bring the opening salvo of a thousand troublesome inquiries, prompting awkward, and inflammatory, answers.

"Did you have any further contact with Mrs. Landry beyond the seminar?"

There it was. An eye-blink later Geoffrey could feel his entire life sucking down a gaping, spiraling sinkhole, his brain locked between truth and lies, unsavory facts and indefensible deceptions. Geoffrey was somehow responsible for Tess's death, as he was for Veronica's, even though Detective Taylor had called a week earlier to tell him there were no matches with his DNA or fingerprints. It didn't matter; he could feel his culpability, guilt pulsing through his veins, firing across his synapses, red lights splashing along the inner lining of his skull. He felt himself separate from his own body, floating like a shadow on the front deck, could hear his voice as if speaking across time and space, explaining to Detective Massanburg about how Tess had given him her room number, how she'd invited him in, how they'd spent the next two days and nights together. He didn't tell Massanburg about the spillage he felt when she laughed, how her lips were like hot butter on his flesh, how her touch made something warm and vital collapse inside him. The perfect whiteness of her skin. The smell of her neck. Her legs entwined with his, and suddenly, Geoffrey felt the evening growing darker, smaller, as if trapped under a shrinking dome.

Massanburg had yet to respond. Geoffrey's chest expanded and fell, his breathing strained, stifled and rough. He recalled the first night with Tess, how he'd placed his hands gently around her throat, how taut the flesh had been beneath his fingertips, how she'd cooed with pleasure, her arms limp at her sides, submitting herself completely. Without pursuing it further, he slid his hands up to cradle her face, kissed her deeply, her hands wrapping his hips, pulling him closer. That was it. The asphyxiation desire gone. He never considered it again.

"Did you see her after you left the hotel that last morning?"

"No. I never saw her again."

"Did she say anything to you about stopping anywhere, or meeting anyone on her drive home?"

"No. Nothing."

"Thank you for your time, Mr. Cannon," Massanburg said. "We may be in touch."

"Sure. Any way I can help."

Geoffrey sat down on the steps. He placed his phone on the wood next to his leg and stared out at the gathering darkness enveloping his property. The trees swayed, the leaves clattering, the breeze honing a cool edge to the evening. Why was this happening? These lovely women. Geoffrey was almost relieved Massanburg had not told him how Tess was killed. And yet he wanted to know. And then, like a premonition, Geoffrey's attention was pulled toward some movement out toward the edge of the driveway that butted up to the trees, back in the brush. Standing up, he sharpened his focus, narrowing his eyes on the shape beyond the poplar trunks and waxy rhododendron leaves. A figure. A bear on its hind legs? It was large, but too still, and seemed to be looking directly at Geoffrey. A man, maybe. Or just a hole in the foliage? A mirage.

"Who's there?" Geoffrey said, and could have sworn he heard a grunt or snort. Just then headlights started up the road, casting long shifting shadows across the driveway and surrounding woods, chaotic shapes that appeared to jolt the thick trees, making them quiver and flicker and dance. As the car rushed past Geoffrey's house, it left a fading smudge of red light along the macadam. When Geoffrey gazed back toward the trees, the figure was gone.

16

SOMETHING HUGE IN THE POPLARS

ORVIN WAS FINISHING his morning coffee, reading the Kleary Creek Press, when he came across a small article on the third page. TWO HIKERS FOUND DEAD. The article went on to say the couple had been hiking the Appalachian Trail and were suspected to have been attacked by a black bear, authorities said. Other than names of the hikers, where they were from and how long they'd been on the trail, there wasn't much else. Locals were hunting the bear, the article said, though they weren't sure it would do any good. This had been the first attack of this kind ever. Bears in high activity areas around the trail had been known to grab unattended backpacks, or come into campsites at night to try to steal food bags hikers hung from tree limbs. Orvin couldn't figure out how such a thing could have happened, unless the couple had confronted the animal. Black bears just weren't that aggressive, unless it was a mama bear with young. Even then, to have killed both hikers would have been highly unusual. Orvin wasn't surprised however that the newspaper had stuck the article on the third page; Kleary Creek was a hiker town and the local A.T. Council didn't want that kind of press.

Orvin turned the page and laughed when he saw that Yellow Mountain was back in the news. He smiled to himself and sipped his coffee. Every couple of years someone would report seeing strange lights up on top of Yellow Mountain. It was known for its massive bald, which the true believers were convinced made a perfect landing site for UFOs. This report would spawn a host of sightings, people trekking up the treacherous six-mile-long trail to camp out and capture footage of Kleary

Creek's cosmic visitors. Of course, hours into the first night these space-ship safaris ultimately devolved into drunken parties and orgies with bonfires big enough to be seen from outer space. Even though most of the reports were hyperbole, eventually the Kleary Creek Sheriff's office would have to enlist the help of the Asheville Police Department to break up the party with their official helicopter. The local police could do it on their own, but the bald was so difficult to get to, even with four-wheel drive. It was easier to just run a chopper up there and scare everybody off the mountain before they caught the whole damn forest on fire.

Amused by the story, Orvin was still chuckling to himself when he folded the paper and set it on the kitchen table. He went out to the garage and loaded the sander into his pickup truck. He was pulling out of the driveway when Colette hailed him from the front porch. She ambled down the driveway to Orvin's window.

"Where're you off to?"

"Mr. Cannon's. Finishing the sanding today."

Colette shook her head, the corners of her mouth pulled down with disappointment. "Why do you have anything to do with that fella?"

"It's work, Colette. Did you happen to win the lottery while I was reading the paper this morning?"

She glared at him. "You've turned ugly, Orvin. Ever since the heart attack."

Orvin closed his eyes, about to apologize, but couldn't find the words; they were locked beneath decades of anger and hurt. He took his foot off the brake and started rolling backward when Colette pushed toward the window. "It's that man! He's the devil, Orvin! He's evil!"

Orvin slammed on the brake and slapped the shifter into park. "Horseshit, Colette! What the hell are you going on about, woman?"

"There! That right there! You never spoke to me like that before! That man is wicked!"

"You talking about Mr. Cannon? Jesus Christ, Colette, the man saved my damn life!"

Colette shot back from the truck as if she'd been slapped, her face twisted with horror. Orvin felt bad but he wasn't going to do this, not now. "I've got to go." He pushed the shifter into reverse and raced backward into the street, almost colliding with an approaching car. The woman slammed on the brakes and laid into the horn, miming her rage behind her windshield; her mouth a spirited hole, her fist a hammer, a soundless but harsh rebuke. Orvin gave her a quick-nod apology, then stuck the truck in gear and sped past the irate woman who was not quite finished with him, rolling down her window to blast him again. A fading scream at best, like a siren speeding away. Orvin barely noticed, but his chest was doing the two-step; his heart didn't need this kind of workout.

He welcomed the twenty-minute drive to Geoffrey's home, the tree-lined highway with its majestic backdrop of mountains. No matter where your eyes landed, they were rewarded with beauty; a sparkling river casting up diamonds, two-hundred-year-old spruce and pines and oaks reaching up to touch the clouds, pristine meadows spotted with cattle, huge valleys holding back vast repeating mountains. Breathtaking.

In several minutes he was turning onto the narrow mountain road leading up to Geoffrey's home. He had enjoyed a peaceful ride, but now Colette's scathing condemnation of Geoffrey droned inside his head like a hornet's nest. Something had happened after his heart attack, but it wasn't due to the man who'd saved his life. A life review, that's what Orvin attributed his impatience with Colette to. All the years of her self-righteousness, her denial of her own immorality, measuring the circumference of everyone else's sins against the expansive territory of her prayers. No one could measure up. Not Jesus himself, and especially not Orvin.

He hadn't planned on being in such a state when he guided his truck into Geoffrey's driveway. Turning off the engine, he got an itchy feeling in his gut, remembering the two naked women in Geoffrey's house the morning he'd stopped. Maybe he should have called. He pulled out his phone and tapped in the number.

"Hello, Orvin, how are you this morning?" Geoffrey said when he answered.

"I'm good," Orvin said. "Just checking to make sure it's okay to come up and finish that sanding."

"Sure. About what time?"

"Hmm. Well, I'm in the driveway if that's okay."

"You didn't have to call. Come on up! Need help with anything?" At this point Geoffrey was standing on the front deck looking out at the driveway in his boxer shorts, the phone to his ear.

"I'm good," Orvin said, looking up at Geoffrey through the windshield, thinking this guy had some definite boundary issues. Dr. Phil would have a picnic with him on his show. Orvin got out and wrestled the sander from the bed of his truck, along with his fifty-foot extension cord. By the time Orvin reached the deck, Geoffrey had gone back inside, hopefully to put on some pants.

Orvin had been sanding for almost half an hour when Geoffrey came out. Orvin switched off the sander.

"Did you see my flyer down by the mailboxes?" Geoffrey said, wearing cargo shorts and an old T-shirt with holes in it, and no shoes.

"Flyer?" Orvin said, leaning on the sander.

"For the mountain party. Two weeks. We'll be ready, right?"

"Sure. I'll get it sealed tomorrow and… sure, no problem."

"You sure? I didn't mean to put you on the spot."

"It's all good. No, she'll be ready."

"Are you coming? You and Colette?"

Orvin's lips buckled with disappointment. "Colette won't come. I'll try to make it, though."

"Is there a problem?"

"Just Colette…" Orvin's gaze swept toward Geoffrey's knees, drawn to the huge scars below each joint. He recalled them from his first visit. "Football injuries?"

Geoffrey bent down over his own legs, as if he'd not been aware of the disfigurement. "Yeah… well, not exactly."

"Sorry. None of my business," Orvin said, uncomfortable with his own intrusiveness.

"No, it's fine… just hard to explain…"

"Well, I better get back to it," Orvin said, ready to switch on the noisy device.

"Hey wait. I wanted to ask you something."

Orvin looked over at him, his finger on the trigger.

"Are there a lot of bears around here?" Geoffrey asked.

"Fair amount."

"I think I saw one the other night, standing right over there. Behind those big trees." Geoffrey pointed to the huge poplars near the end of the driveway. Orvin followed his gaze.

"Behind?" Orvin was puzzled. Amidst the poplars were numerous mountain laurel shrubs with dense leaves and standing at least five feet high, not to mention the rhododendron. Orvin couldn't figure out how Geoffrey could have seen a bear behind those.

"He was right there, behind those little bushes between the trees."

"I don't understand," Orvin said. "You wouldn't have seen a bear unless he was on his hindlegs—"

"He was standing there looking at me."

Orvin's mind shot back to that third page article in the Kleary Creek Press, two hikers killed by a bear. No bear would stand behind those shrubs on his hindlegs unless he was frightened and ready to defend itself, or attack. "Was he making any noise, or rocking back and forth like he was agitated or something?"

"No, still as a post. Then a car came and the headlights must have startled him. He was gone. I thought I might have heard him snort, but couldn't be sure."

Orvin had never heard of any bear who stood around like a nosey neighbor spying on folks from behind the bushes. It was no bear. Maybe it was a curious person, but Geoffrey's closest neighbor was at least three hundred yards in any direction. "The eyes play tricks on us up here in these mountains some time." The statement was lame, but Orvin had little else to offer.

"Yeah, you're probably right." Geoffrey chuckled a little. "Do you want a Coke or anything, Orvin?"

"No, I'm fine." Orvin took his eyes back to the poplars one last time, then switched on the sander, guiding it gently along the freshly cleaned boards.

17
ANOTHER BODY

THE FOLLOWING week passed without going anywhere; that's how Geoffrey thought about it. A Mobius loop. Time was that way. A trap. And Geoffrey was caught in it. Several days earlier Orvin had sealed the deck and Geoffrey had watched through the glass doors, the lanky white-haired man working the oily liquid into the boards with a brush, back and forth, back and forth, the wood changing over time. Geoffrey made lunch and took Orvin a sandwich and a drink and chips and complimented him on the fine work, then receded back into the house, a voyeur, watching though the glass until Orvin finished and drove down the mountain in his truck.

Geoffrey was in a bit of a rut, meditating himself out of his slump numerous times a day. Only to slide right back in. There was yoga, which helped, his mind emptied, until Veronica showed up, then Tess. Then at lunch one day Geoffrey read about the couple who'd been killed on the Appalachian Trail, though he had never heard of that footpath before. A day or so ago a young woman was killed who had been walking some local trail just outside of town, one-minute listening to music on her earbuds, the next, dead. Another bear? Were bears that menacing? Geoffrey had no idea about that either. The town council convened a special session to investigate the recent rash of deaths. A lot of dead bodies for such a small town. Police and Conservation Agents and Park Rangers scoured the area looking for these animals. Local hunters with dogs held in metal pens in the beds of pickup trucks were recruited to help.

Geoffrey slept rough, the sleep of the tormented, which really wasn't sleep at all. When he finally dozed off, the dreams came, but with a price; terrifying images that were stubborn to fade, cold sweats, and shadows, the language of night, which crept across his newly sealed deck.

One morning, Geoffrey called ET and they talked on the phone a while until Edward said he'd drive over. They had lunch on the deck and Geoffrey told him about being fingerprinted and providing a DNA sample in Knoxville, about going to Tess's room, how Tess had been found dead in some woods behind a rest area off the highway a few days later. The Oklahoma City police had called Geoffrey. Asked questions. Then Detective Taylor had called and said the results from the fingerprints and DNA didn't match the ones taken from Veronica's body. He told Edward about the recent killings in the town. But Geoffrey had nothing whatsoever to do with those mysterious deaths either. He didn't even know those people. Bears, it was believed. Edward listened, his face growing graver as he sipped a beer and said nothing. Geoffrey warned ET about Yellow Mountain, that people were on to them, they saw the lights, they were going to be up there watching. Edward shook it off, said it was nothing, it happened all the time, that Geoffrey should never concern himself with such matters. Edward, getting up to leave, told Geoffrey he'd be in touch, not to worry, *they* would figure something out about these killings, about Veronica, and Tess. *They, The Associates. They,* they were the lights on Yellow Mountain, whoever *They* were.

A few nights later, Geoffrey woke to a commotion out on the deck, something large and cumbersome knocking around. It stood at one of the glass doors like a black stain against the starry night sky, unmoving, beastly and cruel. Geoffrey could feel its treachery through the pane, could feel its unholy heart beating in his own chest. A ghastly, unnatural linkage had formed and he felt the tug of a new gravity, sucking at him, drawing at his breath. He spiraled into darkness, a murky tumult of misbegotten dark shapes.

A storm beat against the metal roof, the gray rain of morning painting reflections into the wet boards beyond the glass sliding doors. He drew himself up out of bed. In the kitchen the microwave time indicator flashed on and off, the numbers gone, replaced by indistinct dashes that meant nothing. The power had gone off in the night. Geoffrey ate breakfast and meditated, then tried yoga until Veronica was there wearing red running shorts and that tattered Jamie Cullum T-shirt. Geoffrey walked to the calendar and realized this was the night of his mountain-get-together-shindig. Where had the time gone? He dressed and drove to the supermarket and crammed soft drinks and beer and lunchmeat and cheeses and bread and snacks and dips into a metal cart and ran them past the checker, the register dinging and adding and calculating.

By the time Geoffrey pushed his groceries to the Rover, the rain had stopped, leaving behind a bruised and puffy green sky, as if the heavens had been in a terrible brawl. He drove back home and carried everything inside and spent the afternoon preparing a buffet for his guests, putting out wine and glasses, prepping platters he covered with plastic wrap to keep them fresh, shoving beer down into a huge ice-filled cooler along with soft drinks and bottled water, thankful for the diversion. When he finished getting everything ready, he switched the radio on in the bathroom and showered while listening to the local soft rock station and just as he was shampooing his hair, the news came on. Another body. A middle-aged jogger on the muddy bank of the Flat River which ran through the heart of town. No talk of bears this time. Local authorities were investigating this peculiar string of events. They still weren't calling them murders. But what else could they be?

Geoffrey sat on a mat on the floor of his bedroom wearing a white tunic, his legs crossed, his hands resting on his knees, palms up, thumbs to index fingers. He could normally sit this way for hours. He was only fifteen minutes in when something crashed outside. His eyes shot open and soon he was at the door, staring into a fresh sheet of rain splashing across the shiny boards. Wind tossed the tops of the huge trees, while an enormous limb sat precariously balanced on the railing. Geoffrey put on his rain jacket and slopped to the far end of the deck and pushed the limb over into the yard. It broke into three thick pieces when it hit the ground. Rotten. Geoffrey instinctively looked up to check on the bad tree, as if he could spot which one it was, but something caught his attention at the periphery of his vision. A shadow moving through the woods below. Upright. Not a bear. But huge, and he could almost hear the rumors. Bigfoot. Sasquatch. Yeti. But it faded into the fog-drenched understory so quickly Geoffrey dismissed it as a trick of the wind and mist and laughed at his own folly. He went back inside and put his mat away and changed into shorts and a polo shirt and put on a pot of coffee and picked up a few things lying around, then dusted the bookshelves and kept himself occupied until the first guests started to arrive.

18
THE BEAST

ORVIN WAS LOOKING for a place to park, deciding to just pull his pickup to the shoulder. The road wasn't ever that busy, and Geoffrey's driveway was packed with cars. Orvin was a bit surprised at the turnout. He walked between vehicles toward the front steps, pausing a moment to check the deck. Water from the rain beaded up on the new finish. It looked good, and Orvin felt a surge of pride. Been a while since he'd felt that.

The murmur of talking mixed with music drifted out to meet him. He figured people must be wandering to the deck since the rain stopped. He spotted some folks he knew and said hello, asking about this and that, or if they'd seen a mutual friend over the past year, and shook hands and smiled. He fielded questions about Colette, saying fine, good, a bit under the weather... it was nice connecting with people he hadn't seen in years. When he finally made it into the house, Geoffrey must have spied him immediately.

"You made it," Geoffrey said, shaking Orvin's hand. "I'm so glad... and Colette?"

"No, she wasn't feeling herself," Orvin said, figuring there wasn't much use in explaining his wife's contrariness to Geoffrey.

"That's too bad. I hoped she would come... well, head over here and let's find you something to drink."

"Just some sweet tea or a cola is fine."

Orvin was following Geoffrey to the kitchen when a mad rush of people burst through the doors, laughing and chuckling, covering their heads, sliding the huge doors shut behind them to escape the sudden deluge. The deck sizzled, the rain coming hard, like a train crossing the metal roof. Just then, the whole interior was blasted with bright light, bringing some *oohs* and *ahhs*, then three seconds later, a glass rattling thunderclap that seemed to travel from one end of the valley to the other. A rolling explosion. The house lights flickered a bit, then burned steady again. Geoffrey was laughing, his eyes wide. "Okay, so I don't have sweet tea, but here's a Coke. And... let me get you a glass with some ice."

"I don't need no glass."

Lightning flashed across the mountains, the thunder now a constant rumble. The wind rocked the trees, ripping green leaves from branches, branches from limbs, sporadic lightning flashes revealing a sky crawling with turbulent purples and greens.

Geoffrey handed him the soda, then guided him toward the buffet table.

"You put on quite a spread, Geoffrey!" Orvin said, smiling toward the mounds of food and desserts.

Lightning exploded outside the glass doors, painting everything in blinding white light, immediately followed by the deafening crack of thunder, rattling the glass, shaking the entire house. The lights flickered, then went out, then splashed one more time, until the house went black, leaving everyone in darkness. Silence for a moment, everyone temporarily stunned.

"Don't worry, the lights will come back on in a moment," Geoffrey said.

There were grumblings about candles and flashlights, Geoffrey reassuring everyone that it would be fine. Then he disappeared. Orvin saw Geoffrey walk away, into another room. Then suddenly, the lights snapped back on. People chuckled and laughed and talked about power outages and the Kleary Creek Power Company and how many times it seemed the lights went out in Kleary. Somebody mentioned the generator they owned and how everyone up on the mountain should have one, and the conversations started veering off in the direction of natural disasters and climate change. Geoffrey returned a few minutes later and asked Orvin if he was going to eat.

"Maybe a bit later," Orvin said, confused by the sudden return of electricity. "You have a generator, Geoffrey?"

Geoffrey's eyes seemed to bristle with confusion a moment. "Yeah, yes, the place must have a generator. I wasn't sure how it worked, but, yeah, seems fine..."

Orvin just nodded, certain that this house never had an independent power supply. And if Geoffrey hadn't installed one, where was all this juice coming from? Maybe the power company restored the outage. When Geoffrey excused himself to check on the other guests, Orvin took the opportunity to walk outside. The rain had eased and Orvin walked down the steps to the backyard. He listened carefully, then let his eyes survey the surrounding mountains. Nothing but darkness. No power anywhere. Then he listened to the wind-rustled leaves, rain sizzling along the concrete patio; only one thing missing—the constant thudding of a generator motor. Nothing but natural sounds. He took his attention back to the house, the yellow light silhouetted by the crowd drinking and eating and having fun. Orvin shook his head and headed up the back stairs to the glass doors and went in.

Geoffrey walked over. "You're soaking wet."

"A little rain, is all," Orvin said, suddenly uncomfortable, recalling all the horrible things Colette had said about Geoffrey. *The Devil. Satan. He's pure evil.*

"You okay, Orvin. You look pale."

"Yeah... it's just that... did you buy a generator this past week?"

Geoffrey regarded him a moment, then said. "Uh, no, it already had one."

Orvin shook his head gently from side to side. "I don't believe so, Mr. Cannon. No, this house never had a generator... so unless you put one in, well..."

Geoffrey raised his eyebrows, and gave an innocent shrug. "I guess the power company fixed the problem."

Orvin twisted his mouth to one side. "No, I don't think they did. The mountains out there are black." When Orvin said *black*, the lights snapped off immediately.

People started muttering again... do you have flashlights... where are the candles? Does anyone have matches? Someone thought to use the light function on their smart phone and people chuckled. Great idea. Others got out their phones and shined them at one another and started laughing and joking around. The party resumed in the dark, as if nothing had happened. When Orvin looked back, Geoffrey was gone again. The wind howled, huge trees and bushes near the edge of the yard quaking under a grayish curtain of rain, everyone inside lit a ghastly bluish white from the phones. Lightning flashed and shuddered, thunder rumbling through the mountains. People didn't seem to notice the storm, until the next lightning flash illuminated something on the deck no one was prepared for. People screamed clutching their phones to their chests, fighting back through the others to get away from the glass. A moment later, the thing was gone.

A few men walked closer to the glass, their wives imploring them not to get too close. "What was that?" one woman said. Then another, "It looked like an ape or something!" "It had a human face!" "There was nothing human about that!"

Orvin knew it hadn't resembled anything he'd ever seen before. Maybe the fright of it appearing so suddenly made it seem seven or eight feet tall, and five feet wide with a freakish face and unnatural eyes. One thing Orvin knew for certain—it was huge and ungodly, and evil; he could still feel the prickly charge along his skin, a low voltage warning.

Someone mentioned the hikers who'd been found dead recently. Someone else brought up the lights on Yellow Mountain. "Should we call the police?" "And tell them what?" "That we saw a monster!" This brought a few nervous titters, but mostly people were setting down their plates and cups, rounding up their umbrellas and jackets, heading for the doors.

When the power snapped on a few people stumbled, disoriented momentarily by the sudden light. Orvin swiveled his head back and forth, looking for Geoffrey. A few moments later Geoffrey appeared from the kitchen.

"Hey, is everyone leaving?" he asked, as if nothing had happened.

"Didn't you see that damn thing?" one of his neighbors said. Geoffrey looked over at Orvin.

"There was something out there. On the deck. Some kind of critter I ain't never seen the likes of," the neighbor added, guiding his wife toward the doors.

Orvin said nothing, still under the influence of an eerie, residual spell, as if his bones and muscles were misaligned beneath his skin. He recalled the bear Geoffrey had seen near the trees at the end of the driveway. This was certainly no bear, Orvin realized, fairly certain what Geoffrey had seen wasn't either.

"I'm sorry folks," Geoffrey said, coming to say goodbye, shake a few hands. "I think it was just a bear, probably." Geoffrey made light of it, then: "I saw one near the driveway the other night."

Folks smiled and nodded and hurried down the steps; car doors slamming, engines starting, headlights sweeping in huge arcs across the house and lawn as they fled the driveway. Orvin decided to wait until everyone left, maybe give Geoffrey a hand with clean up, but mostly for curiosity's sake.

Geoffrey had walked the last of the neighbors out, even went down the stairs a few steps to witness the vehicles pulling from the driveway. Orvin watched him from the deck. Geoffrey seemed forlorn, shocked, and horribly sad; Orvin never figured Geoffrey for a man plagued by gloomy emotions. Geoffrey turned slowly and trudged up the steps and across the deck, obviously surprised to see Orvin standing there.

"I thought you left with the others," Geoffrey said.

"Figured I'd give you a hand."

Geoffrey shook his head. "That's not necessary. Really."

They walked inside and Geoffrey didn't even seem to notice his hair was dripping down the back of his shirt.

"You should go dry off," Orvin said.

Geoffrey nodded and picked up some plates off the coffee table and carried them to the kitchen. Orvin followed with glasses and paper dessert plates. He dumped the paper plates in the trash, then loaded the glasses into the dish washer. The storm, with new fury, slashed against the sliders with the force of a power sprayer. Lightning flashed in bright plumes. Thunder boomed and rolled, echoing up and down through the valley below. Geoffrey and Orvin worked in silence, Orvin picking up napkins and soda cans and coffee cups, Geoffrey running his Swifter along the wood floor to grab the crumbs. They worked for almost thirty minutes before Geoffrey went to the bedroom to change his shirt. Orvin was hauling the last of the glasses and cups to the dishwasher when someone knocked on the sliding glass door. At first Orvin wasn't sure he'd heard the sound, with the storm and all, until he spun around to see two dark figures standing at the glass.

19

ON YELLOW MOUNTAIN

WHEN GEOFFREY CAME out of the bedroom, he heard laughter, and Orvin speaking to someone. He was surprised. Everyone had gone. When he entered the living room, two policemen stood smiling, arms at their sides, Orvin sharing something that must have been amusing. "This is Geoffrey Cannon," Orvin said, turning toward Geoffrey.

"You had quite a night," one of the officers said, still chuckling about something. "We had no less than six calls about Bigfoot sightings…!"

Geoffrey looked over at Orvin, who just smiled. "I told him that people had been drinking," Orvin said, "and with the lightning and the power out, and everybody shining their phones in each other's eyes, well…."

"So, you didn't see anything either, Mr. Cannon?" the officer said.

"No, I was in the utility room checking the breaker box," Geoffrey said, not sure why Orvin told the police he hadn't seen anything. "When I came back, people were leaving…"

"We have several descriptions of this thing," the officer said, looking at his note pad, smirking. "Let's see: Dark and Hairy. Almost human. Big. Nothing human about it. Completely hairless. Eight foot tall. Five foot tall. Skinny like a pole. Wide as a truck… not much help." The officer turned to his partner with a broad smile. "Guess we got us our own Kleary Creek Sasquatch!"

Geoffrey said nothing, glancing toward Orvin to see if he would offer them a more comprehensive description. Why wasn't he saying anything?

"We're going to have a look around outside before we leave," the officer said, smiling, then shifted his attention to Orvin. "Make sure you say hello to Colette for me. Missed her at choir the other night."

"I will, Mason. Take care," Orvin said.

The officers walked out and Geoffrey followed them to the door and stood, watching them walk down the driveway. Beyond the trees, diffused smudges of lightning bloomed along the ragged black edge of the mountains. One policeman stopped at the rim of the yard, squatting down to check something. The other policeman walked over and bent down next to him, then got out his phone and snapped a picture. A footprint, Geoffrey figured. They walked near the perimeter where the mowed grass gave way to rhododendron, saplings, mountain laurel and sticker bushes. The officer holding his phone squatted and took another picture with flash, then checked to see if it came out. After he showed it to his partner, they turned and walked to their cruiser. In a few minutes they'd backed from the driveway, headed down the mountain, their taillights reflecting like hot embers on the wet macadam.

Geoffrey went down the steps to inspect what they'd found. "Jesus," he said to himself eyeing the huge footprint. He walked across the yard where the officer had snapped the second photo and found the other one. The rest of the prints must have been lost to the gravel and rock in the driveway, but the ones in the mud were pronounced and disturbing. It had toes, maybe six, maybe four, he couldn't be sure. When Orvin walked up behind it startled him.

"Sorry," Orvin said. "Didn't mean to spook you."

Geoffrey found Orvin's eyes in the low light. "Why did you lie to them?" Geoffrey said.

Orvin seemed to be wrestling with equations and functions that didn't quite total up. "What's going on here, Mr. Cannon?"

Geoffrey wasn't clear why Orvin had reverted to calling him Mr. Cannon again, but the elderly man was obviously vexed. "What do you mean?"

"Look, I know you don't have a generator, so I'm not sure how you wrangled power up here at your place when the whole dang valley was knocked out." Orvin paused, seeming to need a moment to bring himself together. "And the day of the heart attack... you brought me back from the damn dead, Geoffrey! How is that possible?" Orvin stared hard into Geoffrey's eyes. "And I'm not even sure I want to know." Orvin glanced down, squatting to get a better look at the footprint. "And this damn creature tonight... what the hell was that? Did you have something to do with that?" Orvin touched the mud at the lip of the depression, as if to make it real, then stood and washed his palms together.

Geoffrey was shocked. He probably should have expected this, the way Orvin had been acting earlier in the evening, but Orvin's query ambushed him. "I don't know what to say," Geoffrey said, truly at a loss for explanations. He couldn't tell Orvin the truth about the things he did have answers to, and couldn't tell him anything about this so-called creature because he didn't understand what was going on himself. "I'm just trying to help folks. That's it. Just trying to help..."

Something seemed broken in Orvin's eyes as he turned and trekked the short distance down the shoulder of the road to where his truck was parked. Geoffrey wished Orvin would have stayed and talked, but in reality, was relieved he'd left when he did; Geoffrey didn't feel comfortable confiding in him — Orvin would never be able to parse the macabre trajectory of Geoffrey's life.

He went back in the house and phoned ET. When the call went to voicemail, he left an urgent message. "We have to talk tonight!"

Growing impatient, unable to wait for the call back from ET, he hurried down to his Rover. Rain was falling again as he backed from the driveway, the taillights making it glow like a shimmering red curtain.

Driving to Yellow Mountain managed to numb his senses. The monotonous predictability of the rain slashing at the pavement created a barrier in Geoffrey's mind, holding back, at least temporarily, the more disturbing thoughts. High-voltage discharges sparking above the mountains were oddly soundless, harmless tumescent blooms of light and color, nothing but splendorous manifestations. Once again, he found it impossible to focus; Orvin's puzzled expression was etched into the blank space of Geoffrey's thoughts. And the police. Geoffrey appreciated that Orvin hadn't said anything about the creature, slaking the officers' suspicious natures. But the footprint? What did the officers make of those? Obviously they were not the tracks of a bear. Geoffrey imagined police cars and detectives and investigators taking photos and plaster casts. Then more questions. So many questions. The questions would never end. Then there was Oklahoma City. Detective Massanburg. And Asheville, Detective Taylor. What if those two investigations happened to merge, Massanburg and Taylor pooling resources, sharing evidence and statements and fingerprints and DNA. What if they found out about the *U.S.S. Eldridge?* The possibilities were overwhelming. Geoffrey felt a familiar heat in his solar plexus, a disquieting panic upending his sympathetic system, affecting his motor skills, recalling all those years of hiding out, laying low, trying to remain invisible. A faceless life. Anonymity and isolation. He never wanted to go back to that again, and felt as if he were sliding off a crumbling cliff, the vertical drop taking his breath.

Geoffrey almost missed the turn. Slamming on the brakes, he felt the Rover fishtail on the rain-slick cement, before the tread found traction. He checked his mirror and backed up in the middle of the highway, then wrenched the steering wheel hard to point the Rover up the dark, haggard road. Fresh mud sucked at the fat tires, the thick rubber teeth chewing through the silty rock and red clay. A few times Geoffrey was nearly thrown from the seat, the Rover slipping and grinding, then suddenly lurching forward when the tires found purchase, bouncing him through the deep ruts and cratered mud holes. Nearing the top, the path no longer a road but a formless slurry, the Rover slammed into a tree. He backed up, then tried to force the vehicle back to the center, the engine whining, the slick tread falling prey to torque and trigonometry. It took several minutes to get the vehicle righted before he resumed the slow crawl up and over the gutted terrain. Geoffrey was glad to reach the top, the rain coming in grayish curtains against the black trees and brush. When he switched off the Rover's lights, he realized he'd forgotten his headlamp. He dug in the glovebox for his flashlight, then popped the door open, immediately slipping on the slushy earth when he placed his foot down. Brushing the red mud from his trousers, he pulled himself up on the vehicle to steady himself before he stepped away and slammed the door.

The path to the bald was a gloppy mess, the soggy ground sucking at his boots, caking in the tread, the footwear doubling in weight. Geoffrey had never done this before, come to *The Lodge* uninvited. He planned to summon *The Associates* somehow, and hoped ET was with them. Or maybe he could appeal to the beings directly, get their help, plead for their counsel. Thinking of the police, the investigations, Geoffrey was overcome; he could never go back to the life he'd lived decades earlier. Never.

When he reached the bald, he looked up. What was he expecting to see? The ship suddenly appearing, descending as if they'd been waiting for him? At times it did seem as if they monitored his movements. He shined the light toward the clouds drifting above him, the beam powerless against the vast hanging gloom. A faint smudge of moon tried to burn through. The rain had stopped. Stars flickered through the irregular black holes between clouds.

Geoffrey worked the on-off-switch on the flashlight as if it were a signaling device, shooting some disjointed, indecipherable code into the heavens. He should remember Morse from his time in the Navy. But he didn't, and what difference would it make anyway? It wasn't like *The Associates* responded to distress calls. What was he thinking driving all the way up to Yellow Mountain? But it wasn't about thinking. It was about desperation. It was about the ratio of trepidation to optimism, phobia to euphoria, the world tilting in a very chilling and unfavorable direction.

"Where are you!" he screamed, his head torqued back, soliciting some nebulous god floating in the ether. "Where the hell are you!" He pointed his flashlight upward, his impatience like a weighty magnet sucking him down into the mud. He yelled several more times, his heart thudding, a reckless, faulty contraption at the core of his being. "Goddamn it, where are you!"

"Hey, asshole, keep it down!" somebody screamed behind him.

Three figures moved toward Geoffrey in the dark, bright lamps at their foreheads giving them the eerie appearance of a trio of Cyclops. Or maybe a Tri-clops! Geoffrey shined his flashlight toward them. When they got closer, Geoffrey could see they were no more than boys, teenagers, maybe high school age.

"Sorry," Geoffrey said. "I had no idea there was anyone up here."

The boys regarded Geoffrey with cautious disdain. "What the fuck are you doing, buddy?" one of them said. "Trying to call E.T.?" The other two boys laughed.

Geoffrey was caught off guard a moment, realizing the young man was referencing the movie, not his manager, Edward Turley. "Are you camping up here or something? I didn't see a car or—" Geoffrey started to say, but the young man cut him off.

"Why don't you head back down the mountain before we have a problem."

"There's no problem, I just—" Geoffrey started to say, a sudden noise in the brush thirty yards away stealing his focus. The young men's heads swung toward the sound. The branches of a catawba rhododendron shook and trembled as something huge ran out from it, charging at Geoffrey and the young men. Geoffrey was frozen, the boys mesmerized by the peculiar anomaly. When they realized the creature was not changing course, the teenagers turned and shot off toward the cover of trees fifty yards away. Geoffrey, roused from his stupor by the boys' sudden departure, bolted in the opposite direction, his feet catching in the wet oat grass, throwing him to the ground. Before he could get up, he heard the first scream, a horrible cry that split the night. Geoffrey struggled to his feet, unable to see into the seamless black. The next scream was a bleating howl, and for a split second, Geoffrey glimpsed the young man's headlamp, a firefly spinning, flitting erratically through the dark. Geoffrey started running in the direction of the boys when he heard a loud thump and a yelp, a pliant body hitting earth, the sound of sudden death. Geoffrey stopped and stood post-still, his eyes unable to find their way into the dark vegetation at the verge of the bald.

A few minutes later, the creature maundered from the brush, crushing saplings and mountain laurel shrubs underfoot. It was enormous. At least eight feet tall, Geoffrey estimated, though it was very dark. The beast rocked from side to side as it moved, a clumsy, off-kilter gait as if it had no inner gyroscope to correct its balance. Yet, it had no trouble catching those young boys, who looked like football players, or track stars. The creature walked within twenty yards of Geoffrey, then stopped. It spun its massive upper body, fixing its shiny eyes on him. Their mutual gaze seemed to compress between them until Geoffrey could see every detail in the monster's face. Hideous sharp crooked teeth, furrowed blemished flesh pocked with welts and lesions. Tufts of coarse hair grew in blotches along its neck and ears, spreading to a ragged, mangey mane cloaking its head and running down its shoulders. The rest of its body was too dark for Geoffrey to pick out the details. Just then, the creature made a move in his direction and Geoffrey was stuck, literally, his boots sunk in a mud puddle. He pulled at his right leg, trying to free it, until his foot slipped from the boot, which was now cemented in the muck. Trying to free his left foot resulted in losing his other boot, his socks soppy with silt and mud. The only way Geoffrey could move was by high-stepping, raising his knees nearly to his chest, slogging slowly forward, stealing glances over his shoulder to monitor the progress of the beast. It seemed to match his pace, neither concerned or worried that Geoffrey could escape.

With the quality of a dream, a blinding light snapped on from above, the ship swirling and droning with resonant harmonics, a rich reverberation that pulsed in Geoffrey's chest. He looked up, the spinning colorful lights, the enormous craft hovering, drifting slowly down to earth. Majestic, impossible.

Before the saucer settled to the ground, he searched the area. The creature was gone. Geoffrey backed away, feeling a bit woozy, disoriented. He had no idea how long it was before ET was at his side, shaking him by the arm.

"What are you doing here, Geoffrey?"

Geoffrey should have been glad to see Edward, but all he could do was cry. "They're dead. Those boys are dead."

"What are you talking about? What boys?"

"There was a horrible beast… it killed them… it's killing everyone… didn't you see it?"

Edward looked down at Geoffrey's feet, one muddy sock, his other missing, his pants soiled to the knees. "Where are your shoes?"

"Did you hear what I said? The boys are dead. All three of them…"

"Where's your car?"

Disoriented, all Geoffrey could do was point his finger in the direction where he thought he'd parked the Rover. "So many people are dead. I only wanted to help people, and they're dying… and it's my fault."

"Come on," Edward said, taking Geoffrey's arm and leading him toward the trail.

"No!" Geoffrey shouted, jerking free from Edward's grasp. "Let's find them. Maybe I can still save their lives!"

Edward shook his head, grabbing Geoffrey's arm again, pulling him toward the trail.

"What about the bodies? Dammit! We have to do something," Geoffrey said, spinning to face Edward.

"Not us. Not tonight. Let's get you home."

20
CARLY AND MELISSA

CARLY HELD her hand over Melissa's mouth, Melissa's cheeks damp with tears, her body trembling. "You have to be quiet," Carly whispered, peering out the tent opening. She had zipped it down just enough to see what was happening. "Fucking unbelievable," Carly said under her breath.

"They're dead," Melissa mumbled into Carly's palm, sobbing. *"They're dead."*

"You don't know that," Carly whispered, pulling her hand tighter over Melissa's mouth. "You have to be quiet."

All of them had heard someone yelling out in the field beyond their tents. The fellas dressed quickly and were leaving the campsite when Carly had asked them what they were doing.

Renny had said, "Checking on numbnuts over there waking the fucking dead!"

"Be careful," Carly said, zipping her and Melissa's tent, leaving a small opening she could see out. The stranger continued shouting something, Carly couldn't be sure what. Then she heard the guys talking to someone, then some back and forth, not quite an argument. Renny did most of the talking, though it was hard to hear the person they were speaking to. Carly couldn't see anyone, their view blocked by a stand of shrubs and rhododendron. Melissa woke and asked what was going on. Before Carly could answer, the screams came, impossible to tell who they belonged to. Then grunting, or huffing, like a bear, Carly thought, though she'd ever only heard one in movies.

That's when they saw it. "A fucking flying saucer," Carly had said in a harried whisper. "Where's my phone?" She ran her hand along the dark floor of the tent and came up with it, quickly going to the camera to start recording. Melissa was sobbing, but Carly couldn't deal with her yet, trying to video the ship, the brilliant beam shooting down, the spinning, flashing lights. "Fucking unreal," Carly kept saying to herself, watching the ship land on her screen, glancing over the top of the device to witness the real thing. Even after it was down, the ship's lights burned like a forest fire through the brush and trees. Carly kept her video running, then heard talking, someone emotional, having difficulty speaking. She couldn't hear the other person. Now she couldn't hear either of them, but the ship was still there.

Carly scooted closer to Melissa, who was shaking terribly, and pulled her to her chest, trying to calm her. A moment later Carly could tell someone or something was out in the field, moving closer to their tent.

Carly leaned in close to Melissa's ear. "Don't make a fucking sound," she whispered.

As wet as it was, the sedge and oat grass still made a whooshing noise as someone slogged through it. Possibly more than one person. Maybe animals. Carly's stomach clenched, Melissa quaking in her arms. "Shhhh," Carly said softly near Melissa's ear. The presence was closer now. But there were no flashlights or headlamps, and Carly couldn't understand how these things could see in the dark. Or what they were looking for. Carly put her phone down and reached for one of the extra tent stakes. Melissa shook violently in Carly's grasp, rocking her head back and forth, moaning into Carly's palm. "Quiet, goddammit!" she said, her lips pressed to Melissa's ear, tightening her grip over Melissa's mouth.

When the moon peeked out from behind the clouds, the area beyond the tents glowed dimly with a hazy, grayish light. Carly could barely make out the silhouettes of three figures maybe twenty yards away, on the other side of a natural barrier of green alders and mountain laurel. She hoped they couldn't see the tent. The figures appeared to be wearing hoods, concealing their faces. One of them bent down and picked something up, a body, and carried it across its arms toward the ship as if it were nothing. A second one followed, then the third figure, all of them effortlessly carrying bodies. Carly knew not to mention this to Melissa, but it was obvious their classmates were dead. She tried to compose herself, a groundswell of emotions threatening to topple her; fear and sorrow and confusion and grief and terror and awe. It emptied her. Something inside came untethered and she could feel herself sliding apart, her brain unhinged from her body. The thing that brought her back to the moment was the massive ship breaking free from the earth's gravitational pull, pulling at her, pulling up on the leaves and the oat grass and the sedge, pulling up memories of her friends who were now dead, the sound of their laughter rising into the sky, wired to the incredible spacecraft, threatening to rip everything from the face of the earth, floating upward and Carly could almost feel her own body's weightlessness, her own cells warping and twisting, disintegrating, the ship growing smaller, a bright dot in the sky, a new star, a new silence, until it just vanished.

The night was suddenly too quiet. Carly could hear the deafening absence of cicadas and tree frogs, just the residual buzzing in her ears, the soft drone of nothingness. It seemed that the spacecraft had taken the moon, and the stars, leaving behind a perfect, featureless black hole where the world had been. It was then Carly realized Melissa was no longer sobbing, no longer quaking or afraid. Carly slowly removed her palm from Melissa's mouth. When she released her, Melissa held for a moment, then slumped to the floor of the tent. She had passed out. Carly decided not to wake her until she figured out what they should do. One thing was certain, they were not going to spend the rest of the night in a tent on Yellow Mountain.

21

IN THE SILENT WOODS

CARLY SHOOK MELISSA, her palm ready to cover Melissa's mouth if she started to scream. Melissa stirred, moaning.

"Shhh," Carly said. "You have to be quiet."

Melissa's eyes grew bright in the dark, her expression souring as the details of the evening rushed back. She started to speak when Carly covered her mouth. "Don't talk, just listen. We're going to hike down this mountain. We're only going to—"

"In the dark?" Melissa interrupted with worried eyes.

"We're only going to take what we need to get to the car," Carly continued, ignoring her friend. "So, get your clothes on, and find your headlamp. You might need your jacket."

They dressed in silence, careful not to poke or elbow one another in the cramped space.

"What about my backpack?" Melissa whispered. "It's brand new."

"Forget the damn backpack," Carly said. "Only what you need to get down the goddamn mountain."

The girls searched around the tent for anything else they planned to take, then regarded each other with quiet intensity. Carly nodded to Melissa. Melissa's lip quivered when she nodded back, tears hanging at the lower rims of her eyes. As quietly as possible, Carly drew the zipper down. A mattress of fog floated just above the ground as Carly crawled on her hands and knees out of the tent, her hiking pants wetting from the damp weeds.

"Which way?" Melissa whispered.

Carly was still surveying the area, then nodded in the direction of a barely perceptible opening in the woods, not sure if it was the right way, careful to keep doubt from coloring her voice. "Stay right behind me," Carly said softly. "And be as quiet as possible."

The girls moved in unison, matching step for step, Melissa a couple strides behind Carly. They plodded carefully through the tall grass with their headlamps off, the smudge of moon casting enough light to cross the bald, until they reached the woods. Their hiking shoes were soaked, caked with mud, the dampness bleeding through to their socks. Carly stood a moment at the opening in the brush, the path barely visible, as if it had been haphazardly erased. She switched on her headlamp. Melissa did the same.

Carly had hoped to make the trek without their LED lights, but it was going to be tough even with them, the trail sketchy at best; this tread would be inhospitable even in daylight. They hadn't gone fifty yards when Melissa yelped. Carly spun toward her to tell her to shut up, then spied Melissa lying face down on the ground. She hurried back to help her up. "Are you okay?" Carly whispered.

Melissa was crying, rubbing a bloody trail of mud from her knee. "Shouldn't we just stay in the tent until morning?"

"We can't."

"Why not? We'd be safe in the tent."

Carly was fairly sure they wouldn't. They needed to keep moving; with at least five treacherous miles ahead, they'd be lucky to make it to the car before daybreak. Carly led Melissa forward, letting go of her arm when the girl had steadied herself. They walked carefully, pushing aside branches heavy with wet leaves, watching their steps for roots and rocks. Parts of the trail were puddled mud, like quicksand, sucking at their sneakers.

In the silent woods, Carly had nowhere to hide the screams, the cries echoing in the empty attic of her skull. Renny was dead and his father, Mason, would be devastated. Mason was there every Friday night watching his son move the team up the field, throwing Hail Marys to Tommy Jamison, handing off to Kyle Bretton. Those three boys were the nucleus of the Kleary Creek High offense. And great friends. Now they were all dead.

Carly's mind was trampled ground. The death of those three young men, the UFO, the whole weird ass night; she could hardly bear the weight of their bizarre deaths, feeling a strange detachment, as if ripped from reality along some perforated line. She sniffled and almost forgot where she was, then wondered if Melissa was still behind her. When she turned, her headlamp fell on a few tree trunks, rocks and weeds, the trail fading away into a black tunnel. She waited. Melissa couldn't be that far behind, she reasoned. She took a few steps back in her direction, then paused, about to call, the air charged with a precarious current. Her eyes searched the murky woods, her legs weakening with terror. She shook her head, regret triumphing over action, unsure any longer about her decision to abandon the tent. Just then she saw movement in the black abyss between the trees. "Melissa?" she called quietly. "Is that you?"

22

DEEPEST FEARS

GEOFFREY COULD BARELY RECALL the ride back from Yellow Mountain. ET had driven. Geoffrey had been in no condition to get behind the wheel, and spent most of the drive whimpering about the three boys who were killed, then stressing over Veronica and Tess, and remembering the others who had died in the newspaper; a strange concept, dying only on paper for Geoffrey, but he had still felt their passing. Eventually Geoffrey's despair gave way to fatigue and he'd fallen asleep. Edward had driven to Geoffrey's house to pack a suitcase for him, while Geoffrey sat on the couch staring at the wall across the living room. After locking the house, they took off in the Range Rover for Bristol, Tennessee, the venue for Geoffrey's next seminar. Edward planned to stay the night in Bristol with Geoffrey, and got his own room down the hall. He told Geoffrey he was going to leave in the morning, but would be back by the following weekend for the seminar.

"Just spend the week relaxing, use the pool, watch television," Edward told him. "But be by yourself. No visitors or guests." Geoffrey knew Edward's meaning. Then Edward told him something that would dominate Geoffrey's thoughts for days after. It went like this: *"The Associates* have been monitoring the situation, Geoffrey… they believe you released this monster from your subconscious," Edward had told him, sitting in the chair near Geoffrey's bed in the Bristol hotel room. "But, I don't…" Geoffrey said, stumbling with the words, "I mean, how can something like this—" Edward cut him off. "You have to be vigilant," Edward said. "This thing has access to your deepest thoughts and fears, the ones that never make it to your conscious mind..." Here Edward paused, as if calculating the infinite number of possible futures. "There is no telling what it will do." Edward's expression flagged, losing color and vitality. "I warned you, Geoffrey," Edward said after a few moments, shaking his head without superiority or rancor, just sober regret. Edward stood up and walked to the window, then turned back toward Geoffrey. "Don't let it drag you down. We'll figure something out." Geoffrey should have felt relief, but there was something unsaid still lingering in ET's eyes.

Over the ensuing days, the conversation with ET looped through Geoffrey's mind. It seemed to end, then start again, an autonomous discussion which plucked every thread of Geoffrey's attention.

Alone in his hotel room, Geoffrey sat on the edge of the bed, his eyes wired open, the present tangled into the past. Over eighty years ago he'd been salvaged from an unsalvageable calamity, all those lives lost, all those dead sailors embedded in steel. There must have been a reason he'd been spared, something expected in return, some recompense he owed for his miracle. The gifts he was given, to heal, to help, to manifest out of thin air for those in need. The whole reason he'd joined the Navy in the first place was to help those who were being tyrannized and subjugated. He didn't care about medals or adulation or even a pat on the back; helping others was reward in itself. That was his life's mission, he knew it with absolute certainty. It was why he'd been shown mercy in the Philadelphia Navy Yard. It meant everything to him. And as he thought about the fictional Geoffrey Cannon, the make-believe character he'd taken his moniker from, the invented man's generosity and kindness in the novel, the real and pathetic Peter Smithwick sitting here in Bristol felt ashamed, felt as if he no longer deserved to call himself Geoffrey Cannon. He stared at nothing, the conversation with ET starting to loop again, and Geoffrey could hardly believe he'd created something so reprehensible, so vile, that was actually killing people...

23

NEWTON'S THIRD LAW

GEOFFREY COULDN'T JUST CHALK it up to polarity; the state of having two opposite or contradictory tendencies. Yin and Yang. A cosmic teeter-totter. However, Newton's Third Law was pretty clear; for every action in nature there is an equal and opposite reaction. A beast? How was that even possible? His mind grappled helplessly in the darkest corners of the unknown.

With less than four days left to prepare for the upcoming seminar, Geoffrey felt overwhelmed. Normally that would be more than enough time, but now, being unable to function, or even shave, those young men on his mind, and Veronica, and Tess, four days felt like four minutes. He took a deep breath and remained seated cross-legged on the floor of his hotel room, repeating his mantra over and over inside his head. *Om Gam Ganapataye Namah.* His ravaged mind fought the foreign sounds, his fears and concerns refusing to abdicate control.

In front of large crowds, that's where Geoffrey was meant to be. From early on he knew that to help others was the purest form of life, the most perfect way to serve the universe. After his experience on the *U.S.S. Eldridge,* third mate Peter Smithwick learned he had powers, capabilities that went beyond normal understanding, that defied science and rational thought and most of the laws of physics, at least in their current form. Those laws would eventually be rewritten or expanded at some point in the future, but Geoffrey didn't have to wait for that moment; for him, the laws had already been revised.

Over the years, after his marriage with Amanda failed, he discovered

he had the power to manifest material objects, and how to set up resonant fields, separate himself into other dimensions. These spectacular
feats came easy to him after the experiment in the Philadelphia Navy
Yard, possibly also due in part to who he was; the son of a minister and a
harlot stepmother. The contradiction of opposites. His mother had been
sixteen, a prostitute in Philadelphia when Reverend Jacob married her
and brought her to the farm, gave her a chance to reshape her life. She
seemed to relish the simplicity, away from the darker pull of the city, but
the experiment was doomed to fail.

Polarity. Electromagnetic energy, the relative orientation of poles and
magnetism, resonant fields. Geoffrey knew all about mystical amperage;
the ability to evoke images and emotions, create balance between induc-
tive and capacitative reactances. Geoffrey could focus the electrical
impulses of the human body and mind, then connect the current
between numerous individuals, like a massive supernatural generator,
using sound and synchronous vibration and concentration. Once the
field was created, everyone present was part of a unified event, a
powerful transformational tool where one was safe to explore unconscious images and memories and emotions, healing themselves through
shared experience.

He instructed people on how to breathe with intention. To hone their
awareness on the present moment. Put them in sync with one another.
He'd ask for volunteers. Bring them up on stage and give them a
mantra to repeat. Like TM on a grand scale, but more than just meditation, a common thread running through and connecting each and every
mind in the room. The energy became palpable, even visual at times.
People witnessed auras. Whirling vortices of the chakras. The serpent of
kundalini. Even peculiar, and often humorous, mythological creatures
and beings, lights and colors and dimensions, all in the safety of a
communal mind, like watching a movie in a crowded theater. The audience members were treated to a journey inside, and outside,
themselves.

Returning to the experiential world, they opened their eyes, their
faces relaxed, their minds refreshed. Geoffrey would smile out across the
bright faces, people of all races, old and young, women and men, some
balding, some with great statements of hair, a few in wheelchairs, some
with canes leaning against their chairs, people with glasses, or
sunglasses pushed up on top of their heads, wearing hats, or shorts,
dresses and jeans, work boots, or flip flops, or brand-new tennis shoes,

some with watches, or jewelry, earrings and bracelets and piercings and tattoos.

He relished every second. However, to orchestrate this level of engagement required immeasurable concentration, and in this moment, with turmoil stirring his apprehension and despair, he lacked the wherewithal to even order dinner.

Needing to recharge, Geoffrey knew no better way. Feeling slightly reborn, he dressed and rode the elevator to the lobby, hurrying to the front desk, unable to heed Edward's counsel. "I need a car," Geoffrey said, sounding a bit breathless, desperate, as if he were out of time. It had not been an oversight that ET had left him *immobile*, without transportation, hoping Geoffrey would stay put, focus his mind, corral his worst impulses.

"A cab?" the woman behind the desk asked. Edgy and not quite himself, Geoffrey scanned the lobby. A young brunette, wearing sunglasses pushed up on her head, sat in one of the cushy chairs, her legs crossed, her skirt inadvertently pulled back, showing off her tan thighs. She glanced up at Geoffrey, smiled, then took her eyes back to her book.

"A rental car," Geoffrey said.

"Car rental about a mile from here. I'll call them," the receptionist said, looking at a list of numbers on a sheet behind the counter. "They'll pick you up and take you back to their office to fill out the paper work."

When she started dialing, he asked if there was a public computer. She pointed to a desk on the far wall. He hurried over and started typing, bringing up a screen full of search results. He found a notepad and jotted down a few addresses. When he went back to the front desk the young woman said the car rental folks would be at the hotel in about ten minutes. Geoffrey took his eyes back to the brunette in the cushy chair, who was now talking with a friend, an attractive blonde wearing skinny jeans and a tank top. Geoffrey took a deep breath and scrambled out the front doors to wait for the car.

After the paperwork was done, the credit card run, Geoffrey checked the first address on his list. There were plenty of parking spots on the street in front of the soup kitchen. He went inside, saying hello to people eating as he walked by. "I'd like to pitch in," he said to the man behind the counter. The man smiled and handed Geoffrey an apron, guiding him to the end of the line where there was a huge container of donated bread, bagels and rolls.

Already Geoffrey felt his muscles relaxing. He talked with people pushing their trays along the line, sensing their illnesses, smiling as he offered bread and rolls. Some smiled back and took the offering, while others remained grim, beaten, shuffling over to a table to find a seat. When most of the lunch crowd had thinned out, Geoffrey went back to the kitchen to help with dishes, chatting up other volunteers, laughing with them. He sensed that one of the women was anemic, Sally, a woman in her fifties. About to leave, he removed his apron and hung it on the hook, then hugged Sally who was out by the tables talking to the homeless. He held her, seeing the scarcity of healthy red blood cells, picturing an infusion of new ones forming, robust cells capable of carrying fresh oxygen to her organs. In a matter of days, she would start feeling better, finally able to get off iron supplements and meds.

After he left the soup kitchen, he visited a shelter for battered women, speaking with many of the temporary residents, viewing their ailments, curing some covertly, surreptitiously gifting others money. One young woman, whose face was bruised and disfigured, was so frightened she would not come out of the corner. Geoffrey produced a beautiful red rose, then set it on the table near her and smiled, nodding that it was for her. After speaking with other women, he was headed for the front door, ready to leave, when he glanced toward the back corner of the room; the rose and the battered woman were gone. Just then, a woman and a man with a video camera came through the shelter entrance, asking if he was Geoffrey Cannon. How had the press learned he was in Bristol visiting shelters? Eyes and heads shifted toward the commotion at the front doors.

Geoffrey slid past the reporter into the daylight, hurrying down the sidewalk.

"Mr. Cannon," the woman reporter said, pushing her microphone toward him, following on his heels. The cameraman bustled out behind, edging around Geoffrey for a better angle. "How did you know Veronica Carlson? Was she your girlfriend?" the young woman said, her eyes hard, focused.

Geoffrey was about to answer, but what would he say? He looked for his Range Rover, knowing he'd parked across the street. Where was it?

"How about Tess Landry from Oklahoma?" the reporter shouted toward him. People on the street slowed and eyed Geoffrey. "Mrs. Esther Landry? Did you know she was married?"

Some passersby stopped, listening to the reporter ask about the killings in Kleary Creek. "Isn't that where you live, Mr. Cannon? What do you know about those brutal murders? Their deaths were similar to Ms. Carlson's and Mrs. Landry's, weren't they? Do you think they're related?"

Geoffrey finally remembered the rental; he'd been staring right at it, wondering where his Rover was. He hustled across the street and jumped in, the reporter and cameraman scurrying to keep up. She was still shouting questions at him when he was pulling from the curb, watching her annoyed expression shrink in the rearview mirror.

He had planned to visit a few other shelters before heading back to the hotel, but the encounter with the press left him agitated and jumpy, his nerves sparking like faulty electrical circuits. After dinner in his room, which he'd been unable to finish, Geoffrey pushed the food cart into the hallway, still processing the afternoon, replaying what Edward had told him, "Be by yourself." He wished he'd listened.

Not quite ready to sleep, he watched television for a while. Too distracted to follow anything, he switched off the TV and slid down under the blankets, concentrating on his breathing. When he finally drifted off, sleep came like a war zone, dreams shaking him, thrashing him about, chasing him through hostile landscapes, bending him like a funhouse mirror. He woke with Veronica lying naked next to him in bed, her lips blue, her dull, lifeless eyes staring at the ceiling. He jumped up, gulping at the air, pacing the room to purge the images. Several times he looked back at the bed, sure she would still be lying there, the red marks still clearly imprinted on her neck.

He hurried to the bathroom for a glass of water, downing it, then filling the plastic cup again. For a long time he sat in the chair near the small sofa, the lights on, trying to bring order to his dismantled mind.

24

EXTRA EYES

OFFICER CALHOUN PHONED Orvin at seven in the morning asking if he would join the search party on Yellow Mountain. After nearly a week, they were still searching for Mason's son, Renny, and two other boys, Kyle Bretten and Tommy Jamison, and the two girls. Calhoun explained to Orvin that the three boys, and two girls, Carly Rasterson and Melissa Trenway, had hiked up Saturday morning and planned to camp that night and return late Sunday evening, but they never came home.

"Mason and me went up there the other night when them kids didn't show," Calhoun said to Orvin. "We found their tents, and gear, but no sign of them kids. Wyatt phoned Thornhill Sheriff's Office, and they dispatched a chopper, but the woods rimming the bald are so dense they couldn't find anything... It's like them kids was abducted by aliens or something..."

"What? Are you serious?" Orvin said, shocked by Wyatt's ridiculous comment.

"Well, no, of course not, but that's what it looks like, you know... them gone, and all their equipment still up there... Anyway, could sure use some extra eyes."

Orvin was actually relieved that Wyatt hadn't been serious, but still wasn't sure it was a good idea for him to go. "I'd love to help, Wyatt, but I don't think I can hike that trail up there. It's gotta be six miles. That's rugged country."

"No, Orvin, I wouldn't think to ask you to climb that damn mountain. No, we'll go up in the cruiser. Another team's gonna hike up from the bottom… maybe them kids got lost… though, Renny, he knows his way around them woods."

Orvin detected a troubling tentativeness in Wyatt's voice. "How's Mason holding up?"

A bristly pause followed. "He's in pretty rough shape, but won't admit it. He's been up there on that mountain day and night."

Orvin agreed to help. Officer Calhoun said he'd pick him up in about fifteen minutes. Orvin finished the last of his coffee and oatmeal, then went to the bedroom to put on his jeans and some boots and a long-sleeve flannel shirt. Even though it was warm out, the bald on Yellow Mountain was over five-thousand feet in elevation. It would be chilly. He was buttoning his shirt when Colette rolled over in bed and asked what he was doing. Orvin explained about the camping trip, Mason's son, that he planned to help in the search.

Colette clucked her tongue, shaking her head. "I don't know why them kids go up there… nothing but trouble. You saw the paper last week, didn't you?"

Orvin nodded. "Every year somebody thinks they see lights up on Yellow Mountain," Orvin scoffed. "It's become some kind of urban legend… or, I guess a rural legend. Either way, it's all hogwash."

"Don't kid yourself, Orvin. There's something amiss up there… and in this town…"

"What's that supposed to mean?" Orvin spun toward her, aiming his eyes directly at the middle of her face.

"You wouldn't hear me if I told you," she said, swinging her legs over the side of the bed, resting a moment with her hands on her knees.

"Is this about Mr. Cannon?"

Colette sniggered. *"Mr. Cannon. Is that his name?"*

Orvin rocked his head in disgust, not wanting to hear anymore she had to say. He couldn't figure out why Colette was so vexed by the man. The knock at the door was welcomed and Orvin fled the room saying he'd be back later. Once outside, he took a deep breath and hurried down the walk to the cruiser.

It took them about forty-five minutes to get to the top. There were three other official vehicles wedged in near the trees, two police SUVs and a Game and Wildlife truck. Orvin figured more would be on the way. Calhoun's radio crackled. It was Mason wondering where he was.

"Just got to the top," Calhoun said. "Orvin's with me. Over."

"The team has started up from the bottom," Mason said, his voice crackling over the radio. "You and Orvin start there and walk down the trail if Orvin feels up to it. Don't overdo it, Orvin. You hear me…?"

"No sir," Orvin said, leaning toward the mic in Wyatt's hand. "I'll be fine."

"Don't go more than a mile or two, Wyatt, then come up here. And take breaks along the way."

"Find anything yet?" Calhoun said.

"Not much… over and out."

Officer Calhoun looked toward the woods. Orvin pointed to Calhoun's left and said, "I know what Mason told you, but let's head up to the bald."

Calhoun looked at him confused, then said, "But, Mason told me—"

"I know, but there's a trail up there not many folks know about, an old moonshiner path. Kids might a got on that by mistake and got lost… it dead ends about twelve miles from here…"

"Twelve miles…!" Calhoun said, sucking his teeth.

"We're not going that far. Let's just have a look."

Once they reached the top, it took Orvin about five minutes to find the trail. He pointed it out to Calhoun. "You sure that's a trail?" Calhoun asked, clearly doubtful and concerned. Orvin remembered, that from certain angles, the trail was completely hidden, but by moving slowly toward the east the trail would come into view. Orvin figured if those kids were camping and got turned around, they might have seen this trail not knowing it wasn't the right one. Calhoun followed behind Orvin moving east.

"Well I'll be damned," Calhoun said when the trail revealed itself. "Hells bells, I never knew that was here."

They started down, the path difficult to navigate due to years of debris and fallen branches tossed there by storms. A few times they had to climb over the thick trunks of downed trees, Calhoun urging Orvin to take it easy. Orvin would cut him a hard look and keep moving. It was slow going but the path seemed to open up after about twenty minutes. Orvin stopped, spying something off the trail in the woods about twenty feet or so. He pushed limbs aside and broke through the thick cover, high-stepping to get past thick plants and bushes. It was definitely a body, a girl. When Orvin stepped closer he almost lost his breakfast. Her body was degraded by weather and animals and Orvin had to look away. Calhoun tromped up next to Orvin and stood staring.

"You know her?" Orvin asked.

Calhoun only nodded at first. "Could be Melissa Trenway. Junior at Kleary. Cheerleader. Pretty girl. Well, was…" Calhoun pressed the button on his mic and walked away from Orvin and started speaking. "I think we found the Trenway girl, Mason. She's dead. Pretty messed up."

"Does it look like sexual assault…?"

Calhoun cleared his throat. "No, she's dressed and all, but animals have gotten to her…"

Over the length of several heartbeats, Mason hadn't responded, then said, "Is Orvin okay?"

"Yeah."

"Can he keep going?"

Calhoun looked over at Orvin and Orvin nodded.

Officer Calhoun explained about the moonshiner trail and told Mason he'd try to mark it best he could. After ending the conversation, Calhoun drew a small, bright orange flag on a metal wire from inside his coat pocket and stuck it in the ground near the edge of the trail, then asked Orvin to help him wrap yellow police tape around some of the trees, circling the body location. When they finished, Calhoun took a deep breath. "You can never get used to this," Calhoun said. "And I thank God for that."

Orvin led the way down the steep mountain, stopping occasionally to reset himself, give his legs time to gather up more strength. Trying to hold your body back on steep inclines was nearly as hard as climbing up them, especially in muddy conditions, Orvin thought. They'd walked about another hundred yards when Orvin spotted something shiny in the mud. It appeared black in the low light, but reflective like mica, or garnet. When he reached down to pick it up from the mud puddle, he realized it was the corner of a cell phone.

Calhoun said, "What did you find there?"

Orvin twisted toward him and handed him the phone, careful to touch only the edges. Calhoun pressed the power button, but nothing happened. "Maybe the lab up in Asheville can get this thing working," Calhoun said, slipping the phone into a plastic bag.

About then a helicopter rumbled by, apparently searching for Orvin and Calhoun, and the Trenway girl's body. Calhoun got on his radio. "We're nearly right below you," Calhoun said. "Can you see us?"

"We have eyes on you now. Is the girl there?"

"No, back up the trail. I'll walk up there. Maybe you can get a lock on me." He turned to Orvin. "You okay here?"

"Yeah, go. I'll look around."

Calhoun hurried up the mountain, his voice trailing off as he disappeared around a bend in the path. Orvin could hear the chopper pulling away, following Calhoun up the slope. Orvin walked off into the woods where he'd found the phone, his Levi's snagging on sticker bushes and thistle. Mostly he kept his eyes on the ground, the underbrush so dense, but it made him a bit dizzy and he looked up, and froze. Fifty feet away, from a thick wall of vegetation and rhododendron, a pair of eyes stared back. He was about to call out when he realized they were not human. Run was his first impulse, but he knew he wouldn't get very far. In that moment, he wondered why he hadn't brought his gun. What was he thinking? He never went in the woods without a firearm; too many hazards. He had planned to, but when Colette broadsided him with her salvo of theories and conjectures, he plumb forgot.

Slowly he stepped backward, keeping his eyes on the thing, which was now a bit familiar... the creature from Geoffrey's deck the night of the party? Just as he took another step, he tripped over something, tossing him to the ground. He tried to get up, tangled in branches and vines, then flipped onto his side to get leverage, coming face to face with a young woman, her throat crushed, her skin chewed and ravaged. In seconds the forest whirled around Orvin like a tornado, the woods a dizzying blur of leaves and trunks and branches. The ground shook, the rumble deafening; and Orvin's world went black.

Calhoun shook him awake, asking Orvin if he was okay. When Orvin opened his eyes, the dead girl was still lying there, Orvin draped across her body where he'd fallen. Calhoun helped him to his feet. Orvin brushed off his jeans and shirt, then rubbed the pain at his elbow. The rumble and wash from the rotors shook the woods, the chopper directly above them. Calhoun helped Orvin to the trail and had him sit on a downed tree. The helicopter hovered above the canopy of thrashing leaves and dropped a double-loop strop on a cable. Calhoun fixed the dead girl's body into it, then cinched it tight and gave them the signal to hoist her up. In minutes the girl was secured inside and the helicopter soared off to the north and was gone. Calhoun hurried back to Orvin.

"Your face is like chalk," Calhoun said. "You don't look so good..."

Orvin tried to swallow, his throat dry. He nodded, about to tell Calhoun what he'd seen in the woods. Why didn't he? Maybe because the night of the party at Geoffrey's house, he'd lied about not seeing anything, then made light of the whole thing by suggesting folks may have had too much to drink, and then the storm and all... Or maybe Orvin just couldn't allow his mind to believe such a thing could exist...

After he rested a bit, he and Calhoun took a slow hike up the mountain, resting several times along the way. Finally making it to the bald, Orvin was struck by how many men and women had joined the search. Before they walked very far, Calhoun grabbed Orvin's arm and cautioned him about saying anything about the girls they found.

"You don't want to get folks all wound up, okay. Mason's the only one who needs to know at this point."

"Was that the other girl you were looking for?"

"Yeah, Carly Rasterson. Real fireball on the girls' soccer team. Her folks are gonna be devastated... sometimes I just hate this job..." Calhoun paused a moment before walking over toward Mason. Orvin followed.

They talked a bit, Mason breaking from the conversation anytime someone spoke to him on his radio.

"Any luck?" Calhoun asked.

Mason could only shake his head, disgusted, weary and grief-stricken. It was obvious he was starting to buckle.

"You been up here all night," Calhoun said. "Why don't you take a break, drive Orvin back to town... get some rest. I'll stay up here and run the search. You won't do that boy of yours any good if you collapse up here."

Mason exhaled, and rubbed the stubble on his jaw. "No, you take Orvin home, and when you get back... I'll take a nap in the cruiser. I can't leave here, Wyatt. You know that."

Calhoun nodded and looked at Orvin.

"Thanks for all your help, Orvin," Mason said, patting him on the shoulder.

Orvin said he could stay, that he was fine to go on, but Mason insisted. If they didn't find anything by the next morning, maybe Orvin could lead them down into the Dempsey Creek area, look around down there. Orvin had hunted Dempsey Creek for decades.

"Okay," Orvin said. "You just call me, you hear."

Mason smiled and turned away, walking toward the tents, kicking at the ground as if some clue was still to be found in the sedge and oat grass. Officers had been posted around the clock to protect the area from hikers and animals. Mason stopped ten feet away, watching two agents pull out gear and tag it, mark it off a list, while another took photos of everything. Mason had left the campsite as is, Calhoun explained to Orvin, choosing to keep it intact until the FBI had a chance to look everything over, or until they'd found the kids, not wanting to risk destroying any clues or evidence. Some things the agents bagged; others were organized in rows on the ground. Orvin and Calhoun watched from a distance, Mason's back to them, as the FBI agents pulled out Mason's son's belongings, the boy's backpack and sleeping bag, his water bottles, things Mason must have recognized, had maybe given the boy for his birthday, or Christmas. Mason's shoulders started heaving and Orvin could hardly bear to watch any longer.

"You ready to head down to the cruiser?" Calhoun said.

Orvin nodded, exhaling, wishing he'd said something about the creature. But had he actually seen anything? He couldn't be sure now and certainly didn't want to interject something so ridiculous into Mason's grief.

The two men started down the trail back to Calhoun's vehicle, Calhoun in the lead, Orvin watching the young man's feet step around rocks and up over roots, mud falling in small clumps off the young man's soles. It was mesmerizing, the cadence, the fresh air, the snapping of brittle branches, the crunch of leaves from the previous fall. At one point, Orvin almost called out to Calhoun to tell him to stop, wanted to explain what he saw, those unearthly eyes peering back between the big, waxy leaves of rhododendron. Then, without warning, the strangest notion cut across his thoughts; Geoffrey Cannon. Somehow—and Orvin had no idea how it could be possible—Geoffrey Cannon and that beast were connected in some way.

25

STRIEBER MOUNTAIN ROAD

DRIVING ACROSS TOWN, Colette couldn't understand why Orvin hadn't said much when he returned from searching Yellow Mountain. He'd seemed extremely weary, preoccupied, just wanting to eat supper, watch some television and go to bed. The next two mornings he'd been gone by six a.m., helping with the search in the Dempsey Creek Wildlife Area, then Jasper Creek and the western end of Nantahala National Forest. So far, they'd found no sign of the missing boys.

After picking up groceries and stopping at the post office to mail bills, Colette decided to make one more stop. Ten minutes later she was steering the car into the library parking lot. She hadn't been here in a while, and mostly only to use the computer when she needed to check things online, or find a new romance novel.

When she walked past the front desk, Laverne asked where Colette had been keeping herself, and how Orvin was recovering after the heart attack, then shared a bit about her own husband's arthritis. Colette would normally appreciate the small talk and catching up, but she was in a bit of a hurry, wanting to get back home before Orvin returned from the search.

"How's that granddaughter?" Laverne said.

"Oh, fine, but we hardly ever see her now that John and Michelle moved to Virginia." Thinking about the beautiful child, Colette was suddenly sad, and a bit lonely.

"John like his new job?"

"I think so, but he's like Orvin, you know, doesn't say much about anything."

"That's sure something about them kids up on Yellow Mountain," Laverne said, strolling out from behind the front desk. "I don't know why anyone goes up there... nothing but trouble it seems."

Colette had said the same thing to Orvin, but he'd ignored her, something he was doing with greater regularity. "Orvin's out helping with the search..." Colette added.

Laverne's face darkened. "In them mountains after his heart attack? That don't seem so smart."

Colette felt the same way, but there was no talking to him about it. Maybe he wanted to die, maybe he was so miserable he just wanted it all to be over. And why he'd befriended this Geoffrey Cannon fella, she just couldn't understand. She didn't like Mr. Cannon and didn't trust him and was pretty sure he wasn't who he said he was, though she didn't know how she could prove it. Laverne kept talking about the high school kids and mentioned that she had gone to see Carly's mother, Donna, and what a mess she'd been, the poor thing. "Bless her heart," Laverne said. Just then a patron walked to the front desk with a short stack of books.

Laverne walked toward the counter. "Good seeing you, girl," she said to Colette. "Let me know if I can help you find anything."

Colette thanked her and headed for the stacks, unsure if and how the book would be catalogued. She decided to check the computer first, then typed in the title. Adult nonfiction. She wrote down the number. Even though the computer showed that the book was not checked out, she wasn't finding it. Laverne came up behind her. "Having trouble?"

"No... I'm okay," she said, feeling a shiver of self-consciousness. She really didn't want Laverne knowing what book she was looking for.

"You sure, hon? Folks don't always put books back in their proper place. Takes the whole dang staff to find some books." Laverne laughed, her eyes lively, apparently under the hold of a humorous recollection.

"I'll be fine," Colette said, finally spotting the book on the bottom shelf. She let her eyes roam the books up higher, pretending to search the titles, waiting for Laverne to walk away, hoping she didn't linger.

A girl walked up and asked Laverne if she knew where the oversized books were.

"Sure, baby doll, you come with me." Laverne walked away, the girl following. When they were out of sight, Colette bent down and snatched the book from the shelf, looking for a private corner where she could sit uninterrupted. She found a space near the rear emergency door, a little table with one chair and a single lamp. She sat down and stared at the cover. *The Philadelphia Experiment, Project Invisibility.* She read the back cover, then opened it to the first few pages, shuffling through them to find the table of contents. She sampled the first chapter, and was surprised by the quality of the writing. Turning back to the front matter again, she read the author's bio. Both educated men, one of them with a book on the Bermuda Triangle which had sold over ten thousand copies. But what did that prove? That people would read anything...?

Colette couldn't believe she was holding this book in her hands. Never had she allowed herself to slip down through the cracks of what she knew to be true, the solid world. She turned to the second chapter, read a few lines, then the third. It was an easy read, with lots of names and dates. Well researched it seemed, but she wasn't sure this book was going to help. Maybe if she checked it out of the library, she'd have more time to sink into the narrative and find what she was looking for. The thought of carrying it to the counter, then sliding it over to Laverne to be scanned, turned her knees to jelly.

"You found yourself some real seclusion back here," Laverne said, smiling, sliding up near Colette's cubby hole. Colette was mortified, her heart thumping like an off-balance washing machine. Laverne leaned in and read the title.

"You should get the movie," Laverne said. "We have it on the shelf over there, the original, not that crappy remake. I'll warn you though, whew, it'll scare the crapola out of you!" Laverne laughed, her eyes wide, obviously watching the movie play inside her head.

"You know about this?" Colette said. "Is it true?"

Laverne smirked. "Oh, what the heck is true or fiction anymore? But it's a heck of a story, at least the movie... I'll tell you that much. Haven't read that book, though."

Laverne stared at the cover a moment longer. "Project *Invisibility*," she said, laying extra emphasis on the word Invisibility. "I'll tell you what, though... I wouldn't put it past the government to run experiments like that and never tell anyone. You read about them strange lights up on Yellow Mountain a week or so ago, didn't you?" Laverne, waiting for Colette to respond, wore a grim seriousness that distorted her features in a ghastly way.

"Between you and me, I think the government and military knows about them aliens, too... and more than that, I think they're in cahoots with 'em," Laverne stated with almost comical certainty. "I think that's where all this technology comes from, your microwave ovens, your iPhones and computers, and all this fancy electronic stuff." Laverne stared at Colette with stone-sharpened eyes, as if Colette was part of the cover up. "And what about that creature they saw up there on Strieber Mountain Road the other night? Maxine Fredricks was at that shindig... she saw that damn thing. So did her husband, Mort, and several other neighbors. What did the Sheriff do? Nothing... that's what."

"What creature? Strieber Mountain Road?" Colette was confused, but the road sounded familiar.

Laverne cackled, shaking her head, but her eyes were dead serious when they flew back open. "That's just the dang point, Colette... what creature? Not a damn thing in the newspaper... or on the tube! Big cover up, that's what I say. And I know Mason's going through a rough time now with Renny missing and all, but he should have done something about those sightings... maybe his boy wouldn't be missing, if you get my drift..."

A bit relieved, Colette figured she wasn't the craziest person in the library anymore; she wasn't even in the running... Laverne was clearly the Mayor of Looney Town.

"I don't mean to make light of Mason's situation, but... I pray for that boy. All them kids. Well, the boys at least. The girls... well..."

"What about the girls?"

Laverne shook her head, her features sagging. "Both dead, poor things. Brutalized the way I heard it. Horrible."

Orvin hadn't said anything about the two girls, that they'd been found dead... he hadn't said much of anything at all. Why was he being so secretive? Was that why he was so distant the evening he came back from Yellow Mountain? Colette's head was spinning, everything Laverne had told her, it was too much to process, and Colette quickly filed everything she'd just heard under the heading of, *Laverne: gossip and exaggerator. Only a third of what she thinks she knows is true, and even that is subject to scrutiny.*

"I better get going," Colette said, picking up the book.

It took a moment for Laverne's features to unwind. Soon she had her fetching smile back, the one she saved for library patrons and just about every man with a pulse.

"You want that movie?" Laverne said. "Or you going to stick with the book?"

"I'm just gonna put it back…"

"Might as well check it out. Doesn't cost a cent to take it."

Colette nodded, already picturing it in her closet at home, hiding up on the shelf above her blouses, back behind the shoe boxes. She followed Laverne to the front counter. Laverne ran her card under the reader light, then scanned the book. Tina was standing behind the counter pulling books off a cart and scanning them back into the system.

"That there's a good book," Tina said without interrupting her process, her arms and fingers moving with automated precision. "Raise the hairs on the back of your neck."

Colette smiled when Laverne pushed the book across the counter, then wandered out to the parking lot, her brain drifting in some kind of weird fog, her feet not quite locked to gravity. After getting in her car, she glanced at the book in her hand, feeling like the biggest idiot. What had she hoped to find by reading this book? Then: *Strieber Mountain Road.* Orvin mentioned that once and now she recalled why… that's where the mountain neighborhood party was, the one at Geoffrey Cannon's home. Orvin had said nothing about any creature.

26

BAD NEWS IN BRISTOL

THE NEXT DAY, Geoffrey spent the morning visiting other shelters in nearby towns, avoiding Bristol, and hopefully, reporters. He talked with displaced folks, young and old, sensing their ailments, secretly curing them, except for their mental disorders. Geoffrey was powerless against those, and all forms of substance abuse. It seemed those afflictions were disorders of the spirit, and he didn't know why they were beyond his influence.

He made donations at each of the shelters. Later that afternoon he drove to nearby Kingsport and visited numerous shelters, offering any help he could, administering discreet healing when possible. Helping others boosted his own morale, brought him out of a deep despair, the service to others bringing the only true meaning or purpose to his life. Without it, he felt flat as a cardboard cutout, a non-person, non-existent. He remembered what that felt like.

That evening in the hotel bar in Bristol, Geoffrey sat alone nursing a beer. Alone to ponder, he resurrected an inventory he'd begun earlier in the day. Deferred romance. Absence of long-term love. The impossibility of lasting friendships. How the seminars and shelters and soup kitchens were the only sources of substance and importance in his life. Then there was Edward Turley, ET, his only true confidant. What a strange man. He'd replaced Benny Goodman years ago, just showed up at Geoffrey's cabin in Wyoming one day just before the new millennium. For all of the '80's and much of the '90's, Geoffrey had been living a Unabomber exis-tence, a secluded life void of social interaction, but without Kaczynski's violent tendencies. At that point Geoffrey's beard was down to his chest, his clothes in tatters. Most of his time was spent reading, or meditating outdoors, forgetting what it meant to have a conversation with another human being.

There had been a brief interval between Benny Goodman and Edward Turley, when Misty Chott was his go between, setting up meetings with *The Associates,* though during her reign Geoffrey only met with the beings once so they could explain what they'd discovered about his DNA. Geoffrey, an intelligent man, at least book-smart, had understood very little of what they'd told him, but the beings believed what they'd discovered accounted for his superhuman abilities. Geoffrey never formed any kind of relationship with Misty and eventually, like her name, she just evaporated into the ether and Geoffrey never saw her again. "I'll be your manager now," Edward Turley had said when Geoffrey pulled open the wooden door of his drafty hovel. *Manager,* Geoffrey thought. That was new. Benny had always referred to himself as Geoffrey's friend. It wasn't long, however, before Edward Turley eventually wore a new groove into Geoffrey's life, as if they'd known each other their entire lives. Benny and Misty became fading memories, their tracks deleted without as much as a goodbye.

Over the next few months Edward Turley had made numerous visits to Wyoming. One day he brought some groceries and was arranging them on the two kitchen shelves in Geoffrey's shack; it was odd for Geoffrey to watch this impeccably-dressed man standing in his craphole of a cabin, positioning can goods and sacks of flour and sugar on rough wooden planks. "You know, there are other ways of hiding," Edward said, looking over at Geoffrey, who was sitting on his cot, stroking his beard, a tune playing in his head that he didn't recognize.

"Sometimes the best place to hide, is right out in plain view of everyone," Edward added.

"What do you mean?" Geoffrey said, picking some crud from between his toes.

"I mean, what the hell are you worried about? That someone will recognize you? Who? Everybody who knew you as Peter Smithwick from the *Eldridge* is probably dead, or in an insane asylum. The Navy doesn't have any records of you from back then, and even if they did, so what. Any claim that says you're Peter Smithwick would be preposterous. Who would believe them? Look at you, you look like you're thirty years old... you know, except for that Howard Hughes hair and beard, and your sunken gray cheeks! You need to do what the Navy did. Plausible deniability." Edward had explained to him that the Navy created a form letter to send out to anyone who asked about The Philadelphia Experiment. The official line was, *ONR has never conducted investigations on invisibility, either in 1943, or at any other time.*

"*Investigations*, the letter said! But here's the thing, Geoffrey, nobody was inquiring about *investigations;* they were asking about invisibility *experiments*. The letter then stated that, *A scientific discovery of such import, if it had in fact occurred, could hardly remain secret for such a long time.* Well, obviously, it wasn't a secret, or the Department of the Navy wouldn't have received so many requests for information concerning the experiment, so many in fact, they felt compelled to print up a form letter to convince people the experiment *never* took place! They were not trying to hide anything, necessarily, because they couldn't, not completely. Things leaked out, obviously, but they covered themselves and never admitted anything. Plausible deniability."

Geoffrey had just stared at Edward, unsure how to respond.

"You want to know the truth," Edward said, coming over to sit at the tiny wooden table in the center of the room. "Nobody wants to believe this shit actually happens anyway. Invisible ships? UFOs? Bermuda Triangle? Really? No one wants to think the world is anything other than solid and steadfast, ruled by the laws of nature and the tenants of science, so they can drive their kids to baseball practice, and bake cupcakes and watch football on Sunday. The only people who want to believe this stuff, are kooks and nutcases. So the Navy puts it out there, the kooks and nutcases start running around screaming foul, and the rest of the population turns away in horror, because they've seen the kooks and nutcases and don't want to end up like them. End of story."

"So, what are you saying exactly?" Geoffrey asked.

"I'm saying, get out of here, use your gifts. You have incredible abilities and you keep yourself locked up in this godforsaken shithole!"

"And do what?"

"Fuck, I don't know. Split goddamn atoms. Do magic tricks on Broadway. Turn yourself inside out and bill yourself as The Biological Phenom! I don't know, just do something. We'll provide all the necessary IDs and paperwork, birth certificate, SS card, make you a solid citizen on paper..."

"What about helping people?" Geoffrey said.

Edward had hesitated, then said, "Sure. If that floats your boat. You could change your name, and—"

"No, I like this name."

"Fine, then you can be a *different* Geoffrey Cannon, different birthplace, different driver's license, the works."

The start of another new life, writing self-help books, creating seminars. Geoffrey had felt the exhilaration of rebirth, the Phoenix rising from its own ashes, renewed youth, a creative cycle beginning.

Finished with the recollection, Geoffrey tilted the beer back and finished the last of it. He was about to call it a night when he noticed a guy wearing a black cowboy hat sitting alone in a booth across the restaurant. Any time Geoffrey glanced over at the fella, the man looked away. Fifties, maybe, short white hair bristling out from under his hat, cut to a sprinkling of salt around his ears. A spar mustache, clean-shaven chin and jaws. Geoffrey decided to stare back this time, see what the guy would do. Before the contest could get any traction, a young woman pushed herself up on the stool next to Geoffrey. "This taken?" she said, even though she had already claimed the seat.

"No, I was just leaving." Geoffrey dug out his wallet and threw some money on the bar.

"Hey, you don't have to scramble off so soon. Something I said?"

"No, I just have some work to do is all."

"What kind?"

Geoffrey rubbed his chin and could see from the edge of his eyes that the man in the booth was staring over at him. What the hell did he want?

"Sorry, not tonight," Geoffrey said. "Really."

He turned to walk away, glancing in the direction of the man in the booth. The man shifted his gaze, pulling down the front lip of his wide-brimmed cowboy hat, casting his eyes in shadow.

"I think what you do is fascinating, Mr. Cannon," the young woman said.

Geoffrey turned back toward her, smiling. "So, should I know you? From the Asheville detective's office? Maybe Oklahoma? Yes, Oklahoma, right?" Geoffrey turned his head in the direction of the man in the booth. "He with you? Are you detectives?"

She grimaced, looking at the man in the booth, squinching her face. "You must be some kind of national felon or something?"

Geoffrey relaxed, glancing toward the booth; the man was now gone.

Geoffrey hadn't seen him leave. "Look, I'm really beat. Sorry. I'm usually much more up-tempo…"

"I know. I've been to your seminars before. Want to talk?"

"That would spoil the trick, right? I'm supposed to be the one helping you with your problems."

"Hey, even doctors have to go to doctors."

Geoffrey slid back up on the barstool and ordered another beer. "What are you having?"

She ordered a vodka Collins and laid her sparkly purse on the slick bar top.

"You know everything about me," Geoffrey said. "What's your story?"

She chuckled and said, "Now, that really is a boring tale." She appeared to be in her thirties, hair the color of black onyx, attractive in a spontaneous way, not too much makeup, sensible dress and shoes, deep, liquid green eyes. A wannabe reporter at one stop along the road to her dream, she told him. Now she spent too many hours of her life churning out copy for a mid-sized marketing firm, mostly SEO blurbs for client websites and social media posts. "It is so boring I swear my eyes are going to bleed," she said, sipping her drink.

"SEO?" Geoffrey asked.

"No, we're not going to do this… we're not going to act like either of us is interested in this bullshit. Tell me what the police want with you? Should I be scared?"

Geoffrey felt like saying, *Hell, yes, you should be frightened out of your mind,* Veronica suddenly in his head, her trusting eyes looking up at him, his fingers clutched around her slender throat. Then Tess, killed at a goddamn rest area. How was that even possible? How could that happen? Then the screams, those young boys being mangled by some creature on Yellow Mountain. He could still see the damn thing staring at him from across the bald, its eyes a sickly, unnatural yellow, the stench of it drifting over the night air like an omen. Had he imagined the whole thing? At times he could almost convince himself he had. Not Veronica though… he'd seen the photos, her red shorts, the ripped T-shirt … Was Geoffrey dangerous? What a strange question to have to ask oneself. Shouldn't he know if he was a threat to this young woman who had opened herself to him?

"Hey, I was just kidding," she finally said. "It's none of my business."

Maybe it was her business! Maybe her life depended on making it her business! Geoffrey felt something give at the seams, some fabric deep inside stretching and pulling in opposite directions, loosening around his abdomen, his chest, the threads unraveling. What had his neighbors seen that night at his house? Was it the thing he'd seen near the poplar trees in his driveway? The same one on the bald? How many of these damn things are there? Geoffrey pictured an infestation, the creepy things crawling out of the ground. And why had Orvin not said more about it? Was Edward right, that Geoffrey had somehow conjured these things from his own subconscious. If so, how could he get rid of them? If some metaphysical door existed for these things to enter through, then there had to be an exit strategy as well. Some way to rid these things from the world.

"You know, I think I'm going to call it a night," Geoffrey said, unable to finish his beer, followed by a long tenuous pause as he withdrew his wallet again.

"I could come up for a while," the woman said. "Or you could come to my room for a change of scenery. You look like you could use a little diversion."

Geoffrey smiled, stuffing his wallet into his pocket. "You have no idea how wonderful that sounds," he said. "Maybe another time."

She smiled and tilted her glass back, leaving a trace of lipstick on the rim. "See you Saturday, then... unless you change your mind."

"You're here for the seminar? That's not for a couple of days."

"A little me time. Seeing the sights and slumming in the room."

"Well, have a wonderful getaway," Geoffrey said. She slid him her door-key-card holder with the room number and WIFI code.

"Thanks, but I don't think so." He left it lay, refusing the overture.

"Hey, don't break a girl's heart," she said, mocking pouty lips. "At least take it... then toss it later so I don't have to witness the rejection." She smiled.

He took the card and slipped it into his shirt pocket. "Have a great night," he said, walking toward the elevators. Waiting for the doors to open, he checked his phone to see if ET had called. Nothing. Where was he? Geoffrey was feeling as though he wanted to cancel the seminar. It was an unheard-of thing to do, he knew that, but nothing was lining up right. Everything was off. The angles in his head were at odds with one another, the geometry bending back on itself. Illusions. Fake memories. No matter how much Geoffrey tried to bring the world into focus, nothing added up. It was giving him vertigo. Even reality wasn't real.

The hallways in the hotel twisted and slumped. The doors of the elevator slid open and Geoffrey threw himself into the smallish, metallic space. He punched the number. The carriage started moving under a bothersome hum, as if the machinery couldn't be trusted, the cogs and pulleys under the charge of a menacing poacher, a foul entity sent to steal Geoffrey's mind and spirit when he wasn't looking.

When the doors opened, Geoffrey took himself down the long hallway, swiping his card across the lock when he got to his door. Inside he went to the bed to sit, then pulled out his phone to see if he'd missed ET's return call. Nothing.

A knock at the door brought Geoffrey to his feet. The woman from the bar maybe? He hadn't even gotten her name. She must have followed him up, and as good as company sounded tonight, he couldn't risk it. When he opened the door, ET was standing there.

"Oh, man, I'm so glad to see you," Geoffrey said, hurrying back into the room flailing his arms, pacing back and forth. "I'm being tailed."

"Tailed?" Edward said, shutting the door behind them.

"Followed, you know. Police. Detectives. Jesus, maybe even the FBI. Downstairs in the bar. One of them was wearing a cowboy hat, sitting alone in a booth, staring over at me. The other was an attractive woman, who chatted me up, wanted to know why the police were interested in me..."

"How did she know the—"

"It doesn't matter, ET, how she knew. We have to cancel the seminar. Nothing's going right... it's all falling apart, you see. It's all upside down and sideways and I can't do this thing. Do you hear me, Edward? It's not going to work. It's not that I'm off my game... I don't even have a game! You understand? My head's a tangle of loose wires, firing this way and that. We have to do something, Edward. Tonight. Who do we call? Is there someone we can call to get the ball rolling? Get this deal cancelled? I don't care what it costs, Edward. Are you listening?"

Edward regarded him with a flat expression. "When's the last time you ate, Geoffrey?"

"What! Why are we talking about food when—?"

"I'm going to order room service, and sit right here until you've finished every carb on your plate. Understand? You can go take a shower, or watch television, or sit on the floor and meditate until the food comes, but there will be no further discussion until you've eaten."

Geoffrey cleared his throat, the paranoid components inside his skull spinning like the contents of a blender. He felt sick, and weak, and sat down on the edge of the bed. The crumbling sensation in his chest returned, like bones breaking apart. Turning to dust. Edward pushed a glass of water into his hand. He lifted it to his lips, the gear in his elbow still functioning. The water slid down his throat in ball-shaped units, no longer fluid, surface tension squeezing the molecules into the most compact possible shape. Like in outer space.

In a few minutes Geoffrey was beginning to breathe normally again. He took another drink of water while Edward ordered food from the hotel menu. With his feet on the floor, Geoffrey set the cup down and lowered his back to the mattress, letting his eyes crawl the lunar surface of the textured ceiling. A cobweb hung near the corner by the bathroom door. Everything was oddly interesting when viewed from different angles. The unfamiliar terrain brought him an unexpected calm.

He wasn't sure how long he'd been lying there, or if he'd fallen asleep, when Edward wheeled the cart in and rolled it to the pale green cushioned chair near the window. Geoffrey got up and idled over to sit down, lifting the chrome saucer-shaped lids covering the food. Neither man said anything while Geoffrey ate his dinner.

"Feel better now?" Edward asked when Geoffrey finished, rolling the cart toward the door.

Geoffrey nodded, sitting back and letting his weight sink into the cushions. Edward pushed the cart into the hallway, then came back and sat in the desk chair.

"What's going on?"

"I don't know," Geoffrey said. "I'm just… I don't know how to process everything that's happening. I mean this creature or whatever it is, these killings, those boys on Yellow Mountain… I don't kill people, Edward. I help people!" The statement stopped Geoffrey's mind; the flywheel in his head spinning to an abrupt halt. There it was again. The polarity of compassion. *I don't kill people. I help people.* Why had Geoffrey joined the Navy? To protect and save people, to help those who couldn't help themselves. But didn't it hold, that in order to protect one group over here, you had to destroy another group over there? The cosmic teeter-totter, one child goes up, another goes down. Inevitable. But did energy have to flow in both directions in equal measure? Unimpeded? The poles were clear; positive and negative. The Universe always seeks balance. Newton's Third Law. Unavoidable.

Geoffrey shook his head. "I feel like I don't have a world of my own, like I'm watching everything from another planet..." Geoffrey said, "I'm not here, not anywhere... and I can't do a thing about it..."

"This probably isn't the best time to tell you this," Edward said, pausing a moment, as if to gauge Geoffrey's resilience.

"What? What is it now?"

Edward stalled a moment, then looked into Geoffrey's eyes. "There were two girls up on Yellow Mountain that night. Camping with those boys."

"What? Are they okay?"

Edward pulled his lips back. "They're dead."

"Did someone find them?"

"Yeah, as a matter of fact, it was your new best buddy, Orvin, who found them."

"Orvin? What was he doing up there?"

"Helping the police. Authorities have been scouring the entire area, like four hundred square miles so far. Choppers. Dogs. The works."

"What are they looking for?"

Edward seemed confused by this question. "The boys' bodies. They haven't found them."

"Why not? They were right there on the bald!"

"*The Associates* took them. They had this idea they could resuscitate them..."

"Bring them back to life? Did it work?"

"No. Probably a bad idea, in hindsight. If they had just left them in that field, this whole debacle would be over by now."

Edward was wrong about his conclusions; nothing would be over, and the parents would never stop grieving the death of their children. Geoffrey couldn't help but wonder why *The Associates* hadn't been able to revive those boys; they seemed capable of just about anything. But had they really tried, or was their alleged compassion nothing more than a wicked curiosity over how the young men had died? That possibility left Geoffrey disgusted and nauseous.

"One of the boys was the Sheriff's son..." Edward added.

Geoffrey leaned forward in the chair, cradling his forehead in his open palms, then leveled his eyes on Edward. "Don't you care what happened to those kids?"

"Of course, I do. It's tragic. But there's little to be done now."

"Where are the boys?"

"I don't know. On the spacecraft, I think. They're doing more research—"

"Jesus, Edward!" Geoffrey screamed, cutting Edward off. "Put the bodies back! Christ! So the police can find them! So they can have some closure!"

"Sure, we can do that. I'll let you know when it's done. It will all be taken care of, okay. I promise. Now I'm gonna take off. You get some sleep."

"Wait, what about the seminar? I can't do this. We have to cancel."

Edward stood, looking over at the nightstand. "I think that would be a bad idea. Terrible idea, Geoffrey. Bad optics. Let me handle everything, okay? You get some rest. You've got two days before the seminar. Lay low, make sure you eat, and spend some time at the pool. People are depending on you to be at this seminar, Geoffrey. They've driven hundreds of miles. You understand? They need you."

Geoffrey wanted to tell ET about the press ambush at the shelter the other day, but knew if he did, he'd get another earful about not staying in the hotel, being alone. "What about this creature thing?" Geoffrey said. "And the detectives? I mean, could they be FBI?"

"We're working on everything, okay. Keep smiling… and don't act so guilty."

Geoffrey couldn't figure out how any of this could possibly work out. Edward walked to the door, stood a moment with it opened, then left pulling the door shut. Benny Goodman had never been as cagey and cold as Edward Turley; Edward seemed part reptile. Geoffrey got ready for bed, unsure how he would sleep, his mind trying to adapt to the latest bad news; the two girls killed on Yellow Mountain. How did they die? Was it the creature again? Why hadn't *The Associates* known those girls were there? Protect them. Geoffrey rolled over, switching off the lamp, the brassy glow from the sodium vapor lights in the parking lot washing through the room like the reflected light from some alien moon.

27

RUBBERNECKS

ORVIN WAS BEAT when he decided to drive to Geoffrey's house. They'd been searching all day in Copper Gap and the Little Prong River area. Nothing. No sign of those boys. Mason was vexed, and there was no consoling him. Calhoun kept to himself. The other men knocked off around six thirty that evening, and even though Orvin was starving, having only eaten a couple of packages of cheese crackers all day, he needed to speak to Geoffrey. And Geoffrey wasn't answering his phone.

Coming up the road to Geoffrey's house, Orvin was dumbfounded by the number of cars and pickups lining the macadam. He couldn't even get into Geoffrey's driveway; the place looked like a used car lot, people milling around with their phones out. Others leaning against their pickups and SUVs, pulling their legs in when Orvin eased his truck past them. There was barely enough room to get through. Orvin parked up the hill from the house and hurried back down, stopping the first two people he passed, a couple of teenagers. "What's going on here?" Orvin said, distracted by the shifting throng of people.

"The creature, man! This is where people saw it."

Orvin rushed away toward Geoffrey's yard, trying to corral people as he went. "Nothing to see here. This is private property. Come on now, let's get in your cars and head down the road."

People grumbled, sauntering to their vehicles, sneaking glances back at the edge of the yard, toward the woods. Already some folks were pushing through the bushes back into the trees and underbrush. Others ignored Orvin outright, as if they hadn't heard him. He had to confront them head on, let them know they were trespassing and subject to arrest.

"I've already called Sheriff Durn… so, you need to move along." He had managed to get many of the onlookers headed for their trucks, while a bunch of them persisted, traipsing around Geoffrey's deck, looking into the house, standing at the railing drinking beer, holding binoculars.

"What the hell are you doing, people!" Orvin shouted. "You can't be here. This here's private property. Now let's go before the police arrive."

The two at the railing turned and frowned at Orvin, grudgingly walking away.

"Hell no!" Orvin shouted at the couple. "You take them dang beer bottles with you!"

The man walked back and got them off the railing, then carved a sharp look at Orvin as he strolled past.

"That's it folks, nothing to see here," Orvin said, herding the gawkers toward the road. "Come on," he yelled at some people lingering near the perimeter of the yard. "You have to go. And don't come back. Respect folks' privacy. You wouldn't want strangers tearing up your yard, would you? Let's go, keep moving."

Like herding goats, Orvin thought, taking a quick walk around the property after shooing the horde of spectators away. "Jesus H. Christ," Orvin said to himself, realizing that Geoffrey's Rover wasn't in the driveway. He hadn't been able to tell what was what with the gawker parking gridlock.

"Damn," Orvin said. He pulled his phone out and rang Geoffrey.

"Orvin, how are you?" Geoffrey said, picking up. "I was just heading out for an evening walk."

"We need to talk, Mr. Cannon," Orvin said, uncomfortable calling him Geoffrey any more. Like when you have a hog going to slaughter, you don't really want to get too chummy. "Can we meet up tonight?"

"I'm sorry, Orvin. That's not possible. I'm in Bristol, Tennessee. My seminar starts tomorrow morning first thing."

"Do you know what's going on here in Kleary Creek?" Nothing came back. The line sounded dead. "Mr. Cannon? Are you there?"

Geoffrey cleared his throat. "I'm sorry. Yes, I've been keeping up with the news. It's absolutely tragic…"

Orvin was uncomfortable with how to proceed, unsure if he could keep the conversation from veering off the road and over a cliff. "What do you know about all this?" he finally said.

"Just what the news has—"

"No! This creature business? The lights up on Yellow Mountain. What's going on?"

"I don't know what you—"

"I think you do, Mr. Cannon. I don't know how, but I think you know much more than you're letting on…"

Another long silence. This time Orvin waited.

"Can we talk when I get back in town?" Geoffrey finally said.

"I don't know if it can wait. We've been searching for these boys for four days and Sheriff Dunn's a wreck. So are the other parents. They're all suffering. And those two girls. Just horrific what happened to them. And those boys. Mason's boy, Renny. Fine boys, all of 'em. They didn't deserve this. None of them did… And this evening, when I got up here to your place, the property was covered with nosey rubbernecks. I could hardly get my dang truck up the road… It's getting out of hand, here."

More silence. This time Orvin was almost certain he'd lost the phone connection. Just then, he thought he heard a faint whimpering coming from Mr. Cannon's end of the call. He waited, took a deep breath and let it out slowly.

"Mr. Cannon?" Orvin said more calmly. He waited for several long seconds, then spoke again. "Mr. Cannon?" Orvin heard Geoffrey clear his throat.

"Sorry, I thought someone was at the door," Geoffrey said, followed by a sound like a muted sniffle before he spoke again. "I'll be back on Sunday morning at the latest. Maybe late Saturday night. Can we please talk then?"

"All right," Orvin said, displeased and a bit angry.

"I am so sorry for everything that is going on in Kleary," Geoffrey said. "I hope those boys' bodies show up soon. I feel that they will. Can I call you when I get home?"

"How about Sunday morning after church," Orvin said. "I'll drive up around noon."

"That will be great." Geoffrey disconnected the call. Orvin stared at the screen a moment before sliding the phone into his pocket. He walked up the hill back to his truck, bothered by the call. Something hadn't sounded right and Orvin couldn't bring forth the troublesome detail. When he popped the door of his pickup open, the snippet of conversation he'd been searching for was right there in his ears. *I hope those boys' bodies show up soon.* Why would Mr. Cannon refer to those young men that way; no one had said they were dead.

28

BRISTOL: MORNING OF THE SEMINAR

GEOFFREY HAD BEEN grateful for the Navy. The military was where he'd come into himself, learned true discipline, not just following orders, but orderliness and self-restraint. And he loved helping total strangers, people he would never meet but could help just the same. The Navy was the place for that, until that fated day, the green mist encasing the ship, the charged molecules of air, the screams, the dead bodies, his own legs captured in steel. At times he could still see those ghostly images of the crew, vague multi-colored outlines of faces and arms and legs, changing hue, then disappearing altogether, moving through a flickering fog, alive, but not really there, an eerie, nauseating strobing nightmare.

The top brass had not told the crew what was going to happen that day. Or even what could happen. Like a dangerous magic trick in the trial stages. Did the purveyors of this mind-altering feat not know what could go wrong with electromagnetic fields? Was the incident in the Philadelphia Navy Yard an *experimental* experiment, one where the outcome hadn't even been imagined, the possibilities not calculated out to multiple probabilities? Or had those responsible for the research known all along the potentially cataclysmic outcomes, what terrible things might transpire, then figured the risk was worth it? Geoffrey would never let himself be used again. It was important he not be found out. Certainly the Navy and the government would be interested in his abilities. They might even figure they could lay claim to him, body and soul, that since he had been serving in the Navy when the anomaly occurred, it stood to reason they still owned him, property of the state, the utilitarian argument; for the good of the many.

And the press. And behavioral science labs, foreign governments, terrorist groups, anyone seeking an edge. And what about the police, the detectives, the murders: someone was bound to uncover his true identity. All that investigation. Was the FBI involved? Would some obscure clue surface, one Geoffrey had not even bothered to worry about because he wasn't trying to hide anything? His only concern all these years; cloak himself in anonymity. Newspaper articles, photos, or the fingerprints Detective Taylor had procured in Knoxville, and DNA; those were all worrisome possibilities, especially that DNA—there was no fooling that. But would the Navy have his DNA on record from 1943? Was DNA even a thing back then?

Geoffrey recalled being at *The Lodge* one evening, sitting in a smallish cube of a room, much like a doctor's waiting room, only more sterile and dimly lit, with no plants, one chair. The voice of *The Associates*—which had a tinny, tremolo quality, as if spoken through an ordinary house fan turned to high speed—reigned down from a speaker in the ceiling, informing Geoffrey that his DNA had been altered during the Philadelphia Navy Yard debacle. Mutated to great effect, they'd told him, stressing that many of Geoffrey's so called "clutter" genes had been rewired from their inferior state, forming brand new strains, expanding Geoffrey's capabilities, both physically and mentally. Geoffrey hadn't understood the concept of "clutter" genes, and could only stare up at the speaker. Productive, useful genes formed in myriad combinations of three proteins. The beings explained that as much as ninety-five percent of the genes in the Double-Helix were nothing more than *clutter* in normal human beings, thousands upon thousands of repetitions consisting of only one letter of the genetic code; *"Junk!"* Rendering them absolutely useless. But not in Geoffrey's case. Many of these had bound with the other proteins necessary to become useful, directed to perform herculean tasks. *The Associates* were still researching which of Geoffrey's genes did what, but the findings so far were promising to say the least. This was a few weeks after Edward Turley showed up in Wyoming, when Geoffrey was still living the vaporous existence of a specter, yet even now Geoffrey wasn't sure what any of that meant.

Looking at himself in the mirror, Geoffrey could not shake the conversation with Orvin the evening last. He checked his watch to see how much time he had before the seminar. Over ninety minutes. He had time for a short stroll through the parking lot to center himself, breathe some fresh air, forcing himself to think about the sound check, the stage, the lighting, the delightful faces of his audience. He was always in awe of this incredible pool of individuals, their pleasant countenance, their smiles, their gentle eyes. He couldn't help but wonder what they did for a living; bus drivers, construction workers, secretaries, doctors, teachers, Pilates instructors, merchants, checkers, computer programmers, some even unemployed, all looking for something they couldn't find in their everyday life, something that was absent, something important they knew they needed to feel whole. And he hoped to deliver that missing ingredient, at least the knowledge of where to look for it.

Not normally prone to jitters, Geoffrey felt his insides roiling up, an annoying, effervescent discomfort that was now in his blood stream, the sensations bubbling through his veins. He took the elevator to the lobby, then hurried for the warm glow of the morning sun beyond the glass doors. No sooner had he stepped outside than he heard a siren racing closer. Out at the far edge of the parking lot, a knot of emergency vehicles flashed bright red and blue lights, police cruisers, an ambulance, a fire truck. Just then another police car sped into the parking lot, followed by two others.

Geoffrey moved slowly toward the commotion, drawn to the harsh, glaring urgency two-hundred yards away. He knew they were near the mulch-covered walking track that ran through the woods surrounding the hotel parking lot, a tranquil path Geoffrey found the night before after his talk with Orvin. Just the right length for a pleasant half-hour stroll. But the tranquility was splintered now, the lights splashing off shrubs and tree trunks, police hurrying into the woods with guns drawn, EMTs forcing the wheels of a metal cart over the uneven terrain.

Geoffrey now stood less than fifty feet from the fray. More vehicles arrived, two of them apparently unmarked police cars as some hotel patrons craned their necks toward the commotion. It took over fifteen minutes for the EMTs to emerge from the woods, the person on the stretcher covered by a plain sheet. It was obvious the person was dead. Police followed the stretcher from the woods, while detectives from unmarked cars lingered in the thick cover of bushes and trees. A small crowd had assembled, people sending their attention toward the men and women working the scene. A moment later an officer with a huge spool of yellow crime tape carried it back into the woods.

Geoffrey was so engrossed in what was happening, he hadn't heard Edward come up behind him.

"Geoffrey..." Edward said.

Geoffrey spun around. "Do you know what's going on?"

"Not exactly, but it isn't good. The seminar's been cancelled."

Geoffrey didn't care, and was actually relieved it was called off. Edward appeared to be struggling. "The police want to speak with you."

"Me? Why?"

"I'm not sure. But they're inside, in the lobby. You should go."

Geoffrey couldn't have felt greater pain if he'd been kicked in the gut. "I don't understand..."

"Come on... I'll go with you so we can sort this out."

Geoffrey felt suspended by some anti-gravitational repulsion, numbly gliding beside ET as they moved toward the hotel entrance, connections in his brain misfiring, conductors sizzling, components igniting, the current circulating backward, then forward, a dangerous, unpredictable surge.

29

ELIZABETH ZAHN

A WELL-DRESSED man and woman met Geoffrey and Edward as they came through the hotel entrance. The man was wearing a sport jacket and tie, close-cropped hair and soft, oddly adolescent eyes for a man in his forties. The woman's countenance was strained, serious, her dark eyes unreadable. She wore a midnight blue skirt with matching jacket over a light blue blouse. Lieutenants Laticia Melrose and James Curtis. They introduced themselves as detectives from the Bristol Police Department.

"Maybe we could talk over there," Lieutenant Melrose said, looking in the direction of an intimate alcove off the breakfast room. Geoffrey and Edward followed the officers and took seats next to each other. The officers sat opposite them. Detective Curtis spoke first.

"Geoffrey Cannon, correct?" he said, then verified the spelling of Geoffrey's name. He asked how long Geoffrey had been in Bristol, and the purpose of his visit, jotting down the answers in a small spiral bound notebook. Geoffrey explained that he'd been here about a week, preparing for the seminar, and was enjoying some down time.

"What type of seminar is it?" Detective Melrose said.

"Spirituality. Connecting with your higher Self. Being present in your life."

"Why is it called, *Are You Out of Your Mind?*" Melrose asked.

Geoffrey probably needed to change the name of his talk. It was so misunderstood. "The idea of being present in one's life requires taking a journey out of the mind," he tried to explain to the officials, "essentially freeing oneself from his or her own thoughts. Most of us don't even realize how much of our lives are not spent in the present moment, either dwelling on the past, or anticipating the future."

Melrose scribbled notes in her pad. When she finished, she flipped through a few pages, coming to the one she'd obviously been looking for.

"Do you know Ms. Elizabeth Zahn?"

The name was not at all familiar. It's possible Geoffrey could have met someone by that name at any one of his seminars, but he didn't recall it. Geoffrey shook his head. "No, I don't remember a Ms. Zahn. I mean, I meet a lot of people."

Melrose looked at her notes again. "The hotel bartender said you had drinks with her two nights ago." Melrose's gaze seemed to be aimed at the center of Geoffrey's face, like a gun. He didn't recall having drinks with anyone. Detective Curtis held out his phone to Geoffrey, displaying a picture of the dead woman, her black hair spread along the ground like oil, her green eyes fixed unnaturally. It was the attractive young woman from the hotel bar, the one Geoffrey suspected of being an undercover police officer, or FBI; he'd never gotten her name. He couldn't believe she was dead, the peculiar angle of her head indicating that maybe her neck had been broken.

For a moment Geoffrey couldn't speak. "Yes, I do remember her now. We talked a while, then I went back to my room. That was the last I saw of her."

"Do you recall what you and Ms. Zahn talked about?"

"Small talk, really. Not much of anything."

"The bartender recalls overhearing Ms. Zahn asking what the police wanted with you, then asked if she should be scared? What do you think she meant? Why should she be scared?"

Something caught in Geoffrey's throat, the rotor in his chest spinning like crazy, beginning to wobble, grinding at his ribs.

"Do we need a lawyer?" Edward interjected.

The detectives both looked at Edward. "That's up to you," Lieutenant Curtis said, flipping his notebook closed. Melrose looked at Geoffrey. "Mr. Cannon, do you want a lawyer?"

Geoffrey looked over at Edward, who was engaged in an ocular contest of will with Detective Curtis. "What do you think, ET?" Geoffrey said, almost in a whisper, but loud enough for the officers to hear.

Edward finally ended the retinal tug of war with the tall lieutenant and brought out his phone. He tapped his finger on an entry in his contacts, then waited. "Stu, it's Edward. I need you in Bristol right away." Edward glanced over at Lieutenant Curtis, then at Geoffrey. "Bristol, Tennessee." Edward quickly brought up a map of the area on his phone. "Looks like Tri-Cities Regional is the closest airport. Yes, I'll pick you up. Text me the particulars when you have them." Edward disconnected the call and glared at Melrose, then Curtis.

The officers stood. Detective Curtis told Geoffrey to stand, that he was under arrest, that he had the right to remain silent, and so on. While Curtis was mirandizing Geoffrey, he handcuffed Geoffrey's arms behind his back. Geoffrey was in shock, staring at Edward.

"This is ridiculous. You don't have enough to arrest Mr. Cannon," Edward told the officers.

"We have a witness that saw Mr. Cannon enter the hotel nature path between 6:30 and 7:00 last evening, putting him there at the same time as Ms. Zahn," Detective Melrose said. "Mr. Cannon is the last known person to interact with Ms. Zahn. And until we know more, Mr. Cannon will be spending some time with us in Bristol."

Officer Curtis guided Geoffrey across the lobby of the hotel toward the entrance. So disturbed by Orvin's call the night before, Geoffrey truly couldn't remember when he'd gone for his walk. But he'd never seen Ms. Zahn on the nature path. He would have remembered.

"Wait a second," Edward said. "You're arresting him because someone thinks they saw him enter the path? That's insane!"

"Would you like to join us as well, Mr. Turley?" Officer Melrose said. "We have plenty of room at the station."

Edward caught Geoffrey's attention and said, "Geoffrey, don't say another word until Stu and I meet you there. Got it?"

Geoffrey nodded, Officer Curtis steering him from behind. Attendees for Geoffrey's seminar were beginning to arrive, unaware the event had been cancelled. Many recognized him, their eyes bright and wide, softly muttering their shock and surprise, the crowd parting to let the officers through. Geoffrey forced a smile, his heart damaged, the image of Elizabeth Zahn—this beautiful and broken young woman—flashing over and over in his head.

30

THE PLEDGE

SHE PRAYED for her eternal soul, her own salvation, never convinced forgiveness had been granted. The minister had assured her of God's mercy in such matters, but Colette wasn't sure she could leave everything up to faith, or the minister's convictions, not when the destiny of her own eternal life hung in the balance. Orvin sat beside her, staring at nothing in particular, obviously still vexed from the evening before when he'd come home after searching for the missing boys. Colette had pressed him on his somber mood. He waved her off and finished his dinner without a word. The secrets. They had so many now. All these years together, it was bound to happen; keeping things to themselves, burying them so deeply they'd be impossible to find. Wasn't that the point, after all? Make the unsavory details of life disappear. But Colette's never did vanish and she wondered about her daughter, who would be in her forties now, that young baby girl she'd given up for adoption so many years ago. All these years Colette and Orvin's own son, John, never even knew he had a sister. Colette couldn't help but wonder if her daughter, whom she'd only seen once at birth, had children of her own? If so, how many? What were their names? It seemed impossible; it was so long ago and yet she could still see her newborn's face as if the child had been born yesterday. The cruel magic of the mind. An inseparable past and present.

When Orvin looked over at her, Colette felt a moment's chill, as if Orvin, in that precise moment, had glimpsed her hidden history. He never knew about the child. In all the years of marriage, he never once asked about that difficult time in her life. He must have known she was pregnant when she left high school. She'd gone to go live with her aunt up north, have the baby, and give it up for adoption. When she'd returned to Kleary Creek, she heard the abortion rumors. Orvin must have heard them too, but he asked Colette to marry him anyway. Maybe if he'd known the truth about that night, he never would have proposed.

Three cheerleaders for the Kleary Creek Cougars had suggested an incentive for the team to win the state championship; an all-expense paid orgy with beer and food. It started as a tease, more a joke than anything. The joke, however, picked up momentum and started spinning substance into itself, a cocoon of possibility, like perpetual motion, gaining a life of its own, eventually transmuting into a pledge. The unspoken current of the pledge was powerful, like an opiate, drugging everyone in its grip. Bad decisions overwhelmed common sense. Everyone involved was in freefall. A reckless gravity determining the trajectory of all those young lives; all the team had to do was win. And they did.

Colette thought it would be a *kick,* like a party almost, civil and respectful, fun and sex and alcohol. It ended up being the most repugnant night of her life. High school boys with appetites of men, and the carnal instincts of feral beasts. The inhumanity would last till almost dawn. Sometimes two boys at once. A free for all. The girls were defiled, time and time again. One girl passed out from an overdose; her drink laced with drugs. Colette had tried to escape, only to be dragged back into the cabin. Some of the football players left, but other boys showed up, ones that didn't attend Kleary High, friends of friends. Word of mouth. There was fighting amongst strangers, angry drunken brawls over ridiculous arguments, that spilled out into the dark night under a black canopy of trees. One boy produced a gun, prompting the other to do the same. A duel, three feet apart, nearly barrel to barrel. The crowd stepped back. The moment froze, two boys in the center, unwittingly pulled into a deadly face off, neither wanting to be there, neither willing to walk away. The girls used that opportunity to escape, grabbing what clothes they could and rushing out the back door to their car.

No one survived unscathed. The girls were forever damaged emotionally. Remorse and shame in the aftermath of the event took its toll on some male students who had participated. The girl with the overdose spent a week in the hospital. The other girl transferred to another school. Many kids contracted STDs. For days Colette walked around in a haze, unable to tell anyone what had happened. She skipped school. Kept to herself. Watched television in her basement and cried when her parents weren't around. She stopped going to church, her spirit succumbing to the durable weight of her humiliation and shame. Truancy became an issue. The principal contacted her parents. Colette had no explanation. She wept when she told her parents how much she hated school, that she was going to drop out. They were crushed. They argued and fought. Eventually her parents forced her to go back. Her mother would drive her in the morning, pick her up in the afternoons. But Colette skipped out as soon as her mother pulled from the curb, then would wait near the corner when her mother returned. This went on until the school called again. Soon after, Colette had become ill, staying home each day with stomach pains and vomiting. Colette was pregnant. It was impossible to know who the father was. They talked, her and her parents, the three of them bound together by this tragedy. Colette would live with her aunt in Pennsylvania until the baby was born, then give the child up for adoption. Colette's life forever distorted. A crippled, uncertain future.

Eventually she returned to Kleary Creek, got a job at her father's car dealership, living at home with her parents. The three of them worked together to turn the basement into Colette's own room, her own television and refrigerator. Her own bathroom. She would live like an adult under the supervision of her parents, her own money, her own curfew. And she prayed her parents would never find out about the night at the cabin.

Colette had no friends, except for a woman at the grocery store, a checker she would get to know. She even thought about applying there, but her job at her father's dealership was comfortable. Her dad was easy going, joked around with her, made her feel human again. They sometimes went out to lunch together and he would smile at her, tell her how much he loved her. Her heart would detach, a fragile, unmoored feeling, wondering how her father would feel if he knew the truth.

Tired and empty, with the church choir singing a hymn, Colette looked over at Orvin seated beside her. His eyes were heavy, sleepy, but he still had a glow of youthfulness. Orvin only knew the rumors about that time in her life, and she was glad for that; they were far less repulsive than the truth.

When services ended, they stood and Colette took Orvin's hand. He glanced at her, at their hands clasped together, then walked her up the aisle toward the back of the church. Being Sunday, they would normally go out for a mid-day breakfast, but Orvin announced that he had an errand to take care of.

"I can drop you at home first," Orvin said. "Maybe we can go out later for lunch or something."

"I'd prefer to ride along if you don't mind."

Orvin's jaw tightened for a split second. He only nodded, then opened the truck door for her. It saddened Colette to see how untrusting they'd become of one another. The suspicion was obvious on his face when she asked to go with him. Did Orvin think she didn't believe he had an errand to run? Or was he hiding something? Mistrust was a seductive, spiraling trap, nearly impossible to escape.

They drove in silence for most of the trip, the radio playing the news, the picture of their granddaughter on Orvin's dashboard. Colette could barely recall the last time she'd seen the little girl, who had obviously grown since that photo was taken.

"We should get some sandwiches at the deli when you're finished, and eat at that lovely picnic area by the river. It's such a beautiful day."

Orvin glanced over at her, skepticism rippling across his face.

"It would be fun, that's all," she said, taking her eyes out to the trees along the highway.

A few minutes later Orvin's phone chimed. When he answered, Colette was just about to nag him about pulling to the shoulder to talk, but the highway was empty so she dropped it. She could only get Orvin's side of the conversation.

"They did? This morning?" Orvin said, his hand guiding the steering wheel gently, executing minor adjustments. He shook his head, his features marshalled by bad news. A few minutes later he disconnected the call and dropped his phone on the seat. Colette wanted to ask, but decided to wait.

"They found them boys," Orvin said, his eyes more angry than sad. "All dead. Necks broken."

"Oh my... that's horrible, Orvin," she said, reaching over to touch his leg.

"Know where they found 'em?" Orvin said, his voice tight, upset. "Fucking Dempsey Creek!"

"Orvin!"

"Don't start on me Colette. I ain't going to hell 'cause I swore..."

Colette held her tongue, suppressing her righteousness, wanting to apologize to Orvin. Another time maybe. But she was curious why he was so upset. "I don't understand. What's the problem with Dempsey Creek?" she said.

It took several minutes for Orvin to answer. "We searched Dempsey Creek days ago. Crawled over every damn log and rock in that whole dagum basin. If those boys had been there, we'd a found 'em."

Colette was confused. "Are you saying someone moved the bodies?"

He shot a hard glance her way, his lips pressed to a stiff line. He fixed his eyes back on the highway. Fifteen minutes later they pulled into a driveway after winding a mile or so up a mountain road. A few cars and trucks sat near the house, people milling about. She was about to ask whose house this was when Orvin bolted from the truck, yelling at people. "This here is private property! What the hell do you think you're doing! Now get on outta here! Scoot! Let's go!"

Orvin had certainly changed over the weeks since his heart attack. Colette had never heard him use language like he'd been using of late, not even in high school. He'd always been mild-mannered, a bit shy and introverted, never really a pawn to anger and swearing. Now he was like one of those nasty honey badgers with a burr in his backside. Maybe the heart attack had rearranged Orvin's priorities, but the important features of his revised life had not quite surfaced yet, or maybe they had and he didn't know how to arrange this new puzzle. He had always made her feel like the centerpiece of his life; now she wasn't sure if she was even welcome anymore.

The people in the driveway finally left and Colette got out of the pickup, unsure where Orvin had disappeared to. She walked to the edge of the woods, noticing Orvin up on the deck, knocking on one of the big, double glass-sliding doors. The deck looked very nice, like it had been recently refurbished. Then it hit her; this was Mr. Cannon's house. Why Orvin's urgency over driving up here today? What was so important? Colette couldn't help but wonder if the recent birth of Orvin's ornery disposition had something to do with Geoffrey Cannon; every time she thought about that man an edgy darkness spread through her. Maybe her intuition was wrong. She wasn't sure anymore what she'd hoped to glean from the library book, but so far, all it had accomplished was to make it harder for her to sleep at night.

"Colette. Let's go." Orvin stood behind her, his large hands hanging at his sides. She spun around, startled. His voice sounded different now, all the warmth siphoned off.

Orvin turned and stepped briskly toward the truck. Even his gait had changed; he walked with the frenzied impatience of a man half his age. When Colette slid up onto the seat and pulled her door shut, Orvin wasted no time backing from the driveway.

"Stop, please, will you, Orvin?" Colette said, letting her eyes explore the hard lines of her husband's face.

He hit the brakes and glared over at her as if she had just caused him to miss some momentous opportunity, a chance of a lifetime that would never come again. His eyes didn't move from her face, his mouth fixed.

"What's going on? Whose house is this?" she said.

For a long, difficult moment he just stared at her. "What difference does it make?"

"Is this Mr. Cannon's residence?"

"Yes! Happy now? I don't want to hear about him anymore from you. Understand? You made it pretty clear where you stand with Mr. Cannon, okay."

Colette weighed her next question carefully, but asked it anyway. "Is this where the creature was sighted? Is that why those people were trespassing?"

"Creature! What goddamn creature would you be talking about, Colette? Is this from that crazy goddamn book you've been reading? Is that what this is about?"

"How did you—?"

"You left it in the fucking bathroom... what kind of crap is that, government experiments and invisible sailors and whatnot... Really, Colette?"

Colette had to turn away, fighting back tears, wondering what had turned Orvin so cruel. Orvin pulled out onto the road and raced down through the curves like he was late for roll call in hell. She slid down her window and kept her attention on the trees and foliage rushing past, preparing herself emotionally for impact, letting the cool breeze wash the heat from her face.

31

THE DEFECTIVE ALGORITHM

AFTER SPENDING the night in jail, Geoffrey was still seated in the interrogation room, Stu Maitland sitting next to him arguing for release. "Look, you have to charge him or let him go."

Officer Melrose looked down at the stack of papers sitting in front of her.

"It's been over twenty-four hours. Mr. Cannon has been very cooperative," Stu told Officer Melrose. "And we've been extremely patient."

Geoffrey had given them information that Stu vehemently protested to. Geoffrey figured it would move things along if he told them about Detective Taylor in Asheville, about her investigation into Veronica's death. He ran his idea past Stu.

"No, absolutely not, Geoffrey. That's insane."

"But they found nothing linking me to Veronica's death," Geoffrey told Stu.

"Well, what if Officer Melrose does find a link. Then what? You'll be booked for sure and this thing's going to trial."

"But she won't find one, because I didn't kill Veronica, and I didn't kill Elizabeth Zahn."

Stu finally caved to Geoffrey's idea, and it had seemed to work in their favor; Bristol Police took Geoffrey off the top of their list.

Lieutenant Melrose sat a few more minutes, as if debating her next move in a hotly contested chess match. Finally, she said, her accusatory tone not lost on anyone, "You're free to go, Mr. Cannon. We may be in touch in the future, so, don't stray too far."

Stu and Geoffrey walked from the room and met Edward at the front of the station.

"We good?" Edward said.

"It worked," Stu grumbled, jogging his head back and forth disapprovingly. "Big gamble, though."

Geoffrey looked over at Edward, then back to Stu. "Thank you," Geoffrey said, shaking the attorney's hand.

After Edward and Geoffrey dropped Stu at the airport, they stopped for lunch on the drive back to Kleary Creek. Over burgers they discussed the details of the seminar refunding process, Edward explaining it would all be done through the website, but Geoffrey was only half listening, his mind tangled with images of Ms. Zahn, her body lying in the weeds, the only lifeless organism there. The detective had shown Geoffrey numerous shots from the crime scene, as if the sheer number of pictures of Ms. Zahn's dead body would shake some truth loose he'd failed to share. And it had; a deep and aching sorrow over the waste of her unlived life. He was fairly certain the creature had nothing to do with Ms. Zahn's death. Bristol was hours away from Kleary Creek; how could it have traveled this far? He'd felt the same way about Tess Landry's death; even though Knoxville was closer to Kleary Creek than Bristol, the creature couldn't have possibly murdered her either. It seemed to Geoffrey that someone was tracking his seminars and killing women that Geoffrey had some interaction with. But why?

When Edward got up to use the restroom, Geoffrey pulled out his phone and checked messages. Several missed calls from Orvin, with one vociferous voicemail. Geoffrey listened to it and couldn't understand why Orvin was so upset, Orvin demanding they speak right away. He thought about phoning him back from the restaurant, until Edward returned and asked if Geoffrey was ready to hit the road.

The two men walked to Geoffrey's Range Rover; Geoffrey still confused by everything happening. They'd only been on the highway about fifteen minutes or so, when Geoffrey turned toward Edward in the passenger seat and offered up his theory on what was happening to these women at his seminars, that someone must be setting Geoffrey up. Edward held his eyes on him as if Geoffrey had a new appendage growing from his head.

"What?" Geoffrey said.

"Why would you think that?" Edward said, seemingly confused.

"Well, no way the creature could have killed those women... I don't think it could cover that kind of distance undetected and—"

"Geoffrey... I thought you understood!" Edward interjected, sounding almost angry. "It's a phantasm of your mind, unshackled from time and space and the laws of physics." Then: "It will be wherever your mind sends it..."

Geoffrey quickly pulled the Rover to the shoulder, not bothering to check his rearview mirror, a semi blasting its horn as Geoffrey skidded to a stop.

"You can't be serious!"

Edward sat a minute, as if formulating an explanation Geoffrey could grasp without much effort. "Geoffrey, how do you produce those red roses you give to women?"

"I just think about them, and they appear, right in my—" Geoffrey stopped, the color draining from his face, his eyes empty sockets.

"I'm sorry," Edward said. "I really thought you understood."

Geoffrey fixed his gaze on the highway, cars rushing by jostling the Rover, his mind scanning an anthology of undesirable consequences. All these dead people. Women and children. Innocent bystanders; victims of his own chaotic mind, his own untethered thoughts. His hands started shaking on the steering wheel. He clamped his fingers tighter to the leather grip, trying to make the trembling stop, but the current sizzled through his veins, lightning trapped beneath his skin with nowhere to go.

"We have to do something," Geoffrey said. "What about *The Associates*? Do they have any ideas?"

"They're working on it, Geoffrey. They've never witnessed this phenomenon before, so it could take a little time."

"A little time? A lot more people could die in *a little time!*"

"They believe it has to do with your extraordinary ability to manifest out of thin air. If you couple that with your uncanny ability to see illness, and actually transform biology with your mind... well, you can start to imagine the possibilities..."

Geoffrey slammed his right palm down on the leather rim of the steering wheel. How could something so beneficent be bent to such nefarious ends?

"There really is nothing you can do," Edward said. "This isn't your fault. This thing seems to be drawing on energy so buried in your psyche... I mean, you can't just magically call this negative energy up... And this thing can't just be willed away. You just have to be patient."

Geoffrey listened, but felt there had to be a way. Maybe confronting the beast, he could somehow deduce its intentions, find a path into its design, and using that bridge, find the link to Geoffrey's own malfunctioning inner math. The defective algorithm. The erroneous equation. Something was very wrong, and he had to find a way to fix it.

"This may make you feel better," Edward said.

Geoffrey looked over at Edward, aware of his perfectly trimmed silver-white hair, his smooth, shaven jaw, the absolute perfection of his shiny blue eyes. Even his pressed charcoal gray shirt and trousers were impeccable. Unruffled. Composed. Unfazed. What could possibly make Geoffrey feel better in this moment?

"The police found those boys' bodies," Edward said. "In a place called Dempsey Creek."

32

CONCRETE EVIDENCE

A MAN in a black cowboy hat, white shirt and jeans entered the Bristol Police Station and asked for detective Melrose. The officer behind the desk told him to have a seat, then picked up the phone and called her desk. In a few minutes Lieutenant Melrose swung the door to the front lobby open and motioned for the man in the black cowboy hat to follow her.

"Thanks for coming, Mr. Landry," Detective Melrose said.

"Is there a problem?" Landry asked.

"No, we just had a few more questions, if that's all right." Detective Melrose offered Mr. Landry a chair, then closed the door. She asked if he wanted coffee or water or anything. He said no and folded his arms across his chest, then crossed his legs. Lieutenant Melrose was not blind to his body language, Mr. Landry's arms and legs a human barricade, and figured this probably wasn't going to go well. Landry seemed very defensive.

"Just so you know, we had to release Mr. Cannon," Melrose said, hoping to evoke a response from Landry.

"What? He killed her... I saw him enter the woods not ten minutes after she did!" Landry said, the flesh around his eyes tight and red. "I'm telling you... he did it!"

"Yeah, that's kind of what I wanted to ask you about. Why were you out by the nature path? Were you getting ready to walk it yourself?"

Landry's features hardened into a sturdy scowl. "I was getting something from my car. I have a classic candy-apple red '68 Corvette and I always park at the far edge of parking lots. You can't be too careful… people are pigs."

Melrose was rereading Landry's statement, how he'd seen Ms. Zahn first wearing a blue warmup suit approach the trailhead, then stop to stretch a few minutes before jogging off into the woods. Not ten minutes later here comes Mr. Cannon in orange shorts and a plain white T-shirt, wearing a sweatband and orange running shoes. He didn't pause to stretch or anything, just started jogging as soon as he reached the trail. But he left in the opposite direction. That's when Mr. Landry walked back to the hotel. He said he never saw either one of them again until the police arrived. Then he saw Mr. Cannon walk up and stand there, "gawking!" Melrose thought it strange that he actually used that word, *gawking*. It seemed a bit derogatory, as if Mr. Landry harbored some animosity toward Mr. Cannon.

"Why were you staying at the hotel?" Melrose asked.

"I came for Cannon's seminar."

"That explains how you must have been able to recognize Mr. Cannon, but how did you know her, Ms. Zahn? Had you met?"

Landry straightened his back, appearing as though he needed to fortify his position in relation to Melrose. "I saw them together. In the bar the night before. Cannon was hitting on Ms. Zahn and she didn't appear to like it much. She smiled at him a few times, but it was obvious she was just being friendly and wanted him to leave her alone."

Melrose shuffled through some papers until she found the bartender's statement. "According to the bartender that night, Mr. Cannon had been in the bar for an hour or more before Ms. Zahn came in. Ms. Zahn then walked up and sat next to Cannon and initiated conversation."

Landry bristled but never let down his guard. "Maybe so, but what difference does it make who said what to who and when? I know what I saw. Cannon obviously wanted her to go back to his room and she refused and he left angry. Next morning she's dead. What more do you need?"

Melrose checked the bartender's account again which completely contested Landry's claim. Why was Landry lying, making Cannon out to be a cad with an attitude? Melrose had not felt any of that from Cannon when she interviewed him.

"Do I need a lawyer, here? Am I under arrest?" Landry's face was beet red, contrasting starkly against his white sideburns and mustache.

"No, you're not under arrest, Mr. Landry. We're just trying to clear up a few things," Melrose said, hoping he didn't lawyer up. Landry was their best witness, and their only suspect now. Asheville had sent over Cannon's fingerprints and they didn't match any at the crime scene or on Ms. Zahn's neck. Asheville PD also sent Cannon's DNA to the Bristol lab, but Melrose didn't really expect to find anything since Cannon obviously hadn't been with Zahn.

"Your statement says you drove up from Oklahoma City," Melrose said. "That's almost a thousand miles. Do you have other business in Bristol or something?"

Landry shook his head. "You should be spending your time questioning Cannon. He's the one you want!"

"Why are you so convinced Mr. Cannon killed Ms. Zahn?"

Landry's face flushed, his eyes growing bright and wide. "Because he killed my wife!" Landry screamed, then broke down crying. "That bastard killed Tess." Landry bent over, sobbing into his palms. Detective Curtis burst into Melrose's office.

"Everything okay?" he said, looking first at Landry, then at Melrose.

"Come in and close the door," Melrose said to Curtis. He pushed the door shut and stood near her desk.

"Talk to Detective Massanburg," Landry said through tears, wiping his nose. "Oklahoma City Police Department. He'll tell you all about that fucking murderer!" Landry was far from done grieving. Melrose asked Curtis if he would mind taking Mr. Landry down to the lounge and getting him some coffee or something. She wanted to make a few phone calls. Landry stood and walked with Curtis.

Melrose found the number and called and asked for Detective Massanburg. When he came on the line, Melrose explained who she was and asked him about Tess Landry and Geoffrey Cannon. Massanburg explained that there was absolutely no evidence linking Cannon to the Landry woman's murder. Mrs. Landry had been driving home from Knoxville and stopped at a rest area to use the restrooms, then took a short stroll on a paved path in the woods. The groundskeeper found her that evening, her neck broken.

"We had no leads," Massanburg said. "Not much evidence at the crime scene. And no one saw her. You know how those rest areas are. People drive in, then drive out, in a hurry to get back on the road... what's your interest in Tess Landry?"

Melrose explained about Ms. Zahn's murder and that Ward Landry was here in the department accusing Cannon, that he'd seen them together and the details about the nature path.

"Ward Landry's in Bristol, Tennessee?" Massanburg said, a bit surprised. "What's he doing there?"

"He says he was going to attend Mr. Cannon's seminar."

"Oh... okay, a bit odd, don't you think? Especially given the circumstances."

"Absolutely. I have no idea what's going on. The other thing I can't understand is why Landry is so sure Cannon killed his wife."

There was a hesitation from Massanburg. "Tess Landry obviously had a little fling with Cannon when she was at the seminar. They shacked up for a couple of days at the hotel, according to housekeeping. Evidently these two weren't trying to hide anything. Anyway, we investigated it and... well, not much else to it. The affair crushed Landry, though. Once he found out, he was certain Cannon killed her, though there was nothing in the way of proof. He called here every day, telling us we couldn't let it drop. I don't know...." Massanburg sounded exasperated.

"Is Landry dangerous?"

"No, I don't think so. He's an insurance salesman. Home. Auto. Life. The usual stuff. He and his wife have a nice storefront here in Oklahoma City, make several hundred thousand a year. He's harmless... but, you might want to speak with the Asheville PD in North Carolina, though. They might have more on Cannon."

"We did. Listen, thanks for your help. All of this makes a bit more sense now." Melrose thanked him again and hung up. The nagging unknown as to why Landry was in Bristol in the first place still sullied the air. Certainly not to attend Cannon's seminar. Melrose was certain of that.

She went to the lounge to check on Landry. He was sitting at a table by himself, absently running his fingertip down the side of a can of cola, wiping away the condensation. He looked up at her with red eyes. "I'm sorry about that... before..." he said, wiping his mouth. "It's all too fresh."

She sat down across from him. "I am so sorry for your loss, Mr. Landry."

"Massanburg won't pursue it anymore. Are you going to let it drop, too?"

Melrose sighed, and shook her head. "I know this is hard, Mr. Landry, but we can't find anything linking Cannon to these murders, other than a staggering coincidence. But with no further evidence, we can't pursue it."

Landry brought his hands to his lap. He looked over at Melrose. "That's why I'm here... to find concrete evidence. I knew he'd kill again. And he did, practically under my nose." Landry's face slowly crumbled, until he was sobbing into his hands again.

33

FEEDING THE BEAST

GEOFFREY HAD BEEN HOME A WEEK. He ate very little, spending most of his time meditating on what to do about the creature. Orvin phoned every day, but Geoffrey couldn't take his calls, letting them go to voice-mail. At one point, Orvin came up to the house, pounded on the glass doors, screaming that he knew Geoffrey was inside. "Open this goddamn door! Your Rover's in the fucking driveway!" Orvin screamed and pounded. Geoffrey was about to answer, afraid Orvin would have another heart attack if he didn't calm down. But Geoffrey had no idea what to say.

In the evenings Geoffrey waited down at the edge of his yard, staring down into the dark woods, trying to summon the creature that now seemed to have a mind of its own. A few times something stirred in the mountain laurel down the hillside, eventually showing itself as a deer, or a coyote. Geoffrey waited, sometimes until three or four in the morning, before he dragged himself back up to the house. His sleep was ragged and troubled, plagued by freakish images rumbling through the ravaged topography of his dream world. Rushing forward. Falling back. Hiding just beyond the margins of his vision, watching him, spying. He woke sweating. The room upside down for just a moment before righting itself. One night, Tess Landry was lying next to him dressed in a flimsy evening gown, trying to warn him about something, her lips moving but her words were gibberish. He told her to slow down, to take a breath, but the words came faster until her chin and the lower half of her mouth was on a hinge, a ventriloquist dummy, the jaw with painted-on teeth moving so quickly up and down it finally broke loose and bounced on the mattress, landing on the floor. Before Geoffrey could retrieve it for her, it shattered into a thousand pieces.

The sun was just coming up when Geoffrey's phone chimed. Edward Turley. Why was he calling so early? What was so important it couldn't wait?

"Yeah," Geoffrey said.

"You don't sound good," Edward said. "What's going on?"

"What do you want?"

"Just to let you know, all refunds have been resolved for the Bristol seminar, and amazingly enough, we have already sold out for the next one. Which is in Bristol two weeks from today. A lot of people just rolled their tickets over when we announced the new seminar. They're rooting for you, Geoffrey. When your supporters heard the news about what had happened, they couldn't wait to back you. They're loyal, Geoffrey. They love you. Very rare these days."

How could any of this possibly excite me? Geoffrey thought. It seemed Edward was immune to hardship and despair, as if he had no measure of empathy and human suffering. How could Geoffrey celebrate anything while those who'd lost loved ones were still paralyzed by a maddening, relentless grief?

"Have they come up with a solution yet?" Geoffrey asked.

"What?"

"*The Associates.* Have they come up with a strategy for the creature?"

The gap in the conversation lasted several seconds. "Not yet, Geoffrey." After Geoffrey sighed, Edward added, "But they did relay something to me that you need to know… and I'm afraid you're not going to like it…"

"What now?"

"They told me that as long as you mope around fixated on these killings, you are literally 'feeding the beast.' Do you understand? You are exacerbating the situation. There've been three more killings in the past week. I'm sorry to have to bring you this bad news, but you have to shake out of this. You need to get back into life. You have to get past these deaths… *The Associates* told me to reschedule the seminar as soon as possible. Get you back on stage before this thing becomes unstoppable."

Geoffrey didn't think he could possibly fall any deeper into despair. This was an untenable conundrum. If he focused on the killings, they became worse. But if he engaged with his followers, put a smile on his face and went out to help people, the beast could kill those he engaged with. This was a quandary of the worst order. What was he supposed to do with this?

"I know what you're thinking, Geoffrey, a horrible, fucked up Catch-22. Well, you're right. But *they* believe the situation would be better served by you getting these deaths into some kind of perspective, a compassionate attitude where you could view everything through a larger lens, one where you remain a bit more detached. Does that make sense?"

Nothing made sense. Especially this conversation.

"Look," Edward said. "If you can move beyond feeling that you are responsible for these deaths—which you aren't, by the way—then you can begin to process them with the necessary objectivity. True compassion depends on a bit of distance. You are making their deaths about you, but they're not. You have to extricate yourself from the pain in order to empathize with their plight."

Maybe Edward was making sense, or maybe it was all gibberish, like Geoffrey's dream with Tess Landry, her ventriloquist dummy mouth spewing out nonsense until her jaw fell off. But mostly Geoffrey was tired and weary and wanted uninterrupted sleep, a deep rest that might regenerate his burned-out circuits.

"I've got to go," Geoffrey said.

"Yeah," Edward said. "Get some sleep. I'll talk to you later in the week. Let me know if you need anything. And don't forget to eat!"

Geoffrey disconnected the call and walked to the lounger, falling backward into the cushions. He wasn't sure how long he'd been staring at the blank screen of his television set when someone pounded on the glass sliding door. Geoffrey, trying to avoid all encounters, was too slow getting out of the chair to escape to another room; Orvin had already trapped him with his eyes. And by the scowl on the elderly man's face, it was pretty clear Orvin probably thought Geoffrey *was* responsible for the deaths.

When Geoffrey drew the slider back, Orvin rushed in like a winter storm, ranting and railing and Geoffrey could hardly make sense of anything the enraged man was screaming about. Geoffrey pushed the door closed and waited for the charge in the air to dissipate. When the worst of it passed, Orvin could only glower at Geoffrey.

"Would you like to have a seat, Orvin?" Geoffrey said, offering the couch. Orvin paced, as if sitting might dissipate his anger, clearly in no place for concessions.

"Okay," Geoffrey said, sitting back in the lounger.

"I don't even know where to start," Orvin said, searing his eyes into Geoffrey's. "You said we'd talk last week, and then you didn't show. And you didn't return my calls." Orvin seemed to be equivocating, throwing the minor infractions on the table first, leading up to the most appalling grievance. He spun toward Geoffrey, his fists balled at his sides.

"How did you know them boys were dead?" he blurted out with tiny sparks of spittle.

"I don't know what you're talking about," Geoffrey said.

"The hell you don't! You know damn well what I'm talking about. When I told you them boys was still missing, you told me their *bodies* would show up. You seemed to be the only person in Kleary Creek that knew they were already dead!"

Geoffrey leaned forward on his knees and hung his head.

"The bodies showed up in fucking Dempsey Creek, for chrissakes!" Orvin scoffed, the small muscles of his jaw flashing, flexing and collapsing. "We searched that damn place the second day! And them bodies weren't there. And the coroner says they been dead for over a week! What are you playing at, Mr. Cannon? I mean, I've held my tongue about all this... haven't told Mason or Wyatt, and I feel like a damn traitor for it, or worse, a conspirator! I need answers, Mr. Cannon, or the first place I go when I leave here is straight to the Kleary Creek Sheriff's Office."

Geoffrey raised his head. "The boys were killed on Yellow Mountain. I was there that night... I saw it happen."

Orvin's face went blank. He moved backward toward the couch, never taking his eyes off Geoffrey, then sat down.

"That creature you saw the night of my party... that's what killed them. That's how I knew they were dead..."

"Why were you on Yellow Mountain at night?"

Geoffrey shook his head back and forth. "I can't tell you that, Orvin. I'm sorry. And I can't tell you who moved the bodies to Dempsey Creek. There are things I just can't talk about..."

Orvin blinked a couple of times. "Are you involved in all this business somehow?"

Geoffrey nodded.

"Did you cause my heart attack?"

"No, I didn't… but, I knew you were going to have one. That's why I asked you to go for a walk, so you'd have it when I was around to help you."

"Are you a doctor or something? Or one of them psychic fellas?

"Not a doctor, but, yes, I guess you could say I'm psychic." Geoffrey paused a moment, feeling he needed to elucidate, that Orvin would make room in his mind for a truth that might fall outside his present paradigm. "I see diseases in people… and I can cure them…"

Orvin's eyes narrowed as he seemed to reflect on this notion. "You heal people? Like Jesus?"

ET warned about this very thing years ago, bringing up the story of the young Savior, reminding Geoffrey to regard the story of Jesus as not so much about mankind's salvation, but more as a cautionary tale about being too open in regard to one's powers. Geoffrey had attributed this observation to Edward's acute cynicism, and his prickly philosophical take on just about everything.

"It's different," Geoffrey told Orvin, who sat slit-eyed and confused. "It's nothing Divine. I just…" Geoffrey couldn't finish the sentence, couldn't tell Orvin that his abilities were the product of mutated genes caused by an unfortunate, ill-conceived experiment nearly a century earlier.

"Did you *heal* me that day on the road?"

Geoffrey realized he had said too much. "I know you have questions. But, can we get back to what's going on here in Kleary Creek? This creature?"

Orvin nodded, his eyes still wrapped up in something unfathomable, not looking at Geoffrey, but through him. After a long minute or two, Orvin finally said, "I need to tell Mason and Wyatt. We can form us a search party. Find this thing and kill it."

Geoffrey nodded, not at all the direction he saw things going. "Yes, Orvin, a great idea… but maybe before we involve the Sheriff's Office… what if… I go by myself."

"By yourself? You can't be serious?"

"Yeah, I think it's best. That way no one else will get hurt."

"That's suicide. Do you even own a gun?

"No, I won't need a gun."

Orvin leaned forward in the couch, his bony fingers clamped to his hard knees. "You can't go alone. You don't even know these woods. You'll be lost after five minutes."

"No, I'll be fine."

Orvin shook his head. "No, sir, you won't be fine! I can't let you do it!"

Geoffrey started to protest until Orvin stood up sharply and waved his hand. "I won't let you," Orvin said. "I grew up in these woods and hunted every square inch. I'm going with you."

"That wouldn't be wise, Orvin. Not with your heart."

Orvin stared hard down on Geoffrey. After several long seconds, Orvin said, "Well... give me a quick once over with them gifts of yours... you'll see I'm fit to go!"

34

UNEVEN FURY

ON THE DRIVE HOME, Orvin couldn't quite come to terms with Geoffrey's pronouncement, about being a psychic healer, able to see diseases in a body, and cure them. It wasn't that Orvin didn't believe him, he did—after all, Geoffrey had saved his life—but Orvin just couldn't imagine how something like that worked. If it wasn't Divine, what was it? He'd heard of TV evangelists who claimed to be healers, but it all seemed pretty far-fetched. Orvin did wonder if Geoffrey, with his psychic powers or whatever they were, had more to do with the creature than he was letting on.

They'd made plans to search the woods around the Yellow Mountain Bald area in a couple of nights. The only thing Orvin couldn't figure was how they'd find the creature. "It'll find us," Geoffrey had told him. If that was true, Orvin figured, then why go all the way up to Yellow Mountain? Wouldn't it show up anywhere they went? It didn't make sense, but Geoffrey had seemed pretty certain of himself. He said that they should search an area void of people. Yellow Mountain surely qualified on that point. It was desolate, for the most part. Maybe the creature frequented the bald because it lived nearby? Orvin knew of some caves off the south side of the mountain. Good place to hide if you're a big old ugly sonofabitch. Orvin thought about those kids, how unfortunate they'd been camping up there that night. What were the odds? And Geoffrey? What the hell was he doing up on Yellow Mountain?

Orvin pictured the creature at Geoffrey's house that night, standing at the glass doors like it was waiting to be let in. But Orvin could never quite figure out what it was. Some kind of hybrid maybe, or something that escaped from a zoo? Possibly a military experiment gone awry; though he didn't really believe that, trusting someone would uncover a perfectly logical explanation for the thing.

When he pulled into the driveway, he was surprised Colette's car was gone. Book club night, he realized, and walked into the dark house and turned on some lights. He went to the kitchen to make himself a sandwich, then poured himself a large glass of milk. There on the counter, out in plain sight, was the book Colette had gotten from the library. He figured that since he already knew about it, what was the point in her hiding it any longer? He brought the book over to the table and set it next to his plate, reading the back cover, then flipping to the table of contents. Orvin took a bite of his sandwich and read the introduction, which quickly took him places he really wasn't prepared to go. The night had already been strange enough. Geoffrey's bizarre admission earlier, then now, reading this book; it was like trying to digest a double-decker sandwich of wacky. Navy ships disappearing and reappearing, invisible crew members, experiments with electromagnetic energy, psychological damage, death, coverups, camouflage, toying around with the basic building blocks of matter, space and time. Orvin sipped his milk and started reading the first chapter. He wasn't sure why Colette had brought the book home in the first place, but he could understand now why she hadn't stopped. It was infectious. Orvin expected the writing to be over the top, the way most sci-fi novels were, but this wasn't a novel, and it wasn't crazy, which made it all the scarier.

Each chapter built on the previous, and Orvin could almost imagine that the Office of Naval Information, faced with such outrageous accusations, would react exactly as the book described whether the accusations were true or not. How else could they respond? If it was false, of course Navy officials were going to deny that anything happened. By the same logic, though, they had to deny it completely if it *had* happened; how could they go public with such research, especially given the disastrous outcome. After all, people were severely affected, psychologically harmed, even killed. And who in the public was ready to accept the science fiction tenants of invisibility and bi-location, the ship in one place one second, then hundreds of miles away the next, then back again; no way would any government agency own up to such claims. The U.S. government had to present a sober front, a rational face; anything like this was too crazy. Too dangerous. This was just the kind of technology enemies and foreign governments and terrorists killed for. Orvin could barely weigh the consequences of any government or group in possession of a weapon such as *invisibility*, not only for its troops, but its armaments of war. The potential was mind-boggling. The U.S. kept the Manhattan Project a secret, until the devastating weapons were used at Hiroshima and Nagasaki. Their deployment in Japan would hopefully serve as *deterrents* to future wars. But invisibility of war ships and aircraft, no, that capability would serve much greater advantage if no one knew it existed, at least for the proprietors of such technology.

Orvin got up and put his plate in the sink, then poured himself more milk and took the book to the living room. At every turn of the page he wanted to discount the entire treatise as farcical and without merit, but the authors presented the facts in a clearheaded, serious fashion, admitting that they had undertaken the project to disprove the entire incident ever happened, that the myth was just that, a fabrication of the weirdest kind. The problem was, each time the researchers of the book attempted to discount some shred of evidence, they instead received a new form of confirmation, sometimes an anonymous account leading them farther down the sinister rabbit hole.

Orvin was a few pages into chapter four when Colette bustled through the front door clutching a couple of grocery sacks in her arms. She gave him a quick hello and hurried past into the kitchen. The refrigerator door opened and closed several times, then the cabinet doors, before she returned to the living room where Orvin was reading.

"I see you found my book," she said, sitting in the chair opposite his.

He looked up. "It wasn't like you were hiding it."

"No, I suppose not," she said, clearing her throat. Orvin, smelling the floral scent of her perfume, studied her odd expression for a moment.

"Something wrong?" he said.

"What do you think about the book?"

He opened it to where his finger marked his place and scanned the pages, as if the answer to her question was written there. "Uh... well, it's interesting. I'm not sure if I believe any of it yet, but these fellas make a compelling argument, I guess." He wet his lips with his tongue. "Why are *you* reading this? I know you have relations in Philadelphia. Is that why you have this book?"

She regarded him with a somber expression. "Actually, I was at the library and Laverne suggested it. I'm not sure why... it's a very old book."

"Do you like it?"

"Not really," she said. "I prefer romance…"

Romance? All he'd ever seen her read were detective novels, cookbooks, and memoirs. He searched for a piece of paper to use as a bookmark, finding an old magazine and tearing off the corner, then offered the book to Colette.

"No, you hang onto it. I read as much as I wanted to. When you're done, I'll take it back to the library."

Orvin nodded, feeling like she had more on her mind she was wanting to offload. He opened the book and started to read again. The fact that she was sitting near the edge of her chair, her eyes seemingly caught in the vacuum of her thoughts, distracted him from concentrating on the text.

"Orvin," she said after several minutes of silence.

He looked over at her.

"I need to talk to you, okay," she said, fat tears cresting the bottom of her eyes.

"Is everything all right?" Orvin said, setting the book down, the magazine page corner sticking out where he'd left off.

"I wasn't at book club tonight." Her eyes were so tortured now Orvin wasn't sure he wanted to hear whatever she was about to tell him. "I had a meeting with Minister Lockton."

Orvin knew that Colette and the minister were close, that he was a fine young man in his early fifties, married with four children. He knew Colette confided things in the minister she'd never trust to him, but he'd known that going in, like one of those prenups rich folks sign, so there's no confusion about what's what and who's who. Colette and Orvin never signed anything saying that he would not be privy to her thoughts, or the anthology of her past, and he was okay with that, never quite sure what the bargain ended up costing their marriage in the long run.

"There are things about my past you don't know, or at least I don't think you do," she said.

Colette shared the history lesson through a curtain of constant tears, details about football players and a secluded cabin in the woods, and two other girls, and drinking and drugging, and violence and Colette had to pause several times to gather herself, shaking, ringing her hands, staring at the whirls and knots in the brocade oval rug on the living room floor. Orvin had been aware of some of the story from his high school days, at least a version of it, but nothing ever this graphic, or repugnant. He'd never heard about the prodigious drug use, the fights, the abuse, the violence, the gang rapes, the inhumanity of these high school boys. A merciless heat rose along the taut skin of Orvin's face, his heart beating an uneven fury beneath his ribs. Colette went on, explaining about the showdown outside the cabin, barely more than children, pointing guns at one another, the onlookers with a remorseless craving for carnage, screaming, encouraging, burning to see what a bullet at close range would do to human flesh. Young people with no true compass for the impermanence of life, or how durable death was.

That's when they escaped, the three girls, practically naked running across the uneven forest floor in the dark, sticks and rocks and leaves cutting their bare feet, dashing for the car, the young girl in the driver's seat crying, spinning the tires as they fled the scene, never slowing down until they were almost home.

Orvin could almost feel himself drifting into a fugue state, some suspended condition of awareness, soundless and cold. He fought the encroaching darkness behind his eyes, tried to focus on the details of each tear that rolled down Colette's cheek, each one swollen with unspeakable history. But the story was far from over. Any enduring and agonizing struggle is always rife with bitter consequences. This one was no different; sexually transmitted diseases, mental anguish, loss of direction, missed opportunities, and in Colette's case, unwanted pregnancy.

It was hard to hear she'd gone to live with her aunt for those several months, enduring her pregnancy virtually alone. Then returned to a ruined life; no high school yearbook memories, no prom or dates, no falling in love. Orvin wasn't sure she had actually ever loved him. She agreed to marry him when he asked, and he was over the moon by her acceptance. Even so, he knew that only a part of her stood on the alter and kissed him when the preacher pronounced them man and wife. The rest of her was gone, maybe forever, possibly never to return. And for whatever reason, Orvin had been happy with just a slice of Colette, as if there was so much to her that even a sliver would always be enough. But it hadn't, not really.

After a long while, with tissues piling up on the floor, Colette raised her tear-ravaged face to Orvin, but said nothing; everything was out in the open now.

"I can't begin to imagine how horrible that was for you, Colette," Orvin said. "I am so sorry you went through that."

Colette tried to fight back the next wave of tears. "Orvin, I am so sorry," she said, trying to dab them dry. "All these years I've wasted between us. I've been so closed down. And then it seemed, after your heart attack, you were pulling away from me and… I can't imagine my life without you. I should have told you all of this so many years ago. I've been so ashamed, and I've taken my humiliation out on you for so long. I just hope you can forgive me…"

Orvin was so shocked by the contents of the entire day, it was difficult restoring balance, the world wobbling under some new, unfamiliar disorder. "I'm just sorry I couldn't be there when you needed someone," Orvin finally said, his own eyes wetting. He got up and led her to the couch and they sat holding each other. This night would last until dawn, he knew, both of them trying out honesty as if it were a new language, neither of them adept at navigating the buried emotions that would undoubtedly be stripped bare.

35

NIGREDO, TENEBROSITAS

HE'D BEEN READING and taking notes all morning, certain that clues to this creature could be found in books. Texts on psychology, novels and scholarly works from the library covered the coffee table, with several notepads and volumes strewn helter-skelter along the floor. The story of Dr. Jekyll and Mr. Hyde provided clues in a philosophical sense, but it would take more than theories and fiction. *Nigredo, tenebrositas* — the chaos and melancholia of the inner life — possibly inched closer to identifying some connection to the beast, yet was far too abstract to be of any use.

By midafternoon, he stopped to toast a bagel and took it out onto the deck and sat in one of the chairs. Everything he'd read all made sense while he was immersed in reading, until he unplugged from the text—like now, eating a bagel on his deck—that's when some cog in his brain, one ruled by reason and logic, fought every concept maneuvering for a spot in Geoffrey's scheme; which was now suddenly the thoughts of a madman. Of the deranged and unhinged. How could this beast be the somatic translation of Geoffrey's deep-rooted phobias and fixations, whatever they were? Yet, his entire adult life had been governed by forces from the outer rim of accepted reality. Regardless of how crazy it all seemed, he was nevertheless moving forward with his plan and it needn't involve Orvin.

They had decided to begin the hunt in a few days, but Geoffrey couldn't wait. Besides, he could think of no reason to drag this elderly man along on his dark safari; no one else should be exposed to danger.

That was one aspect he had no trouble imagining, the danger of this proposed strategy, which, at its core, was vague and risky.

The next morning he drove into town and purchased a new head-lamp, and new boots; his old ones most likely still mired in the mud on Yellow Mountain. He wondered if the police had found them, and if so, had they offered them in to the evidence locker? Certainly they must be teeming with his DNA. Or had *The Associates* swept the area for anything that might incriminate him? Unable to entertain any more deadening thoughts, he jumped back into a book by Johnson.

After reading a few more hours, the light outside rippled with purples and deep, bloody reds. It was time to get dressed. In the bedroom, while pulling on his new boots, a snake of apprehension slith-ered through his gut, a squirming, liquid sensation that poured down into his legs. A bit shaky, he grabbed his new headlamp off the bureau and fitted it onto his forehead, then checked it in the mirror, unsure what he was hoping to find.

He had phoned Edward earlier in the day, and told him his plan. For a long while, Edward had said nothing, then assured Geoffrey he'd get everything set up. "I'll meet you up there," ET said.

Giving the house one last look, Geoffrey hurried down the steps to his Rover and threw himself inside. Everything he'd read over the past twenty-four hours was oddly gone from his memory, leaving in its place a dank whirling residue, a furtive bottomless vacuum.

36

A GREAT STORM

SITTING in a sterile room in *The Lodge*, Geoffrey explained to Edward about growing up on a farm in Pennsylvania with his preacher father and stepmother, Lauralee, his father's harlot wife. Even Edward winced a bit at Geoffrey's use of the archaic term for prostitute. Geoffrey went on, with as much as he could remember about his past, now nearly a hundred years ago, telling Edward about Lauralee and John Bennett sleeping together when Geoffrey's minister father was out preaching the Gospel in neighboring towns and cities for donations. Geoffrey paused in his story every so often, knowing *The Associates* were listening from somewhere on the spacecraft, frustrated he could not speak to them directly. Edward assured Geoffrey that *The Associates* were hearing every word, that a face-to-face meeting wasn't necessary.

"What if they have questions?" Geoffrey said, unwilling to accept the surreptitious nature of this approach, feeling like an idiot glancing up toward the ceiling as if he might spy a microphone, even though the ceiling was nearly blank, except for that big black eyeball looking thing. He pictured a bunch of little aliens sitting around a table looking at him, listening to his voice over tinny, metallic speakers, all of them laughing and slapping each other's backs. Geoffrey's imagination around the situation was absurd, for sure, but with nothing else to work with …

Edward assured him if *The Associates* had questions, he would pass them along to Geoffrey, assuring him nothing would be lost in translation.

Geoffrey regarded Edward a moment, then said, "I think my father killed Lauralee and John. I think he killed them in his own bed. With a shotgun..."

Edward listened, nonplussed by the disclosure. "Anything else?"

Geoffrey shook his head, the memory so vague as if to be a mirage, or the contents of a book he'd read once. Memories, if anything, were often faulty, especially ones nearly a century old.

"I was eleven, maybe twelve," Geoffrey said. "It was 1933. The Great Depression had left its mark on the entire world. I can't recall exactly. I was young, I know that. Just a boy. The effects of the depression had rippled out to the heartlands, the farms. The aftershock lasted for years..."

Edward nodded, then said, "Okay, now I want you to just relax, hold those memories close. In a few minutes you'll feel like you've fallen asleep. A few technicians will come in and hook up monitoring devices to your skin, chest and brain. They need to measure your galvanic reflexes, capillary hydrostatic pressure, dorsal root ganglia response, evaluate brain activity and other physiological functions."

"Why?" Geoffrey asked.

"In order to gauge how accurate your recall is. When you're finished, they'll score the veracity of your memory on a scale of 1 to 100. Anything over 90 is fairly accurate, at least close enough to help us understand what's going on."

Edward had explained earlier that the state Geoffrey would be put into would not be sleep, but something more akin to a deep, hypnogogic state, so they could get past his conscious defenses to the dark material of his buried psyche. "You'll experience your memory as if it were a story about yourself, young Peter Smithwick, as if you're watching yourself as an eleven-year-old boy in rural Pennsylvania. Don't judge the images. You shouldn't experience any fear, either, as you'll be acting as an objective observer of your own life."

"Will they know what I've remembered?" Geoffrey asked.

Edward shook his head. "No, they'll only know how accurate the memory is. But you'll recall everything, and much more vividly than you do now."

Edward used a controller to ease Geoffrey's chair back into a more comfortable, prone position.

"What if I fall asleep?" Geoffrey asked.

"You won't," Edward said, the lights dimming in the room. On his way out, Edward told him to just relax, that everything will be fine.

Before Edward even shut the door, Geoffrey was already fading, not drowsy exactly, but losing his present consciousness, suddenly aware of a series of tones and beeps playing in the room, the pure notes methodically spaced, some kind of sound pattern, until they were the only stimuli left, as if they originated inside his skull, echoing there. Geoffrey —eyes open or closed, he had no idea, nothing but blackness with no sense of time or presence—did however feel odd sensations along his scalp, along the flesh of his arms, his chest, his face, vague points of pressure, pulsing with subtle current.

Were technicians affixing electrodes to his skin to measure his physiological responses? Was that what he was feeling? Wasn't that what Edward had told him? How odd, that he felt completely and utterly alone, yet beings might be right there with him, touching him, observing him.

A moment later his thoughts dissolve like salt in water, the tones in his head elongate, pulling him inward, spiraling down a tunnel with nothing to see, just the sensation of movement, enclosed, though not claustrophobic, until he himself feels erased, replaced by the shorter days of autumn descending into winter, the sun traveling a lower road in the southern sky. A pale blanket of light spreads across the yard, Peter Smithwick sitting on the wooden porch, watching two hounds.

Kotter's beagles had been humping furiously for so long, that the male dog ended up stuck inside the female. When the male beagle tried to dismount the female after the long and vigorous encounter, he only succeeded in getting turned rear to rear and was unable to withdraw. Now the dogs are coupled together like two locomotive engines facing in opposite directions. When the female moves forward, the male yelps, stumbling backward in an attempt to follow. The two are a sight as they fumble around the yard, yelping and kicking up little clouds of dust.

Peter has been watching the beagles from his front porch steps for some time. He is eleven years old and has lived his entire life on a farm, but never has he seen anything like this. Peter watches, laughing at the comical sight, as the dogs struggle to free themselves. He wants to help them but isn't sure how.

So enthralled with the scene, Peter fails to notice the sky growing dark and ominous. A dust devil rises from the sparse yard near the dogs —a whirling genie, harbinger of a tremendous storm. The weathervane spins wildly, rattling and whining a pathetic alarm, the shutters slap against the peeling clapboards, trying to shake themselves free from their hinges. Dust sweeps out from under the weathered porch, swirling like a tornado, forcing the boy to shield his eyes.

Down on the road, maybe a mile out, a dark shape heads toward the house, its progress dragging a long plume of dust in its path. The boy stands to see it better. Out of the corner of his eye he sees the beagles still struggling, now a bit more frantically. Peter ignores them; his attention fixed on the unknown object heading up the road. In a minute or so it's close enough that Peter can see it's a wagon. Behind and above it, a greenish storm cloud in the shape of a monstrous beast towers over the distant hills and fields, as if at any moment this *beast* will open its gigantic jaws and swallow the wagon, the road, and the entire valley.

It is then Peter recognizes the driver. The minister! The boy is surprised the old man is back so early. No one expected him for at least two more days. With just a slight tug on the reins, the driver brings the buckboard to a halt in the front yard. Anxious over the minister's unexpected return, Peter considers running inside, warning *them* he's home. He glances toward the front door, then back at the minister seated in the wagon. No time! If he can just stall the old man in the front yard long enough...

Savage, spiraling gusts lift small stones mixed with dirt high into the sky, dropping them all around the boy as he runs out to meet the old man—who's dressed all in black, climbing down from the wagon. Standing near the huge wheel, Peter rubs the grit from his eyes.

"Pa!"

The large figure—a man in his sixties with a face craggy as broken shale—has his back to the boy. Long hair tangled yellow and gray, the texture of corn silk, streams out from under the old man's black hat and down across his square shoulders. The minister turns toward the boy, then uses a weathered hand to anchor his brimmed hat against the wind. His eyes glint out from the dark hollow between his angled cheeks and the ledge of his brow.

"What are you doing home?" Peter asks. "Lauralee said you wouldn't be here 'til Saturday!"

"How come you ain't inside, boy?" the old man says as he motions toward the house with the newspaper in his free hand. "What's got you so occupied to keep you out in a storm?"

Not home for one full minute and it seems the minister already knows what Peter's been up to. *They're just some silly ole beagles!* the boy thinks, feeling shame slither through his stomach, a feeling he's become accustomed to around his father.

The old man eyes the tangled dogs for just a second, then says, "Peter? You been watchin' them mongrels fornicating?" Peter can't bring his eyes to the minister's face, those sunken gray cheeks, deep and bruised like the stormy sky racing above their heads.

"It's okay, Peter. It's a good thing. Now you can see how God deals with fornicators. The Lord will lift them up to heaven just as they are for their judgement day, still lashed together in sin." The minister's lips are drawn and cracked as a dry creek bottom. "There's no hidin' sin from the Lord!"

Wind howls through the valley as Peter stares at the ground. He feels the preacher's heavy gaze upon his head, like a beam of light trying to burn a hole clear through to his soul.

"Boy, take the wagon to the barn and unhitch the mare... give her some hay. You might oughta brush her down a bit too 'fore you come back to the house."

Peter reaches up and pulls at the bridle, still pondering the preacher's words when he realizes that he has to stop him from going inside. "Pa, do you want to hear what I learned from the Bible today?"

"Best get busy, boy. Tend to the chores I give ya. That's a mighty storm building this evening."

Peter leads the horse and buckboard to the barn, the tops of trees tossing and swaying. The wind no longer gusts in bursts, but rolls steadily through the fields like a ghostly machine. Grit and dirt swirl up from the ground, stinging the boy's cheeks and eyes. Trying to protect his face with his left hand, Peter's thoughts drift back to Lauralee and the minister; suddenly he doesn't care if the minister catches them. Serve them right! Peter thinks. All of them!

Almost to the barn, the old nag protests, frightened by the surly weather. "Come on girl. You don't wanna be outside when this thing comes down on us." He tugs harder at the reins until she follows. Peter's mind flashes back to the beagles, laughing to himself at the site, glancing toward the porch. The minister is already inside and the beagles are gone. Peter tilts his head back to the roiling sky and thinks about the minister's words, imagining those beagles stumbling around on the clouds before God, yelping and sidestepping, looking forlorn. *If God don't laugh at that, He's more serious than the preacher.* Peter laughs harder now, sure he'll be struck dead by lightning where he stands, and for a moment, he forgets about the minister, and Lauralee.

The hogs in the pen are becoming animated under the lightning flashes and thunder, grunting and shuffling, butting each other, confused and anxious, the smaller ones squealing, aimlessly scurrying along the perimeter of the large pen. Peter can't recall if he fed them this morning, another thing the preacher will throw a fit about. Maybe he should check on the pigs once he gets the mare settled down.

Peter unhooks the old nag and puts her in the stall. "Here girl, eat some hay. It'll get your mind off that ruckus outside." She fidgets, too nervous to eat. Wind hammers the barn until it shakes as much as the horse. "Calm down, girl. Eat that hay I give ya. Everything's gonna be just fine."

While Peter is brushing her, a board rips free from the roof exposing a large rectangle of greenish gray sky. Peter looks up just as a lightning flash fills the opening, etching a black shape of the hole behind the boy's eyes, temporarily blinding him. The nag bucks and kicks even before the thunderclap rumbles the earth beneath their feet. "Whoa, girl! Whooaa!" Peter tries to settle her but she spooks. He dives out under the gate of the stall, but her hoof catches him before he gets free. He screams, grabbing his ankle, using his good leg to push himself backward away from the stall.

Rain pours through the opening in the roof. The barn door slams shut, then sucks open violently. Peter pulls himself up and hobbles from the barn; the mare crashing her hooves against the weathered boards of the stall gate. The barn door slaps maniacally against the wooden slats of the outside wall; sheets of rain slicing through the darkened barnyard. Peter tries to force the barn door closed, but the wind fights back, crashing the door and Peter against the side of the barn. Dazed, Peter falters a moment, then falls backward into the mud. Before he can regain his footing, the frightened mare splinters the stall gate, bolting from the barn and galloping past him off across the field. "Come back here, damn you!"

Covered in mud, Peter gets to his feet, watching the horse disappear into a solid curtain of gray rain. *The minister's gonna whoop me good for lettin' that damned ole nag get away!* The barn door sucks shut, then bursts open again, knocking Peter off balance. He stumbles, able to regain his footing and limps toward the house. A loud but muffled crack rips through the hissing rain. Peter looks up thinking it might be a limb about to come crashing down, deciding a second later the sound came from the direction of the house. The rain comes in dark waves making it almost impossible to see. Shingles fly from the roof like startled bats from a cave. A window, illuminated by an oil lamp, provides the only beacon back to the house.

Another loud crack, this time more like an explosion, issues from the direction of the house. With his ankle throbbing, Peter hobbles as fast as he can. Wind shoves and teases at his back; a fallen limb grabbing his good foot, dropping him to the soggy ground. Mud sucks at his small wet frame. The moist earth seems to speak to him in his head. *Stay down this time. There is nothing you can do.* Wind roars, shifting through his damp clothes, bringing him a chill.

Peter is face down on the earth when he hears another loud crack, but this time he no longer cares. The tip of his nose is inches above a muddy puddle; a fragrance rises up from the ground, familiar and welcome; the smell of damp earth, planted fields, new life. He waits completely still, until he no longer hears the wind, or feels the stinging rain on the back of his head and arms; until the pain in his ankle dissolves, and the faces of the minister and Lauralee and John grow translucent and finally disappear. He waits until the dark clouds part, sunlight exposing a vast field of large sunflowers swaying back and forth. Comforting warmth spreads over him like a blanket. The darkness inside his head turns golden and luminous, building until a dazzling white glow fills the dark cavity of his skull. Nothing moves. Everything perfect; perfectly still.

All at once he feels himself rising up, out of the mud, off the ground, suspended, and knows at that moment, he's dead. *Of course! I'm dead and going to my judgement. I am going before God!* He's astonished and terrified all at once. *Oh God, I hope You thought them beagles was as funny as I did.* He opens his eyes, expecting to see himself floating up through shining white clouds. But everything is black, the dark sloppy earth moving past a foot below his face. From the blurry edge of his perspective, he spies shiny black boots caked with *dried* mud, which seems odd. The minister has him by the back of his trousers, carrying him like a bucket of water toward the house. The sky has lightened somewhat while the wind still howls. The old man sets the boy down next to the angled wooden doors of the root cellar. Pulling open one side, the minister motions for the boy to climb down.

"Go on, Peter. Go down in the cellar until the storm has lost its fury."

Peter reluctantly steps into the dark hole. "But Lauralee and…"

"No time for talking, son. Just do as I told ya."

The boy steps down, then looks back. Peter is wet and cold and wants no part of the damp cellar. But the old man's resolve is firm, his face like a statue. The minister holds the wooden door effortlessly, even though the wind tears at the shutters without mercy. The boy takes another step down.

"Peter, when everything falls quiet, I want you to head straight for town and find Miss Sarah McCoy. You tell her you need a home. Tell her Jacob sent you."

"But Pa, I…"

The old man reaches into his pocket, bringing out a hand full of cash, the deed to the farm, and a chain with a tarnished silver cross. Peter recognizes it as the minister's.

"Folks are still struggling. Now take these things and make sure Sarah and her husband get them. The cross is for you…" Jacob holds his hand out to Peter. Peter reaches up to take everything. With his hands full, he isn't sure what to do, seized by a sadness he's never felt before.

"Peter," says Jacob, gently touching the boy's wet head. "I fear I invoked a pact with Satan … and we are certainly damned."

When the minister finishes speaking, his gray eyes flicker like the ashes of a dying fire. Peter stares deep into the old man's eyes, which are now cold and lifeless, then back into the black hole of the cellar. Rain slides down Peter's hair and face, his shirt and pants soaked. Somehow, though, the preacher doesn't appear to be wet at all.

The minister slowly lowers the storm cellar door, Peter looking up at the old man, trying to recall the sunflowers swaying in the field. But the reassuring image can't be found, while a new darkness sweeps around the boy, his pale face a fading moon in a narrow sliver of blackness.

37

BARBARIC HUNGER

THE DRIVE to the top of Yellow Mountain passed faster than Geoffrey had imagined. He was still wrestling with the NHI hypnosis experiment *The Associates* had performed the night before, giving Geoffrey's recollection a score of 57. Edward explained that the memory was quite faulty, but not to worry. "They want to perform another Neural-Hypnagogic Induction procedure in a week or so," Edward had told him. Geoffrey wanted to do another the next day, but Edward and *The Associates* cautioned against it, wanting Geoffrey's psyche to have time to further process the stagnant memory, assuring him the first NHI would help to loosen things a bit, bring the accurate recall closer to consciousness.

Geoffrey had decided to go to the bald alone, without Orvin, squeezing by on a couple hours' sleep and just enough food to sustain life and brain function. Nevertheless, he felt fine, renewed by his decision to pursue an approach that wasn't conditioned on *The Associates* NHI procedures, or one that involved guns; he was certain Orvin would have insisted on firearms for this little odyssey.

Geoffrey slammed the door of his Rover and was stunned by how silent the woods fell, as if hermitically sealed against all sound and life. Not a bird, tree frog or cicada, nothing to make the darkness more tangible. Until a loud screech took his breath, throwing his heart into an unrhythmic, fibrillating cycle. It took several minutes to compose himself. The screech came again, but this time he was ready; his mind had already tossed in a picture of a harmless owl for Geoffrey to match to the unnerving noise.

Trudging up the trail to the top of Yellow Mountain, he wondered if he would encounter other campers, people out for a nature getaway, getting back to the basics. Maybe a campfire, and marshmallows and ghost stories. Geoffrey had no idea what a real camping trip would be like; he'd never been on one. When he reached the bald, he started thinking about what Orvin had said about getting lost. Geoffrey didn't think it would be a problem, but now, in this blackest of nights, he wasn't even sure which way to start walking.

The headlamp provided all the light he'd needed coming up the trail, the glow falling on tree trunks and bushes along the edge, but here, on the bald, the beam seemed to fall on nothing but sedge. Crossing the barren expanse, he felt disoriented under the black plasma sky stretching out above him, charged with billions of stars. If he had a sextant, and actually knew how to use one, he could navigate by that. The musing brought him a moment of calm as he traversed the desolate field. When he reached the treeline on the opposite side, he searched the under-growth for the continuation of the trail. It took several minutes before he spotted the narrow opening in the brush. Just as he entered, a low, guttural sound put him back on his heels. Something moved through the brush ahead, but the beam of his headlamp couldn't reach it. For a few minutes Geoffrey stood still, his headlamp moving side to side with his head, painting the forest in slow, luminous strokes. Nothing. Something moved behind him, spinning his attention a hundred and eighty degrees, until the sound was in front of him again. At this point Geoffrey had turned in place so much, he wasn't sure if the idea of *front* and *back* was even pertinent anymore. Whatever made the noise certainly couldn't change positions that fast. Auditory illusion. Trick of the tympanum.

Geoffrey stepped forward into the forest edge, pushing brush and limbs aside, the headlamp finally finding traction on trees and plants along the trail. Moving through the darkness in this way, with only a small portion of detail revealed in any moment, it felt like he was standing still and the forest was moving past him. Ahead, a massive tree had fallen across the path. He lifted one leg over, straddling the log as if he were riding a horse, then eased his other leg over until he was on solid ground again. The bushes twenty yards away rustled with life. Something made a hasty escape, not bothering to conceal its noisy depar-ture. Just then he wondered if snakes would be out at night. He knew that whatever fled wasn't a snake, but the idea of the frightened critter making a racket brought to mind its opposite; the soundless escape;

which conjured images of thick, ropey serpents squirming undetected along the forest floor. One could slither between his legs and he wouldn't even know it. Unless it bit him.

He brought his eyes down to his boots wondering if they would protect against such an attack. In that moment Geoffrey knew he was out of his element, that he didn't belong here. When he raised his head, the beam of the headlamp swept the area in front of him, revealing two tiny bright spots ninety feet away, suspended in the dark void. The light couldn't reach the trees at that distance, but managed to reflect with crystal clarity off two yellow eyes staring back. The world turned impossibly still. The night air didn't move for the longest time. Then the slightest breeze, not even a breeze, but some movement of molecules. Maybe the breath of the beast gently brushing along the fine hairs on Geoffrey's face. He felt it and didn't, a sensation lighter than the touch of a falling feather, yet bringing with it a fusty, rotting stink that filled Geoffrey's nose and head. He recognized the stench at once, the odor etched into his synapses, but couldn't call back from memory where he'd encountered it.

About the time Geoffrey began to wonder when the stalemate would end, the creature started moving slowly toward him, through the woods, cracking limbs and uprooting small trees like a bulldozer. Geoffrey's first inclination was to run, but what was the point of that; he'd come all this way to face this thing.

The beast gave off the overwhelming fetor of decay, as if it were already dead. Geoffrey tried to steel himself, the headlamp beginning to define the hair along the creature's jawline and head, framing its face much like the mane of a lion, but not regal; knotted, greasy and unkempt. The skin of its face was blotched and veiny with the raw-meat look of an exposed organ, a liver maybe, or a spleen. Between its smell and appearance, Geoffrey could barely stand to witness its approach. But he knew not to look away.

When the creature came within ten feet of him, he felt himself take a step backward, a twig snapping beneath his boot. The sound excited the creature, causing it to lunge forward through the understory, in a racket of clattering branches and limbs until it was on Geoffrey. Geoffrey threw his arms forward to protect himself but the counterattack was useless, the beast slapping away his hands, slashing its claws across his face. The burn of the ripped flesh burrowed deep into Geoffrey's nerve endings, the pain a white, hot torch sizzling along his skin. Another blow caught the side of his head, near the temple, igniting an explosion inside his skull. He was losing consciousness. It grabbed him by the hand and dragged him over rocks and broken limbs and sticker bushes, thorns and rough stones scraping at the flesh of his back and ribs. The creature let out a guttural shriek as it sped away, dragging him effortlessly, Geoffrey unable to break loose from its grip. The small bones of Geoffrey's wrist seemed to bend near breaking, his legs torn to shreds on the gnarly, naked ground.

As quickly as the creature had seized him, it released him and fled into the woods. Geoffrey groaned, trying to turn himself over, but the pain at his ribs howled under the slightest movement. No longer able to support himself on one elbow, he let his face sink to the ground, the earthy smell of the soil flooding through him. A moment of relief, maybe shock, maybe temporary unconsciousness, until the facts of his wounds throbbed through his bloodstream, bright, charged, agonizing currents. The amperage of his lacerations burned in every cell, the torture so complete Geoffrey lost all sense of himself to the pain. Relief came as a gathering gloom behind his eyes, sucking the last of the world down a dark, spiraling hole.

When Geoffrey woke, the air was cold and dark. Before he could fully open his eyes, his injuries alerted the receptors in his spinal column, transmitting the messages directly to his brain, pain radiating out then looping back, a pitiless reminder of the extensive damage. Struggling to his knees, he wasn't sure he could get to his feet. Before he could test his stamina and strength, he realized his headlamp was gone. Even if he could stand, there would be no getting off the mountain without a light. Sitting up, he sent his eyes in all directions, hoping to find a smudge of illumination coming up through the weeds. Maybe thirty yards away, a gauzy beam glowed along the lower branches of a large tree. How odd it looked, as if a portal to the center of the earth had opened in the tangled woods. To his right he found a sapling to pull up on, the excruciating sensation at his ribs nearly causing him to lose his bowels. Finally to his feet, he held his side as he hobbled toward the light, cautiously squatting down to retrieve it, careful to keep his torso straight as he stood and fixed the strap onto his forehead. Broken ribs, he figured. Like nothing he'd ever felt before. It hurt to breathe. With the light on his forehead, he scanned the gashes, scrapes and lesions along his arms and legs, his flesh streaked and stained with blood. A hard knot throbbed at his temple and cheek, like a fiery golf ball trapped beneath his skin. From the pain, he could almost imagine what his face must look like.

He surveyed the area, trying to figure out which direction to head. The woods seemed impenetrable and he hoped *The Associates* would rescue him; otherwise, Geoffrey might be stuck until morning. The creature had dragged him so deep into the woods off the verge of the bald, Geoffrey couldn't begin to figure out how to get back. And just as Orvin had predicted, Geoffrey was lost. As if trying to initiate a miracle, Geoffrey looked toward the heavens, at the impersonal flickering specks of light tossed like salt across the black sheet of sky. Geoffrey raised his wrist slowly and wiped the blood from the crystal of his watch. Seventeen minutes after one. At least five hours until the first vague smear of dawn. The sensible thing to do now was find a place to rest for the night, but Geoffrey wasn't comfortable doing nothing. He had to find the trail. He had to get back to his Rover and head home. The encounter had been a complete failure, leaving him nearly crippled with pain.

In absence of any logical approach to finding the trail, he opted to trust his intuition. After walking for nearly twenty minutes, he encountered nothing but downed trees and sticker bushes. When he felt himself heading down the mountain side, he turned around, needing to travel *up* to get back to the bald, figuring he could walk the perimeter until he came to the trail. Meandering through the dark gave Geoffrey time to think about the creature, how he could get close enough to the beast to sense its intentions, understand the source of its barbaric hunger. But he'd sensed nothing, which was distressing; he needed to learn where the beast had come from in order to send it back.

Resting on a boulder, Geoffrey checked his watch to see that it was a little after three in the morning. He was exhausted. Original pain had eased somewhat, or he'd gotten used to it, while other injuries were just making themselves known; a tender ankle, a tightness in his back, stinging at his buttocks and hip from being thrashed along the ground, a throbbing burning knot at his shoulder. Over time his neck had begun to stiffen, making it uncomfortable to turn his head. He was about to push up from the rock when he heard a low growl, a harsh, slow rumbling. He swiveled his head gently until the headlamp snagged a glistening pair of yellow eyes. The beast was no more than fifty feet away. Why hadn't he smelled the damn thing before it got this close? Geoffrey sucked in a large ball of air, trying to decide what to do, but the decision was made for him when the creature burst through the weeds and small trees.

Geoffrey didn't have time to react, the attack sudden and savage, knocking him to the earth, the pain centers igniting fires throughout his body. The blows came one after another, the beast hammering him with huge gnarled paws. Balling himself to a tight knot, Geoffrey hoped to thwart the worst of it, but that was impossible. His body took the punishment until his consciousness had endured enough, removing Geoffrey from the fierce assault into a dark, vacuous space, temporarily free from pain.

38

A NECESSARY LIE

ORVIN HADN'T SPOKEN to Geoffrey since the night at Geoffrey's house when they planned the hunt for the creature on Yellow Mountain. Orvin pulled the wooden box from the gun safe, then opened the lid and lifted the .45 from the felt-lined interior. The pistol was locked and loaded. He slid a couple of extra magazines from the shelf and stuck them in his jacket pocket.

"What are you doing, Orvin?" Colette said, stopping on the steps to the basement.

He looked up at her and didn't want to get into it tonight. They had been doing so well since their talk a few nights earlier when he'd returned from Geoffrey's house; he and Colette had actually made love a couple of times, something they hadn't done in years. He'd been struck by his rekindled desire at seeing Colette naked, her body lovely, unravaged by her sixty plus years. She wasn't a jogger or gym junkie, but seemed to possess a natural vitality, a tendency toward a comely figure. Now she stood on the steps in her nightgown, her long hair down to her shoulders.

"Are you going out?" she said, taking another step down the stairs.

"Another search party tonight," he said.

"I thought they found all those kids."

Orvin couldn't get back on the lying track again; they'd made a pact to be honest with one another. "They did. I'm going with Mr. Cannon." Orvin preferred to address Geoffrey by his surname, to dissuade any notion of friendship between the them. He knew she hated Geoffrey, or at least distrusted him, but couldn't understand why. Colette didn't respond, coming down the steps until she stood in front of Orvin. She leaned in and kissed him tenderly on the lips.

"You know how I feel about that man," she said softly. "And I hope you know how I feel about you, Orvin... I would prefer you didn't go... I'm worried."

He slipped the .45 into the holster behind his back and pulled her close. "I love you, Colette," he whispered into her ear. "I always have... and nothing will ever change that."

When he pulled back, she had tears in her eyes. "I'm sorry I wasted so much of our lives," she said. "I don't want to waste one second more." When she held his gaze, Orvin recognized something in her expression, some unsaid words floating on the reflections in her eyes. "I'd like to go with you tonight," she said.

He frowned and shook his head. "You don't want to muck around in the dark," he said, unwilling to tell her how dangerous it could be.

"What are you searching for?" she said.

Orvin had to tread lightly here. A small lie was in order, because the truth was as yet unverifiable, and potentially frightening. "I think a rogue bear's been killing these hikers and such," Orvin said, hoping his eyes wouldn't betray him. Black bears weren't normally a threat to humans, and if it became one, a bear's method of killing was never as precise and clean as snapping a neck, or smashing a windpipe; it was a messy and brutal business. Colette stared at him.

"I know you're lying, Orvin... so I won't even ask why you're going with Mr. Cannon. All I know is you must have a very good reason for keeping the truth from me, especially now..." She raised up on her toes to kiss him on the lips, then turned and headed up the steps. Halfway up the staircase, she turned toward him. "Don't let yourself get hurt."

Orvin watched her climb, then listened to her small bare feet thump across the kitchen floor toward the living room. She'd watch a couple of shows on television, then read until she got sleepy. After that, she would go to their room and ready herself for bed, brushing her teeth, removing any makeup she had applied earlier in the day, then brush her hair in front of the bathroom mirror. In bed she would slip beneath the sheet and covers, then lie on her back a few moments as if to give gratitude for the day before rolling onto her side, away from Orvin's half of the mattress. Minutes later she would purr softly, a gentle breathing, signaling to Orvin she'd fallen asleep, drifting quietly in the custody of her dreams.

Orvin felt horrible for his deception. He tried to push away the sticky regret, leaving the house by the basement door. Outside, light fading, night less than an hour away. By the time he and Geoffrey would reach Yellow Mountain, a moonless world would be upon them; a very black night indeed.

Cranking the engine of his pickup, Orvin was about to back from the driveway when he received a text from Deputy Calhoun. *Orvin, thought you might be interested in this clip the lab boys pulled off Carly Rasterson's phone.* Carly Rasterson? It took a moment for the name to register; the young girl he'd found that day on Yellow Mountain, her phone lying in a muddy puddle. Orvin figured the device had been ruined. He tapped the video, the night footage grainy at first, slowly gaining focus, revealing a circular pattern of spinning lights rising from the bald into the night sky. "What the hell?" Orvin said to himself.

The five-second video continued looping, the lights rising over and over into the darkness above Yellow Mountain. After a minute or so, he stowed his phone and pulled from the driveway. On the ride to Geoffrey's house, his mind played back the video from the phone. It was impossible to deny what it looked like, but he had to entertain other possibilities, like kids playing with those remote-control drones fitted with colorful lights, a prank to post on YouTube, maybe send to the Kleary Creek newspaper for their website.

After a twenty-minute drive, Orvin arrived at a dark house with an empty driveway; his first thought—Geoffrey foolishly left without him. Orvin hurried up the front steps to the glass doors at the living room. He knocked several times hoping he was wrong, then pulled on the handle. The door slid open. Finding the light switch, Orvin flipped it on and was dumbfounded by the clutter of books and papers scattered across the living room. He glanced at a few titles, words like *shadow* and *individuation* and *psychology* jumping out at him. After checking Geoffrey's bedroom, he went to the kitchen, the sink stacked with dishes, cups and silverware. Orvin went back to the living room and stood in the middle of the maelstrom, trying to figure out what to do next. Where was Geoffrey? How long had he been gone?

At first Orvin thought to drive up to Yellow Mountain, but wasn't sure if his pickup would traverse the rutted muddy road; his vehicle didn't have four-wheel drive like Geoffrey's Rover, which could leave him stranded and a long way from help. Maybe he would drive back home. But what if Geoffrey was in trouble, or worse? A chilling emptiness settled in his gut.

Deciding to wait at the house for Geoffrey to return, he figured he'd better call Colette and let her know he may not be home until morning. Her phone rang several times before she picked up.

"Orvin! Is something wrong?"

"Did I wake you?"

"No, I was just getting ready for bed. Is everything okay?"

"He's not here. Mr. Cannon. He must have gone by himself."

The silence stretched to several long seconds before Colette finally said, "Are you coming back home?"

"Uh… I thought I'd stay until he gets back. I'm worried." No matter what he thought about Geoffrey personally, he knew he was indebted to the young man. Owed him his life and would do whatever it took to clear the tab.

Colette seemed to be thinking, the sound of water rushing into the bathroom sink. "I'll join you, okay?" The water shut off.

"It's late, Colette? What would you do over here?"

"Be with you," she said. "Just give me the directions… it'll be fun…"

Orvin was going to protest but the truth was, it did sound like fun. He couldn't remember the last time they'd been anywhere together overnight other than at home. He gave her directions and told her to be careful. When they hung up, he checked the time on his phone so he'd know when to expect her, then went out to the kitchen to clean up the dishes.

39

SOMETHING IN THE ROAD

COLETTE HAD NEVER INTENDED on lying to Orvin about her reason for sharing the story of the worst night of her life, about the Pledge and the football team, the hedonistic party at the cabin. Because of her shame over the event, burying it all those years, she truly had been pushing Orvin out of her life through her cold detachment and prickly veneer. The minister had told her that maybe sharing her harrowing experience with Orvin may open a dialogue between them, and possibly ameliorate some of her guilt and humiliation. "You can't keep this hidden any longer out of a fear of rejection," the minister told her. "Orvin's reaction might just surprise you." What she never told the minister, or Orvin, was that part of her motivation for setting the past straight and getting everything out in the open, was Geoffrey Cannon. She'd felt a distinct recognition of the young man the first time she met him at the hospital—when Orvin was recovering from his heart attack—but knew it was impossible, unless... unless Mr. Cannon was some kind of wicked apparition, a messenger from Satan come to claim her immortal soul for her past misgivings. She found herself in a spiraling panic, unsure how much time she'd have to make things right. Orvin had explained how Mr. Cannon had touched his chest and ushered him back from the dead. And even though Colette had downplayed the event with Orvin, she knew of only two entities in the world capable of such a task, and was fairly certain Mr. Cannon had not been sent by God.

Even though the highway leading from Kleary Creek was deserted, Colette nevertheless switched on her turn signal to make the left onto

Bennet Mill Road. Guiding her Ford along the deserted highway heading for Strieber Mountain Road, she couldn't help but wonder at the things she might find inside. That was part of the reason she'd suggested coming to stay with Orvin at his house; a bit of spying. The other was a photocopied article she'd received in the mail from a library in Philadelphia. She had contacted them, requesting any information they might have on microfiche regarding a man named Peter Smithwick. After an exhaustive search of their archive of news reports dating back to the late 1800's, the researcher had only been able to find one article. It was a short blurb. Colette read it over numerous times, hoping for some clue that would prove her theory, but never found a thing. The article proved nothing.

Colette—with everything cycling through her mind; her own past, her disclosure to Orvin, the newspaper article about Peter Smithwick, her crazy suspicions—tried to focus on the dark highway, the dashes of bright yellow lines shooting toward her like arrows. Houses and dark buildings she didn't recognize swept past her windshield. She drove over a bridge that crossed a river, the current swirling in pools beneath a lone street lamp. She glanced at the scrap of paper with the directions Orvin had given her to Mr. Cannon's house. Her eyes had only been diverted a second, but when she looked up, something huge was crossing the road. A bear, she figured, up on its hind legs. Colette slammed on the brakes and swerved the car into the oncoming lane, which must have startled the creature. Even though it had started to run, Colette clipped it with her front fender, shifting the steering wheel back and forth to regain control of the car. The creature loped off into the woods along the side of the highway. Colette, with the car under control, inched toward the shoulder to assess the damage.

This stretch of highway cut through farmland, mostly fields and silos and fences, but no houses or buildings, except for a barn here and there, no street lamps lining the road. She left the motor running and got out and walked to the passenger side front fender, cringing when she saw the metal crumpled back like aluminum foil. Glancing down the highway, she wondered if the animal had been hurt, then walked along the dark shoulder to the spot where she thought she'd hit the bear, her mind reenacting the event. It was big as a bear, she knew that, but something was off; it walked upright very naturally. She'd seen a bear once on its hind legs, but when it walked, it had moved stiff and ungainly, rocking back and forth like Frankenstein or something. This creature's movement was fluid on two legs; standing upright was obviously instinctual. Could it have been a man with a large coat? The thought shot a cold dread through her. She scanned the edge of the woods, checking the road periodically to find where she'd hit the thing. Twenty feet ahead she spotted broken plastic, glass and ruined chrome trim scattered across the pavement. After checking both ways, she walked into the middle of the deserted highway to inspect the area. She could find no blood, no sign of anything other than the wreckage from her car.

Walking back, Colette heard something rustle in the bushes near the shoulder. If it was a person, they may be unable to call out to her. "Hello? Is someone there?" She walked closer, listening for a response. "Hello?" She thought she heard a low grunting sound, like someone hurt. She stepped closer to the bushes. "Is someone there? Are you okay?" No answer.

Just as she got out her phone to dial 911, a car came speeding down the road. A second later the blue flashing lights snapped on. The police car slowed and pulled to the shoulder where Colette was standing and came to a stop. The officer got out with his flashlight and shined it toward her.

"Ma'am, is everything— Colette? Is that you?" the officer said.

Colette shielded her eyes from the bright beam. "Who is that?' she said.

"Wyatt Calhoun!" Calhoun brought the beam of his flashlight to the pavement and walked up next to her. "Are you okay?"

Before she could answer, something spooked in the bushes near them and ran away through the underbrush, snapping limbs and branches. Calhoun swung his light toward the commotion. "What the heck was that?" He stared at the spot in the brush for a long moment.

"I hit something with my car," Colette said. "I don't know if it was a man or a bear... or something else..."

He shifted his attention toward her. "Something else?"

"It was big, but it was walking on two legs..." She wanted to tell him it was Bigfoot, until she pictured Laverne at the library going on and on about UFOs and Sasquatch and all brands of nonsense.

Calhoun scratched his head. "Well, whatever it was didn't sound all that injured. I doubt it was a person, though." He spotted the debris in the middle of the road and turned his flashlight on it, following the beam out onto the pavement. "No blood here," he said toward Colette. He walked back over and escorted her to her car. "Bit of damage. In the old days, that would a been a few hundred bucks, but anymore, with all these dadblamed newfangled trim and plastic and specialized whatnot, that could set you back a few bills. Orvin might be able to get the parts at the junkyard and do it himself. Save you a bundle."

Colette felt the night chill settling in. "I'm not worried about the car... I just hope no one was hurt."

"Now don't you give that another thought," he said. "No way a person got hit and run off like that. No, that was some critter. A tough ole bear. He'll probably be fine. They got some thick hide." Calhoun seemed to ponder his own statement, as if recalling some moment in time. "Say, what are you doing way out here? Where's Orvin?"

"I'm going to meet him at a friend's house," Colette said, not really wanting to go into details.

Calhoun bobbed his head a few times. "Will she drive all right?" he said, looking at her car.

"Yeah, I don't think the metal is rubbing the tire or anything."

"Well, okay... hey, we should all get together some evening, you and Meg and Orvin and me. Go to the movies."

Colette nodded. "Sure. Sounds good."

"Orvin really helped us out with finding them girls," he added abruptly, as if he'd been holding it in for some time. "He tell you about that?"

"No... I don't think he was comfortable talking about it."

The deputy toed the gravel at his feet. "Yeah, not really great dinner talk." His face collapsed under the weight of a dismal memory; the man suddenly looked ten years older, Colette thought.

"I better be going or Orvin will be calling the Sheriff's Office to go looking for me," she said, giving him an awkward little chuckle.

"Well, it's been too long. Now let's get together soon, all right?"

Calhoun smiled and started walking back to his cruiser. Colette watched a few moments, then went around to the driver's side and got in. She'd forgotten the engine was running and grinded the starter when she turned the key again. "Oh, sugar!" She checked the rearview mirror. Deputy Calhoun seemed to be waiting for her to pull out first. She put the car in gear and slowly pulled from the shoulder, checking the directions to Mr. Cannon's house one last time.

40

FULL MEASURE OF THE DAMAGE

WHEN COLETTE WOKE, she looked over at Orvin asleep on the floor next to her. It had been fun, like a campout or something, the two of them sleeping on makeshift bedding on the hardwood floor of Geoffrey Cannon's house. Orvin had been worried when she was late, and had worn a troubled look when she told him about hitting the creature on the highway; but it hadn't been the damage to the car that vexed him. And he would never tell her what was bothering him. The night before, they had sat out on the deck, a blanket wrapped around them like high school kids at a Friday night football game, talking about their life together, remembering all the times with their son growing up, how they both missed their granddaughter. "I guess we need to make a trip to Virginia," Orvin had said. "Not sure when those two are gonna bring that little girl down here."

At one point they were about to make love, but Orvin said he couldn't push away the notion that Mr. Cannon could pull up at any moment and find them naked on his deck. Orvin still half-expected him to show up, at least that's what he'd told Colette. She told him about Wyatt wanting Meg and them to go to a movie. Orvin hadn't immediately warmed to the idea, and Colette knew he hated going to the cinema in town, sitting in a crowded theater, listening to people crunching popcorn and slurping cola through their straws.

A moment later Orvin stirred, yawning, seeming surprised it was daybreak, looking around as if he couldn't remember where he was. He looked over at Colette, registering shock at seeing her beside him on the floor. "Good morning," she said, reaching her hand out to touch the whiskers on his jaw. "I think you're getting more handsome every year."

Orvin laughed. "Could be your eyesight's failing," he said, bending down to kiss her. After a moment, he looked around, his expression turning gloomy. Colette knew he was troubled that Mr. Cannon hadn't returned. Orvin threw the blanket off and walked toward the bathroom. The night before, Orvin had given her a brief tour of Mr. Cannon's house, and she was relieved for some reason by how ordinary the interior was. Bookcases and a television, couch and chairs, kitchen table and all the normal things one expects to find in someone's home. She wasn't exactly sure what she'd expected to find.

When Orvin returned, he asked what she wanted for breakfast.

"What's the plan today?" she said, pushing up on one arm. When she felt her bare breasts shift beneath her nightgown, she suddenly felt sexy, a sensation she hadn't experienced in decades. Maybe it was sleeping on the floor of a stranger's house, or the way Orvin was looking at her in that moment; her desire felt natural and welcome.

"I have to drive up to Yellow Mountain," he said with a trace of anxiety in his voice.

"Let's grab breakfast on the way."

Orvin gave her a slowly changing look of confusion. "You can't go," he said. "It's too dangerous."

"What's dangerous about it?"

Orvin shook his head, his lips glued in frustration, until, like a valve under too much pressure, blurted out, "Dadgummit, Colette, can't you just do what I ask you?

"Okay... so I don't know what's got your underwear in a bundle, but I think I'll be fine. I mean, you slept with that dang .45 strapped to your back all night."

Orvin rocked his head side to side, then walked away mumbling about why things had to be so complicated all the time. Cabinet doors opened and clapped shut. After a few minutes Orvin shouted from the kitchen. "Cereal okay? Some kind of Chocolate Goobers or something..."

"That's fine," she said, changing into her clothes in the living room.

After breakfast, she loaded up their things, while Orvin washed the few breakfast dishes. They tidied up a bit, then walked to Orvin's pickup truck. Before Orvin got in, he stood a long time with his eyes fixed down the road. Colette could almost guess Orvin's thoughts; he was hoping

Mr. Cannon would come up the mountain any minute and save them from making this trip.

For most of the drive they rode in silence, the wind rushing through Colette's open window. Sitting out on the deck the previous evening, wrapped in the blanket with Orvin, she regretted she had waited so long to tell him about the horrible orgy in high school. She couldn't even recall when the word "orgy" had even become part of her vocabulary.

"Why don't you call Mason or Wyatt to go look for Mr. Cannon?"

Orvin cut her a sour look. "Cause then I'd have to answer a bunch of dadblammed questions like I'm answering now," he said, letting his scowl linger on her retinas a moment. The tires droned on the pavement for quite a while before Orvin turned to Colette. "I don't mean to be cross, but... I just can't explain everything right now..."

"That's okay," she said. Then after a moment, she tried to lighten things with a joke. "I was just wondering... do I need a gun, too?"

Even though Orvin didn't react positively to her quip, she was glad to have her sense of humor beginning to return from the dead.

When Orvin turned onto the dirt road and started up the mountain, Colette was shocked by how rough it was. She held onto the handle attached to the headliner, always wondering about its purpose; now she knew. Orvin never took his focus from the rugged terrain, and kept the vehicle moving forward, upward, jouncing harshly through the gulleys, stumbling over large stones.

"Shouldn't we slow down?" Colette asked, feeling her bottom bounce off the seat several times.

"If I slow down we'll be done for," he said, his eyes out the windshield. The truck rattled and clunked, then mired down, shooting free a second later when the tread caught. They had gone a few miles when the front end dipped severely and the front tires caught in a deep rut, wrenching the steering wheel in Orvin's hands. "Damn!" The back tires started spinning, throwing mud, smoking and whining. He slapped the steering wheel with his palms. He mashed down the gas pedal again and Colette feared another heart attack if he didn't calm himself. Jerking the shifter into reverse, he got the vehicle to nudge backward before he punched it back into drive, the truck lunging forward into the culvert, ripping the steering wheel from his hands again. When he took his foot off the gas, the engine died, smoke still rising from the rear tires. He sat staring out the windshield before he glanced over at her. "I have to walk the rest of the way. You wait here."

"I'm not waiting here," she said, surveying the densely wooded area draped with thick writhing vines and plants. She popped open her door before Orvin could protest, then looked at the mud puddle below. She stepped down, the mud reaching the bottoms of her jeans. "Damn," she said under her breath.

Orvin climbed out and stood waiting for her, glancing up the mountain. He absently reached behind his back to feel the gun, which gave Colette a moment's hesitation; what was he expecting to find up on Yellow Mountain? They trudged up the muddy road without talking. And if Orvin hadn't appeared so concerned, she thought this little adventure might be exhilarating. As it was, it filled her with anxiety.

With the forty-five-minute hike to the top, Colette could feel how out of shape she was. Her nightly walks in the neighborhood after supper, and her stretching exercises in the morning, had been no conditioning for this mountain. Orvin was feeling it too, bent over, holding his knees when she finally caught up to him.

"You okay, Orvin?" she said, walking up next to him. She placed her palm on his back. His shirt was soaked. Just beyond Orvin was a vehicle, a dusty Range Rover.

"Fine," he said, taking in deep breaths. He stood up straight, stretching his back, his hands on his hips. "I'm fine now." Orvin was a kind and generous man, but Colette couldn't understand why he would go to all this trouble for a virtual stranger.

"Is that Mr. Cannon's truck?" Colette asked, walking over to it to inspect the interior, half-expecting the young man to be asleep inside.

Orvin looked over at her. "Let's keep moving."

When they reached the bald, Colette was knocked out by how beautiful it was, mountain vistas in all directions, the sedge swaying under a soft breeze. Orvin started across the field as if he knew where he was going. They searched a long time, crisscrossing the bald, entering the woods that surrounded the area. After an hour or so, they took a break on a downed log. Orvin checked the gun at his back again. Colette knew better than to ask why he was so nervous. He appeared deep in thought, glaring at the ground, then letting his eyes drift toward the bald.

"Maybe we should split up," she said. "We might find him quicker.... if he's still up here…"

Orvin glowered at her, his eyes hard. She thought he would burn a hole through her face, until his gaze shifted, his attention fixed on something behind her.

"What's that out there?" he said, standing suddenly. When she turned to look, he was already on the move. Colette got up and saw what he'd been looking at, but it appeared to be nothing more than a boulder near the edge of the field. By now Orvin was in a trot heading for the object. Colette hastened her pace to keep up. That's when she saw the object move, then stop again. When Orvin reached it, he let out a howl, "Oh gracious Mother of God!" Orvin knelt down next to it. That's when Colette saw it was a man. When she came closer, she recoiled involuntarily, repelled by the bloodied, twisted form on the ground. She forced herself forward, tears coming when she witnessed the full measure of the damage.

"Is that Mr. Cannon? Is he dead?"

"I don't know how he isn't," Orvin said, trying to untangle his arms a bit to see his face. "Oh my God! Oh my God!" Orvin dug into his pocket for his phone, tapping a recent number, letting his eyes dart around the bald as if he anticipated some kind of ambush. "Put Mason on now," Orvin screamed into the phone when someone answered.

Orvin waited a few moments, his eyes flitting between Mr. Cannon and the woods along the perimeter of the bald, occasionally finding Colette.

"It's me, Orvin. I'm up here on Yellow Mountain, Mason. You need to send a chopper up here. Medical emergency..." Orvin waited, his eyes moving constantly, as if wired to impending danger. Colette moved closer and knelt down next to Mr. Cannon, brushing back the hair from his face, her stomach filling with heat. She wished they had brought a couple bottles of water.

"Please, Mason, hurry. This fella ain't gonna last much longer," Orvin said, his features pressed. "I'll fill you in later. Just hurry, okay!"

Orvin shoved the phone into his pocket, standing to survey the area. He looked down at Mr. Cannon. Colette wiped some twigs and detritus from Mr. Cannon's face and hair, wondering how this could have happened. And how Orvin was aware of such danger up here? And what could possibly have compelled Mr. Cannon to venture here alone? The questions were mounting when Orvin seemed to notice something that put him on edge. He quickly withdrew the pistol from the holster at his back and pointed it toward the far trees. Colette let her eyes follow the barrel to see what he was pointing at. She didn't see anything, not at first. Then it came into view. The image was a vague shape, nothing more than a dark smudge against the densely-packed woods. Colette thought it might be just a thick cedar tree, until it moved. The shape shifted to the right a few feet, keeping its distance, then disappeared like a fading stain into the vegetation. She had been looking directly at it and still couldn't see where it had gone, as if it just disappeared.

The sudden rumble of the helicopter eclipsing the bald took Colette's breath, and set her heart bumping in her chest. Orvin holstered his pistol, then waved his arms at the aircraft, always keeping an eye on the vast field between them and the edge of the woods. When the craft landed, three emergency medical technicians rushed across the bald with a folding stretcher. One of the technicians ran back for a neck support. Once they had Geoffrey secured on the gurney, the oxygen mask in place, two of the EMTs lifted the mechanism until the legs locked beneath it, then carefully rolled it toward the helicopter, one of them monitoring Geoffrey's vital signs. Orvin and Colette walked over with them and stood in the opening, watching them start an IV. Colette looked at Orvin, and said, "How are we going to get down the mountain?"

Orvin seemed to ponder their dilemma a second. One of the technicians must have heard Colette's question.

"We have room if you need to go with us."

When she looked over at Orvin, he nodded. She climbed in and Orvin followed. It was cramped but she didn't care; she didn't want to have to deal with getting the pickup unstuck. Her eyes found Orvin, who seemed tangled in a distressing problem, his attention fixed on the desolate bald beyond the craft.

41
NOT LIES, EXACTLY

MASON MET Orvin and Colette at the hospital helipad. When Mason witnessed Geoffrey Cannon being brought down out of the craft, his eyes narrowed, the life leaving his face. He looked over at Orvin. "What the hell happened?" Orvin knew exactly what happened, though he wasn't sure why Geoffrey was still alive, why the creature hadn't broken Geoffrey's neck the way it had all those kids. And even with the fifteen-minute helicopter ride from Yellow Mountain, Orvin had still not managed to concoct a believable account for Mason, or how to explain why he and Colette had been on the mountain in the first place.

"How did you... do you need a ride?" Mason said.

Orvin nodded and followed Colette to the cruiser. He was about to put Colette in the backseat, then decided to put her up front next to Mason, let her explain everything; it would be the most honest and uncomplicated account, since she didn't know all the unspeakable details.

"Do you mind coming by the station to fill out a report?" Mason asked, looking in the rearview mirror to find Orvin. Orvin nodded and said, "No problem."

Shifting his attention over to her, Mason said, "Are you okay, Colette? You look a little peaked."

"No, I'm okay now... it was just pretty shocking to see Mr. Cannon in such a state."

"You knew him?" Mason said. Orvin let out a breath he felt he'd been holding since they'd left the bald.

"Oh, sure," Colette said. "We went up to Yellow Mountain looking for him. Orvin was pretty sure Mr. Cannon had gotten himself lost. Right, Orvin?"

Mason looked over at Colette, then checked his mirror. Orvin didn't let his eyes find Mason in the rearview mirror, keeping his own attention focused out the side window.

"How do you know Mr. Cannon? A relative? Friend?" Mason asked Colette.

"Actually he's a new customer of Orvin's," Colette said. "Orvin just did his deck lately. It's really beautiful."

Orvin's attention came back to Colette, to the new tone in her voice. Where was she going with this?

Colette said, "Mr. Cannon, well, Geoffrey, is new to the area. And I guess he was interested in seeing that bald up at Yellow Mountain, especially after..." Colette stopped and turned toward Mason. "Oh, Mason... Oh Mason, I am so sorry. How could I be so stupid! I am so sorry about Renny..."

Mason drew a deep breath, keeping his eyes straight ahead, his shoulders tight against the seat, his uniform crisp and squared away. They rode in silence for a while and Orvin knew Colette had not staged that moment; she truly had forgotten about Mason's tragic loss. But Mason would never forget and the ongoing investigation had to be tough on him. Orvin knew that officials were still looking into the murders. Investigators knew the boys' bodies had been moved, but didn't know why, or who had killed them, and how those three boys together had not been able to overcome their attacker. They were all on the football team, top shape, fast and strong and young. It didn't seem possible for one attacker to systematically kill all three boys one at a time by breaking their necks, without the other two intervening. Deputy Wyatt Calhoun had called it a *vexing conundrum.*

When Mason pulled into the parking lot of the Sheriff's Office, a call came over the radio, a 10-16 he said he had to respond to. He was sorry but asked if it was okay if Colette and Orvin could fill out a report inside.

"I really appreciate it," Mason said. "Wyatt or one of the other officers will help you out. Good seeing you Colette. Orvin, take care."

Orvin and Colette got out and stepped away from the cruiser. Mason sped away, lights flashing, the vehicle accelerating down the road. A moment later the siren snapped on and faded slowly toward the west side of Kleary Creek. When Colette started for the front doors, Orvin snagged her arm.

"I didn't lie," she said, a bit defensively, as if she had expected some kind of admonishment from Orvin.

"I know you didn't," Orvin said. "No, you did the right thing. You told him what you knew, that's all."

Colette let her eyes fall to the pavement. "I did make up the stuff about Mr. Cannon wanting to go up there to see—"

"No you didn't. You never finished telling Mason what Mr. Cannon was doing up there or why he wanted to go…"

"I feel kind of bad…"

"You shouldn't, Colette. For all you know, Mr. Cannon was just interested in knowing more about Yellow Mountain. I mean, with the stuff in the newspapers, lots of people would be." Orvin hoped the video on his phone that Deputy Calhoun had sent him never went public, or made the news. That would drive a whole lot of curiosity seekers up to that bald, and right to that monster. Orvin couldn't even imagine the carnage if that happened.

Colette seemed satisfied with Orvin's rationale, and had just started walking toward the front doors of the station when she stopped and spun toward Orvin. "Who's going to do the talking once we're inside?" she said.

"You start… and we'll go from there… if you're okay with that." Orvin looked into her eyes to see if he could detect any reluctance. She smiled, then leaned in and kissed him on the lips. Orvin followed her into the building and sat next to her as she related the events of the morning, not telling Calhoun they had spent the night at Geoffrey's house, or how he'd been gone for a couple of days, or any of that. Calhoun asked a few questions to clear things up, Colette answering them flawlessly. It wasn't a deception, exactly, Orvin thought; she truly had no idea what was going on, and Orvin wasn't quite ready to explain, since the whole deal with the creature and Geoffrey seemed preposterous. Orvin still could not figure out Geoffrey's connection to that thing, and by the blood, lacerations and contusions, Geoffrey hadn't figured it out either, and it nearly got him killed. Just then, a prickly suspicion interrupted Orvin's thoughts, a disturbing notion relating to the UFO video on his phone… was the creature an alien? Was Geoffrey?

"So, where were you heading last night when I saw you " Calhoun asked, a little confused reading the statement Colette had just given him.

"Oh, that was just another friend of ours. No, we didn't drive up to Mr. Cannon's place until this morning. Orvin wanted to check on some painting Mr. Cannon wanted done, and when he wasn't home, Orvin started to worry."

Calhoun shifted his eyes toward Orvin, then back to Colette. He nodded, then looked over the report before bringing his attention back to Orvin.

"Guess you-all's gonna need a ride home?" Calhoun said, shuffling the papers into a neat stack on his desk. "When do you want to go up and get your truck out of the mud?"

"I'll take care of that," Orvin said, standing to leave, hoping Colette didn't say anything about her car being at Geoffrey's house; they'd get a neighbor to drive them back to his place. "Floyd's got that four-wheel truck with a winch," Orvin continued, glad to veer the conversation in a new direction. "You might need to get someone to drive Mr. Cannon's Range Rover down the mountain though."

"You have the keys?" Calhoun asked.

Orvin shook his head. "No, sure don't. He must still have them."

"Yeah, you're probably right. I'll call over to the hospital…" The deputy stood a long, uncomfortable moment before he finished his thought. "From what I heard about Mr. Cannon's condition, he's darn lucky to have a *contractor* like you looking out for him."

Orvin gave him a smile, picking up the hint of sarcasm, as he placed his hand on Colette's lower back guiding her toward the door.

"Orvin, hold up a second," Calhoun said, hurrying out from behind his desk.

Orvin knew what Wyatt was going to ask, surprised he hadn't posed the question while filling out the police report. "Any idea what happened to Mr. Cannon? I heard he had some nasty wounds."

Orvin rocked his head side to side, as if flummoxed. "Bear, I guess." Orvin held Wyatt's gaze a few moments, then turned, pressing his palm to Colette's back, guiding her toward the exit.

42

A TIMELY ACCOUNT

GEOFFREY WAS SURPRISED to see Edward sitting next to the bed when he opened his eyes. ET evidently had come every day to the hospital the nurses had informed him, but Geoffrey had only regained consciousness the day before. They had yet to talk, and Edward just sat by, reading a magazine or book, or watching television. Occasionally he would step out, go to the cafeteria for something to eat, usually leave the hospital around five in the afternoon, then return after lunch the next day. Today he was early. Geoffrey wasn't exactly sure what time it was, but he could tell it was still morning.

Geoffrey picked at his breakfast plate, offering ET a piece of wheat toast with butter. Edward declined with a wave of his hand. Geoffrey took a bite of the toast and laid it back on the plate, then picked up a grape and slid it past his lips. Chewing was difficult, but he was managing.

"You don't have to come every day, ET," Geoffrey finally said. "But I appreciate it. I do."

"It's not a problem," Edward said. "Do you feel like talking today?"

Geoffrey knew this moment was coming. ET had barely said a word to him yesterday, but Geoffrey, even though he was conscious, had been so out of it due to the morphine drip, that he would not have been able to respond anyway. He actually felt much better today and wondered if the nurses had changed the painkillers in the IV.

"Sure," Geoffrey said. "What's on your mind?" He still wasn't sure what had happened, or how he got to the hospital. His mind had not caught up to this new reality yet.

"Well, for starters, how are you feeling?"

"Okay. Much better than yesterday." Geoffrey moved his right arm, the pain in his shoulder telling him to stop. He moved his legs under the blankets. They were sore, for sure. He was afraid to see what his face looked like. With his neck in a brace, it was nearly impossible to turn his head; he hoped the immobility was from the brace and not something more serious.

Edward leaned in toward Geoffrey, scooting his chair closer to the bed, then looked around to see if anyone was in earshot. "So, should I deduce that you went looking for this thing… and that you found it?"

Geoffrey nodded, memories of that night coming in sharp jabs and muted colors, like some furtive kaleidoscope of brutality. He could still feel the blows, smell its awful, rotting breath, the grunting and growling, the howls, flashes of red and white exploding into bright angles of pain. Disparate images, disconnected from each other yet streaming as one continuous moment.

"How did I get here?" Geoffrey finally asked.

"Your friend, Orvin. He and his wife went up to Yellow Mountain looking for you."

Geoffrey cleared his throat, which was dry and raspy. He grabbed the plastic cup from the tray and finished the last of the water. Edward reached over and refilled it from the pitcher. Geoffrey didn't recall seeing Orvin or his wife. The last thing he remembered was sitting on a large rock, resting, trying to recover from the creature's attack. He sort of remembered the creature attacking again, but his memory was so fragmented, he couldn't be sure if he was just recalling different aspects of the same assault as separate and distinct from each other. Except for the pain, which was very real, the entire night lingered in his mind with that murky quality of a cruel nightmare.

The oddest notion broke in on Geoffrey; if he could heal others, why couldn't he heal himself? He had no inner vision of his wounds, could only see the outward bandages and abrasions. He could easily see other's ailments and illnesses nestled deep inside their organs and cells, but not his own. It seemed as though his ribs were broken, but he could only tell that because it hurt to take a deep breath.

"Have *The Associates* been working on the problem—of this creature?" Geoffrey asked. "Have they come up with a solution?"

Edward looked directly at Geoffrey. "They've killed it three times. Even took its lifeless body up and ejected it into the cold vacuum of outer space..."

"Seriously?"

"It just keeps coming back. It's not real, like you and me. I mean, it seems to die, but then... they know it has to do with you, but they can't figure out how to go about stopping it. Obviously, you confronting it physically isn't the answer. This is deeper than that. Something psychosomatic."

"Like it's all in my mind? That can't be... it's killing people."

ET nodded, but offered nothing else.

The notion of this beast being immortal was unacceptable. It had been born, so to speak; it should be able to die. It came from somewhere, and he had to figure out a way to send it back, rid it from his psyche, bleach it from his subliminal thoughts and desires. Maybe making those thoughts known? But how does one make conscious that which seems hell-bent on remaining hidden?

"What about another NHI?" Geoffrey said. "Drill down deeper into my subconscious. I'm willing to try anything."

Edward nodded. "Yeah, they want to, once you're feeling better." Then, after a moment: "I hate to bring this up right now, but we have to talk about the next seminar." Edward sat back in his chair. "It's a little over a week from now... are you going to be in any condition to do it?"

He had forgotten all about it, and frankly, it seemed unimportant given everything that was happening. Nevertheless, he felt he could do the seminar. It had only been a few days and already he felt he was on the mend. Even doctors could do nothing for the cracked ribs except give him painkillers and keep them wrapped. But what about *The Associates*? They could do so much more in a shorter time.

"What if I got out of here... and went to *The Lodge?*"

Edward seemed to be thinking on the suggestion, then started nodding. "I think that's an excellent idea. When are they supposed to release you?"

"Day after tomorrow, I think. They want to run more tests."

"I'll do some checking ... but we don't want to raise suspicions by taking you—" Edward stopped talking as two people entered the room. Geoffrey followed Edward's gaze.

"Orvin!" Geoffrey said, surprised. "Colette!"

Orvin nodded at Geoffrey, then looked over at Edward. Geoffrey introduced them all and asked ET if he could find an extra chair. Edward said he had to be going, but he'd be by later that evening with news.

"Nice meeting you both," Edward said. "And thank you for finding my boy here."

"Geoffrey's your son?" Orvin said, as if confused. Colette looked surprised.

Edward shook his head. "No, I'm his business manager." Then, to Geoffrey: "I'll see you later." Edward touched Geoffrey's foot through the sheet before he left.

"Please, sit," Geoffrey said, directing his attention to Orvin and Colette. "We've got so much to talk about."

Geoffrey did most of the talking, asking them questions, finding out what they knew, what they saw. Geoffrey felt like he'd thanked them every five minutes, and was stunned that Colette had been with Orvin on Yellow Mountain, that she had come to look for him; her attitude toward him had obviously mellowed. She was actually sympathetic about his injuries, and his recovery, asking him a few times if the pain was bad, if he had sustained any permanent damage from the attack. Colette was the first to ask what had happened.

"Were you attacked by a bear?" she said. Orvin glanced over at her, then looked at Geoffrey with an expression of concern, as if wondering how the young man was going to bridge this difficult gap. Geoffrey had so hoped he could get Orvin alone for a few minutes to know what he had told her, and the police. So far, with him unconscious until twenty-four hours ago, the police had not come for a statement yet. He figured Orvin hadn't told her about the creature.

"I really don't know," he said. "It all happened so fast." Geoffrey thought he'd just lay out some details and hope it comported with the overall arc of whatever fabrication they had floated. "I just went up to have a look around… I guess I should have waited for Orvin. I was curious is all, about the lights people saw. It was stupid. I hadn't seen anyone around, but I think someone jumped me from behind. It was really dark. I never really got to see what happened."

Geoffrey then changed the subject, asking how they got up there, and if anyone had driven his Rover down the mountain. Edward had said nothing about it.

"It's at your place," Orvin said. "When Floyd drove me up to get my pickup out of the mud, I drove my truck down the hill, and Colette drove your Rover."

Geoffrey could not understand this turnabout with Orvin's wife, but he was so relieved to have whatever animosity she'd felt toward him behind them now. He really liked them both a lot and hoped they could be friends. "Thank you, Colette," he said.

"That thing drives like a tank," she said. "I followed Orvin down the mountain just in case he got stuck again."

They sat a few moments not talking, as if they had exhausted every last bit of commonality between them. "Now if you need to rest, just say the word and we'll be going," Colette said into the silence.

"No, really, this is great," Geoffrey said. "It's so wonderful seeing you both, and I can't—"

"Please," Orvin said. "Don't thank us again. Just consider you and me even."

"I don't feel like I could ever repay you for what you did for me. Coming to find me, risking your life..." As soon as the words left Geoffrey's mouth, he wanted them back. Colette's face registered a shock that Orvin might be left to explain later if Geoffrey didn't dig himself out. "I just meant it was really scary for me..." Geoffrey quickly added. "And dangerous... I mean, because I know nothing about the outdoors. That's all I meant, Colette. It was so kind of you to help, is all."

Colette seemed satisfied with the lame recovery, but Orvin appeared a little perturbed. Geoffrey figured Orvin was sitting with his tongue clamped between his bicuspids to keep from yelling at Geoffrey for his stupid decision to venture off by himself.

When Orvin stood, Colette regarded him as if she thought he was getting ready to leave. She grabbed her purse. Orvin said, "I'm going to the cafeteria for a coffee and something to eat. You want to join me, Colette? Or you want me to bring you something?" He looked at Colette, then at Geoffrey.

"I'll wait here if that's okay," she said, smiling up at him. "Coffee and a Danish sounds good, if they have it."

Though glad for her company, Geoffrey was surprised Colette chose not to go with Orvin.

"You, Geoffrey?" Orvin said.

"Coffee. Maybe some cream and sugar."

Orvin nodded. After leaning over to kiss Colette on the cheek, he turned and walked out. Colette wasted no time getting to her agenda for staying behind.

"I don't know how long Orvin will be gone, but we need to discuss some things," she said, opening her rather large purse. Geoffrey had no idea what this was about.

"We met once," Colette said. "A long time ago. It would be nearly impossible for you to remember me, but I remember you like I saw you yesterday."

"I'm sorry. I don't recall—"

"At a library in Philadelphia," she said, breaking in. "I worked for a while until my baby was born. I was eighteen and very pregnant."

Geoffrey was trying to mash up some quick math to figure out how long ago that might have been. Over forty years, at least! He wasn't completely sure how old Colette was, but he figured her for early- to mid- sixties. Even so, he didn't remember her, and said quickly, "I'm sorry, I don't mean to be rude, but that would be impossible. I mean, I probably wasn't even born when you were eighteen."

"You were reading this when I spoke to you." Colette drew the library book from her purse. "I remembered the book. It was strange, because my aunt lived in Philly for years and never heard of this experiment. That got my curiosity up."

When she handed it to Geoffrey, he recognized it immediately, feeling the cold chill of a wraith surround his body. 1979. That was the year the book came out. Then he remembered Colette, though they never exchanged names, but he recalled how beautiful she was, how lucky she was to be pregnant, to be starting a family, imagining an overjoyed husband lying with her at night, sharing meals, and how sad it made him feel that he would never have that for himself.

"Peter Smithwick," she said. "That was your name then. I asked a few of the other women at the library if they knew who you were. And of course, they did, by all the books you had checked out over the years. I guess I had a bit of a crush on you at the time. You were always studying, so focused on so many subjects, things I'd never heard of before. It was dizzying to imagine where you stored it all."

Geoffrey had to be careful here. She had no real proof, just a belief she'd seen him. "I'm sorry, Colette. I understand how confused you must be, but I promise, it wasn't me. I've never even been to Philadelphia."

Colette gave him a wide grin, not mean or accusatory, but a knowing smile, with enough warmth to put him at ease. At least for the moment. "That's okay... I didn't really expect you to own up to any of this. I read this book hoping I could find some clues in it about you..." She stuffed the book back into her purse.

"Then I did a bit more checking," she said, bringing a folded piece of paper from her purse. She handed it across the bed to Geoffrey. He opened it. A photocopy of an old newspaper article. The Smithwick Farm Murders, dated 1933. No photo. Geoffrey started reading. The article recounted the brutal murder of Lauralee Smithwick, and her presumed lover, John Bennett, survived by his wife Margaret Bennett and their children. It explained that John Bennett owned the farmland adjacent to the Smithwick land. The details of the love tryst between the two was vague, but authorities believed that Reverend Jacob Smithwick, returning from a traveling mission of hope and prayer, had found them in bed together and shot the two lovers in the Smithwick bedroom. Both Lauralee Smithwick and John Bennett died from shotgun wounds to the face and neck, nearly decapitating the two lovers. It appeared Reverend Smithwick then placed the shotgun under his chin, committing suicide.

The Smithwick's son, Peter Smithwick, who was fourteen, reportedly had been locked in the Smithwick's root cellar waiting out a terrible storm when the killings took place. Authorities found the boy when they checked on the property after Mrs. Bennett contacted the police when her husband had not returned home the next morning after a trip into the city. The police had been routinely checking neighbors to see if anyone had seen John Bennett. That's when they discovered the dead bodies in the Smithwick bedroom, and the Smithwick boy in the cellar.

Contrary evidence surrounding the Smithwick Farm Murders surfaced when detectives found traces of blood on the back porch railing. Authorities finally decided that Reverend Smithwick, distraught by finding the two lovers in bed, shot them first, then ushered his son to the cellar, inadvertently touching the railing and leaving a trace of John Bennet's blood behind. Then, gripped by grief and guilt, the minister killed himself. It was later reported that Lauralee Smithwick, originally Lauralee Shaw, had worked for a time as a prostitute in downtown Philadelphia before marrying Reverend Jacob Smithwick. Peter Smithwick was Reverend Jacob Smithwick's son by a prior marriage. No blood relation to Lauralee Shaw.

Authorities also reported finding over fifty dead hogs at the Smithwick farm, the deaths of the animals believed to be part of the Agricultural Adjustment Act under the leadership of Secretary of Agriculture Henry Wallace. It appeared that some of the pigs had been slaughtered by gunshot wound to the head, but the majority had died from slit throats. Authorities are still investigating the peculiar choice of extermination of these animals. It was reported that the hogs were successfully transported from the Smithwick farm to a nearby plant to be processed into inedible meat and bone meal.

Geoffrey couldn't believe the inaccuracies in the newspaper account. He hadn't been fourteen years old at the time. He'd been eleven. He hadn't known about them being nearly decapitated and tried to recall that morning, seeing his stepmother squeezed into the narrow space between the bed and wall. Certainly her neck could've been damaged, he figured. But not Mr. Bennett. He was lying there with his insides exposed, his head on the pillow, normal as could be. And all the pigs were alive when he left that morning for the McCoy's. Nobody had shot any of them or slit their throats. And Geoffrey, back then Peter, hadn't even been around when the police arrived. He let himself out of the root cellar that morning and went to the McCoy's, distraught by the dead bodies in the house. The police didn't talk to him until several days later. Geoffrey couldn't understand how the reporter could get the story so wrong, and had been so engrossed in disputing the erroneous facts of the article, he failed to notice Orvin's return.

Geoffrey looked at Orvin first, then the coffee cup on his tray, afraid to take his eyes to Colette; she would notice his discomfort immediately. "Thanks, Orvin," Geoffrey said, sipping the coffee.

"What you got there?" Orvin asked, taking a bite of his sandwich. Colette was busy with her Danish roll, but occasionally looked over at Geoffrey, her eyes serene, knowing.

"A newspaper article," Geoffrey said.

"Kleary Creek News?" Orvin asked. "Is it about your ordeal?"

"No... no, it's not about me," Geoffrey said, handing the photocopy back to Colette.

"Are you sure?" Colette asked.

Orvin reached over and took the article from Colette's hand and started reading. "Well, hell's bells, Colette, this article's from 1933! This happened before *we* were even born! How could this have anything to do with Geoffrey?"

Colette nodded, never taking her eyes from Geoffrey. "I don't know... I was hoping he could tell us."

Geoffrey recalled what ET had told him years ago, something to the effect of—never admit to anything. Nobody can prove you have any association to Peter Smithwick, and if they claim so, they'll be certified as insane. Geoffrey had to concede that Colette had no actual proof that the boy in the article, Peter Smithwick, was actually him.

"I'm sorry, Colette," Geoffrey finally said. "I know you believe what you believe, but this is impossible, of course, and I don't know a Peter Smithwick."

"Did you dig up this article, Colette?" Orvin yelped. "You think Geoffrey had something to do with this? That's nuts, Colette! What in the hell were you thinking?"

Geoffrey's denial, along with Orvin's rant seemed to have no effect eroding Colette's resolve, as if the facts in her mind were arranged in such a way as to be indisputable. She sat placidly sipping her coffee.

"Who is Mr. Cannon supposed to be in this scenario, Colette?" Orvin continued. "Can you tell me that?"

"He's the fourteen-year-old boy. Peter Smithwick." She pulled out the library book about The Philadelphia Experiment and proceeded to tell Orvin how she'd met Geoffrey years ago when she was pregnant and living in Philadelphia with her aunt. She'd been working at the library until her baby was born. Of course, then, he was Peter Smithwick. "And he looked exactly as he does right now," she said, staring directly into Geoffrey's eyes, as if she could see his lies imprinted on the back of his skull.

Orvin looked at Geoffrey, then at Colette. "None of this makes any sense," Orvin said, waving the photocopy in his hand. "You know how many Peter Smithwicks there must be in the world? And maybe you just saw someone who looked like Geoffrey back then. I mean, that was what, forty-five years ago? Jesus, Colette, how could you recall a face from that far back?"

"I just do," she said. "Peter was special back then, had a real appetite for knowledge, kind of like those books stacked up at his house the other night. All those notebooks. That's when I knew for sure. That's what his table at the library would look like. All those books. I couldn't even figure out how a person could keep all that information straight. No, Peter Smithwick was special. And so is Geoffrey Cannon, aren't you?"

Orvin's mouth opened for a second, as if to say something, but he just shifted his eyes toward Geoffrey. Orvin must have noticed his wife's calm demeanor, her unwavering certainty, and that would surely mean something to him after being married for so long. Orvin would certainly be replaying all the odd things that had happened since he'd met him. "Is any of this true?" he asked Geoffrey.

Geoffrey cleared his throat. He didn't want to lie to either of them. But how could he possibly explain the truth? No, he had to heed ET's advice for once and do the smart thing.

"I'm sorry to both of you, but, no, none of this is true," Geoffrey said. "I do understand your confusion, Colette. I would be too, if, you know…. But… I don't know what else to say…"

Colette stared at him, a soft smile easing across her face, her eyes sparkling as if she'd just uncovered all the proof she needed that her theory was correct. "Are you ready to go, Orvin, so Mr. Cannon can rest?"

Orvin stood, then handed the article back to Colette. Colette regarded the photocopy a moment, then dropped it on his food tray. "You should keep this."

Geoffrey glanced at the folded paper, then looked at her. She stepped close to the bed, then leaned in and kissed Geoffrey on the cheek. "I really hope you feel better soon," she said, giving him a warm smile. Orvin came closer and touched Geoffrey's arm. "Take care," Orvin said, then was about to add something, but just turned away. Colette gave Geoffrey one last look as she walked out in front of Orvin, who never turned back.

Geoffrey, whose juggernaut of optimism had always kept him afloat in the worst of times, was struggling to unravel the mess Colette had made of his brain. Some trapdoor had opened inside him, and something crucial to his survival had fallen through it and was still falling, tears streaming down Geoffrey's cheeks.

43

A POWERFUL THOUGHT

EDWARD PICKED Geoffrey up at the hospital a day early. The doctor told him to take it easy for a few weeks, and handed him a prescription for painkillers. "And don't hike alone anymore," the doctor said, half in jest, his smile fading as he shook Geoffrey's hand, as if the doctor never quite believed his story about being jumped from behind and never seeing his attackers.

Edward and Geoffrey walked in silence to Edward's SUV. Geoffrey had still not completely recovered from Colette's investigative work and her resulting supposition. Orvin and Colette had not returned to the hospital after that day, and as much as Geoffrey enjoyed their company, he was glad they stayed away; he wasn't sure how long he could shore up the ruse, or himself, under such scrutiny. He would have loved to just tell them the truth. Maybe they could have accepted it and would have agreed to keep his secret. What harm could it do? Then he wondered if Colette had told anyone, and if Orvin had finally submitted to her camp. If so, Orvin would never look at Geoffrey the same again.

When they pulled from the parking lot, Edward turned toward Geoffrey. "You're pretty quiet."

"I think I have a big problem," Geoffrey said, proceeding to explain everything that had transpired during Orvin and Colette's visit. He was recalling the book he'd been reading in 1979, The Philadelphia Experiment, as well as the article she'd somehow unearthed from 1933 about the murder of his stepmother and her lover, Bennet, and his father's suicide. Geoffrey remembered meeting Colette at the library when she was eighteen and pregnant. What shocked him was that Colette could recall that encounter after forty years, even if Geoffrey looked exactly the same, which he was fairly certain he probably did. And it was that very day when he'd spoken to Colette, that he'd gone home and his wife, Amanda, had confronted him about why she was aging and he wasn't.

"What are the odds?" Edward stated casually when Geoffrey finished.

Geoffrey's head shot around in his seat. "That's all you have to say?"

Edward gave a little chuckle. "Well, you have to admit, that, wow, that is some freaky synchronicity, right? I mean, not so much that she ran into you back then, but that she remembered. And then you just happen to live in the same town. I mean, that's crazy, don't you think?" Then, after a few more chuckles: "Must be some crazed, all-powerful trickster running the whole show, right?"

The whole show? Was ET referring to the universe, life in general, or just *Geoffrey's* life? He wasn't exactly sure what ET meant, but it was obvious ET didn't grasp the seriousness of the situation. If Colette somehow made her case to someone who could actually find definitive proof of Geoffrey's real identity, his life of touring and seminars would be over, and his life of hiding and seclusion would begin again. He'd be hounded by believers and disbelievers alike, by the press, by talk show hosts, as the freak who doesn't age. Or the con artist, the fake, the *healer! The New Messiah.* The brand of publicity he had always shunned. And the beast. What was to be done about that? Geoffrey felt something separating, like a second skin peeling from his body, floating away, leaving only the heavy husk of his corporeal self behind to deal with gravity and ridicule and embarrassment. That new heat rose inside again, like the day when Orvin and Colette left his room, taking all the air with them, leaving Geoffrey alone with his tears.

"Don't fret," Edward said.

Geoffrey sniffed, his head bent toward the window. "Sure, yeah."

"Hey, everything's going to be fine. It is. *The Associates* will get you fixed up like new and you'll be back on the road, all of this behind you..."

"Really! How about the fucking monster, ET? They can't even figure that out... how are they going to help me if they can't even take care of that damn thing!"

Edward fell quiet, his eyes on the highway. Geoffrey turned back to the window, the mountains and trees rushing by, the simple truth of nature, the easy lightness of a predictable world. Geoffrey wished for that now, and would give up everything, his ability to see disease and heal it, and especially the slow aging process which made it impossible for any true permanence with another being. How odd, he thought. Permanence was Geoffrey's greatest advantage—he'd live a ridiculously long time—and also his greatest curse against anything lasting or *permanent*. Was this the balance Edward warned him about? That the world sought balance in everything. Newton's Third Law. Maybe Geoffrey should have admitted to Colette that she had figured out the riddle, then he could skulk away on his own terms, find solitude before anyone could find him. But couldn't he do that now? Just vanish? But then what? He had come, in a relatively short time, to hate his life in Wyoming, the crappy small cabin, the lack of interaction with other humans. But he had so convinced himself that his life was okay, that he was content to sit and read and live in the woods alone—he was broken, after all, and that was the best he could ever hope for.

The ruts in the road leading up to Yellow Mountain jolted Geoffrey from the numbing reverie. It was already dark and Geoffrey had not seen the day change to night, so lost in his own thoughts. They had stopped for dinner and ET had run some errands, but Geoffrey couldn't figure out where the day had gone.

By the time they reached the top, it was completely black out. Geoffrey popped the door on Edward's SUV and got out, suddenly aware that they were unprotected, and the creature could be anywhere. Edward's face was lit by the interior dome light when Geoffrey looked at him. "How are we going to make it to the bald?" Geoffrey asked.

Edward reached over and hit the glove box lid, flopping it open, and withdrew a rather stout pistol, thick barreled and shiny. Geoffrey had no idea what it was, but it looked deadly enough. What was Edward hoping for? Did the gun have *silver bullets*, or some other supernatural killing power? Did it fire little crosses, or wooden stakes? Garlic? *Kryptonite?* Geoffrey's mind was calling up every ridiculous ammunition from decades of moviegoing and reading that proved lethal against otherworldly anomalies. For whatever reason, it seemed his mind needed some kind of fictional time out from the situation, some hope of a weapon that would actually work.

After holstering the gun in his side stirrup, Edward got out and slammed the door. He turned on a flashlight and walked over to Geoffrey. "Here, take this," Edward said, handing him the light. Geoffrey swished the beam around on the ground, then painted it across a few trees.

"You think that gun will do any good?"

"It'll kill that thing long enough for us to get to *The Lodge*."

It was odd to Geoffrey that even when he and ET were alone, they still referred to the flying saucer as *The Lodge*. And the aliens as *The Associates*. Following behind ET, Geoffrey was still trying to figure out the beast's immortality, or its *provisional* immortality. Evidently it would die, but then would just come back to life. What entity does such a thing? After a moment, it hit Geoffrey. A *belief!* A stubborn *belief* can seemingly die, but only recedes into the shadows, never truly vanquished. Is that what they were dealing with? A living, breathing *belief,* with huge claws, tusks and a sadistic hostility toward humans? If so, what was this persistent, hidden *belief?*

They didn't have to wait long before the spacecraft descended on the bald. Edward handed Geoffrey the blackened goggles. "Must I?" Geoffrey said, twirling the curious eyewear in his hands.

"Just put them on, okay. Let's don't go through this every time."

Geoffrey fitted them over his eyes, then let Edward guide him toward the ship.

44

A PACT WITH SATAN

WHEN SOMEONE WALKED IN, Geoffrey, still groggy, wasn't sure where he was, and didn't recognize the visitor. The light in the room was dim, the source undetectable. And other than a low, pervasive hum, the smallish room was completely still. When the person moved closer, Geoffrey recognized him. Edward walked toward the bed, appearing to wobble like gelatin, and a bit vague at the edges, smeared and undefined. Geoffrey closed his eyes to refocus, then opened them. Edward was now sitting, his body still quivering, his outline shifting in a weird wavering pattern, making it hard for Geoffrey to keep him in the frame of his vision.

"What's going on?' Geoffrey said, a bit anxious. "You're like rubber or something…"

"It'll wear off in a while," Edward said. "How are you feeling?"

The chair and small table by the wall were wobbling, too. "I've got vertigo or something," he said. "I'm feeling sick to my stomach."

"It'll pass," Edward said. "Here, drink this."

Geoffrey sat up a bit and took the glass and sipped. The liquid was white, with an odd but sweet taste, and the viscosity of cream.

"Drink it all," Edward said. When Geoffrey finished the last of it, the room started coming apart at the edges, then rearranging itself until all the corners aligned and stopped moving.

"Is that better?" Edward said.

"Yeah, much."

"Take a deep breath and move your arms and legs," Edward told him.

Geoffrey was able to breathe deeply without pain, and had full range of his extremities, as if nothing had happened. He checked the cuts and lacerations on his arms. They were completely healed. "I feel great," Geoffrey said. "And crazy hungry. Are we still at *The Lodge*?"

Edward nodded. "I'll bring you some food in a few minutes. But you need to rest for a while."

Geoffrey laid back and closed his eyes. The room was neither cool nor warm; no sensation at all, not even of gravity. It wasn't that he felt as though he might float away, but he didn't register the normal pull of the earth either, a sensation one would never notice until it was absent. While waiting for Edward to return with food, Geoffrey's mind occupied itself with thoughts of the creature, what could be done about it. He was rather surprised *The Associates* had not figured out a way to controvert the thing; they seemed capable of miracles. Memories of the encounter with the beast shifted through his thoughts, impressions and recollections of the vicious attacks, but those were interspersed with bizarre images, vague at first, until they took shape; the Reverend Jacob flashed once in his mind, then his birth mother—whom he hardly knew—then the farm and Sarah McCoy and her husband, the people who took him in when the Reverend killed himself. He hadn't thought about any of those people in years. Suddenly the newspaper article was back in his head, the one Colette had found, the details playing like a movie, no words, just faces, and storm clouds and an unmoving landscape of rotting pig carcasses. Then the Reverend's words echoed in Geoffrey's head, "I fear I invoked a pact with Satan … and we are certainly damned."

Geoffrey opened his eyes to flush the narrative from his brain.

Edward was moving a tray of food toward him on some kind of metal cart. "What's going on?" Edward said. "You look spooked."

"Have you followed the news?" Geoffrey said. "Has anyone died in Kleary Creek over the past week?"

"An elderly woman at a nursing home, if I recall. And then… some guy in a bad car accident the other day. That was about it. Why?"

No one had been killed by the beast since Geoffrey interacted with it. Had things changed? Had that confrontation been enough to send the thing back into the ether from which it came? Only one way to know for sure.

"I have an idea, ET," Geoffrey said. "Just hear me out."

Edward had already erected a barrier that showed clearly on his face.

"I need to go out and face the creature again," Geoffrey said. "I think I'm making progress…"

Edward reached over and took one of the fries from the plate and bit it in half, then popped the rest into his mouth. "You're mad, Geoffrey," he said flatly, as if there were no point in discussing it further. "It will kill you next time."

"No, it won't, ET. It can't kill me because it knows if it does, it will die too. That's why it didn't kill me."

Edward nodded slowly, as if Geoffrey's notion still made no sense, even if he was correct. "Why would you put yourself through that punishment again?"

"Somebody has to do something."

"We're working on it…"

"How many people have died since you've been *working* on it, ET? And it seems I'm the only one who can fix it."

Edward sat staring at Geoffrey, his eyes fixed spots on his face. "So, the plan is, you go do battle with the beast, then *The Associates* patch you up again, then push you *back* into the ring again, and again…? Is that what I'm hearing?"

Geoffrey shrugged and flipped his eyebrows up. Edward shuffled his head back and forth. "You're insane. The very definition of insanity, doing the same thing over and over expecting a different result." Then: "How does this end, Geoffrey?"

Geoffrey felt like he was on the cusp of a cosmic reckoning, if he could just sustain himself with the creature long enough to make a breakthrough. It was true, Geoffrey had no idea how such a *breakthrough* would manifest, or if he'd recognize it when it did, but he trusted he'd know what to do. Regardless, he had to go back and confront the creature again. It was the only way.

Edward stood and prepared to leave Geoffrey's room. "If they agree to this," Edward said. "When do you want to go?"

"As soon as possible."

Geoffrey held back his usual smile, knowing ET would read Geoffrey's pleasant demeanor as a sign he was not taking the situation seriously enough. When Edward walked out, pulling the door shut behind him, an unsettling, pressurized silence filled the room. Geoffrey could feel the current bristle along his skin. Nearly inaudible words filled the dead space—*I fear I have invoked a pact with Satan... and we are certainly damned*— the words repeating back into space as if they had always lingered in the shadows.

45

THE MANTRA

AN IDEA that sounded good in the sanctuary of *The Lodge* suddenly took on a duller luster in the solid blackness of a soundless night. Geoffrey watched the ship rise into the sky, soon becoming an indistinguishable bright speck in the dispassionate universe. It seemed *The Associates* welcomed the idea much more readily than Edward had, which gave Geoffrey a moment's pause, as if *The Associates* had no clue as to what to do about the creature, and seemed to have little compunction over Geoffrey's pain or suffering, willing to sacrifice his wellbeing and comfort to learn more about the phenomenon. Everything was merely research to them, trial and error, evaluation and analysis. They assured him, through ET, that they would find him as soon as possible after the engagement. Edward had offered to accompany Geoffrey, so if the beating got too bad Edward could shoot the creature and rescue Geoffrey from further damage. Geoffrey declined, feeling as though that kind of interference might be counterproductive.

"Counterproductive?" Edward had scoffed, shaking his head. "That's what you're worried about?"

Geoffrey tried to focus, flush all extraneous thoughts from his mind. Crossing the bald, he repeated his yoga mantra in his head trying to calm himself. He hadn't walked very far before he thought he noticed something moving near the perimeter of thick trees and shrubs forty yards away. Within seconds the creature was moving toward him, not running, or in a frenzy, but as if it were a planned meeting, like a luncheon between friends. Geoffrey tried to enlist his ability to read diseases, his uncanny gift of seeing the inner workings of humans, with no success as he concentrated on the creature. He tried to steady his breathing, counter the beast's ferocity with his own calm. The mantra in his head came faster now, an endless loop of vowels and consonants blending to a single, dynamic and monotonous drone. He felt the current building along his extremities, the mantra sparking through his synapses until he sensed his entire being filling with a blinding radiance. The creature kept moving toward him, then stopped ten feet away. The noxious stench of the beast filtered through the air, a smell unlike any other. It stared at Geoffrey, as if maybe it recognized him, the beast's eyes appearing to glow in the strained, peculiar darkness. Geoffrey held the mantra in his head, the separate sounds now one continuous, quickening buzz inside his skull. The beast stepped closer, getting to within five feet. At this close range, Geoffrey finally gained a sense of how large the creature was; at least a foot, maybe two, taller than Geoffrey. He was trying to read the thing, attempting to tap into its thoughts, learn its driving motivation, when it bared its yellow teeth and growled, a chilling, guttural sound that reverberated to the marrow of Geoffrey's bones. In that instant, Geoffrey lost the thread of his mantra, his mind seized with horror, and the beast struck instantly. The first blow ripping across Geoffrey's cheek, followed by the next to his temple, the creature on top of him, the weight of it crushing his chest. Geoffrey tasted the hot metallic brew of blood and saliva filling his mouth, red and yellow lights burning behind his eyes. A claw came down on his throat, trapping the air in his lungs. Unable to breathe, Geoffrey tried to throw the thing off but couldn't budge its suffocating weight. Just then the beast jumped up and grabbed Geoffrey by one foot and started running across the bald dragging him like a puppet over sharp rocks and sticker bushes. With the pain collecting, Geoffrey on the verge of unconsciousness, he felt himself become suddenly airborne, weightless, flying across the bald several feet above the ground, landing harshly on the solid turf, an elbow snapping in a blast of white searing pain. Geoffrey braced himself for the next attack when he heard an explosion. He tried to find the source of the discharge, but couldn't focus, the ground swelling and tilting, until he couldn't hold onto the world any longer.

A day or so later Geoffrey woke in the austere, smallish room of *The Lodge*, feeling better, never truly aware of how bad his injuries were. Edward sat with him a long while until Geoffrey could get some sense of who he was, where he was. When Geoffrey drank the white liquid, the room stopped morphing into other shapes. He glanced over at Edward.

"No more, Geoffrey," Edward said with a finality that froze him.

"I was close," Geoffrey said, his throat still parched and rough.

"Yeah... to death."

Geoffrey could almost recall seeing something in the creature's face just before it attacked, some recognition that was fleeting, so brief Geoffrey couldn't be sure what it was. From what he could reconstruct, it had been more of a human face, one he recognized but couldn't bring back in the moment. Geoffrey was about to argue his case again, but could see by the look in ET's eyes it was pointless. If he could only speak with *The Associates* directly, he could convince them to let him try one last time. As if anticipating Geoffrey's stubbornness on this issue, Edward produced a small handheld mirror. He reached it over to Geoffrey.

"Take a look at what I'm seeing," Edward said.

Geoffrey took the mirror and lifted it until his face reflected inside the oval. He could barely recognize himself, his face appearing lopsided and disfigured, scarred, bruised and ruddy. One of his blue corneas seemed to be floating in blood, the other eye nearly closed off by the ruddy swollen flesh above and below. His nose was misshapen, his cheek drooping as if the structure beneath it no longer existed.

"*The Associates* will fix your face, but I wanted you to see it first," Edward said. "And your elbow, that may never be right again. That thing refractured many of your ribs—now they're as scarred as your knees. And you're lucky *The Associates* were able to reconstruct part of your spinal cord or you'd be paralyzed. You may be right that this creature won't kill you, but it will fuck you up so bad you'll wish you were dead."

Geoffrey had never heard Edward use profanity before. He set the mirror down and closed his eyes to rest. He felt fine. *The Associates* must have given him some kind of beta blockers that didn't make him groggy or loopy, while disguising quite effectively the extent of his injuries. When he opened his eyes, Edward seemed to be dozing. He wanted to ask if Edward had shot the beast, if that was the loud explosion he'd heard. If so, what had happened when he did. Did the thing just die, or did it lope off into the woods like an injured animal? When Geoffrey gazed up, Edward looked away, as if struggling with information he wasn't sure he wanted to share.

"What aren't you telling me?" Geoffrey said, growing impatient with his mercurial mentor.

"In 1983," Edward began, his tone grave, "someone I knew was at the Montauk Air Force Base when scientists performed controversial experiments involving electromagnetic radiation and psychotronic evaluations. According to my associate, that base was the petri dish for the most sordid and secretive research projects in U.S. history." Edward went on to explain that after WWII, Nazi scientists were recruited by the U.S. government under *Operation Paperclip* to bring their extensive human experimentation experience to the Montauk Project. Edward's *friend* had told him about underground bases, crazy experiments with enormous generators, and a huge rotating radar dish that made people sick and nearly insane. Geoffrey was having trouble following the thread of ET's bizarre tale, and couldn't help but wonder why Edward was telling him all this; what did this have to do with the beast? Unaware of Geoffrey's impatience, or just not caring, Edward went on to explain that along with mind-control, and horrendous human trials and studies, scientists were also tasked with time travel experimentation.

"What does any of this have to do with this monster?" Geoffrey said, vexed by Edward's seeming inability to get to the point.

Edward scratched the back of his neck, then aimed his eyes at Geoffrey. "Many surviving crew members from The Philadelphia Experiment were brought to Montauk in '83 for the *witness effect*. It's an occult term, roughly meaning *connected* or *related to*, like a lock of someone's hair might be the link for creating a spell or enchantment. Because these sailors were *connected* to The Philadelphia Experiment, scientists believed they would create a successful *link* to the new experimental trials, a link across time back to the 1943 experiment, the one you were involved in."

"I still don't understand!" Geoffrey said, a bit forcefully.

"A beast was photographed after the experiments, a huge dark entity on the base that showed up on film, but wasn't viewed directly by the photographer," Edward said. "No reports of anyone killed by this *thing*, but *The Associates* believe what happened *then* may be related to what's happening now..."

"They were at Montauk Air Force base?" Geoffrey blurted, a painful knot forming in his chest. "During these experiments?"

Edward nodded, shifting his eyes away from Geoffrey.

Geoffrey couldn't believe what Edward was telling him. First The

Philadelphia Experiment, then the Montauk Project! Who are these *people,* and what are they up to? None of this sounded good.

"What did they do about the monster back then, in '83?" Geoffrey said.

Edward stood up. "You should get some rest, Geoffrey. Don't worry about it."

46

NO LONGER ABSTRACT

COLETTE SAT in front of the laptop researching Mr. Cannon's seminar website. It appeared that the next scheduled event was less than a week away in Bristol, Tennessee. She wondered if they still had tickets, and if Orvin would want to go with her. She wasn't sure why, but she felt she wanted to experience first-hand what Mr. Cannon did at these events. But it was more than that, she felt some kind of connection, as if Geoffrey needed them in some way, or she needed him. It was confusing. And even though he had denied everything Colette had brought forth—the newspaper article, their chance meeting at the library in Philadelphia—at least for her, he hadn't been very convincing in his rejection of her suppositions. Was it possible that Mr. Cannon actually *was, is,* the Peter Smithwick of the newspaper account, the young man forty-five years ago she met in Philadelphia? If so, how was that possible?

When she met Mr. Cannon weeks earlier, when he'd visited Orvin in the hospital, she herself had been closed off, wrapped in darkness, and could only see Mr. Cannon as the personification of darkness itself, evil and iniquity. But when she visited him in the hospital several days ago, she had felt much lighter, more optimistic—her life with Orvin having transformed in many ways—and she was able to perceive the unusual young man in an entirely new way, as a purveyor of hope and good-ness. Just as she had seen Peter Smithwick all those years ago, as someone she had admired, was even attracted to at the time. It was a bit of an epiphany. What was curious to her now, was that when Orvin had originally told her how Cannon had saved his life, she had only been able to view it through the lens of wickedness and villainy, as if the entire event had been some unspoken contract for possession of Orvin's soul. With Colette in a more uplifted place herself, she could appreciate what Geoffrey had done for her husband as the miraculous gift that it was.

Orvin came in the front door and walked over to Colette at the desk in the living room. "What are you doing?" he asked. She closed the lid on the computer, not ready to broach the matter of the seminar.

"Nothing. What have you been up to?" she said.

He looked at her, then at the computer, then sat on the couch. "I picked up a house painting job today."

"Will you have to get help on it?"

"No. Ranch style. One level." Orvin sat with his hands on his knees, his eyes straight ahead, and seemed to be mentally chewing on something. Colette waited a moment before she asked what was going on. Obviously troubled, Orvin finally said, "I know we talked about this already, but I still don't understand why you had that article about that Peter Smithwick fella." Then, barely a beat later: "I mean, I can't connect the dots, Colette." He finally looked over at her, his eyes pressed with confusion.

"I knew his name from the library back in Philly, and I just... you know, asked the researcher to have a look through the archives for anything on a young man named Peter Smithwick. That article was all they came up with."

The muscles in Orvin's face twitched and tightened a few times. "I'm still trying to grab the tag end of this deal," he said. "So, what you're saying is, that when you met Geoffrey Cannon a few weeks back, you recognized him as this Peter Smithwick fella from the library forty-five years ago?" Orvin said, fixing his eyes on hers, anticipating some kind of response. She nodded. He continued. "Okay, then, since..." Orvin started to say, but stopped, seemingly flummoxed again. "How could he look the same after forty-five years, Colette? That's the part I don't get!"

"I don't get it either, but... he looks exactly the same..."

"But how could you possibly remember what some fella looked like all those years ago? Hell, sometimes I can barely picture my own mama..."

She was growing impatient with Orvin over his line of questioning. It was becoming obvious he couldn't accept her speculation that these two men were one and the same. And that was understandable. "I just do," she said. "I had a little crush on him back then… and I saw him plenty of times at the library, so—"

"A *crush?*" Orvin's face hardened. "On Mr. Cannon? This is the first I heard about any of this…"

"Not on Mr. Cannon! On Peter Smithwick… decades ago, Orvin. I was living with my aunt and several months pregnant and I was feeling pretty alone…"

Orvin took his eyes to the living room carpet, his head nodding gently, his brow knitted, as if forcing himself to understand.

"I mean, maybe I'm mistaken," Colette finally said. She had considered that the whole thing was some false recollection on her part. After all, it was crazy, especially now with Orvin bringing the implausibility into sharper focus. But it wasn't just that she recognized Mr. Cannon's face, but something much deeper, more penetrating, something she'd *felt* when he'd walked into Orvin's hospital room that day. That same helium sensation of emptiness and euphoria, both exhilarating and disturbing, as if she were losing cohesion, turning to vapor. She'd felt that only one other time in her life; when Peter Smithwick entered the library in Philadelphia over forty years ago, a sensation she'd misinterpreted at the time as falling in love. The moment their eyes met in Orvin's room, though, the memory of Peter Smithwick had rushed forward with unsettling clarity. For all those decades the young man had been erased from her life and suddenly she could recall every detail about him, his glowing smile, the dimples that opened near the corners of his mouth, his hair, uncombed but never messy. Even the sweet lime scent of his aftershave. She could see him sitting at his favorite table in the library, books everywhere. She could picture each cover, read each title, like a highly-detailed photograph. None of her normal memories ever held that level of lucidity and crispness, every smell and fragrance from that long-forgotten time renewed, keenly fresh, lingering in the air around her.

"I'm probably wrong… Mr. Cannon probably thinks I'm a nutcase…" Even as the words left her mouth, she knew she was right about Peter Smithwick and Geoffrey Cannon, but why was it important to make Orvin accept her hypothesis? It wasn't. She knew she could live with the uncertainty of the situation, the preternatural quality of someone not aging, then meeting him again after all this time. It was bizarre, absolutely, and easy to dismiss, but because it couldn't be proven that Smithwick and Cannon were the same person, the premise was abstract at best. A fallacy, nothing more. Nevertheless, Colette could entertain this notion in the abstract, was okay with the possibility, no matter how odd.

Orvin couldn't.

He fell silent on the couch, his eyes gazing past the opposite wall.

"Why does it bother you so much?" Colette finally asked.

The look he gave her was that of a stranger, a vacant, mesmerizing stare that was unsettling. She was about to ask what was wrong, when Orvin said, "There is something not right about Mr. Cannon." Then, with a flutter of discomfort shifting across his face: "I've known it from the first time I met him." He looked over at her, his eyes trying to conceal some frightening truth. Orvin appeared to have more to say, but was having difficulty getting out the words.

"I don't want to scare you, Colette, but I need to tell you some things," he said, then went on to explain about Mr. Cannon's mountain party, and the creature that people saw at the glass patio doors of Mr. Cannon's house that night. "I saw it too, Colette, and it wasn't no damn bear. I've never seen anything like it before." He went on to tell her that he believed that the *creature* was killing all these people, and the kids on Yellow Mountain. "That's why Mr. Cannon was up on that bald. Hunting that damn monster... and I think he found it, and that's what tore him up so bad... not sure why it didn't kill him, but I have an idea..."

She waited for Orvin to finish, trying to hold back the questions careening around in her head.

Orvin's eyes came at her like bullets. "I think he's connected to that damn thing in some way," he said. "I can't quite wrap my brain around it..."

"I don't understand any of this," she said. What Orvin was telling her caught her completely off guard. It got her wondering if her original impressions of Geoffrey Cannon were correct after all, that he was some emissary of darkness. Before she could gather herself, Orvin pulled out his phone and scrolled through some pictures, then handed the device to her and hit play. She watched the video loop several times, the colored lights flashing up through the tree limbs and shrubs, before disappearing into the night sky. After numerous playthroughs, she hit stop and handed the phone back to Orvin.

"What is that?" she said.

Orvin laid his phone on the coffee table. "That's video from Carly

Rasterson's phone the night she was killed on Yellow Mountain. Wyatt sent me the footage."

Colette was dumbfounded. Laverne at the library went on about strange creatures and aliens and such all the time, but that was Laverne. This was Orvin talking about such things, fierce monsters, a video that looked like a UFO. This was no longer abstract. An eerie chill sidled through her, and she wasn't sure she wanted any more to do with Geoffrey Cannon.

47

A LIFELESS HUSK

IT TOOK SOME CONVINCING, but Edward and *The Associates* decided to let Geoffrey have another go at the beast, but only with Edward along. Geoffrey told them he felt he was making progress, that the beast was transforming in appearance; it once had fangs, almost like a mandrill, but now had the tusks of a wild boar. The creature's face had even come to resemble a swine somewhat, the extended snout, the small, wide-set eyes. Its skin was no longer a thick blanket of bristly hair, but now possessed a leathery veneer blotched with tufts of hair, large muscles and protruding veins clearly visible. Geoffrey wasn't sure what it was becoming, and it was certainly no less ominous.

The plan was that Edward would stay out of sight, armed with a rifle this time, and night vision scope. Geoffrey was not to move from the designated spot, and wait for the creature to come to him so Edward could get a clear shot if necessary. Geoffrey was also armed with a stun gun kind of device, though no one knew if that would really do any good.

If *The Associates* had come up with a better plan to deal with this thing, Geoffrey wouldn't be testing this stunt again. But he felt he had no other choice. Fortunately, the moon was bright, making it easier to see. The spacecraft had already departed, leaving Geoffrey in the middle of the bald alone. He wasn't sure where Edward was, but felt certain Edward had him in his sights. It didn't take long for the beast to show, coming from the opposite edge of the bald. It was walking differently now, a casual gait that gave it the appearance of being out for a stroll.

And it appeared a bit smaller than it had last time. Right now, it was nothing more than a dark smudge working its way across the sedge, directly toward Geoffrey. Geoffrey's lungs tightened as it came closer. Obviously the beast was not planning to attack, or perhaps wanted to catch Geoffrey off guard with its unthreatening approach. Geoffrey was well into his mantra, a freight train of sounds rushing through his mind, a new energy cycling through his veins, when it came within ten feet and spoke. "Hello," it said.

Geoffrey would have been shocked, but a half-second earlier something in Geoffrey's mind registered that it was a man.

"Sorry, didn't mean to startle you," the man said, moving closer until Geoffrey could see it was a hiker with a large backpack. Then: "Out enjoying the stars?"

Geoffrey hadn't even noticed the sky above him. "Yeah," he said numbly.

"It's been nice not having rain these past several days," the hiker said, who appeared to be middle-aged, maybe a bit older. He had a headlamp, but it was turned off. "Finally got my gear dried out a couple nights ago."

"Where're you headed?" Geoffrey said, feeling uncomfortable with the man's presence on the bald, wondering where the creature was.

"Just out for a week," he said. "Headed to Milbur Falls. Got a car parked there. Should arrive day after tomorrow."

"Kind of dark to be hiking, isn't it?"

"Not with this moon, especially out in the open. Lost some time in the rain and I'm trying to make up some miles. But I don't mind. Beautiful night."

Geoffrey could only nod, his eyes searching the surrounding area for movement.

"Well, I better get going. Hope to find a nice spot to camp," he said, then started looking around at the bald. "This actually doesn't look too bad here."

Geoffrey wanted to say something to discourage the man. Before he could think of anything, the man said, "According to my weather app, though, they're forecasting a storm for tonight… can you believe that?" he said, as if thinking out loud. "This would be a bad place to get caught in a lightning storm. I best keep moving," he said, then told Geoffrey goodnight and continued across the bald.

Geoffrey watched him depart, hoping he would be okay. The man soon disappeared over the far ridge of the bald and the silence of the night spread over everything. A few minutes later Geoffrey heard a rustling behind him. He turned to see something approaching, something large with an ungainly, stuttering walk. Geoffrey rebooted his mantra, working it up to peak voltage, his heart thumping just as quickly. The beast approached rapidly now, some weird loping, jouncing slog that made it appear unable to control its own movements. Its eyes glowed with an intensity Geoffrey had not noticed before, the stench of the beast reaching Geoffrey twenty feet away. But it wasn't slowing this time and Geoffrey kept his eyes focused on the thing and it was on him. Geoffrey tried to brace himself for the impact, but the creature stopped abruptly, its huge maw hanging over Geoffrey like an awning, its rank breath seeping into Geoffrey's nostrils. Geoffrey continued the mantra, letting his mind open to the beast's thoughts. Slowly, Geoffrey raised his eyes only, trying to see what the thing was doing. But it was so close, Geoffrey couldn't see anything but the bottom of its muzzle and its huge tusks. He had to raise up, and hoped the movement wouldn't set off a vicious attack. Geoffrey brought his head up gradually until his eyes were in line with the creature's. The yellowish glow of the beast's eyes with their intense blue irises, unsettled Geoffrey at first, until an uncanny equilibrium rose up between Geoffrey and the thing, some strange balance that almost felt like communication. Geoffrey held its bloodless stare, enduring its horrible breath, hoping to garner new information, some agenda the beast might have beyond mindless killing. When nothing came, Geoffrey felt a perplexing discomfort, feeling as if the only way to end this encounter was with some kind of reaction. What at first had felt like some kind of symmetry of awareness, now seemed more akin to a maddening stasis, a lit fuse that would not end well.

The creature held Geoffrey's gaze, its eyes fixed and unblinking in a treacherous way. Barely did its mouth show signs of life. Its horrible stained teeth showed through the narrow space of its disarming grin, as if it were amused, but Geoffrey knew it to be the natural curve of its jaws. No, it wasn't grinning, merely tolerating Geoffrey's presence. The first blow came as an agonizing surprise, the world flashing red and bluish white. Geoffrey had not registered that anything had changed, until the creature struck him, then struck him again and again, shocking Geoffrey's nervous system, overloading brain circuits, taxing his pain centers. Geoffrey couldn't tell if he himself was on the ground or still standing, the world tilting in an unexpected way, the sensation of gravity lost, the molecules charged with frenetic lunacy.

A loud crack. Maybe a bone? A leg, an arm? Geoffrey couldn't be sure, caught in a hammering machine, pistons pounding his flesh, pulverizing tiny bones to mush. Another loud crack. A breath later the mechanism stopped and from the margins of Geoffrey's bloody vision, he watched the huge beast topple, a lifeless husk falling to the earth. Just beyond the unmoving creature Geoffrey saw something or someone running toward him. The world lit up in bright flashing lights descending from the heavens. In the aftermath of the struggle, Geoffrey, beginning to lose consciousness, tried to reconstruct the final moments as the beast was falling, how its facial features shifted, became nearly recognizable, someone Geoffrey knew intimately; his own father, Reverend Jacob.

Later, when Geoffrey would become conscious again, he would ask Edward what the creature looked like when Edward, still holding his rifle, came over close to it to make sure it was dead. Edward would say it was a hideous thing with sharp teeth and huge tusks, small dead eyes, and a hole in its chest the size of a skull. Geoffrey would ponder what he saw for days after, wondering if he had imagined seeing his father's face on the monster, if it had been nothing more than a hallucination brought on by the loss of blood and the excruciating pain of broken bones.

48

MIRACLES

THE DUAL NATURE OF REALITY. The material and non-material aspects of the physical world. One no more real than the other, and it seemed that everything in the universe pointed to this indelible truth of opposites. Yet much scientific thought had concluded long ago that the non-material realm was all delusion, the idea of free will and choice merely constructs of a frightened mind, needing to believe there was more to the experience of being alive than science's materialistic approach could provide. Scientific discourse had previously elected the brain as the organ that ran the whole show, while the corporeal being was just along for the ride; that we were all just *prisoners* of our own cellular processes and that's how it's always been, and would always be. Yet even that notion suggested something *other* than the body and brain, that *other* which could *hold someone prisoner*, and that which *could be held prisoner.* What could that *other* be? It seemed that even by science's own definition of reality, some organism which didn't fit into the category of brain or body, something beyond the material, was capable of thinking about itself as separate and apart from the brain-body model. But what could that be if the non-material realm didn't exist as science once imposed? The Decade of the Brain, a ten-year gallop of extraordinary research and discovery, changed all that, at least for many.

That is what Geoffrey wanted to talk about today to his attendees, the dual nature of reality, the majesty of the mind. Most of Geoffrey's seminars were about freeing oneself from the sabotage of incessant thought, but another aspect of this magnificent entity, one Geoffrey never spoke much about, was the miracle of the mind. Geoffrey wanted to talk about miracles.

Waiting backstage for the seminar to kick off, Geoffrey was busy trying to focus, his mind looping back to a week or so earlier on Yellow Mountain, facing the beast. Seeing the image of his father in the dying creature was more like a false memory now than a solid-state recollection, one that Geoffrey couldn't quite trust. Then there was his stepmother, Lauralee, whose colorless oval face had flashed for half a second, a faulty, superimposed image over his father's leathery visage. And yet, Geoffrey couldn't help but consider his mind was the artist here, a trickster painting around the unfortified edges of Geoffrey's thoughts.

"Five minutes," Edward said, coming up behind Geoffrey. Geoffrey looked up at ET and for the briefest moment didn't recognize his long-time partner. "You okay to do this, Geoffrey?" Edward added, obviously noticing the vacancy in Geoffrey's eyes.

Geoffrey nodded, recalling the first blast from Edward's rifle that night, then the second, which finally took the monster down, the faces of his father and stepmother snapping across the creature's lifeless expression. In the dark space of Geoffrey's skull, the gunshots kept exploding, the beast kept falling over dead, its dying breath a rotting potpourri of blood and rotten eggs.

Edward stared at Geoffrey's face a long couple of seconds before Edward said, "Man, that thing really messed you up." *The Associates* had done all they could, and would perform more marvels once Geoffrey returned to *The Lodge* after the seminar ended, but Geoffrey had seen his own discolored face in the mirror, the lacerations on his neck, the swelling around his left eye and cheek, his scraped forehead. It still hurt to take a deep breath, the air forcing apart his fragile ribs. The wounds on his legs were stubborn and ruddy. "You sure you're up for this?" Edward asked.

Geoffrey stood, wearing his signature cargo shorts and polo shirt, and tennis shoes with no socks. "Just make sure to dim the lights before I walk out," Geoffrey said, ambling toward the curtains marking the edge of the waiting area. A moment later, to applause and a slowly darkening auditorium, and without the customary spotlight, Geoffrey presented himself to the audience. He waited a moment for the adulation to wane, then, in a somber tone, said, "Please, everyone, close your eyes."

The room fell silent except for a few coughs, shoes shuffling, chairs creaking, people trying to set themselves into a comfortable position while shutting their eyes.

"Take a deep breath… and let it out slowly.

"Now breathe normally, focusing on your breath. Try to keep it even and relaxed," Geoffrey said, his lavalier mic whispering his words out into every ear. After a few moments, he began again. "I want you to imagine an ocean spreading out before you that is turbulent, huge swells capped with white, the water dark. Above the ocean the sky is bloated, purplish-green with towering specters of rumbling clouds. Enormous waves rise and crash down on one another, beating silvery-white tendrils across the dark green water. Wind roars and whips the surface into sucking swells and exploding ridges. Now, move your intention just beneath the surface of the water. You breathe easily and effortlessly here beneath the ocean surface. Now look up, see the froth and bubbles roiling above you, hear the sizzle of the water blistering and discharging, feel the pressure of the waves pounding into themselves. Currents still push and pull you." Geoffrey paused just a moment. "Move your intention deeper now, farther below the surface of the chaotic ocean, just out of reach of the ebb and flow of the storm. Be aware of the calm starting to surround you. Watch the surface tear itself apart while you observe the turmoil, safe from any harm, comfortably protected from its fury. Now move your intention to the ocean floor. Notice how the soft sand barely stirs when you settle down on its cushy surface. Feel the peace surround you, envelop you. The light is dim, pleasant and calming, yet crystal clear, infused with a rare luminance. You are safe here. It is utterly silent, serene. Exotic, colorful fish swim without caution, dart and glide and play. There are no predators here, nothing that can harm you." Geoffrey allows a few moments for them to sit with this sensation. "This is your mind free of distraction, absent of the constant dialogue of everyday life. Sit with that emptiness a few moments."

After a brief interlude of complete silence, Geoffrey spoke: "Now, I'd like you to move your intention slowly back toward the surface, noticing how the light changes ever so slightly, becoming brighter as you approach the upper layer of water. Everything has changed, the surface smoother now, dimples of refracted sunlight playing above you. When you move your intention above the surface you see the sky is a perfect blue, the ocean a remarkable mirrored glass reaching to the horizon." Then: "Now, please, open your eyes."

Geoffrey positioned himself in the middle of the stage. He waited for everyone to return their awareness back to the room. When they began to move naturally, Geoffrey motioned for the lights to come up.

"Welcome everyone, to the, "Are You Out of Your Mind?" seminar," Geoffrey said, a wide smile across his face. People started to applaud, which soon devolved into rumblings and murmurs of surprise and shock. Geoffrey knew they were reacting to his battered face and arms.

He laughed gently. "You can probably see I've had one heck of a week," he said joking. People laughed nervously with chortles and gasps of reserved amusement.

"Before we get started," Geoffrey said. "I'd like to remember someone who died here two weeks ago. Some of you may have even known her, and maybe heard about her tragic death. Elizabeth Zahn was a lovely young woman with her entire life ahead of her. If we can, let's take a moment, close our eyes and let our hearts connect with her indelible spirit."

Everyone sat quietly for a short time.

"Thank you all," Geoffrey said. "It is so great to be here today with so many joyous and vibrant beings," Geoffrey said, spreading his gaze across the conference congregation.

"Miracles," Geoffrey said. "Let's see a show of hands for everyone who believes in miracles." Hundreds of hands shot up toward the ceiling. Geoffrey smiled. "Now, how many of you have actually witnessed a miracle?" Most of the hands went down, about a fourth remaining up, and with more reticence, as if people weren't sure about the veracity of their claims.

"I am here to tell you, that each and every one of you has witnessed a miracle, are witnessing one right now." He paused, letting his eyes scan the audience, then: "Now you may think that what I am about to tell you isn't truly miraculous, but trust me, it is the most amazing miracle you could imagine." Geoffrey paused again, distracted by someone in the audience, someone he recognized but didn't know. It was the man from two weeks earlier, the one wearing the black cowboy hat who had been staring at him in the hotel lounge. At the time, Geoffrey had thought the man had been an undercover policeman, or FBI. Elizabeth Zahn had struck up a conversation with Geoffrey, and Geoffrey had thought maybe they were working together, both undercover officers. The same man was now in the audience, wearing his black cowboy hat and western-style string tie, and a black leather jacket. Geoffrey couldn't see the man's eyes, cropped by the shadow of his hat brim.

"If you look at your neighbors around you," Geoffrey continued, pushing away his curiosity, "you are witnessing a miracle. Each and every one of us is a walking miracle. What does that mean? It goes to the fact of the dual nature of reality, the material and non-material realms of existence…"

Geoffrey glanced back at the man, who was stationary and fixed, like a gargoyle, in the fourth row. That's when Geoffrey's eyes snagged on two other people, about nine rows back. Not only did he recognize these two people, he also knew them.

"Now… anyone familiar with my books and seminars knows that I am a believer in uncluttering the mind," Geoffrey said, trying to continue his talk, "taking back the present moment from all the static in our heads, as we did a while ago with the guided meditation. But today… I want to *celebrate* the mind, talk about its non-material quality that we take for granted, missing out on the most profound aspect of our experience and what true miracles we all really are. I want you all to consider for a moment, how you came to be, cells dividing, then dividing again, until they've formed into a human being in the womb. And you may be saying, 'Well, Geoffrey, science has explained all that.' True, science has explained the *process*. But here's the part science can't explain; 'how' it's possible. Science can't explain the unknown source of intelligence that informs those cells to create the human, a human that doesn't even have a brain yet! Miraculously, each cell knows its exact and unique job in your biology, even as it's forming! Cells that will become your skin, the retina of your eye, the tissue of your lungs, the lobe of your ear, the nail on your big toe, all these cells knowing exactly each task they're to perform to make you into a human being! Forming your skeletal structure within a magnificent tapestry of ligament and muscle, veins and arteries, wrapped within a flexible and resilient skin. The cells know exactly how to form the brain, that will become the center of thinking, the lungs that will provide our most precious lifeline, and that incredible organism, the heart, which will beat from the moment of its inception until the moment of our death. The heart and lungs and all the organs will operate with no help or commands from us, while we sleep, watch television, drive our cars, performing no matter how distracted we are with other matters; the mundane, the dramatic, the sorrowful, the exciting. The heart will continue on, beating beneath our ribs, mostly forgotten by us in the frenzy of our everyday life. And yet, if we steal a moment of stillness, our heart is working away quietly, methodically, miraculously, through the din of our everyday trials, setbacks and victories.

"But the miracle persists throughout our lives. These cells die and replicate, replacing themselves, renewing every centimeter of our bodies continuously, remaking us unceasingly, executing myriad complex processes that keep you functioning, sending blood where needed, adrenaline when called for, calories, vitamins and nutrients to replenish, and millions of microscopic tasks too numerous to count, all without any input or help from us... and this process continues..."

Geoffrey stopped, smiling, so moved by seeing Orvin and Colette in the crowd, he found it hard to go on. "I'm sorry, but I must take a moment to mention a couple of my dearest friends. Colette, Orvin, please come up here so I can introduce you. What a surprise!"

Heads swiveled trying to find the couple. Orvin shook his head and Colette covered her face. "Please, come on up, Colette! Grab Orvin and bring him up here." Colette smiled and looked at Orvin, who shook his head no. Geoffrey implored the crowd to applaud until Orvin got out of his seat. Which they did, and Orvin finally stood and escorted Colette to the front of the room. Geoffrey went down and hugged Colette, then shook Orvin's hand, pulling him closer for a brief hug, guiding them up on stage. Orvin was clearly embarrassed, but Colette seemed to take the moment in stride. Orvin fidgeted next to Colette while people applauded. She gave everyone a wide good-natured smile, a bit sheepishly, her eyes sparkling with delight.

"Please welcome Colette, and her husband, Orvin!" Geoffrey said, sweeping his hand toward the modest couple. Geoffrey waited for the applause to die out, then: "This lovely young couple saved my life a week ago," Geoffrey said, nodding thoughtfully. "I'm not kidding. I, being new to the area where I live, did not heed the sage advice of my dear friend, Orvin, here, and I went up in the mountains, at night, alone..." Geoffrey was shaking his head, admitting how foolhardy it had been. Orvin glanced over at him, blanked-faced.

"When I didn't return," Geoffrey said, "these two took a hazardous ride up to the top of a huge mountain on a road that hasn't really earned the designation of *road*, but more a rough, guileless mess of a path. They then hiked to the top and searched for me until they found me lying on the ground, barely able to move..."

Geoffrey smiled over at Colette, then Orvin, noticing movement at the edge of his sight. People in the audience clamored, some shrieking with fright, jumping up and moving away from their seats. Geoffrey spun around to see a man standing in the newly vacated crater left behind by people scattering to the far ends of the aisles. The man pointed a pistol at Geoffrey. It was the man in the black cowboy hat, the man who had fixated on Geoffrey two weeks earlier in the hotel lounge. A couple of large men a few rows back started moving forward toward the gunman, when Geoffrey put up his hand, told them to stop. Most people were headed for the exits, calling on their cell phones.

"You slept with my wife," the man in the cowboy hat said. "Then you killed her!"

Geoffrey motioned for Colette and Orvin to leave the stage by the side entrance where Edward was watching the drama unfold. Colette looked around and was about to take a step when the gunman told her to stop. "Nobody's going anywhere," he shouted, pushing forward toward the stage, knocking chairs out of his way, never taking his eyes from Geoffrey and Colette, until he was within twenty feet of them.

"I think you must be mistaken," Geoffrey said, trying to keep Colette and Orvin behind him. "I'm sure I don't even know your wife."

"Is that right!" The man took another step forward, the gun pulling his arm straight out toward Geoffrey. "How about Tess Landry, you bastard! You killed my wife and the police won't do a thing about it. Why didn't you have a little memorial for Tess the way you did for Ms. Zahn, the other woman you killed!"

Edward sauntered out from the side entrance to the stage and the gunman told him to halt, pumping the gun at him before swinging it back toward Geoffrey. Geoffrey held out his palm to stop Edward, motioning for him to go back.

"Let's have Colette and Orvin, here, leave the stage, okay?" Geoffrey said to the irate gunman, placing his hand on Colette's arm. "Then we can talk about all this before someone gets hurt."

"You stay the hell where you are, lady, or you'll be joining my wife!"

Colette started to sob, tucking in behind Geoffrey. Orvin had just made a move toward his wife when the gunman rushed forward a little. "You stop right there, motherfucker," the man yelled at Orvin. "As a matter of fact, get your scrawny ass off the stage. Just Cannon and your wife. That's all I want to see."

Geoffrey didn't like the trajectory of this standoff, but nodded toward Orvin to leave the stage. "No way am I leaving Colette out here with that goddamn madman…"

"Oh, Orvin, please, just do what he says," Colette cried. "Please, I'll be fine..." She was shaking in Geoffrey's arms now, Geoffrey trying to keep his back between the gun and Colette, looking at the gunman over his shoulder.

"Go ahead, Orvin," Geoffrey said. "We'll be fine, okay?"

Orvin licked his lips and stared hard down on the man, his jaw fixed and shiny. After a moment, Orvin turned and ambled toward Edward standing in the wing, his head swiveling between Colette and the gunman. Four policemen appeared at the back of the room. The gunman spun around and told them to stay put or Cannon and the woman would die. The policemen drew their revolvers and waited.

"Now that the police are here, I want you to admit you murdered Tess Landry," the gunman said. "Do it now, or you're both gonna die, I mean it." The man's gun arm turned rigid, steady, steeled against the recoil. The police moved closer, officers congregating slowly at the edges of the stage. One officer told him to put the gun down, that everything was over.

"It's over when I say it's over," the man yelled to the officers. "And if you come any closer, it's going to be over damned quick!" The gunman was between Geoffrey and the police.

Just then, someone backstage knocked over a chair, causing Geoffrey to reflexively spin from the perceived danger, rotating Colette away from the loud bang. The gunman fired. The explosion corresponded with Colette going limp in Geoffrey's arms, a bright red stain blossoming on the chest of Colette's dress. Geoffrey cut a hard look at the gunman in the audience, then back to Colette as she slumped toward the floor. Orvin screamed, running toward his wife. The gunman got off one last bullet before the police shot him dead under a barrage of gunfire. Geoffrey was kneeling, holding Colette by the shoulder off the floor, a bright, new searing pain at his abdomen. The police rushed the gunman, who was lying motionless on the floor. Geoffrey was trying to hold his consciousness, could feel his own blood wetting his shirt. Orvin knelt down next to them. "Colette! No! Colette!"

Geoffrey's breathing was labored, his consciousness flashing in and out. He moved his forehead closer to Colette until it rested against hers. Closing his eyes, Geoffrey could see the bullet, the path of its entry just missing her heart, the puncture in her spleen, the blood drooling out, the blood mixing into the organs. In a few moments, Geoffrey, with his right hand behind Colette, pressed his opened palm against her back, concentrating on drawing the slug toward his hand, could feel it beginning to move until it touched his palm. He closed his hand over it, making sure he had it, then let the bloody bullet drop to the wooden stage. Orvin looked down at the mashed lead covered in blood, then at Colette, saying nothing. Geoffrey was having difficulty breathing. He looked up and saw Colette floating above the stage. He shook his head no when she stared at him from above. "No, Colette," Geoffrey mumbled, closing his eyes, letting his intentions trace the lethal path through her spleen, healing the wound, stemming the bleeding. Above him, Colette floated further away. Geoffrey sent his intention back in, finding the spot where the bullet had grazed her stomach. He repaired that lesion and worked to siphon off the excess blood inside her body.

A moment later Colette came conscious, her eyes lidded, distant.

"Oh my God, Colette," Orvin cried. "Oh my God!"

In a few seconds, Colette climbed to her feet, stunned and groggy, and a bit shaky. Orvin hugged her to him, the blood on her dress staining Orvin's shirt. Outside, sirens rushed toward the hotel. Edward was standing with two other men. The police assured Edward that the EMTs would arrive any second, but Edward ignored them and told the two men to pick Geoffrey up. The police protested, but the men, followed by Edward, hustled Geoffrey out the back entrance of the event room and into a waiting black Suburban with darkened windows. The doors slammed. The vehicle lurched forward, racing toward the parking lot exit, nearly colliding with two police cars escorting other emergency vehicles speeding in.

49
DEAREST FRIENDS

POLICE LINGERED near the back exits, keeping out reporters and onlookers, while officials circled the dead body of the man in the black cowboy hat, taking photos, securing his pistol and checking his finger-prints with a mobile scanner. Policemen stood near the rows of chairs taking statements from witnesses who'd been sitting nearby when the gunman bolted upright and approached the stage. Orvin was trying to find a way to exit the huge event room without being noticed, guiding Colette from behind. She seemed dazed, not sure where she was or what was happening. Orvin was a bit shaken as well when he spied a side exit from the auditorium. A police officer had just come in from the parking lot through the metal doors and hurried toward the back of the room. Orvin could see that the doors led out onto the parking lot, making it possible for him and Colette to avoid the hubbub at the back exits. They were nearly to the edge of the stage when an officer rushed up to them.

"Please, stop, ma'am," the policewoman said. "You look hurt. Are you shot?"

Colette looked at the young woman officer who had worried eyes, then glanced down at the blood stain on her dress, before looking over at Orvin.

"Someone said a woman was shot. Is that you, ma'am?" the officer asked again and Orvin wasn't sure how to answer. It would sound stupid to say she *was* shot, but she *isn't* anymore. And how could he explain the blood? The officer seemed to be growing impatient, clicking her eyes between Colette and Orvin.

"This is my wife, and no, she isn't shot," Orvin said. "We were on stage when the guy started shooting. My wife was trying to help Mr. Cannon... he was shot... that's where the blood came from. It's Mr. Cannon's." Orvin feared the officer would see that he was dissembling, trying to explain too much the way the guilty often do. And weirdly, he did feel culpable, not for the attack, but trying to cover up Geoffrey's miraculous restoration of Colette. Orvin was fairly certain Colette had been dead, though he could never be sure, but she had not responded to his words or touch.

"Ma'am, you don't look good," the officer said, rushing over to grab a chair from the edge of the stage. "Here, please, sit."

"No, she'll be fine," Orvin said. "She just needs some fresh air." Colette sat down anyway, not really present, her eyes floating in empty space, unfocused, disconnected from reality.

The officer asked Orvin's name, and his wife's, then said, "You were on stage when Mr. Cannon was shot?"

Orvin said they were, explaining that Mr. Cannon had invited them to come up when he recognized them in the audience.

"So you knew Mr. Cannon?"

"Yes, I did some work for him."

The officer wanted details about the kind of work Orvin had performed, if Orvin was a professional house painter, and why they, he and Mr. Cannon, had become so chummy. The woman officer asked how long they've known each other. Orvin explained that they lived in the same town, Kleary Creek, and since Geoffrey was new to the area, he asked about Orvin's church and the area and such. Orvin was already tired of the interview and just wanted to leave, wondering where Geoffrey was, if he was dead. The shooting looped in Orvin's head, accumulating more information and details with every replay.

"Did you know the shooter?"

Orvin shook his head.

"What did the shooter say to Mr. Cannon?"

Orvin knew exactly what he'd said, but wasn't keen on sharing that with the authorities, still feeling an odd allegiance to the strange young man, even though he was completely flummoxed by him. The truth would be best, Orvin finally figured, with plenty of people in attendance who must have heard the attacker. "He accused Mr. Cannon of sleeping with the man's wife..." Orvin finally admitted, "and killing her."

Another officer walked over to the policewoman taking Orvin's statement and handed her a piece of paper. "It says here the shooter's name was Ward Landry from Oklahoma City, Oklahoma. His wife was Esther Landry, went by Tess. She was murdered several weeks ago..." The officer then looked up at Orvin. "Are you sure you don't know Mr. or Mrs. Landry?"

"No, never heard of them until just now," Orvin said, a bit perturbed and unsettled, as if he were being accused of something, had had some part in this macabre incident. The officer asked for more information, address, phone number and such and Orvin provided everything she needed, his mind snagged on the word *murdered*—Orvin had never considered that Mr. Landry might actually be telling the truth, that Geoffrey had slept with the man's wife... and had killed her? The killing was hard to imagine, but the sleeping with his wife, well, Orvin thought back to the morning he first met Geoffrey, the two naked women walking around in his house. Orvin had never quite been able to parse that scene, and chalked it up to young folks and social media and a new relaxed morality.

"Can we go now?" Colette asked, looking up at Orvin with confusion. Orvin met the policewoman's brown eyes as if to ask if they could leave.

"Do you attend all of Mr. Cannon's seminars?" she asked, not quite ready to relinquish her authority.

"First one," Orvin said.

"Why today?"

Orvin was frustrated now. "I don't know. Colette wanted to come for some reason... and didn't want to drive all this way by herself. So I said sure." What was this officer looking for? They had their shooter lying dead on the floor. What else did she need to know?

"Did Mr. Cannon ever talk to you about his seminars?"

"No."

"Did he mention the woman who was killed here two weeks ago, a Ms. Elizabeth Zahn?"

"He mentioned her in his talk today."

"Never before that?"

"No. We never spoke to each other about his seminars, or much about his personal life."

The officer cleared her throat. "Really, that's odd," she said, looking at the paper in her hand as if she might find something incriminating. "Don't you think?"

"I don't know what you're talking about," Orvin finally said.

"It sounds like you hardly knew Mr. Cannon at all, and yet, he stops the seminar when he spots you in the audience, then invites you up and introduces you and Colette as his 'Dearest friends.' Isn't that odd?"

"I don't know why he said that. I guess he doesn't know anyone in Kleary Creek yet, and just figured, you know…"

"Actually, I don't know. 'Dearest friends' sounds pretty intimate. I have about three people in my life I'd call my 'dearest friends,' and they're people I've known for ages. Somehow you and Mr. Cannon are dearest friends after only a month or so. And yet you know none of his personal history, or what he does for a living. Have you read his books? Or listened to his lectures on YouTube?"

"No," Orvin said, careful not to add that he didn't know Geoffrey was an author. "Some folks, especially extroverts, think everyone they meet is their *dearest friend!*" Orvin recalled a few people like that, customers and acquaintances that seemed to have more *close friends* than Orvin had hairs on his head.

Now the policewoman appeared as exasperated as Orvin felt, but she had an edge of anger to her frustration as evidenced in her voice, as if Orvin was lying.

"Did you know that since you've known Mr. Cannon, there have been several investigations around his possible involvement in three murders?"

Orvin felt like he'd been tased, current sizzling along his skin, certain the shock had registered on his face. "No, I knew nothing about any of that," he stated, maybe a bit too emphatically, wondering what Geoffrey was into, picturing the beast at Geoffrey's home the night of the mountain party, all those dead high school kids on Yellow Mountain, how badly Geoffrey had been hurt when he and Colette found him on the bald, the lights of a UFO on the Rasterson girl's phone, and all the strange happenings since Orvin had met the eccentric young man.

"I don't feel well," Colette said, trying to stand up, her eyes lidded, dull.

"Let me get you to the car," Orvin said, not bothering to ask if it was okay to leave. If it wasn't, he figured he'd find out soon enough.

"We'll be in touch, Mr. Littney," the policewoman said. Orvin looked at her over his shoulder as he guided Colette toward the exit. When they finally got outside, Colette magically transformed into a living, breathing member of the human race.

"Jeez, I thought we'd never get out of there," Colette said, walking briskly toward her car as if to avoid any more interaction with the police.

"You're okay, then?" Orvin said, quickening his pace to catch up to her.

"I was a bit loopy at first, but I feel fine."

When they reached the car, Colette pulled out her keys and unlocked the doors, then headed for the driver's side. "Want me to drive?" Orvin asked, concerned she wasn't completely herself yet.

"No, I'm good," she said, throwing herself into the front seat. "I need some food. How about you?"

"Sure, I could eat."

Before she started the vehicle, she looked over at Orvin. "What really happened back there?" she said, her breezy demeanor suddenly on hold. Orvin wasn't sure where to start.

"You were shot, Colette." Orvin didn't want to add that she was also dead, never completely certain, but either way, didn't like thinking about it.

She nodded. "Yes, I thought that, but... how is it that I am sitting here with you?" She looked over at him, bewilderment marshaling her features. Orvin reached into his jacket pocket and pulled out the bloody slug and opened his palm toward her.

"What's that?" she said.

"That's the bullet Geoffrey pulled out of your body..."

She regarded Orvin with curiosity, her features seemingly drawn into a memory she couldn't quite make sense of, yet. She reached down and twisted the key until the engine hummed, then checked the rearview mirror before pulling from the parking space.

50

TWO HUNDRED AND FORTY MINUTES

EDWARD'S female assistant monitored Geoffrey's vitals. The woman looked over at him and gave him a quick shake of her head, letting him know it wasn't good. He figured Geoffrey's health was already compromised from the encounters with the beast earlier in the week, and that's why his body wasn't responding more robustly to this latest trauma. Geoffrey had a profound physiology. *The Associates* had discovered this shortly after the invisibility experiment at the Philadelphia Navy Yard. It was part of the reason they had chosen him, that, and the fact of his background, the death of his parents at a young age, his resilience, both mental and physical, in coming back from that early childhood tragedy. His military profile reflected his durable nature, his optimism and buoyant personality, his eagerness to help and care and protect his shipmates. Plus, his intelligence scores would have been remarkable for anyone, but especially so for someone who had only completed the eighth grade. No, Peter Smithwick had been the perfect candidate, just the subject *The Associates* had hoped to produce from the risky electromagnetism experiment from over a half-century earlier. From all their previous research, they knew the human genome could be altered and enhanced through this type of directed and powerful energy, that the experiment, if successful, was capable of switching on dormant genes, ones that most humans never have advantage of. Even though *The Associates* had never mastered the math completely, they were nevertheless thrilled to discover—after extricating Peter Smithwick from the bulkhead—that they had inadvertently created the perfect research subject, becoming the beneficiaries of the most profound, and somewhat unexpected, miracle.

Now it seemed they could lose Geoffrey at any moment.

Edward pulled out his phone and punched a number from his favorites. "Edward Turley. I need a medivac out here on Interstate 81, stat."

He waited a moment until the person came back on the phone. "We have your location. We'll scramble someone to your location in five minutes. Look for us. Plenty of vacant farmland next to the highway."

"Good," Edward said, ending the call. "Keep your eyes out for it," Edward told the two men in the front seat. Edward looked over at the medical assistant. She was injecting something into Geoffrey's portable IV, her attention focused, her eyes grave.

After several long minutes, the man in the passenger seat spoke over the back of the seat. "It's landing up ahead."

Edward looked through the windshield between the two men. The chopper was coming down thirty feet from the shoulder of the highway. The only thing between them and the craft was a deep gulley and a barbed-wire fence.

"Can you get over there?" Edward said.

"No problem, boss," the man said, motioning for the driver to plow through the flimsy fence and get close to the chopper. Edward leaned down against Geoffrey, trying to steady him for the rough ride. They always brought a medical assistant to Geoffrey's seminars, but Edward was now rethinking that strategy, believing that having a chopper standing by made more sense, with a full medical array of equipment and two medical technicians; Geoffrey Cannon was a precious and irreplaceable commodity; *The Associates* would not be pleased if Geoffrey Cannon died on Edward's watch.

The Suburban slowed somewhat, then kicked up a tumult of dust and stones crossing the shoulder, rocking and jouncing through the gulley, tossing the passengers against the doors and headliner as the SUV shot up the other side of the ravine, smashing through the barbed-wire fence, dragging it and weathered posts across the tall weeds toward the helicopter until the fencing snapped. Medical attendants waited with the gurney, rushing over to the black Suburban when it came to a stop. The rear door flew open and the female assistant held the IV as the medivac EMTs lifted Geoffrey from the car onto the gurney, lashing him down, then hustling him across the rough field. In minutes they had him aboard the craft, lifting off.

Edward told the drivers to get back on the highway before they attracted attention. This had been a risky move in daylight, but so far so good, no highway patrol or local sheriffs. The driver steered the big vehicle back across the barbed-wire lying on the ground, then through the gully and back onto the highway, Edward instructing them to head back to Bristol so he could get his car.

The medivac chopper destination was an isolated ridge in the Bays Mountain range near Kingsport. Detection was always a bit chancy during daylight hours, but the situation called for furtiveness, and *The Associates* had mastered stealth. They most likely had Geoffrey aboard already, performing their stunning feats. At least that's what Edward hoped. The whole maneuver had taken about forty minutes, but Edward had his car now, finally back on 81 headed for Kleary Creek. He would rendezvous with them later that evening on Yellow Mountain. Not knowing how Geoffrey was doing tied a knot in Edward's stomach, the same one that started appearing the previous week with Geoffrey's insistence on confronting the beast. *The Associates* tried to assure Edward that everything would be all right, that most likely Geoffrey was correct in his assumption that the creature would never kill him, the creature knowing on some level that if it did, it would eliminate itself as well. And that assumption had borne itself out—the creature could have killed Geoffrey at any time, yet hadn't.

Edward took his focus to the road, suddenly hungry. He pulled off at the first food exit, and settled on some burgers and fries at the drive-through window, tucking the bag between his legs. He unwrapped the sandwich with his teeth and free hand, lettuce and sauce dripping into the open sack. It would take him three hours to get back to Kleary, and another forty-five to get to Yellow Mountain, then another twenty to hike to the bald. It would be just around four hours before his meeting with *The Associates*. But not knowing Geoffrey's condition, that two-hundred-and-forty-minute trip would feel like a lifetime.

51

IN LEAGUE WITH DARK FORCES

THREE DAYS since Mr. Cannon's seminar in Bristol and Colette still couldn't parse what had happened that morning. Orvin had told her she'd been shot by a gunman, but she couldn't recall any of that, had no memory of pain or discomfort. She remembered the man standing up and pointing the gun, then Mr. Cannon shielding her from the attacker with his body. She really couldn't say what had happened to her that day, but something had definitely changed. In the bathroom mirror Colette didn't see a woman transformed, necessarily, but she felt some new drift inside, some movement, lighter and more buoyant like the Colette she'd been in high school. Adventurous, but no longer reckless. No longer the risktaker. Mellowed in life-affirming ways, but unfortunately, never free of the looming specter of regret coloring every thought, every desire. Why had she wasted so much of her life feeling ashamed and humiliated? So much squandered happiness, so much lost joy between her and Orvin. For years she convinced herself she'd married Orvin out of some kind of fire-sale mentality, that if he was willing to accept damaged goods, then why not. But she grew to love his gentleness and boundless heart, his patience and authenticity. And he'd always been handsome, growing more so as he aged. It was easy now to understand why she loved him, though having difficulty understanding what *he* saw in her.

"Oh, sorry," Orvin said, walking in on her still naked from her shower standing at the mirror. He turned away and was leaving when she said, "No, it's okay. Come back, I want to show you something."

When he stepped back in, Colette cupped her left breast and lifted it slightly.

"I'm not sure what I'm supposed to be seeing here," Orvin said a bit brusquely, locking his eyes on hers in the mirror, as if embarrassed looking at her breast as she was touching herself.

She spun toward him and tapped the small mark beneath her breast. "Look," she said.

Orvin leaned down closer. "What is that?"

"It's the scar from the bullet... where I was shot," she said, her eyes wide, her face blank.

"I'll be damned," he said, easing back from her, turning her slowly until he could see her back, bringing his fingertip to a pale mark no larger than a nickel. "A small scar here too." Then: "I guess that's where he removed it... somehow..."

She released her breast and stood facing Orvin, who looked perplexed. "It wasn't that I didn't believe you," she said. "But it just made no sense." And yet, she harbored this vague memory of floating above her own body on that stage, her dress wetting with blood, Geoffrey looking up at her with fierce determination as if he wasn't about to let her pass. Maybe that's what was new, the sudden and pervasive sense of her own mortality.

"He changed us," she finally said.

"What? Who?" Orvin said.

"It doesn't matter," she said, a velvety warmth spreading through her. She led Orvin to the bed and sat on the edge, positioning him until he was standing between her knees so she could undress him. They made love and fell asleep under the blankets.

The next few days were routine. Then, one night at supper, Colette asked Orvin about Mr. Cannon. He'd taken up refuge in her thoughts, not in an annoying way, yet always present, and she couldn't shake the feeling that he may not be okay.

"Not a word," Orvin said, chewing a bite of salad. "Called him several times. No answer."

"Have you driven up to his place?"

Orvin looked at her. "Why do you care? Don't you think it best we're free of him?"

"Why do you say that?"

Orvin asked if she remembered what the policewoman had told them after the shooting. Colette shook her head. Orvin started explaining about the dead women, that the police had been investigating Geoffrey for the three murders, but had found no connection.

"Do you think he had something to do with those women?"

Orvin sucked at his teeth and took a drink of iced tea. "I don't know, Colette, but... something's not right with that young man." Orvin just stared at her a moment. "And how about them kids on Yellow Mountain. Mason's boy, Renny, and them others?"

"You think he was responsible for those kids?"

"I don't know, Colette, but there's more you don't know about him."

"Like what?"

Orvin scrunched up his face, as if he'd just opened a can of pork and beans that had gone bad. "I told you about that *thing* I saw at the mountain party at Geoffrey's place that night, well... I think he has something to do with that. Hell, it ain't just me... Geoffrey himself thinks he might be responsible for it. That's why he went up to Yellow Mountain that night, to see if he could figure things out... that's what messed him up so bad. He's lucky it didn't kill him..."

Colette couldn't understand how Mr. Cannon could have anything to do with a creature like the one Orvin described, but she knew Geoffrey was unusual. He had powers that were not easily understood. She said, "I know I told you that I thought he was evil... but... I don't think he is." Even though the stories Orvin had just shared with her made a strong case that Mr. Cannon was in league with dark forces, she no longer felt in her heart that he was wicked. Now she sensed a deep and simple goodness in him, ever since that night she had looked around inside his home. She felt it again the day of the seminar, and at the hospital when she presented the newspaper article to him. His denials had been based in truth; she was almost certain of that. Nevertheless, he had withheld something that day, but not for nefarious reasons. And at the seminar that morning—he had not faked his excitement over seeing her and Orvin in the audience. She would have known. He'd been genuinely thrilled they had attended.

"I don't think it's wise to have any further contact with the man," Orvin said. "I already feel guilty I never told Mason or Wyatt what I knew about this creature and Geoffrey and all that." Orvin shook his head, his eyes on his plate, his large hands resting on the table, unmoving. "I mean, Mason lost his only son... and I..."

"What good would it have done?"

Orvin's face reddened, his eyes squeezed to hard lines. "I can't believe you'd say something like that!" His features softened over a long interval of bristly silence, as if he were running all the scenarios in his head. "I suppose you're right," he finally said. "Them kids was already dead. Having to accept the existence of some crazy monster, and having to chase it through the mountains would have been more than anyone could handle."

They finished their supper without further discussion. Colette could tell Orvin was still troubled when he didn't say anything while they washed dishes. Afterward, he just retired to the living room and Colette heard the television come on. The sound kept changing—voices clipped mid-sentence, a few notes of music, partial sirens, five words of an announcement, laughter cut off—and Colette knew Orvin wasn't watching the television as much as babysitting it. She dried her hands and put a few things away in the fridge, then went to be with Orvin. As soon as she walked into the living room, Orvin shut the television off. She sat down and was about to ask why he'd done that.

Orvin spoke first. "I know we don't know Mr. Cannon, not really, but... he did save my life, kind of... I mean, he sort of put it in jeopardy in the first place, I guess. But he did save your life on that stage... I know that for a fact... but, I guess if he hadn't been messing around with that feller's wife and... oh, hell, I don't know. I'm just so damn confused about the whole dadblamed thing."

Colette came over and squatted down next to Orvin's lounger and put her hand on his knee. Orvin looked at her, shaking his head. "Now don't twist this into something it's not, but I'm not in the mood for more lovemaking right now. I've been really... you know... enjoying it, if that doesn't sound stupid, but right now—"

"I just wanted to go get ice cream," she said, smiling, so thankful Orvin had stuck around long enough for her to feel all these things. "I love you so much."

Orvin sat forward and placed his hand on hers, his eyes softening to liquid. "I don't know what I ever done to deserve you, Colette," he said. "You're as radiant as the first day I saw you back in high school."

They both stood and Colette hugged him, kissing him on the lips. They held the embrace for nearly half a minute before Colette leaned back to look into Orvin's eyes. "Maybe after ice cream, we could go for a drive. How does that sound?" Colette said.

Orvin nodded, kissed her again, then said, "And if we find ourselves near Geoffrey's place... I suppose we could take a run up the mountain to check on him..."

52

THE AGRICULTURAL
ADJUSTMENT ACT

WHEN GEOFFREY WOKE, he wasn't sure where he was. A blinding light directly above him made it hard to see. Maybe it was a hospital in Bristol, an operating room with lots of machinery beeping and blinking, but no doctors. No one at all. Someone came in and walked over to one of the metallic counters, their back to him. Geoffrey was about to say something when he noticed how strange the person looked. Geoffrey assumed it was a man by the person's build, but the long straight hair threw him off a bit, until the person turned to the side a bit and Geoffrey could see the full beard and mustache. When Geoffrey's eyes focused more clearly, it seemed the man had some kind of glow around his head, and Geoffrey thought maybe it was the IV in his arm, the drugs offering up the strange illusion. As the man exited the room, he looked over at Geoffrey and smiled, pulling his hood back over his head, finally gliding away. He had a dark, Mediterranean complexion. But as the tall man walked out, Geoffrey noticed his long robes, like vestments or something, a red garment draped over one shoulder and lashed at his waist, trailing down over a white cassock trimmed in gold. He hadn't meant to think of *Jesus*, or at least pictures he'd seen of the enigmatic savior, but that's where Geoffrey's mind went. And he couldn't be sure, but it seemed the man was wearing sandals.

A few moments later Edward walked in. "I see you're still among the living," Edward said, and smiled, genuinely happy to see him, Geoffrey thought.

"Where am I?" Geoffrey asked.

Edward hesitated a moment, then said, *"The Lodge."*

"What about the dark glasses? Why am I not wearing those?"

Edward shrugged. *"The Associates* didn't think it was necessary anymore," Edward said. This notion worried Geoffrey. It had been necessary for over seventy years, why not now? Were *The Associates* done with him, ready to dispose of him so he could never divulge anything he knew about them? Or was he already dead? That notion knocked him back a little.

Before Geoffrey could speak, two military officers walked in and called Edward aside. They looked like generals, with ribbons and medals dangling from their chests. Edward walked over and conversed with them. Two more military personnel walked in and stationed themselves at the doorway. More people entered now—as if some break had ended and everyone was coming back on shift—men and women in lab coats, and other beings wearing long brown robes like Druids, with hoods completely concealing their faces in shadow. These beings moved about the interior as if on a cushion of air, while the white lab coats had all the mechanical movement of normal human beings.

Edward drifted back over when he finished with the brass, who had left the room. Everyone else was busy doing important-looking things, pushing buttons, taking readings, punching in calculations on hand-held devices, examining readouts and studying data. The Druid characters communicated with one another in a series of low, strange sounds, then worked with equipment of a sort Geoffrey had never witnessed before. Even though the physical attributes and garb differed greatly between the white coats and the Druids, he intuited an unspoken harmony, everyone working in concert, never getting in one another's way. The scene had the bizarre quality of a dream, or a sardonic B-grade movie. Geoffrey assumed it was the drugs flowing into his arm—he felt no pain, nothing of the gunshot or the wounds from the beast—and decided that nothing he was seeing was real.

A young woman walked over to the metal bed Geoffrey was lying on and added a new bag to the IV stand, then fiddled with the plumbing and valves.

"They're going to put you out again, Geoffrey," Edward said softly. "They're gonna run some scans. I'll see you when you wake up."

Before Geoffrey could protest or ask questions or inquire into whether this was a ruse to end his life, the new bag of drugs was smooth and precise, the liquid quickly finding the off switch in his brain.

When Geoffrey woke this time he knew exactly where he was, the smallish, austere room that provided his temporary accommodations during his visits to *The Lodge*. Here he would be monitored through the camera mounted on the ceiling, which had all the charm of a department store security system, the dark, Big-Brother eyeball staring down from above, always observing, always present.

Edward walked in and closed the door behind him.

"What's going on?" Geoffrey asked, sitting up, a bit frustrated with the weirdness of his situation. "I mean, what's with the military big wigs, and the Druid things? And who was the priest guy? Is he here because I died, or might die? Are we in outer space right now, like flying around planets, or just orbiting earth? Or is this some elaborate Hollywood movie set somewhere underground in the middle of the desert? How long have I been here? Do I ever get to leave?"

Edward sat down in the only available chair and sighed. "Feeling better?" he said.

Geoffrey shook his head. "What's going on, ET? Don't I deserve some answers?"

Edward shrugged. "Deserve? I don't know about that, but… you've been here for almost two weeks. And yes, we're in outer space, but not orbiting earth. Far away from any detection systems. And yes, of course you get to leave… eventually. But they want to make sure you're okay. And they wanted to run further tests to see how things are progressing…"

Edward sat a moment, looking into Geoffrey's eyes.

"Progressing?" Geoffrey said.

"Well, not progressing, I guess. I'm not a scientist. They've been mapping your genome, want to check stuff out, you know, searching for any changes in your genes or anything…" Then, Edward said with a frown: "How do I know? All this science gives me a headache."

Geoffrey wanted more answers than this, suddenly gloomy over the memories that surfaced in his ride from the seminar in Bristol. "I killed them," Geoffrey blurted out. "I killed my stepmother and her lover. That memory came back to me all at once… when I was dying on that chopper from Tennessee…"

Edward remained quiet, nonplussed, regarding Geoffrey with mild curiosity, like an insect, then said, "You don't know that for sure, Geoffrey. Memories are mercurial at best… *The Associates* want to perform another NHI on you…"

"Okay, good... then you'll see! Let's get it going!"

Edward stood up nodding, then told Geoffrey to close his eyes and relax. He wasn't sure when they would start it, but it didn't matter, as long as Geoffrey was lying down. "And if you fall asleep, that's fine. They'll bring you into a state more conducive to memory recall." Edward didn't smile, had shown no emotion at all as he glanced back at Geoffrey before closing the door.

What other purposes did Neural-Hypnagogic Induction serve other than memory recall? It must have been developed for some greater, or diabolical, use; it was far too complex and specific in its function. Why would *The Associates* even need technology this advanced solely for the purpose of mining memory from the subconscious, especially when hypnosis could maybe yield similar results? How often would they even need it? Something gave Geoffrey pause, especially recalling the military presence on the ship, and what Edward had said about The Montauk Project and mind control. Before he could explore his apprehension much further, a series of tones and beeps sounded in the room, the source undefinable at first, but then, a moment or two later, the sounds moved inwardly, now emanating from within his head. Time and space slowly devolved into a hollow, all-encompassing darkness, pin-point sensations along his scalp, his arms, chest and face, pulsing pressure points, the black void moving inward, spiraling down, nothing to see. Awhirl in movement, he vanishes, the world growing brighter, the farm rough and ignored. Peter Smithwick is fourteen, quite large and strapping for his age, due in part to the Reverend Jacob selling the mule two years earlier to afford repairs on the wagon, leaving Peter to plow the fields without help. The task and the sun and the harsh conditions grew the youth quickly, creating muscle and sinew where there had only been smooth, boyish flesh. The day before the storm, Peter's father, Reverend Jacob, instructed Peter on slaughtering all the pigs, that the only way they could keep the farm going was to accept the money from the government's Agricultural Adjustment Act, put in place to help raise the price of pork, and keep farmers from going under. It was a controversial move, given how much hunger and starvation the country was undergoing, but the Smithwicks, like most farming families, had no choice, they needed the money—while some people jumped out of windows and fell to their death on the days following the crash in 1929, many folks, even four years later, especially farmers, were still falling.

"You have to kill the whole passel of them young pigs, boy,"

Reverend Jacob told Peter. "Except them pregnant sows... government has other plans for them."

Peter didn't really know who the government was, but the way the Reverend spoke of them, they must have been in league with the devil. Now, it seems, this *government* is going to pay them to kill all their pigs, and Peter can't figure out how that makes any sense.

Reverend Jacob hands Peter a small box of ammo for the pistol. Seven shiny brass bullets sit in the bottom of the carboard box, and they have over fifty pigs.

"I can't afford no more bullets right now," the Reverend says. "So, you have to slit their throats." The Reverend's eyes are hidden in the shade from the brim of his black hat.

Peter imagines the mess it's going to be, the chaos, and doesn't relish killing them at all. He slaughtered hogs before, usually one, maybe two, but not over fifty in an afternoon. He isn't even sure how he will manage the massacre.

"The government boys'll be by in a few days for the head count. They'll haul off the dead carcasses," the Reverend explains to Peter. Later that afternoon the preacher packs up the wagon and leaves for his soul-saving-gospel-spreading goodwill tour of the nearby counties. Reverend says folks need the word of God more than ever now, with all the hardship and destitution, they need to believe in something, need to prop themselves up with hope.

The next afternoon John Bennett drives up in his old Model T and parks around the back of the house, out of sight from the dirt road. Peter is headed for the pig pen with the pistol. John climbs the back steps to the house, glancing over at Peter, smiling midstride, then opening the back door and letting himself in without knocking. The screen door slaps shut and Peter stands a moment, staring at the empty space on the porch where the man had been seconds earlier. After loading the pistol, Peter opens and shuts the gate to the pigpen, then sits on the ground with the gun lying in the dirt next to him. Several pigs hurry over to him. They are used to Peter, to his smell, have become familiar with him providing food, supplying plenty of water. And Peter has grown accustomed to them, not as pets, but as living creatures worthy of care and consideration. So it is hard when he grasps the first pig and presses the pistol against its head and pulls the trigger. The pig squeals and breaks loose and Peter is shocked the creature isn't dead. It runs in circles, screeching, bleeding from under the flesh of its neck and Peter jumps up to chase after it. Finally catching up to it, he aims for its head, striking it near the front haunch, dropping it to the dirt, blood pouring from the wound as the pig squeals, exciting the other pigs to start squealing. Running over to it, he puts the next bullet in the pig's head, silencing it, the bullet passing through the skull. By now the other pigs are swarming the dead one, lapping at its blood, rooting into the wounds with their snouts for the warm red juice. Peter tries to shoo them, but the small creatures are like magnets, drawn irrevocably to the blood. Peter kicks at the shrieking, ravenous creatures, pushing them away, but more come, fighting, biting at one another. Unable to fend them off, Peter shoots another through the skull, then another, and another, until the gun is empty. Now the pigs gather at that end of the pen, sopping up blood, squealing, shrieking.

"What the hell's going on, Peter!" Lauralee screams from the back porch, bent forward, her elbows resting on the railing. Her breasts are clearly visible from the drooping neckline of her nightgown. She is petite, and though she is only in her twenties, possesses a coarse mature beauty forged through difficulty and strife. "Why in the fuck are you killing all our goddamn pigs? Are you out of your mind?"

John walks out behind her in his long underwear. Wrapping his arms around her waist, he presses up against her from behind, smiling. "Has to," John says, reaching his palms around to fondle her breasts, "if you want that government money, sweet cheeks. The AAA."

Lauralee spins her head around as if the answer might be found in John Bennett's eyes. Clearly she doesn't understand what he's talking about. "Agricultural Adjustment Act," John says, the tip of his tongue sliding along the upper lip of her mouth. "Had to kill mine, too."

Lauralee shifts her eyes back to Peter, her attention clearly on what John is doing to her from behind. She arches her back and moans, eyes closed, her slender white fingers clenched to the railing. As Peter watches the couple, John slips his hand up under her nightgown to clutch her breast. Peter is woozy and disoriented, an uncompromising new angle to the world, the pigs dying over and over behind his eyes, the blood spurting, the smell of them, their screeching and shrieking like tormented wraiths still circling his feet, slurping at the blood. Lauralee moans louder, head back, her white neck exposed like the stem of a fragile lily, while John, with eyes closed, pumps his hips into her. Peter had witnessed something like this a few years ago with Kotter's beagles in the front yard.

A warm, cloying acid rises into Peter's esophagus, his body shuddering under a disturbing current—revulsion over his stepmother and John, but mostly over his own arousal. He drops the empty pistol in the dirt, then opens the gate to the pen. His shirt and trousers are blotched with fresh blood where he'd tried to pry the live pigs off the bleeding ones. Withdrawing his knife from his pocket, he glides up the steps of the porch on silent feet, placing himself a foot away from John, who is of slight build, a few inches shorter than Peter, and not nearly as strong. John, with his senses tuned to a different reality, is completely unaware Peter is standing there.

Peter grabs John from behind and in one fluid, practiced motion—his muscles remembering all the hogs he's slaughtered in his lifetime—slits John's throat. It is so easy Peter can't understand why killing the pigs with the pistol had been so damn hard. Lauralee spins around, trying to piece together this odd puzzle, John lying in a heap at Peter's feet, blood gurgling onto the porch planks, Peter visibly aroused. She regards John with the indifference of someone who witnesses death on a daily basis, then says to Peter, "What are you doing?" Peter steps closer to her, pulling her to him, pressing her against his body. His hands slip up along the slender shaft of her pale neck, his fingers tightening over the tendons beneath her skin, the knife lying on the floor at his feet. Lauralee, apparently misreading the gesture, lowers her fingers to undo his trousers. Peter tightens his grip and she smiles, then turns in his arms, pushing her naked bottom firm against his groin. She starts to bend over but he brings her back straight. She seems to welcome the rough play and relaxes into him, pushing against his crotch and moaning. When he turns her to face him, she smiles, lifts her left leg, propping her foot on the chair so he can enter her from the front, his large hands closing on her throat, his thumbs pressing into her windpipe. Grinning with pleasure, she closes her eyes, mewling, then wriggles desperately in his grip when the next breath doesn't come, her hands coming to her throat, trying to pry off his thick fingers, her expression bristling with concern, then fear, until her eyes disconnect from the world, her knees falling prey to gravity. Peter catches her mid fall, adjusting his hands beneath her armpits to keep her shoulders and head suspended.

Peter drags her limp body across the porch, her dirty, bare heels bumping along the weathered boards. Elbowing the door open with one arm, balancing her against his stomach, he drags her inside to their bedroom and arranges her naturally on the mattress, leaning her against the headboard, her neck bruised and discolored. He then drags John to the bedroom and, in less than fifteen minutes, has reunited the lovers, both of them braced against the headboard, John's neck lined with blood, both their heads drooping like ragdolls.

Finished, he walks back to the pig pen to slaughter the remainder of the passel, slitting their throats, battling the tide of cannibalistic animals feeding on the lifeblood of their brethren. Then silence, no more squealing and shrieking, just the faint rumble of distant thunder from the green storm building in the eastern sky.

Peter has no idea how long he sat on the ground in the middle of the carnage, carcasses everywhere. Near dusk the Reverend's wagon works up the dirt road and rattles to a stop in front of the house. The Reverend comes over to inspect Peter's task, then walks over to where the boy is seated, the bloody knife still clutched in the lad's maroon-stained hands.

"Peter? Are you okay, boy?"

Peter isn't sure he hears the Reverend speak, but knows the old man is standing before him. He hopes the government men come soon, before all these pigs start rotting and reek worse than they already do. The stink has burrowed into Peter's clothes, into the cells of his skin, deep into the marrow of his bones, a stench that will never leave. The Reverend helps the boy to his feet, pulls his shirt over his head, then helps him remove the trousers until Peter stands naked—his pale white figure stark against the blackening sky. The Reverend guides the boy to the rain barrel and splashes water on him, using the shirt like a rag to wash the boy down.

"Go put on a fresh shirt and trousers," the Reverend tells him. The elderly man follows Peter into the house. When Peter comes to the kitchen dressed, the Reverend ushers the boy outside. In the backyard is a small fire and Peter sees his bloodstained clothes singed and smoking in the throat of the flames. The two of them walk over to the hatch of the root cellar where the Reverend orders Peter down the steps. Before he closes the wooden doors, the Reverend says, "Peter, no matter what happens, boy, you are never to speak of this day again. To anyone, for any reason. Do you understand me?" Peter isn't sure of anything, not even what the preacher means. Other than slaughtering the pigs, which the Reverend had told him to do, there wasn't much else to tell. Peter wants to ask if the preacher's trip was successful, if the Reverend helped a lot of people, gave them hope, but mostly Peter wanted to know if he, Peter, has done a good job with the pigs. They're all dead, and yet, they keep dying, every few minutes, dying over and over again, squealing and shrieking, interspersed with moments of calm before they start dying again—Peter wonders if they'll ever stop, if they'll ever be silent.

"Not a word, Peter. Promise me, not one word about any of this."

As the wooden doors squeak shut, they bring the darkness with them, a container of solid black air that Peter cannot trust or connect to, as if he's floating through a starless night sky. He hears the preacher wedge a metal crow bar between the handles, locking the hatch from the outside. Peter has no food, no water, and knows he'll be dead in a matter of days. But it's okay. This is a good place to die, away from those rotting pigs, their dead eyes and maddening noise, their stench and disgusting proclivities, their indecent ways.

Peter finds a place in the corner of the cellar, where he can hear the patter of tiny feet scampering across the earthen floor. Rats, he figures. At least they don't smell. Just as Peter starts to close his eyes, a loud blast echoes through the house above him, shaking loose old dust from between the floorboards above his head. Peter had forgotten all about the Reverend's shotgun. Then another blast, followed by a moment of silence, stretching endlessly across the empty void of the dusky cellar. The silence has barely settled, when a third blast rocks Peter's nerves, making him jump, followed by a loud metallic clattering along the wooden planks, then a single, solid thud coming down hard on the boards.

Later that night, Peter hears the storm bending the house above him, the rain beating on the cellar hatch like an angry spirit. Peter sees puddles of blood expanding through the pig pen inside his skull, congealing into rivulets seeping beneath the fence. Lumps of pink flesh lie lifeless in the mud, throats slit, heads bent at disturbing angles, legs stiff and unmoving. He remembers blood on the back porch near the railing, where Lauralee had yelled at him about killing the pigs. With his eyes closed, Geoffrey can see blood dissolving under slanting walls of rain, dripping through the wood slats onto the dark untouched earth below the back-porch boards. He's unable to recall how the blood got on the boards in the first place. His only hope is that if he ever gets out of the root cellar, if he doesn't die in the dark alone, to be eaten by rats, he prays he never has to witness so much blood again.

53

NEVER UNDERESTIMATE FEAR

GEOFFREY WAS NEARLY GAGGING on the words he needed to say out loud, feeling like he could puke at any moment.

"I have to turn myself in," Geoffrey said.

"Turn yourself into what?" Edward said with more than a hint of sarcasm.

"This isn't a joke, ET," Geoffrey said, explaining to Edward about the memory that came during the NHI procedure, about killing all the pigs because of a governmental mandate. Even now, Geoffrey could still see all the blood, hear the squealing. "My stepmother came out on the porch barely dressed, with John, her lover. They started fucking right in front of me," Geoffrey told Edward. "I was covered in blood, sick to my stomach, pigs screeching and attacking each other. And Lauralee. I hated her, all her cheating and screwing every time my pa was away. I don't know why the Reverend ever married her in the first place." Geoffrey stopped to gather himself. "I just lost it. I was so repulsed by what they were doing, by what I was doing to those pigs... and by my own arousal... everything was spinning out of control. Before I slaughtered the last of the pigs, I walked up on the porch and... and..." Geoffrey flushed with shame, horror, unable to bear the weight of this epiphany, the knowledge of his wickedness a reality he could never escape through good deeds— this horrendous, appalling event, Geoffrey thought, will be the moment I relive over and over for the rest of my life...

A long silence sat between the two men. Geoffrey wondered if

Edward was outraged, or disgusted, as he himself was. "That's why I have to turn myself in," Geoffrey finally said.

Edward sat forward, shaking his head.

"I killed two human beings!" Geoffrey shouted. "And then my father killed himself because of me, to hide my crime, then locked me in the root cellar to give me a credible alibi! It isn't right."

Edward was quiet for a short spell. "You can't turn yourself in," he said flatly. "First off, that was 1933. Over ninety years ago! You think anyone is going to look at how young you are and ever believe you...? They'll just think you're crazy, and if you do something as stupid as confess to a crime from almost a century ago, one you committed when you were a kid, then maybe you are crazy..."

"How do you know what year it was?"

Edward chuckled a little. "Do you think *The Associates* just happened to save *you* during that invisibility experiment in Philadelphia, out of everyone that could have been saved? You think they just randomly chose *you?*"

Geoffrey was confused. He had no idea why they salvaged his life above others.

"They know everything about you," Edward said. "Hell, they may even be aware that you killed your stepmother and her lover, for all I know. The point is, they don't care about such things. You're special, Geoffrey. You're bigger than your stepmother and her secret admirer."

"Nobody is above their crimes, ET."

Edward scoffed. "Oh, brother. The most disturbing part of that statement is that I know you're serious."

Geoffrey didn't know what to make of any of this. Why was Edward taking this so lightly?

Even so, Edward seemed to be struggling with something. The dapper man looked up at the ceiling, at the big dark eyeball staring back with bloodless detachment. He waited a few moments.

"Okay, so, I think it's okay to tell you what I am about to say." Edward explained that the aliens, the *Druids* as Geoffrey had called them, are working with top-secret government operatives, run by General Martin now, but has been passed along for decades, different personnel, new operatives, new generals, all in an effort to study Geoffrey, who, because of his unique enhanced DNA structure due to The Philadelphia Experiment, developed amazing special skills. One of which was the effect that he could impose on crowds, the ability to stream their minds into a single, cohesive conduit, to alter their will.

"They've been researching mind control for over two hundred years," Edward said. "That's what The Montauk Project was all about. But this, what you're able to do… a whole new stratosphere. A game-changer. No one ever expected anything like this. The mother lode of all Magical Mystery Tours. Superhuman, Geoffrey. The fucking Übermensch! Nietzsche's wet dream." Edward paused as if to let this information register completely in Geoffrey's mind.

"That had been the main thrust of the research," Edward continued, "until the *beast* showed up." Edward laughed with excitement. "Man, was that ever the fringe benefit of the century, quickly becoming the new focus of this covert military research. I mean, this beast you conjured up out of thin air… man, that's power, Geoffrey. That's real control-the-fucking-world power—an immortal, invincible monster! Are you kidding me? We need to know how it works. And we'll figure it out, okay? Just be patient. And the delayed-aging thing… fantastic. You are the human of the future; the American of tomorrow. And we'll get there. All in time, Geoffrey, and we've got plenty of that."

Geoffrey's mind was unspooling, a whorl of hallucinations tumbling along the inside of his skull, images and notions and information spinning into a maelstrom of datum he could not find storage for, the circuits jamming, electrons firing out of sequence. Suddenly dizzy, he tried a mantra, which felt like bubblegum in his brain, clogging the thought process, his equilibrium failing, his motor-skills faulty. He tried his eyes and found only darkness, his lungs suddenly failing devices in his chest. The world was collapsing in on itself and Geoffrey could do nothing but follow the current into the dark chasm opening inside his head.

One of the medical team brought Geoffrey back to the world, and was taking his pulse when he opened his eyes. A beautiful woman in her thirties. A pleasant fragrance floated on the air near Geoffrey's face when she stood to leave. "He'll be okay now," she said to Edward, then opened the door and walked out.

Geoffrey looked over at Edward, still groggy, his tongue like wet plaster. He looked around for his glass of water. Edward reached over and handed it to him. When Geoffrey emptied the glass, he put it down and said, "How do you do it? How do you keep all these people, like that attractive young woman who was just here, how do you keep them from exposing all of this to the world?" Geoffrey made a wide gesture with his hands, as if to encompass the entire spaceship and everyone on it.

"Dedication. Loyalty. More money than they could hope to earn in three lifetimes." Edward said. "I don't know. They're patriots, Geoffrey. They love America. They want this country to succeed, but more than that, to dominate. Despite the politics and bullshit, which is merely white noise against the backdrop of what we're accomplishing on this ship. We have a good thing going here in this country, and if we can stay in the lead, we can affect real change in the world."

Geoffrey didn't believe for a second that Edward believed what he was saying.

"Rule through example..." Edward said, "and superiority. And never underestimate fear."

Finally, the real crux... that's what Edward really believed. Geoffrey said, "What about the beast? Have we made any progress on that?"

"*The Associates* believe it's a non-issue now," Edward said, sitting back in his chair. Edward went on to tell Geoffrey that *The Associates* believed the beast was most likely vanquished after this last NHI, upon Geoffrey's realization about his past, that Geoffrey's deep buried secret provided the fertile soil to birth the monster. "The unconscious material of your psyche was like a subliminal petri dish," Edward said, seemingly amused by the simile for some reason. "If it will put your mind at ease; not one suspect murder anywhere around here in over two weeks."

"Two weeks?" Geoffrey said.

"Yeah, Sleeping Beauty. You've been getting some much-needed R&R."

Geoffrey's entire existence had been a sham, with all the gravitas and impact of a cheesy magic show, smoke and mirrors, trapdoors and false bottom-boxes, silly illusions that added up to nothing. How they had used him. Was anything real?

"What was the point of the seminars?" Geoffrey asked. "Why the ruse?"

Edward grimaced. "They weren't a ruse," he said. "Those were profoundly important, Geoffrey. Don't start down the pity path, thinking you've been *used* and 'woe is me' and all that crap. You have been at the hub of world-altering discoveries. *The Associates* had researchers at every seminar, studying the effects of your talks and the mental mastery you displayed over entire audiences. They were astounded by your abilities.

During your talks, they recorded brain activity, both yours and the audience members who were part of the research team. These volunteers were implanted with probes and attended strictly to provide neural and cognitive feedback. It was invaluable fieldwork. The kind of data *The Associates* gathered was light years ahead of the most sophisticated brain research available. Other scientists could only hope to collect even a fraction of this kind of data with their million-dollar fMRI machines. No, Geoffrey, your contribution is unparalleled. All of this," Edward said, spreading his arms in an all-encompassing gesture, "would be impossible without you. I hope you understand the importance of what you're doing; it will change the very way we live on this planet."

The disclosure gutted Geoffrey. He was struggling to process this information, realizing that all this time he was just being used. And no matter how crucial Edward tried to make this research seem, Geoffrey wanted nothing to do with their agenda. He needed to free himself from the bonds of government involvement in his life. And the aliens, whoever they were; he wanted to be free of all of them. Geoffrey was trying not to spook, fighting to conceal his outrage from Edward, but he desperately wanted off this ship, to get away from *The Associates,* and vanish from Kleary Creek for good.

"When's the next seminar?" Geoffrey asked.

Edward's face clouded over. "That's the thing, Geoffrey," he said, scratching his neck. "*The Associates* aren't sure these seminars are a good idea anymore, with all this negative publicity and everything. They're thinking of making an announcement that you died from the gunshot wound, that your private physicians did everything they could. Then they'll give you a new identity and we'll move forward. Maybe some other changes. How does that sound?"

"The seminars are everything to me, Edward!" Geoffrey said, suddenly claustrophobic, not at all wild about the *other* changes *The Associates* were proposing, whatever they were. And pronouncing him *dead.* How convenient. Maybe he was more expendable than Edward let on. Geoffrey felt hemmed in, the walls pressing in closer. What was he supposed to do until all of this happened? Sit in this crappy little room like a prisoner?

"That seems a bit drastic, don't you think?" Geoffrey said.

"What, discontinuing the seminars?" Edward said. "Or killing you off?"

Geoffrey couldn't swallow, his heart drumming, circuits shorting out inside his skull.

"You're absolutely white, Geoffrey! It was a joke... did you not hear anything I told you before? You're the golden calf, the pride of the fleet... no one is going to harm you..."

Geoffrey tried to restart his lungs without being obvious he was starved for air.

"Hey, nothing's certain yet," Edward said, reaching over to pat Geoffrey's shin. "If you feel that strongly about the seminars, I'm sure they'd be open to working something out, maybe move the venue across the country, spin the "crazy gunman" stuff to advantage. I don't know, but nothing's insurmountable. I'll have a chat with them. In the meantime, you need to rest and get yourself in shape again. You've had a hell of a few weeks!"

Edward stood to leave.

"Edward, can I head to the house, grab my research books?" Geoffrey said. "I'm going crazy here with nothing to do."

Edward looked quizzically at Geoffrey, then said, "Lots of time to meditate..."

Geoffrey sighed to himself.

"You have no sense of humor these days," Edward said. "Sure, it'll do us both good to get away from the manufactured gravity of this place for a few days. Get some greasy fast food and real beer."

Geoffrey forced a smile. "Did anyone bring my car back from Bristol?"

When Edward seemed to ponder that a moment, Geoffrey was afraid ET had read his thoughts. "I don't think so, but I have my ride. I can drive you," Edward said. "Get some rest. I'll be back shortly." Edward started to walk out.

"Hey wait," Geoffrey said. "Can I get up and walk around, you know, leave this tiny room?"

Edward hesitated. "Let me check," he said, about to leave.

What was the big deal? It wasn't like Geoffrey could find an emergency exit on the spaceship and sneak out. And Edward was impossible to measure—inscrutable one moment, joking the next, then staring sphinxlike at Geoffrey as if he'd mentioned something so worrying that Edward would have to take it under advisement. Like being trapped in a carnival funhouse, Geoffrey had grown weary of the uneven floors and wavy mirrors, Druid aliens and shifting illusions, being denied access to the real world. He had to figure out a way to get off this ship, and away from Edward long enough to make his escape.

With Edward at the door, Geoffrey sat up quickly and said, "Wait, ET... can we land? On Yellow Mountain? There's something I have to do."

54

ONE LAST THING

EDWARD WASN'T wild about the idea but Geoffrey didn't care. He had to make sure. Once he was standing in the middle of the bald, a trillion stars wheeling above his head, the spacecraft lifted slowly from the earth, the sedge and surrounding trees tossing wildly under its departure until the ship was gone from his view. A raw, eerie silence fell over the dark mountain. If the creature was gone, there'd be nothing to fret about. He and Edward had gone back and forth on that point, Edward arguing that the thing was gone, so why risk life and limb anymore, with Geoffrey contending if the beast was truly gone, then so was the risk. "At least let me hang behind with a rifle," Edward had said. Geoffrey had laughed, convinced they were lying to him. "You're not sure it's gone, are you? None of you are! Why would you lie to me?" Edward then grimaced and shook his head. "You are so paranoid, Geoffrey." Then, a few seconds later: "Fine. We'll put you down there and you can see for yourself."

That was over twenty minutes ago. Currently, standing in the middle of the bald, Geoffrey waited, his eyes scouring the far edge of the woods. Maybe Edward was right, maybe it was gone and Geoffrey was being paranoid. *The Associates* had said they'd give him an hour or so, then come back and check on him. "That should be plenty of time to satisfy your paranoia," Edward had said, obviously vexed by Geoffrey's persistence, as if Edward had pressing business somewhere else in the universe. Now Geoffrey was starting to think they were right, that the beast was gone, but it still bothered him that no one on the damn space-craft seemed to be sure of anything.

Geoffrey had just walked over and sat on a boulder, his eyes adjusting to the dark, when he spotted movement at the verge of the coppice, maybe fifty yards away. He stood slowly, watching the spot intently. Had he imagined it? He could feel his own breathing, aware of his own beating heart, which thudded with brittle anticipation. A moment later, he spotted it, stepping from the thicket, gnarly and foul as ever. *They lied, goddamn it!* Geoffrey wanted to believe Edward, believe *The Associates*, trust that they had everyone's best interest at heart, but they didn't. They were as wicked as the beast! As if it had heard him, the monster came to life, becoming agitated, stomping back and forth, like angry pacing, until it turned toward Geoffrey and charged him. At first Geoffrey tried to calm himself, settle his breathing, but his heart wouldn't have any of it. Run, he told himself, then realized, what's the point? No, just stand here and let it kill him, let it kill them both, then they'd be dead, he and this demon, and it would finally be over. That seemed to be the most fitting end to Geoffrey's guilt, a final chance to satisfy justice, rid his evil from the world once and for all. His crime against Lauralee, and John Bennet, even his own father, would finally meet with proper punishment, a just and fitting condemnation.

The creature was less than fifty feet away, closing fast, and Geoffrey thought he could feel the ground tremble from its mighty approach, each footfall like Thor's hammer slamming the earth, until it was upon him. Like a freight train it hit him. Geoffrey went down hard, the creature landing on top of him, the weight of the behemoth making it impossible for him to get air. Gasping, panic filling Geoffrey's body, he tried to let go, give himself to this fate, when the weight of the monster seemed to ease somewhat. Geoffrey stole a breath, then another, everything changing, the beast beginning to whimper, its sobbing low and mournful, the creature now light enough for Geoffrey to push it off.

Getting to his feet, about to flee, Geoffrey noticed a young man kneeling on the ground next to him, the man naked, his head resting against the dirt, his body convulsing under waves of tears. Unsure what was happening, Geoffrey edged away from the curious anomaly, putting distance between him and this new variant. The young man looked up, into Geoffrey's eyes, tears running down his cheeks. The young man was himself at fourteen, large and strong for his age, but still a boy for all his sinew and muscle. The frightened youth opened his mouth to speak, but nothing came out. Geoffrey eased closer and took him in his arms. The adolescent melted into him, holding him around the shoulders, his body shuddering under a rush of emotion.

"How can you ever forgive me?" the boy muttered almost unintelligibly through weeping and mewling. Geoffrey held him tighter, unsure what to say, when the boy was suddenly gone, Geoffrey's arms empty. Geoffrey looked around, nothing but darkness, a new gauzy light from the moon rising above the distant trees. Had he imagined the young man? He felt his shirt; it was soaked from the boy's tears. Geoffrey brushed off his pants, then looked around, going back over to sit on the boulder.

Twenty minutes later the huge saucer descended like a new sky, the lights snapping on suddenly, casting the natural setting into a swirling wash of carnival light. In moments it was on the ground. Edward walked over, Geoffrey meeting him halfway. They stopped and regarded each other in silence, a breeze shifting across the bald.

"You good now?" Edward said, cocking his head to the side to study Geoffrey's face. "What happened?" Edward reached over and touched Geoffrey's cheekbone, making him flinch. It was where the creature's head had collided with his cheek when the beast landed on top of him.

"I tripped. On a rock," Geoffrey said, not wanting to discuss what actually happened. Nevertheless, Geoffrey was finally satisfied the monster was gone for good. Even so, something was still wrong, and Geoffrey was not feeling great about the direction of things, especially with how certain Edward and *The Associates* had been that the creature no longer existed. Obviously, they had been wrong... or outright lied.

55

THE ESCAPE

ON THE DRIVE to Geoffrey's house, Edward explained that Geoffrey should grab only what he needed and leave the rest to him, that Edward would sell the house and furniture, the Range Rover and everything else he didn't need or want. "Think of it as an exciting new beginning..." Then, after a few seconds: "By the way, how's your French?" Edward quipped.

Geoffrey didn't get the joke, and wasn't sure this was *exciting*, or a *new beginning*. He wasn't sure what it was, but didn't want to wait around to find out. If he was going to escape, he'd have to do it before Edward drove him back to *The Lodge*, which is where they were headed once Geoffrey gathered what he needed from the house.

If his plan was to work, he knew it would depend on Orvin's goodwill, if there was any left after the crap he had exposed the elderly man to since they'd first met. Especially Colette getting shot. Geoffrey wondered how she was doing, if his efforts to save her had been in vain, if she'd died. A ruinous foreboding swept through Geoffrey just thinking about her; if she hadn't made it, Orvin would be devastated.

He glanced across the seat at Edward, who appeared lost in his own thoughts, his hands mechanically adjusting the steering wheel, his eyes fixed to the highway. The pervasive drone of rubber on asphalt filled the space between conversation. Edward was catching Geoffrey up on the latest thoughts of *The Associates*, explaining that maybe the seminars could continue, that they still had much to study in that arena. "Maybe a different venue," Edward said, glancing briefly across the seat. "How does France sound? Or Great Britain, Italy maybe? Spain? Greece? They saw these countries as thrilling opportunities."

Geoffrey just nodded and agreed, even at times thinking it would be exciting, but never losing his prime directive, which was to get away from all of them.

When Edward stopped for gas, Geoffrey knew this might be his only chance to escape. He was about to excuse himself to the restroom, when Edward started the pump and walked toward the entrance of the small building, leaving Geoffrey alone in the SUV. Geoffrey looked around, calculating his best route. Edward would come looking for him as soon as he discovered Geoffrey had fled. But he'd have a few minutes to hide and make a phone call.

Popping open the door, Geoffrey glanced toward the service station entrance, then walked toward the back as if looking for the restrooms. Once out of view of the entrance, he rushed up the small weedy slope at the rear of the building, then hurried through the stand of scrubby bushes and trees separating the back lot of the gas station from the country road. The gas station was now hidden from his view and he had no idea if Edward had returned to the vehicle. Even if he had, it was too soon for Edward to realize Geoffrey was gone. He trotted down the road toward a concrete bridge over a small creek and scrambled down the embankment to sit underneath, pulling out his phone. He dialed Orvin and waited for him to pick up, hoping he still would when he saw who was calling.

"Geoffrey!" Orvin said. "You're okay! We've been worried about you!"

Geoffrey was relieved to hear Orvin use the plural pronoun, meaning Colette had survived the gunshot. "Hi Orvin," Geoffrey said. "Colette's okay?"

"Yes. She's just fine." Then, a long hesitation followed by: "Can we talk about what happened that day?"

"Yes, of course, but I have a little problem right now and need your help."

Geoffrey quickly explained that he needed transportation out of Kleary Creek, and asked if Orvin could drive him to a bus station. Orvin agreed, then asked, "Are you at the house?"

"No, I'm... I'm under a bridge on some road called Multry Meadows Drive. Do you know it?"

"Under a bridge?"

"It's a long story, and I'll tell you everything… but right now, I just have to get out of Kleary."

"You know the Bristol Police are looking for you?"

"For me? Why? I was the one who was shot?"

"Yeah, that's kind of what they want to talk about. They've called me twice over the past couple of days, wondering if I heard from you…"

Geoffrey didn't want to put them in jeopardy with the authorities. "Okay, I'll figure something else out. And don't lie to the police if they call you again. Tell them you heard from me, and what I told you—"

"It'll take me about ten minutes to get over to Multry. I've painted a lot of homes over that way."

"No, Orvin, you can't. You could get in trouble with the—hold on a second!" Geoffrey said, pulling the phone away as a car approached the bridge. The car slowed, then stopped and idled above him on the road. Geoffrey looked around for a place to hide, settling for a few bushes near one of the support pillars. He squatted down close to the ground behind the rather sparsely-leaved shrubs and felt stupid, knowing that Edward would see him if he came down the steep bank.

"Are you still there?" Orvin's voice came over the phone.

"One second, Orvin," Geoffrey whispered, having not heard a car door open and shut yet. Just then another vehicle approached and honked the horn. The first vehicle on the bridge moved off slowly, as the other vehicle rumbled quickly over the bridge. Geoffrey had no idea where the first vehicle had gone, if it had driven off, or just pulled to the shoulder ahead. Geoffrey waited, his eyes fixed on the steep slope at the far side of the creek, expecting to see ET scrabbling down through the weeds, regarding Geoffrey with contempt. After waiting a brief time, Geoffrey climbed out of the ravine, carefully searching both sides of the road for parked cars.

"Orvin? You still there?" Geoffrey asked, slipping back down the hill to get out of view, then tucking himself back up under the bridge.

"I'm here," Orvin said. "We're coming to get you. Be there in ten."

"Are you sure?"

"Yeah, we're sure," Colette said. Orvin must have put Geoffrey on speaker. "Sit tight," Orvin added.

"Wait!" Geoffrey said, suddenly uneasy with the plan. "Don't come until dark, okay?"

Orvin must have been doing the math. "That's a couple of hours," Orvin said. "You gonna be okay till then?"

"Yeah, I'll be just fine. Thanks."

When the call disconnected, Geoffrey clambered back down the scruffy hillside and squatted near the creek, cupping his hands into a bowl to lift fresh, clear water to his face.

56

THE LONG DRIVE

COLETTE WAS behind the wheel parked on the shoulder, the car idling, her eyes on the rearview mirror, nothing but dark road behind and in front. A moment later two figures appeared at the car, the doors opening, the dome light shining brightly in the small interior. Colette smiled at Geoffrey as he slid into the backseat. When Orvin got in and shut the front passenger-side door, the dome light cut off.

"Thank you both so much," Geoffrey said as Colette checked her mirrors and pulled from the side of the road. "I'm so glad you're okay," he said, touching Colette's shoulder.

"I'm just fine," she said, asking if Geoffrey needed anything to eat, or drink. He said he was good. Colette guided the car onto the highway heading out of Kleary Creek. After they'd driven several minutes, Geoffrey asked how far it was to the closest bus station. Colette found him in the rearview mirror, then looked over at Orvin.

"We're gonna drive you wherever you need to go," Orvin said.

"I can't let you," Geoffrey said. "The bus station will be fine."

"We already decided," Orvin said. "Them buses is no way to travel."

"But I'm heading out west, like way out west, like Montana west..."

Orvin glanced over at Colette who nodded. "That'll be just fine," Orvin said. "How 'bout we stop and get some supper, then fill up this cooler with some snacks and drinks. Sounds like a road trip to me, Colette..."

Colette chuckled. "Sounds fun!"

Geoffrey settled back into the seat, becoming part of the darkness in the smallish interior. Colette could barely make out his eyes, which appeared miserable and distant. After a while he closed them and seemed to drift off. Colette felt terrible they had to wake him when they pulled off the Interstate to refuel and have a late supper at a truck stop.

When they finished eating, Geoffrey wandered into the connecting store and came back to the car wearing a new hoodie, sunglasses and a new pair of dark sweat pants. When he slid across the backseat, he asked Colette where Orvin was.

"Just grabbing a few things for the trip."

"I'll help him…" Geoffrey said, about to jump out when Colette stopped him.

"He can manage," she said, wanting to get Geoffrey alone for a few minutes. "Orvin explained what happened at the seminar," she said. "What you did for me was nothing short of miraculous."

Geoffrey didn't speak at first, taking his eyes out the window. "It was my fault you were shot," he finally said, his face growing gloomy under the bright, buzzing lights of the service station. Orvin crossed the parking lot carrying a paper sack and the cooler he'd taken in with him. He opened the back door and set the cooler on the floor.

"That won't crowd you will it?" he asked Geoffrey.

Geoffrey shook his head. When Orvin got in, Geoffrey handed Orvin a thick wad of twenties over the seat. "What's this for?" Orvin asked.

"Everything," Geoffrey said. "And please just take it, okay. No arguments. Please…"

Orvin gave Colette a look that made her shrug as she pulled back onto the Interstate. After jamming the money down into his jeans pocket, Orvin put his eyes back on the road. They drove in silence for a couple of hours until Colette announced she needed a break. When Orvin took over the wheel, Colette stretched out in the backseat, covering herself with a blanket they'd brought from home, but she knew she wouldn't be able to sleep. It was around four in the morning when Orvin said he was bushed and pulled into a rest area off the Interstate. Colette sat up and asked if he was okay.

"I'm fine," he said. "Not used to marathon driving anymore."

Geoffrey told them he could drive, that he was in good shape, plenty rested. Orvin took up residence in the backseat, wrapping himself in the blanket Colette had been using, then folded his knees and laid down. Colette took the front passenger seat before Geoffrey eased back onto the road. After a while, Geoffrey looked over at Colette and said, "You've both been pretty patient, not asking what any of this is about."

Colette smiled, glad the young man had not sensed how many times she wanted to ask a thousand questions and had held her tongue, a pact she and Orvin had made at the truck stop when Geoffrey went to the connected store. "We can't bend that man's ear for thirty hours," Orvin had said to her. "I know," she told Orvin. "But if he wants to talk, I'm going to listen." To which Orvin replied, "Well, just make sure he *wants* to, okay?"

Geoffrey shifted his gaze toward Colette and added, "If and when the police call you again, tell them I was headed for Montana. They don't need to know you drove me, okay? I don't want to bring any trouble down on you."

Colette nodded, looking over at Geoffrey, his eyes burdened with sadness and grief. She knew the feeling.

"What I'm going to tell you may be hard to believe," Geoffrey said. "And I hope you'll keep it between us, you and Orvin and me."

Colette glanced over the seat at Orvin, who seemed to be asleep, but it was so dark she couldn't tell.

"The day you said you remembered me from the library in Philadelphia... I lied. That was me," Geoffrey said. Colette, even though she had thought it was him, hadn't truly believed that it could be. Which now, left her more shocked than ever to hear it from his lips, the questions rolling like storm-driven waves through her mind. Geoffrey went on to explain about the book he'd been reading that day, *The Philadelphia Experiment*. "I know you had the book with you that day at the hospital. Did you read it?" he said.

"Yes. So did Orvin."

Geoffrey nodded, taking his eyes back to the highway. "I was there," Geoffrey said. "In 1943 when the Navy ran the experiment. It changed me forever. Changed something to do with my aging gene or something."

"So, you don't age?" Colette said, knowing she was supposed to only listen, but she couldn't help herself. Geoffrey explained that he aged, but at a rate much slower than other humans. Orvin sat up in the backseat but said nothing. Geoffrey shifted his eyes to the rearview mirror for a second, then took them back to the road.

"The newspaper article," Geoffrey said after a few minutes. "About

Peter Smithwick... the one you showed me... that was me. And it was correct. I was fourteen in 1933, and..."

"I'm so sorry," Colette said. "That must have been horrible having your folks die like that..." Geoffrey cut her a hard look, his eyes filling with tears. "I'm sorry, Geoffrey," Colette said. "I shouldn't have said anything."

Geoffrey wiped his eyes, then his nose. He cleared his throat and sniffled a bit. "It's okay... it's just... it's hard to talk about..." Then, after a moment: "I just wanted to set things straight. You've been so kind to me, and it hurt to have to lie to both of you."

They drove in silence until the sky lightened to a dull shade of grayish blue over the highway. After a quick stop at a rest area, they returned to the car, Geoffrey assuring them he was okay to keep driving. Several hours later Orvin suggested they stop and have breakfast. They ate without talking. Afterward, Geoffrey grabbed the check off the table.

"I heard some of what you told Colette in the car," Orvin finally said.

"I'm sorry for the deceptions, Orvin. I really am."

Orvin waved it off. "You saved my life... in more ways than you know."

Geoffrey gave him a weak smile and stood to pay the bill, Orvin and Colette walking out ahead of him. Colette waited near the car, reaching her arms over her head, while Orvin paced the surrounding grassy area to stretch his legs. She was exhausted, but was having fun—the trip was exhilarating. She and Orvin had never done anything so adventurous, unless you counted getting married at nineteen on the strength of a lukewarm love affair and few prospects for the future. Watching Geoffrey cross the parking lot, she couldn't believe how different he seemed now, as if he'd lost all vitality. Orvin, back from his little walk, looked over at her and smiled. "Want me to drive for a while?" he said.

Geoffrey spun toward them both. "I'm okay to keep driving," he said. "I prefer it if you don't mind."

Orvin nodded at Colette and told her to sit in the front seat. "I'll snooze in the back," he said, slipping into the space behind them. Colette fastened her seatbelt and handed Geoffrey the keys. "Just hang onto them until we switch drivers," she said.

He smiled and pointed the car toward the Interstate. Colette checked the map and told Geoffrey where he had to turn. "About five miles ahead," she said, telling him which highway they needed to take. They drove without talking. After about an hour on the highway, Orvin's snoring came from the backseat. "Does that bother you?" Colette said. "I can wake him…"

"Not at all."

"Can I ask you a question?" Colette said.

Geoffrey briefly glanced at her and nodded, pinning his eyes back to the busy highway.

"How did you do that?" she said. "How did you remove the bullet from me?"

Geoffrey explained that he could see diseases and abnormalities in the human body, and was able to repair defects and damages from accidents and the ravages of illness. But that he didn't use this ability very often, not openly. He had been warned about plying his *gifts*, and recently learned that employing them without proper attention could have devastating effects, that he regretted he hadn't listened to his mentors. Colette could think of no downside to healing people, and to have that capability and keep it hidden seemed such a waste. Nevertheless, she could see the contrition in Geoffrey's eyes and realized that whatever had happened, it was weighing on him.

Geoffrey fell quiet and Colette didn't press him further, though it seemed something was still on his mind. After a while, Geoffrey said, "Have you ever heard of Sai Baba?"

Colette turned toward him. "No. Who is that?"

Geoffrey told her about the great mystic, a man with many of the powers Geoffrey possessed, especially healing, and manifestation, and even bilocation. Sai Baba, he told her, had lived an ascetic life, had dedicated himself to years of study and meditation and prayer.

"But you have the same amazing abilities," Colette said.

"The difference is, Sai Baba's abilities were divine. He was an enlightened being," Geoffrey said. "His years of mastery and rigorous practice prepared him to handle such potential. Me… my abilities are the product of a freak experiment and mutated genes. No one like me should ever have this capacity. I lack the discipline and wisdom to wield such powers responsibly."

Geoffrey turned back to the highway, his eyes glassy, unhinged. "All I ever wanted to do was help people," he said almost in a whisper, as if speaking to someone beyond the windshield. "Just help people… but I can't even help myself."

When they stopped at a roadside mom and pop motel to spend the night, Colette took Orvin aside and told him she was concerned about Geoffrey. "I think he's falling apart," she said. Orvin seemed to weigh her statement, but offered food as his only suggestion. "Let's get something to eat," he said. "We're all just road-weary."

Orvin and Colette waited outside the motel for Geoffrey to come out of his room. "Hope I didn't keep you waiting long," he said, pulling the door closed.

"We just got out here ourselves," Colette said, telling a little fib. They drove to a pizza place in town, just a few miles off the main highway. After eating, Orvin said, "I haven't had a beer in a long time. What say we pick some up on our way back to the motel?" Colette wasn't wild about the idea, but she hadn't had a beer since high school. Geoffrey didn't react one way or another, just nodded as he tilted back the glass to down the last of his Coke. Back at the motel, Orvin carried the beer into their room and told Geoffrey to join them if he wasn't too tired.

Orvin stuffed the cans into the small fridge beneath the TV console and offered Colette one. She popped the top and toasted Orvin, clinking their cans together. "Do you realize this is the first beer we've ever shared together?" she said. Orvin chuckled to himself, then said, "Well, let's not make it the last, okay." Colette sat in the chair next to the bed, thumbing the remote searching for something watchable on the TV. Orvin stretched out on the bed, his back against the headboard, some leftover pizza sitting in the opened box next to him. A knock came at the door and Colette got up to open it.

"Come in," she said. Geoffrey moved past her and sat on the desk chair.

"Beer's in the fridge. Help yourself," Orvin said. Geoffrey opened one and took a sip. Colette started to tell Geoffrey that this was her and Orvin's first beer together, and began the story of their courtship, which eventually led her to tell Geoffrey about the darkest chapter of her life. Orvin bristled a bit, obviously uncomfortable with the rehash, and excused himself to the parking lot explaining that he just needed some fresh air. When she finished, Geoffrey's features had lifted somewhat. "I was so envious of you when we spoke at the library," Geoffrey said.

"Why? Pregnant at eighteen, unmarried and about to give up my first child?" she said. "What could you possibly have been jealous of?"

"I looked at you and saw a young woman who was beginning an

amazing adventure, starting a new family with a husband who loved her..."

"And none of that was true..."

"I had no way of knowing that, so to me, you represented all the things I knew I could never have..."

"Why can't you have those things?"

Geoffrey explained that he'd had a wife he loved for almost thirty years, but when she realized she was aging and he wasn't, the marriage ended. "I guess it's lucky we never had children. Or maybe it's not luck at all... maybe I can't, with all the messed-up genes. Doesn't matter anyway, it's not part of my journey."

Colette had never considered that aspect of Geoffrey's delayed aging. She experienced some strange comfort in seeing Orvin age right alongside her, especially now since they'd become so close, followed by a pang of sadness their time now was limited. Consequently, it also made it more imperative they not waste a second. Geoffrey finished his beer and crumpled the can, dropped it in the trash next to the desk. Geoffrey looked at her, then from behind his back withdrew a single red rose.

"Here," he said.

She looked at him, then at the rose. Before she took it from his fingers, the fragrance had filled the air around her. It was real, no doubt, but where did it come from?

"Thank you," she said. Just then Orvin walked in and spied the rose, then looked at Colette, then at Geoffrey.

"What did I miss?" Orvin said, standing near the door. Geoffrey got up to leave and handed Orvin a round, gold pocket watch on a chain. Orvin opened it to a picture of Orvin's granddaughter on the time face. "What's this?" Orvin said.

"I saw that picture on your dash and thought you might like something a bit more permanent," Geoffrey said. "You can hang the chain from your mirror."

Orvin looked down at the photo, then back to Geoffrey. "I don't know what to say."

"Your original picture is still on your dash," Geoffrey said. "What a lovely grandchild. You're both so fortunate." Geoffrey patted Orvin on the arm and opened the door.

"Whenever you're ready to leave in the morning, just give me a holler," Geoffrey said, pulling the door shut behind him.

Orvin held the gold locket in his palm, then brought his eyes to Colette and the fresh rose in her hand. "Where did that come from?" Orvin asked. Colette wasn't sure how to explain, but she would try her best, as soon as she was able to convince herself of what had just happened.

57

FIFTY MILES FROM BOZEMAN

AFTER A LATE BREAKFAST, they were on the highway by eleven that morning. Orvin had driven most of the afternoon, until Geoffrey offered to take over when they stopped for gas. After supper, Orvin took the front passenger seat while Colette snoozed in the back. Ninety miles from Bozeman, the sun slipped beneath the edge of the earth, leaving behind an enormous indigo sky slashed with brilliant pink and orange strokes. Geoffrey could already feel the pressure of loneliness swelling inside his chest. The past few days with Orvin and Colette had been a gift, their quiet, reassuring presence, their unconditional acceptance of Geoffrey's bizarre life story. Geoffrey had almost felt normal, enjoying pleasant conversation spaced comfortably against a silent backdrop of effortless companionship. And until thirty minutes ago, the future had been a distant planet orbiting Earth, without substance or magnitude, unreachable and beyond consideration. Now it had the urgency and seriousness of an approaching asteroid streaking toward the world, a constant, white-hot threat. Geoffrey could feel its thrumming pulse beneath his skin, could feel the dreaded rumble of its mass smashing through the atmosphere, sucking every last molecule of oxygen from the air.

They passed a sign for Bozeman, sixty-five miles. The sky had lost all its amperage, reduced to a listless, dusky gray. Geoffrey glanced across the seat over at Orvin, his large hands on his thighs, his back straight and his eyes pointed toward some distant moment that seemed beyond his grasp. Geoffrey took his gaze to the rearview mirror, hoping to catch Colette's soft face caught in the narrow rectangle of reflection, the shiny glass only sending back a constellation of bright headlights. Colette must still be asleep.

With his destination approaching, Geoffrey was seized by a foreboding anxiety, but couldn't understand why. He'd spent so much of his life alone, and it had never felt burdensome or ominous. When he and Amanda split up after almost thirty years of marriage, it had been tough, even devastating for a while, but never felt perilous. He'd made it through, always aiming himself forward, certain the right thing awaited him around the next turn, the present moment pulling him forward like a friendly tide. But something was different now. Every atom in Geoffrey's universe seemed hazardous and unyielding, as if he were in danger of losing stability, gravity failing, leaving him floating directionless in an infinite, black void. His throat closed for a second and he instinctively gulped the air, testing it along with his own vulnerability.

"You okay?" Orvin said, turning toward Geoffrey.

Geoffrey swallowed the hardness in his throat and nodded, taking his eyes back to the dark highway. Several minutes later Geoffrey could see the familiar green sign approaching.

Bozeman. Fifty miles. A fusty, humid heat rose in Geoffrey's throat as he pulled the car to the shoulder. Orvin spun toward him. "What's wrong? Something with the car?" Orvin said.

Colette sat up in the backseat rubbing the sleep from her eyes. "Everything okay?"

Geoffrey slid the shifter to park. "This is where I'll be getting out," Geoffrey said, nearly in tears. Orvin looked around, then back at Geoffrey. "There's nothing here," Orvin said. The traffic had thinned, the occasional eighteen-wheeler whooshing past, shaking the compact car.

"Don't you want to get to Bozeman?" Colette said, her voice pressed with concern.

"No, this is good," Geoffrey said. Another eighteen-wheeler rumbled by. Colette looked at Orvin as if to implore him to convince Geoffrey to go on to Bozeman. Orvin shrugged his bushy eyebrows turning his palms up. Geoffrey checked the side mirror, then got out the driver's side door and walked past the headlights to the shoulder. Orvin got out and opened the door for Colette. They joined Geoffrey in the cool night air.

"Are you going to be okay out here?" Colette asked, wrapping her arms around herself, patting warmth into her body.

"I'll be fine." He embraced her. "Thank you for everything," he whispered to her. When he let her go, Orvin said, "You sure about this?"

Not at all, but Geoffrey nodded, then stepped forward and hugged Orvin. It took a moment for Orvin to return the hug, but when he did a tear came to his eye. Geoffrey smiled at him. "I am so glad you stopped at my house that morning," Geoffrey said. "What a privilege to know you both."

Orvin swiped a quick finger past his eye, then pursed his lips and smiled.

"So, now what?" Geoffrey said. "Back to Kleary Creek?"

"No, we're headed to Virginia to see that precious little granddaughter of ours," Colette said. "I think we've got some of this road magic in our veins now!"

They all laughed a little, restrained expressions of amusement to vent the underlying sadness. Geoffrey opened the back door and grabbed the paper sack that contained a few things he'd bought at the truck stop the evening before, toothbrush and paste, a comb and some snacks.

"Do you need anything?" Orvin said. "Money… or…? Just call if you need help or anything… I mean it, Geoffrey…" Colette nodded her agreement.

Geoffrey smiled. "Thanks… I'll be fine. I'll try to write you when I land somewhere, but it could be a while."

Orvin put his arm around Colette's waist, pulling her to his side, nodding, smiling. "That would be nice," Colette said. She got in the passenger-side front door, giving Geoffrey a smile through the glass. Orvin gave Geoffrey one last glance as he crossed to the driver's side, popping in and shutting the door before another eighteen-wheeler rushed past. The crunch of the gravel under the tires as Orvin pulled onto the highway sounded like the last crackling of a dying planet. In moments, Orvin spun the car in a huge semicircle on the deserted highway, flashing the lights once before the taillights disappeared over a small ridge and evaporated into the brittle night air.

Geoffrey pulled his hood up and started walking along the shoulder. He wasn't sure what time it was, but the frequency of big trucks had slowed. After an hour or so a light drizzle showed itself in the headlights of the occasional passing vehicle, though he couldn't feel it through the thick sweatshirt. Not going all the way to Bozeman must have confused Orvin and Colette, but Geoffrey had no intention of going there, instead planning to head for Spokane to get supplies, then to a small Washington town called Wenatchee, where he could hop on the Pacific Crest Trail and sneak into Canada. But he wanted Orvin and Colette to have that *plausible deniability,* as Edward had called it, concerning his whereabouts, in case the Bristol, Tennessee authorities kept pestering them.

He had walked about another hour along a deserted road off the main highway, when a car passed. The vehicle went about thirty yards when the brake lights brightened. The car stopped briefly, then backed up toward Geoffrey. When the car was even with him, the window swept down into the door under an electric hum.

"Need a ride?" the man said.

With the rain coming heavier now, Geoffrey welcomed the unanticipated offer. He pulled the door open and was about to jump in when he recognized the driver and stopped.

"Come on, Geoffrey," Edward said. "You're getting soaked."

Geoffrey had finally gotten past the vacuum in his gut when Orvin and Colette had pulled from the shoulder, and had managed to redirect his focus to an uncertain future in Canada; staying in Vancouver, finding work, a place to live until he could figure out something more permanent, or at least sustaining, since permanence for him was impossible.

"How in the hell did you find me?" Geoffrey said, a maelstrom of emotions trampling his calm mind.

Edward laughed. "Geez, Geoffrey, you still don't get it. *The Associates* can find you any second of the day if they want to. Do you know how many resources they've allocated to studying you? Do you really believe they're just going to let you wander off?"

Geoffrey toed the gravel, rain dripping from the front of his soaked hood. He got in and shut the door. Until he felt the warmth of the car, he hadn't realized how chilled he'd been. Edward pulled away and asked where Geoffrey had been headed.

"What does it matter?" Geoffrey said. "You taking me back to Kleary?"

"No, you're done with Kleary Creek," Edward said, shifting his eyes between the road and Geoffrey. "Hey, don't look so down. *The Associates* have some great ideas for your future. I swear you're going to love 'em."

"You don't get it, ET," Geoffrey said, pulling his hood back. "It's my life to plan… not theirs…"

Edward shifted in his seat, though Geoffrey couldn't read his expression in the dark.

"Hurricane Ian," Edward said, guiding them along the wet, winding road. "2004. I had moved to Kleary Creek a year earlier. Anyway, when Ian headed for the Greater Antilles, this couple who lived in Florida decided to bail and head for their summer home in the mountains of western North Carolina, about forty miles from Kleary Creek, where they could wait out the worst of it. So crazy Ian comes up through the gulf, and it's still a category 3 when it reaches landfall, where it makes this huge loop up through the southern states. The wind was considerably less when it pushed through the Carolinas, but Ian was dropping insane amounts of rain. Even though the wind was snapping telephone poles and swelling the creeks and rivers in Western NC, the Florida couple felt they made the right decision coming north, until the mountain towering high above their home starts to crumble. It's called a debris flow. Took out every house along Chambers Creek, including the Florida couple's North Carolina home, killing them in the process."

Geoffrey sat a moment, hoping for more to this story. Edward went quiet.

"So... what's the point?" Geoffrey said.

"That was their life, Geoffrey. Their fate," Edward said. "They couldn't escape it, even by driving nearly eight-hundred miles."

"What does that have to do with me?" Geoffrey asked.

Edward glanced in Geoffrey's direction, then took his eyes back to the road. "Look, the day they flipped that switch in the Navy yard in 1943, this became your life, Geoffrey. Your fate... just as it became mine."

"Yours? I don't get it."

Edward explained how he had been on the Eldridge that day, that they didn't know each other then, that his name had been Henry Downing. "Nobody had to cut me out of the bulkhead, but I was messed up pretty bad. Mentally. *The Associates* helped me through the worst of it." Edward adjusted the heat back a little. "Like you," Edward continued, "I have the slow-aging gene, just none of the other bells and whistles. You're the showroom model for sure."

"But, you don't—" Geoffrey started to say, confused by Edward's appearance; he seemed to be in his fifties.

Edward smirked. "Yeah, *The Associates* did some work on me years ago, when I was married, so my marriage didn't meet the same fate as yours. A few crow's feet, a little extra skin at the jowls, a few laugh lines, adding just a touch every few years or so…"

"You're married?"

Edward shook his head. "No. It was fated as well. Even if it looked like I was getting older, I wasn't, but she was. She finally succumbed to her aging body."

Geoffrey was stunned, angry, and defeated by this new set of facts. There was some relief in the knowledge that ET would age as Geoffrey did, which now felt painfully slow, but the idea that Geoffrey's life could never be his own was unnerving. He would always serve these enigmatic beings and the military personnel, whose occupants would change over time, and even the new recruits would hold sway over Geoffrey's future. Total strangers would determine where he lived, his identity, his livelihood, always under the microscope. Was this really his fate?

"Hey, don't despair, Geoffrey. They got some pretty great ideas for your future," Edward said. "Give them a chance to show you."

"Do I have a choice?"

"Look, I know it's tough… the more you can accept this, the better your life will be…"

Geoffrey wasn't sure how great his life could be if someone else held the reins to his destiny. They rode in silence for a long while. When Edward passed a truck stop on the Interstate that boasted food and snacks, he asked if Geoffrey needed anything. Geoffrey shook his head, thinking about *The Lodge, The Associates,* his last visit to the ship. How strange it had been, the generals, the beings dressed like Druids. Where were *The Associates* now, and where was Edward headed? Geoffrey was about to ask but figured what was the point.

"Who was the long-haired guy at *The Lodge,*" Geoffrey finally said after a few moments. "The one wearing all the robes and stuff?"

"The one who looks like Jesus?"

Geoffrey nodded.

"Yeah, kind of weird, huh," Edward said. "I've seen him a couple of times, but I have no idea who he is."

It figured that Edward didn't know either, Geoffrey thought. Another mystery wrapped in confusion and misdirection. Geoffrey settled back in the seat, thinking about all the *wondrous* plans *The Associates* had for his life, unable to sidestep his own cynicism. Then, like Hurricane Ian, the past circled back through Geoffrey's mind, the Reverend Jacob, the farm, the USS *Eldridge,* trying to place a crewman named Henry Downing, recalling his wife Amanda, and all those lost years shambling around the country, Kleary Creek, the lovely Veronica Carlson... then the most crushing realization interrupted the seamless reverie—Geoffrey could live for another eight hundred years; how could the human mind possibly bear the burden of that many memories?

58
THE VEIL OF ILLUSION

WHEN GEOFFREY WOKE, he was instantly aware they were driving up a rough country road, reminding him of the one leading up to Yellow Mountain, but that wasn't possible. He sat up straight, looking out into the narrow cone of the headlights burning through a black desolate void.

"Where are we?" he asked.

"Still in Montana," Edward said. *"The Associates* want to see you."

In the sanctity of sleep, Geoffrey had escaped the deadening sense of defeat he'd felt under the control and watchful eyes of *The Associates.* And now it sat in his chest like wet shifting sand, that oppressive realization his life would never be his own.

They jounced along, the road seemingly leading up into the cloudless sky, countless stars flickering, the car lights crawling along the rutted, gravel road, past weeds and stunted brush and bushes. The area seemed free of trees. When Edward stopped the car, he turned off the engine and lights, and they sat in a soundless nothingness, innumerable stars scattered across the infinite blackness beyond the windshield. In moments the ship descended in a swirl of lights and sounds, low tones against a modulating, ceaseless hum. When the ship was settled, Edward popped his door open and got out. Geoffrey did likewise, then looked over at Edward.

"What about the—" Geoffrey started to ask.

"I told you, we're done with the black goggles," Edward interrupted, walking toward the ship. Geoffrey fell in behind him, uneasy with this meeting. He had seen inhabitants of the ship last time, but thought that was a fluke. Nevertheless, Geoffrey felt a weird buzz in his veins, his defense mechanism on full alert. Certainly they wouldn't have come all the way to Montana just to kill him. Edward could have done that at any time, while Geoffrey was asleep, then dumped his body in the middle of nowhere.

A ramp came down showing the entrance to the ship, a bright light issuing forth. About to follow Edward up the metallic-looking incline, Geoffrey was suddenly aware he'd never actually witnessed entering the ship, always wearing the dark goggles, or had been completely unconscious.

Once inside, Geoffrey saw no one, could only hear mechanical noises, like air releasing, interspersed with a peculiar clanking, reminding Geoffrey of an old jalopy. He chuckled at the odd irony as Edward led him to a spacious room with banks of blackened windows, like some kind of observation room. It was spacious, with no furniture, no chairs or tables. Nothing really, but the windows, or at least what looked like windows. Geoffrey had never been here before, at least that he could recall, wondering if *The Associates* were on the other side observing them now. All Geoffrey could see in the glass was Edward's and his own reflection.

When Edward turned to leave, Geoffrey followed.

"Where are *you* going?" Edward said, stopping to smirk back at Geoffrey. "You need to wait here…"

Geoffrey's mouth was dry as a cotton ball. He shrugged, not sure what he was supposed to do, starting to appreciate the black goggles and being led to some designated room on the ship, avoiding altogether this awkward clash between free will and protocols. Wanting nothing more than to be back on the highway, the constant thrum of the road, Geoffrey stared at Edward, silently pleading to leave, escape back to familiar surroundings.

"Relax," Edward said sternly, with a trace of disappointment, as if he'd read the fear and discomfort in Geoffrey's eyes. A few seconds later Edward was gone, an unnerving vacuum taking his place. Geoffrey's mind was awhirl with images of *The Associates*, imagining the aliens who resembled Druids with their dark hoods, unable to stop picturing them as maniacal creatures with huge distended jaws bristling with large menacing teeth, their eyes black, dead, always watching blindly. Geoffrey didn't have to wait long for his answer.

In walked the man in robes, dark skin, beard and mustache, his sandaled feet padding across the polished floor. The *Jesus* guy, Geoffrey thought.

"Geoffrey," the man said, smiling, his eyes compassionate, friendly. Geoffrey was about to extend his hand when the man embraced him with an unanticipated hug, holding him warmly, Geoffrey feeling a peculiar peace spreading through his body.

The man drew back, grasping Geoffrey's arms just above the elbows and smiling, before turning toward the wide bank of darkened glass. Geoffrey was tall, but this man was at least six inches taller. Just then, the blackened windows cleared, revealing a vista of outer space that weakened Geoffrey's knees, made him swoon for a few seconds. They seemed to be moving but it was impossible to tell with nothing for reference.

"Call me Ishmael," the man said, and laughed. "Sorry, I couldn't help it... that's my favorite novel of all time."

For all Geoffrey's reading, he had no idea what this man, Ishmael, was talking about. Before Geoffrey could clarify the statement, Ishmael walked closer to the windows, myriad stars and galaxies reflecting in the tall man's dark eyes.

"Alienation," Ishmael said, never taking his eyes from the glass. "Isolation." Then, after a moment: "That must be what you're feeling, Geoffrey. Alienation. Isolation. It's understandable, with your retarded aging process, the inability to form lasting relationships. No one really understanding what you've gone through..."

When Ishmael glanced back at him, Geoffrey felt exposed, uncomfortable, then stepped forward toward the glass, to be on the same plane as the tall enigmatic man.

"But Moby Dick is also about fate. Or at least the speciousness of fate. Have you thought about your own destiny, Geoffrey?"

Of course, he had, long before Edward brought it up earlier; it was the only way he'd survived all these decades, by accepting his providence, his gifts, *or curses*, depending on the circumstances, or the outcomes. Where was Ishmael going with all this?

"Project Übermensch," Ishmael said, smirking playfully, almost laughing. "Nietzsche's superman—'The superior man who justifies the existence of the human race,'" Ishmael added with a wide grin, as if amused by Nietzsche's notion. "When the Disentians assisted the U.S. Navy with their cloaking experiment, these advanced beings had their own agenda—"

"Disentians?" Geoffrey said.

Ishmael swiveled his large head toward Geoffrey. "That's what we call 'em. The little guys with the hoods. The ones that resemble Druids?" Ishmael smirked at something, adding, "That's what we call them... humans are incapable of pronouncing their real name. Anyway, their appearance can be off-putting to humans, so, they wear the hoods. But they're actually pretty humorous and good-hearted, mostly. I mean, they have their dark side, like all of us."

Geoffrey could only nod, his mind swimming. "Off-putting? Like—"

"They have no eyes," Ishmael said. "Nor ears. But they see the world as it is, as the movement of energy. They see and hear energetically. They see *source*, unlike humans, whose minds translate that same energy into trees, water, flowers. You know, objective reality... right? You, Geoffrey, you see energetically, people's diseases and such... and then your mind... well, anyway," Ishmael hesitated, as if recalibrating his thought process. "The Disentians had their own agenda during that experiment, basically, to create the Übermensch. Though they had a different name for it." Ishmael paused, as if trying to callback the moniker. "Oh, it doesn't matter, they, the Disentians have pretty amazing powers of their own; second sight, telekinesis... They believed humans were capable of these things and much more, based on their DNA structure. The Philadelphia Experiment proved to be the perfect testing ground for their theories, though it was a bit of a mess. However, the Navy got what they wanted, stealth technology.

"The Disentians, though, had practically given up on the experiment as a failure, until they came upon you," Ishmael said. "They read your aura, your energetic field, and were hopeful with your initial readings, so they excised you from the steel and brought you here."

Ishmael turned to Geoffrey. "You are nothing short of amazing, beyond their wildest dreams, Geoffrey. And, ooooh, man!" Ishmael chortled. "When you created that monster! Wow, even the Disentians were shocked and awed. I mean, sure, manifesting baubles and trinkets and flowers is one thing, but complex lifeforms from thought! I mean, wow, that was some feat!"

Geoffrey had no control over creating that monster. A dangerous, murderous fluke, nothing to be trifled with.

"Several decades ago, after the Montauk Experiment, a monster was photographed lurking around the facility in New York, big hairy thing. The Disentians could never figure out where it came from... or where it went." Ishmael chuckled as if the memory were somehow amusing.

Ishmael, his eyes wild, spun toward Geoffrey. "Exciting, isn't it? The possibilities!" The tall pleasant man seemed intoxicated with these anomalous potentials. It was disturbing to Geoffrey, unleashing aberrations willy-nilly, but his unvoiced condemnation was soon quashed as they approached the surface of the moon, or what Geoffrey could only imagine was the moon. It sure as hell wasn't earth.

Ishmael seemed not to notice, or had seen it so many times it had become unremarkable. The Sea of Tranquility, Geoffrey thought as they passed over an enormous crater. He'd seen pictures in a book.

"Maybe your fate is that of the rescuer, the 'superman,'" Ishmael said, interrupting Geoffrey's fixation on the lunar surface passing many miles below the craft. Geoffrey wouldn't have been able to respond to Ishmael even if he'd had words, fixated on the gray, mesmerizing moonscape. "Imagine a world with healers like yourself, Geoffrey," Ishmael continued, "able to see diseases, anomalies, and fix them, without medication or drugs or harmful and expensive procedures. And your immune system, they've never seen anything like it; part of the reason your expected life-span is close to a thousand years. That's what we're working on, Geoffrey. That's the Disentian vision... a calmer, more peaceful world..." Ishmael's thoughts seem to linger a moment. "But it will take time."

Geoffrey could barely break himself free. Why were they showing him this, talking to him like this, about his fate, the Disentian's vision for humankind? What did they have to do with anything?

"Mainstream society is not ready for *messiahs*, Geoffrey, people who can heal others, and manifest out of thin air. Look how that went with our last messiah? Not so great, right? That's the problem now, figuring out how to introduce this incredible potential into earth's population without a ferocious backlash. You know, that whole *Satan* mentality, how powers like yours are quickly assigned to dark forces." Then, facing Geoffrey. "But the Disentians felt you were doing pretty well with your furtive healings... until the monster!" Again Ishmael brightened, amused.

"It's not funny!" Geoffrey said, perturbed with the odd man.

"No, you're right. Absolutely." Ishmael became serious, almost grave, no humor in his voice, but Geoffrey couldn't be sure if Ishmael was just feigning concern.

"Why are you telling me all this!" Geoffrey said a bit forcefully.

Ishmael took a moment to consider Geoffrey, staring at him with dark, infinite eyes. "The Disentians understand your consternation, your alienation, how difficult this has been for you. They wanted you to know your importance to humankind, to the planet, the role you're playing to move the world's population into a new, energetic paradigm of joy, profound health and well-being! This has been their dream since their own planet, their own species, was decimated by disease when a tiny asteroid hit their planet. A minuscule event, of no consequence because of its diminutive size, if that tiny rock hadn't been carrying a very resilient strain of bacteria that quickly decimated their population, killing everyone who remained. They even knew it was approaching, but there was nothing to be done, except to escape with a small fraction of the population to the nearest inhabitable planet. Here." Ishmael paused. "Where we've been ever since."

Luckily, for his own sanity, Geoffrey couldn't fully grasp the impact of what Ishmael was telling him, that he somehow had become an unwitting "savior," so to speak, the implications too troubling to contemplate for long.

"I still don't understand why—" Geoffrey started to say, more than a little flummoxed, when Ishmael interrupted.

"I know you think I've been overly flip about all that's happened, finding amusement in the creation of the beast. And I know people died, Geoffrey," Ishmael said, then, a moment later: "Maya. The illusion or appearance of our phenomenal world. It's all illusion, Geoffrey. Nevertheless, the *illusion* is profound, isn't it? Miraculous and terrifying and heartbreaking and spectacular and savage, and yet we cling to it with every fiber of our being. It's our playground, Geoffrey, our stage to experience all that is possible and impossible, all that is tragic and wondrous while wearing these corporeal, fleshy suits. And still, it is all illusion."

"I don't..." Geoffrey started to say, never able to grasp that concept of objective reality being illusory, but was too dumbstruck to finish his thought.

"You're free to go, Geoffrey," Ishmael finally said, smiling warmly. "You never asked for this role, and the Disentians realize that, as well as how much you've suffered. Because of you, we now know so much about the human genome ..." Ishmael paused again, as if waiting for Geoffrey to catch up. "Because of you, we now know how to manipulate your retarded aging gene, how to rid you of all your gifts, actually restore your immune system to that of others like you, so that you can live a normal life, get married, have children, grow old and die, like a normal human being..."

A normal human being. A stifling emptiness opened in Geoffrey's gut, making him feel hollow. This is what he'd hoped for most of his life, to be normal, but now, faced with an option that had eluded him for decades, he was confused, but more than that... frightened; this is the only life he's known for nearly seventy years.

"Before you start wondering if you'll suddenly be ninety years old and fall over dead, you won't," Ishmael said, smirking. "At least the Disentians don't think you will. It's a bit speculative, but—" Ishmael smiled, chuckling. "I'm just kidding. You'll be fine. They figure you could live another fifty, sixty years, even more. And they'll help you with any vocation you wish to pursue. You could keep writing, doing seminars, or you could do something totally different, like cleaning swimming pools, or accounting, or—"

"So, that's it? They're done with me?" Geoffrey said, feeling relief, with an undertone of gnawing vacancy in his chest. "What about Edward?"

Ishmael smiled. "You're exhausted, I can see. You need time to think." Ishmael eased toward Geoffrey, placing his palms on Geoffrey's upper arms. He hugged Geoffrey, then drew back. "Edward's waiting for you."

Geoffrey turned away, and like a sleepwalker, drifted mechanically toward the door. He glanced toward him once, at the inscrutable man staring back, Ishmael's indomitable smile, a mesmerizing glow circumfusing the curious man's face.

59

A LIFE OF NORMALCY

WHEN GEOFFREY WOKE, it was nearing daybreak, the sky a dusty slate gray along the horizon. He had no idea where they were. About then, Edward pulled into a filling station—the lights glaring and abrupt—and asked if Geoffrey wanted anything from the convenience store.

"Where are we?" Geoffrey asked, his mind still a jumble. It hadn't been a dream, he knew that, but it hadn't been real either, his discussion with Ishmael. Was it?

"Idaho," Edward said, peeking his head back in through the open window after he started the pump. "I'm heading for Seattle. Have you ever been to Strathcona Provincial Park on Vancouver Island? It's incredible, Geoffrey. I guarantee you'll love it! Want anything from inside? A snack or something to hold you until we stop for breakfast?"

Geoffrey shook his head, Edward ambling lopsidedly away from the car as if his legs were stiff. Geoffrey got out to stretch, the cool air refreshing, letting his senses drink in everything around him, smelling the gasoline fumes, then the faint scent of honeysuckle, some kind of meat broiling in the convenience store, his senses tuned to nuance, every detail, every molecule sparking through the air. Would his heightened sense of his surroundings diminish when the Disentians *rewired* his DNA? Who would he be without his abilities to see diseases, heal them, manifest anything he needed at any moment? How would the knowledge of his impending death impinge on his relationship to life? Would it occupy every thought, every waking moment, haunt him until the day he finally died? He had no idea. And could he live with the emptiness of not having his gifts, which had brought him so much joy, and pain? How could he even consider not going through with it, condemning himself to as much as eight hundred more years on the planet, maybe more? But if he did, it was like throwing his entire life away, as if everything to this point had been a dream. An illusion! There was that word again, and it was crazy, and confusing, and he felt suddenly short of breath.

Edward returned and shoved the gas nozzle back into the pump with a loud clunk, then threw himself into the front seat, stripping down the shoulder harness, buckling the belt across his lap. Geoffrey got in and did the same, though without the gusto Edward had displayed.

"Don't need to use the restroom?" Edward said, squinting over at him, a strange expression trying to form.

Geoffrey shook his head.

Edward started the engine, then eyed Geoffrey before pulling off. "Why are you so morose?" Edward said. "Everything's gonna be fine."

Geoffrey sucked a deep breath, then cleared his throat. "Yeah, I know…"

Scoffing, Edward put the car in gear, then checked his rearview mirror before pulling from the station. Soon he was guiding the vehicle onto the highway, the day blossoming, the blue sky beyond the windshield radiant and vast, free of the misty fog.

"Where were you when I was talking to *The Associates?*" Geoffrey said into the road-droning silence.

"Coffee and a donut," Edward said. "Why? Did you miss me?"

What was Geoffrey expecting him to say? He wanted to know what Edward thought about the offer the Disentians had made him? Did Edward know about it? Did he even know the Disentians, or did he only know them as *The Associates?* Geoffrey wanted to talk about what happened at *The Lodge,* but how? What if Edward knew nothing about the scenario Ishmael had set out? How would Edward feel about Geoffrey relinquishing his profound abilities? Would he even care?

Then, Geoffrey thought, and far more troublesome; what if everything Ishmael had told him was a lie, to keep him on the hook, to make him feel important about his purpose so he'd quit whining and stop trying to get away from them? Or worse, what if the conversation with Ishmael never happened at all, another phantasm of Geoffrey's imagination, like the monster? How could he know? And the moon? Had they really flown over the lunarscape? It looked real enough, but was it?

"Stop the car, ET!"

"What!" Edward said, startled.

"Pull over," Geoffrey shouted. "Quick."

When Edward swerved the car onto the gravel shoulder with an abrupt stop, the car wavered and Geoffrey bailed, hurrying toward the tall weeds along the barbed wire fence thirty feet from the pavement. He sucked in a long, deep breath, closing his eyes for a moment, the past several weeks a deafening rush inside his head, faces, people, places, events, memories of his life shifting past like taunting, seductive billboards, his chest steel-banded and tight.

Edward walked up behind and placed his palm on Geoffrey's back. "Geoffrey," Edward said softly. "You're bleeding." Geoffrey looked back at him, unsure what Edward was referring to, unaware he'd been gripping the barbed wire. When Geoffrey withdrew his palms, blood spread from the deep punctures, dripping onto the weeds at his feet. Unthinking, he brought his palm to his mouth and tasted the blood; salty, metallic. It tasted real, but was it?

"We need to get those cleaned up," Edward said, handing Geoffrey a couple of damp paper towels to press to his palms. "Come on. Let's get you fixed up, get some food in you..." Edward guided Geoffrey back to the car and got him inside. Geoffrey was numb.

"How can you tell what is real, and what isn't?" Geoffrey said.

Edward laughed. "Those bleeding stigmata on your palms are real. And the infection if we don't get to a drugstore soon for some peroxide will be real. And the breakfast of pancakes, eggs and toast with a side of hash browns will be real, if we ever find a damn restaurant!"

"Everything's a joke to you, ET."

Edward spun his head toward Geoffrey. After adjusting the heat, he said, "No, Geoffrey, I just remember what you've said at every seminar, 'This is the most important moment of your life. The present moment is the only one there is.'" Edward paused, then: "Isn't this moment, right now, real enough for you?"

Geoffrey was confused, queasy, stuck in the prospect of some nebulous future forged by strangers, unseen entities determining the direction of his life for what would feel like an eternity, guiding the lifeblood of his existence for centuries to come. But they, the Disentians, at least according to Ishmael, had offered him an out. A life of normalcy; aging, illness, death. Was Geoffrey truly the lynchpin of a new civilization, as Ishmael had indicated, or just the unwitting dupe of government funded exploitation? Or worse, a guinea pig for alien manipulation?

And the past—no matter how hard Geoffrey tried to ignore it—was woven inextricably into the fabric of his being. If he allowed himself to be *rewired* by the Disentians, would he regret his decision, haunted by ninety years of memories, helping people in unimaginable ways, people he didn't even know. Yet, eight hundred years of living felt more like a sentence than a blessing. But would other humans eventually live extended lives? And Edward would most likely be around. *The Associates*? Ishmael? They would be in the picture, too, at least some version of them, wouldn't they? The possibilities, and the potential consequences of his decision, were too confounding to consider.

Geoffrey pressed the switch for the window. The glass slid down, bringing in a wave of fresh cool air past his face.

"Hey, Geoffrey," Edward said, shooting a brief and caring glance across the seat. "Just relax. Everything's gonna work out, you'll see."

Geoffrey nodded, forcing a smile. Up ahead, a sign for a restaurant was approaching, *The Lumberjack Skillet.*

"What do you think?" Edward said, putting his turn signal on.

"Sure."

Edward pulled in and found a parking spot near the entrance. Geoffrey got out, the air cool, the sun warm on his bare arms, taking some of the chill he'd been feeling. As they walked toward the front doors, a middle-aged woman came out escorting an elderly man with a cane who shuffled cautiously, bent at the waist. Edward and Geoffrey paused, waiting for them to step down off the sidewalk. Geoffrey assumed the SUV in handicap parking belonged to them and was less than ten feet away. Edward had just started to say something to Geoffrey when the elderly man went down, missing the curb, landing hard on the asphalt. He yelped, crying that he'd broken his arm, holding it on the ground, his face wracked and pulled with pain. The woman panicked and knelt down next to him, her face red, her eyes teared. "Dad, Dad! Oh my God!" She was terrified when she brought her eyes to Geoffrey and Edward. "Help please, help me!"

She started to help the old man up but every time she touched him he grimaced and howled with pain. Geoffrey hurried over, Edward following. "Let him lie still for a few moments," Geoffrey said, reaching over to place his hand on the man's chest. The man opened his eyes and looked up at Geoffrey, his face beginning to relax. Geoffrey smiled, then gently put his hand on the man's damaged arm, and in his mind saw that the thin wall of the ulnar humeral joint had separated. He gently placed his palm over it, easing it back into position, the man resting comfortably while the bone healed.

"Are you a doctor?" the woman asked, wiping her tears away.

"He's an EMT," Edward quickly said. "He knows what he's doing."

After a moment, Geoffrey looked up at the woman. "It's not broken," he said to her, then to the elderly man. "You know how tender elbows are. That ole funny bone!"

The woman let out a nervous cackle, reaching out to touch her father.

"Thank you, young man," the old man said, trying to get up. "Feels better now."

Edward and Geoffrey helped him to his feet, while his daughter retrieved his cane. They ushered him to the SUV and got him into the front seat. He smiled, and touched Geoffrey's arm.

"That was quite a thing you did, Sonny," the old man said, soft enough that only Geoffrey could hear. Like a nearly imperceptible flash, the old man's eyes twinkled for a split second, then went dull as he turned his head away. The woman got in next to him, started the engine, then rolled down her window. "Thank you so much!" she said to Edward and Geoffrey. She smiled over at her father, who stared straight ahead, then backed out of the spot and eased toward the highway.

"Let's eat," Edward said, turning to go inside.

Geoffrey watched the woman guide her vehicle into traffic, and then it was gone. He felt odd about the encounter, especially in light of the conversation with Ishmael. When he turned toward the entrance of the restaurant, Edward was holding the door open.

"Did you have anything to do with that, Edward?" Geoffrey said.

Edward wrinkled his lips, his eyes fixed on Geoffrey. "You're tired, I can see. And a bit paranoid."

For a moment Geoffrey couldn't move, disoriented, feeling like the last remaining pawn in a very elaborate game of dimensional chess. Had that little incident been staged for Geoffrey's benefit, to clarify his position? Force him to evaluate his own heart, his gifts, his future? He felt duped, and inadequately equipped to deal with such mercurial beings as Ishmael, *The Associates*, even Edward, who seemed to possess many more skills than he let on. Edward let the door go shut and walked closer to Geoffrey.

"This is a time like no other," Edward said, in a tone reserved for momentous secrets. "How could you consider even for a second not being part of it?"

Geoffrey held Edward's eyes, time collapsing; the past ninety years, the next hundred, and the next, hundreds of years more on this planet, hundreds of years to help others, bring about change, *a new, energetic paradigm of joy, profound health and wellbeing,* as Ishmael had said. But could Ishmael be believed? How could Geoffrey ever know if *The Associates* were truly benevolent, or merely insidious hucksters? And the generals at *The Lodge;* why was the military involved? Would the military ever be invested in a *paradigm of joy?*

Ambiguity would always be a part of Geoffrey's life with these beings. The energies of evil and good were so closely aligned it was nearly impossible to tell them apart. Geoffrey started to think that maybe there was no real distinction between the two, that they were the exact same energy viewed from different perspectives. Even within oneself, these two forces were difficult to distinguish. How could one ever know for sure which energy he was operating from? For instance, curing a person's disease; was that really helping that person, or taking away their only true impetus for change? The abstruseness of the philosophical questions was maddening, reducing every decision down to a paralyzing debate. A call to inaction. Geoffrey couldn't live that way, forever questioning his desire to help others, always doubting the gifts he was given. No, he would move forward, utilize his talents, work in concert with *The Associates* and dedicate himself to his own highest truth, unless it changed or revealed itself to be harmful, or odious, or downright wicked. If that happened, he would alter course, figure out how to move forward at that point. For now, though, he would strive to stay vigilant, stay present, trying his best to remain clear while trusting that he was doing the right thing.

The hostess grabbed two menus and showed them to a table.

Geoffrey picked one of them up, Edward already immersed in his, seemingly removed from the incident moments earlier with the old man in front of the restaurant. Feeling ragged and fatigued, Geoffrey couldn't swerve his mind away from it, something off about the peculiar event, as if it had somehow been staged, the knowing in the old man's eyes when he spoke to Geoffrey. Then it hit him, remembering back to the night the police officer who had stopped to question Geoffrey and Edward. Geoffrey had been driving ET home from Yellow Mountain after meeting with *The Associates,* and the officer had bizarrely "lost interest" in them, even though Geoffrey and Edward had looked damned suspicious on that road in the middle of the night, pulled to the shoulder. Geoffrey believed Edward had done something to the cop to make him leave, some kind of mind trick.

"You were there, weren't you ET?" Geoffrey said suddenly.

Edward lowered his menu and set it on the table. "Where?" the enigmatic Edward said, a faint smile lending a strange glow to his features.

"Montauk. For the mind control experiments. You were one of the sailors they brought from The Philadelphia Experiment to Montauk in 1983..."

Edward sighed through his unsettling smile. "The turkey club is sounding good to me. What are you having?"

The turkey club? Geoffrey *had* thought it sounded good, and planned to order it, but now he couldn't be sure if the idea was *his,* or had been planted by Edward? Geoffrey bristled, his stomach churning over the notion that not only was his life not his own, that even his thoughts were unnaturally forged and supplanted. Feeling the sticky heat of subjugation, he was poised to burst from the booth, flee the ambiguity, but where could he run that they wouldn't find him?

"Relax, Geoffrey," Edward said in a low, empathetic voice as the waitress approached. "You're getting worked up over nothing. No one is tricking you, especially not me." Edward shifted his eyes toward the middle-aged woman who waited statuesque with pencil and pad, then said, "The turkey club and iced tea."

Just then, staring past Edward, past the windows of the restaurant, past the trees on the other side of the highway, the power lines, diesel trucks rushing past, Geoffrey's world fell apart; the past and future, the women he's known, the conferences, the audiences, Orvin and Colette, the beast, the hooded beings at *The Lodge,* the generals, Ishmael in robe and sandals, the USS Eldridge, Geoffrey's marriage to Amanda, the preacher, Lauralee and John Bennett, pigs bleeding and squealing, over ninety years of strangers' faces and voices smashed to shambles, swirling like debris and rubbish in the grip of a tornado, roaring inside his head.

"And you?" the waitress said to Geoffrey. "Do you know what you want?"

ABOUT THE AUTHOR

Lonnie Busch is an award-winning author whose short fiction has appeared in *Southwest Review*, *The Minnesota Review*, *The Baltimore Review* and other magazines. Among his awards for fiction are the Clay Reynolds Novella Prize for his novella, *Turnback Creek*, finalist in the Tobias Wolff Award for Fiction, the *Glimmer Train* Very Short Fiction Award, and others.

Busch is also a painter, animator and illustrator, and has created artwork for numerous corporations, ad agencies and institutions, including the "Greetings from America" and "Wonders of America" Commemorative Stamps for the USPS.

See Busch's books at:
https://lonniebusch.com

(More books by Busch on following pages)

WITHOUT A FACE

Kurt and Alice barely escape an abduction attempt in the middle of the night, but now they're on the lam, unsure who, or what, is pursuing them...

"This is a fully immersive novel that is as emotionally compelling as it is captivating and thrilling." — *Lorena Padureanu, for Bestsellers World*

Read on Kindle Unlimited

ASSIMILATION

When Kercy's mother sells their secluded island cottage, she implores Kercy to never return. "Even after I'm dead…don't ever go back there!"

Something unthinkable lurks in the depths of Soshone Bay

ASSIMILATION

LONNIE BUSCH

[CONTENT ADVISORY: Intended for adult readership and contains scenes of violence, sexuality, rape, aliens, and language that may be uncomfortable for some readers.]

ALL HOPE OF BECOMING HUMAN

Earthquakes rock the planet, revealing huge metallic objects, vast subterranean graveyards, and creatures with only one goal…killing humans.

"This absorbing, realistic near-future tale brims with unrelenting mystery and tension." — *Kirkus Reviews*

CARGO HOLD 4

Years into a deep space mission, eight scientists load artifacts from a planet onto their ship...along with a dangerous entity that rages within Cargo Hold 4

"An engrossing SF thriller. The explosive ending is sure to blow readers away." — *Kirkus Reviews*

THE BALDWIN HOTEL

Past and future collide when Theodore meets his new boss, who has a connection to Theodore's past, and a pivotal role in determining his future!

"It reminded me of "Scarecrow Has a Gun" by Michael Paul Kozlowsky which also raised questions about science while being thoroughly entertaining." *— Caroline Lewis, Goodreads*

THE CABIN ON SOUDER HILL

In the Southern Appalachian Mountains, a woman stumbles into dark family secrets, backwoods justice, and seemingly impossible events that threaten to rip apart her world.

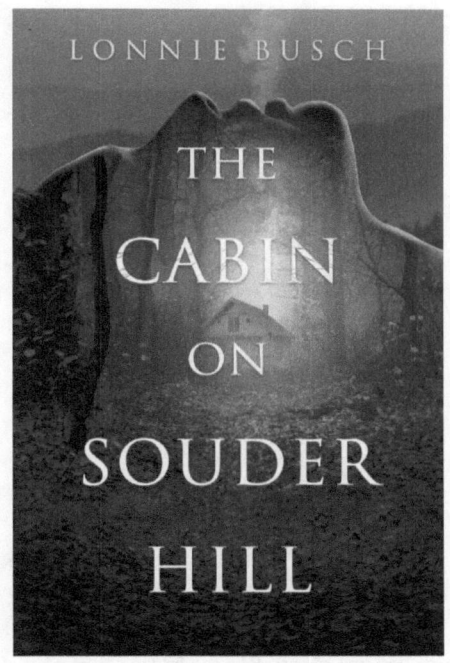

An io9 Pick of Best Books of the Month and Audible Bestseller

THE ANYTHING ROOM

Martin Moffett is given an opportunity that no one should ever get — a second chance to start a new life with his wife... who's been dead for eleven years.

"The intoxicating pull of nostalgia, the fragile nature of grief, and the human yearning for second chances" — *Untold Reads*

PUSH ME
FEISTY STORIES OF LOVE & LOSS

Life-affirming stories through the lens of humor and compassion, exploring the marvelous complexity of human love.

"There's no shortage of emotions throughout the collection—Busch knows exactly which buttons to press to evoke feelings, and the characters, no matter the situation, feel raw and real. A well-written and engaging collection with a lot of heart." — *Kirkus Reviews*

TURNBACK CREEK

A NOVELLA & SIX STORIES

This bittersweet tale of a confrontation of one old man with mortality defies the gravitational pull into despond and emerges as a very nearly inspirational story

Winner of the Clay Reynolds Novella Prize

MY BOOKS ARE AVAILABLE AT ALL THESE FINE BOOK RETAILERS

BARNES&NOBLE

Rakuten kobo

Everand

OverDrive

hoopla

Borrow Box.

Gardners

Ƀ Bookshop.org

SIGN UP FOR BOOK RELEASE DATES, SPECIAL OFFERS, FREE ARCS & GIVEAWAYS!

(Unsubscribe at any time. Your email will never be shared or sold.)

https://lonniebusch.com/